SCREAM OF THE FALCON

BY

R. A. WINTERS

Tate Publishing, LLC

Published in the United States of America
by Tate Publishing, LLC
127 East Trade Center Terrace
Mustang, OK 73064
(888) 361–9473

Names were of the utmost importance in ancient and medieval times. They represented the life and character of those who carried them. Authors such as Nathaniel Hawthorne thrived on drawing parallels between character's names (or the way names sounded) and the character's lives within his novels. Many of the names found herein are of author's creation and are therefore without formal meaning. Name meanings contrived by author are noted by "Connotation of" wherein the author felt that certain names provoked certain thought relationships or patterns for the reader.

ISBN: 1–5988616–6-2

THIS BOOK IS LOVINGLY DEDICATED TO B.J.
MY BEST FRIEND AND PARTNER
IN THE ADVENTURE OF LIFE,
AND TO M.Z. WHO GAVE ME THE EARLY
TRAINING I NEEDED IN ORDER
TO FIND MY VOICE.

PREFACE

After extensive research, I chose to use a blend of medieval and ancient historical data from earth's own history to create the food, culture, dress, and settings (land, cities, and royal houses) of this fantastical world called Berynth as well as paralleling some characters and concepts with biblical inferences. These more realistic data were carefully woven into a fantastical setting so that commonplace things would be recognizable and even tangible to the reader.

The clothing described within was unlike those of later eras that used fasteners such as buttons or hooks for closure. It is necessary then, as a point of reference and to avoid confusion, for the reader to understand that the clothing of this time would have all been fastened onto the body by laces and knots, which were sometimes hidden behind draping. Conversely, these knots and laces were sometimes intentionally highlighted by the clothing designers for decorative purposes and in many instances, the entire garment or garments were actually sewn onto the wearer, which would account for the length of time needed to dress anyone of a royal house. A good example then for the reader's comparison would be the togas worn at the peak of Roman occupation and the tunics and leggings of the later Middle Ages.

The cooking is descriptive of the more simplistic dining of the Middle Ages, as obviously all food was cooked over open flames on a hearth or in large stone or clay ovens. Since food was not easily preserved, it had to be cooked carefully with the heavy use of spices, herbs, and sauces to mask any deterioration of the original quality, a fact especially true of meat. Wine and fermented drink were widely consumed (sometimes even by the young) as they were considered "safer" to drink due to the disease carrying nature of the available fresh water. Another instance of an ingredient appropriate to the time would be the use of honey as a sweetener rather than sugar, which was not available at the time. Most cooking ingredients moonlighted as medicine and even doubled as discerning tools when necessary as nature was the basis for every supply, there being no synthetic copies in sight.

The societal structure, too, was created as a blend because the royalty described in this book are not true royalty as would be found with sovereign kings and queens, but rather depictions of the heads of clan houses. The clan houses and heads of patriarchal societies were generally decided by birth/war and could go to either a male or female progeny or relative although a male was preferred having complete legal power over himself, the land, and the wealth of the clan under the laws of the time. Conversely, a woman was often used as a figurehead whose worth was only as good as her spouse or father, who would have been the controlling parties behind the title. The wealth of a clan would have directly related to an early version of the fealty system. Villages and farms were protected under this system by a governing body (such as a clan chieftain or the lords of later times) that had all the training and gear necessary for making war and keeping the peace as well as allotting the amassed wealth and provisions to the commoners during times of famine or siege. The villages and farms would in return for this protection and future planning offer up the largest portions of their services and products to their chieftain. Alliances between clans were also a key necessity for the continuing survival of any given clan as the agreements made between alliances were the source of the given laws for an area.

Many of the lyrical names in the first book of this series may be recognizable to some readers as being either Celtic or Latin in origin, as I envisioned a world similar to the European cultures (Nordic, Roman, Norman, Germanic, and Celtic). Again, the timeline of which is a blend of the Middle Ages and ancient times.

The battle scenes were created from my knowledge of the strategies and formations of the Roman armies particularly (and their supporting supply trains). The sword fighting scenes come from my first hand knowledge of fencing (especially the epee and saber styles), following a happy participation in a very limited number of classes at a state college. I also used occasional queries into the progression of Olympic fencing and fencing techniques as described on the web for use in the realism of my writing. The mechanical devices noted within and physical descriptions of weapons or stratagem again were patterned after known examples of ancient and medieval creation.

Biblical parallel is most notably displayed in the prologue that refers to the Creation story and the entry of evil into Berynth (the name of the world in which the characters live, which connotes being bereft without the presence of God). It also refers to a master plan to restore communion with God through redemption. In the Bible, God created the world and the humans in it. The humans were warned by God not to eat of the tree of good and evil that was in the midst of the garden, because they, like children, were unable to handle certain conceptual realities such as good and evil. Satan, a fallen angel of God, convinced them to eat of the tree. When Adam and Eve ate of the tree, they unknowingly consigned themselves to a life of what we call "free will" or independent thought, a fact, which although attractive, in reality means making our own way as in a very great darkness without the benefit of being completely filled up with the presence of God. Imagine going from having conversations with and first-hand knowledge of the Creator of the universe to being aware of only the direct here and now and your own sudden mortality—something that beforehand would have been a complete unknown. The only way then that God could restore creation to himself once again (or that original state of perfect communion) was to have humans choose to serve Him from generation to generation, via sacrifices and a strict code of law. The boundaries of formalism would create pseudo-perfection acceptable enough to allow a person to stand before the true perfection of God. However, human perfection is impossible and following the law and sacrifices perfectly was also impossible–unending redemption then could only be gotten through a creature of perfect character. Humans who were sinful could only produce sinful heirs who would have to continue to follow a strict code of laws and sacrifice. Therefore, God planned to give a human woman a child not gotten by man but by his own spirit, the resulting heir of which could provide redemption by offering Himself as the perfect ultimate sacrifice. Prior to God's son Jesus being born and subsequently offered up for the sins of mankind, God searched constantly for those who would do their utmost to follow him not only because of fear or self-preservation but because they had true love for Him and obedience to His laws. He knew that this foundation of faith passed on to others would create a basis for understanding and accepting the great gift that he had planned to give to mankind.

The heroic characters in this book are reminiscent of King David's line. King David was just such a man—with a heart full of love towards God and enough humility to obey God's word. The Bible says he was a man after God's own heart. King David had great communion with God even though he was hardly "lily white" by modern religious standards. King David was a warrior by nature, which did not make it possible for him to directly serve as a priest to the Lord, one who was able to offer sacrifices. His love for God and constant choice to remain soft to the voice of God is what set him apart and constantly redeemed him despite sins of murder, adultery, and pride. He suffered for his sins (being outside of the will of God), but was never far enough to have escaped God's great grace and love for him. In his zeal and despite his inability to serve as a priest, David was able to fund the progression of Judaism into the rest of the known world with the gains of his warfare. Interestingly enough, Jesus, by whom human salvation was ultimately made possible, came from King David's line. The first book of the trilogy then parallels the Bible's Old Testament foundations or pre-redemption.

The above being said, it was not nor is my intent to offend any educated reader who is knowledgeable about the Middle Ages, ancient times, warfare, or the Bible nor to misquote any source. Since the historical data (or references to culture, dress etc.) were compiled over a long period of time, the fallibility of the contents as historical parallel should be considered high. Again, my research was done to create a tangible framework for the reader. No direct sources other than the Bible have been mentioned intentionally as no direct quotes from sources were used. I used the King James and Amplified versions to gain greater understanding of the few biblical inferences used but always paraphrased the scripture avoiding direct quotes, which would look odd in a fictitious novel. I do not claim in any way to be a scholar or teacher of the Bible nor am I a student of history. My research was done for the purpose of enriching my writing.

HISTORICAL CHARACTERS
FROM THE ANNALS OF BERYNTH

Alida:
Small Winged One (Heir of Falda)

Scribe's Notation:
Alida is a changeling or creature that is able to walk in animal or human form according to their choice at any given moment. Changelings are born to walk in only two forms (human and a single animal form). Changelings have spiritual insight meaning that they can see the spirit world as it seamlessly blends with ours. This insight is only possible when they are in or converting to their animal form. In Berynth, they are largely distrusted, as most humans believe they are the result of sorcery. In the ancient times of Berynth, changelings were revered whenever their identities were discovered. However, due to growing hostilities, the practice of destroying changelings has become more common. It is largely unknown that their changeling capability is the result of heredity rather than magic. Changelings appear to be normal humans until the beginning of the conversion of their animal side to natural independence. For instance, meat-eating beasts eventually graduate from milk and regurgitated meat provided by their parents to the ability to consume fresh whole meat that they have captured and killed on their own. A changeling whose second form is as a meat-eating beast would convert for the first time from its human form to the form of the beast around the time this conversion from dependence to independence takes place. It occurs in changelings in roughly the same number of years that it would take its counterpart to convert to in that number of months or days, since humans generally experience slower growth and longer lives.

Crynlaird:
Connotation of a creeping or devious lord (The Banished Apprentice)

Deive:
The Deep (Nursemaid and then Advisor and Friend of Alida, Heir of Falda)

Scribe's Notation:
Deive is an eltar. Eltars have the specific distinguishing features of pointed ears and almond-shaped eyes with a cat-like irises and pupils. They are like humans coming in all skin colors, shapes, and heights but are often rejected by humans as being mad, weak, or of a lower value because of their strong unpredictable spiritual inclinations and because occasionally they are born with other odd features or personality traits. Eltars have a strong sense of the spiritual world although they do not have the actual spiritual sight of a change-ling. Eltars fulfill roles similar to prophets, seers, or priests but can easily be turned to sorcery due to their strong spiritual connections. These holy men and women are *born* into the priestly role they fulfill, having received no training beyond that which they seek out themselves. They come into Berynth at birth, having a knowledge of all that is beyond their human-like sight but have to discover for themselves a way to define the things that they naturally sense. They are separate from humans who have similar gifts of discernment or pro-phetic abilities.

Eldridge:
Mature Counselor (Keep Advisor, Head Counsel to and Friend of Ulrich)

Kellen Grost:
Of the Spring, surname a connotation of a Gristle like Strength (Chieftan of Kinterden Dell)

Landres:
Connotation of one who is Civil, Strong and Steady (Captain of the Guard of Drachmund Heights, Best Friend of Ulrich)

Quirin Laucher:
Traitor's Stone, surname a connotation of Lecher (Mercanery Sorcerer and Conquerer of Falda)

Savine:
Pronounced Säveen, connotation of Savin, a plant that has medicinal proper-ties but is rarely if ever used in humans due to its high toxicity (Chieftess of Lyrnne, and Aunt to Alida, Heir of Falda)

The Red:

"The" is an address of respect for a leader or king of the Northlands; this address is always followed by a specific and noticeable characteristic. For instance, a clan leader having meaty fists would be called "The Fist", "The" is a way of depicting their status as "The" king, the one of greatest power (Chieftan of Brögen Fjords)

Tremain:

From the house by the rock (Captain of the Guard of Lyrnne)

Ulrich:

Noble Wolf (Chieftan of Drachmund Heights)

HISTORICAL PROVINCES & HOLDINGS FROM THE ANNALS OF BERYNTH

Falda:

Folded Wings (Alida's Homeland)

Lyrnne:

Connotation of Lyrical (Savine's Holdings)

Kinterden Dell:

Connotation of Fertile Dells, a place Populated by Children (Kellen Grost's Holdings)

Drachmund Heights:

Connotation of Dragon's Mountain or Dragon's Seat (Ulrich's Holdings)

Brögen Fjords:

Connotation of Broken or Splintered fjords (The Red's Holdings)

BERYNTH

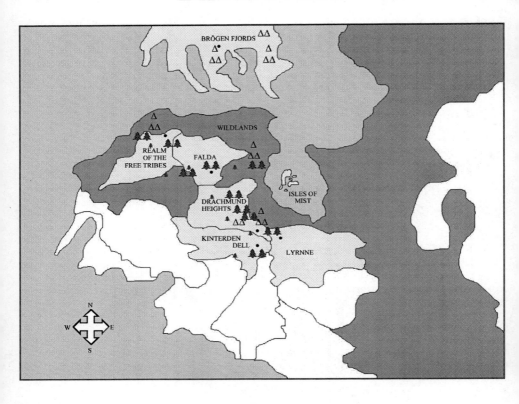

• = Main Cities of Clan Holdings

(Note that most cities are close to clan borders in order to protect clan interests from surrounding lands.)

🌲🌲= Heavy Forestation

Δ= Mountainous

The wildlands are unclaimed/unprotected areas of country considered free to travel. Traversing directly through a protected land would require permission of the clan concerned. All main byways would follow the path of least resistance through the wildlands.

INTRODUCTION

LONG AGO, in a dimension beyond our own, where the air was always scented with jasmine and crushed rose, the one of many names sat at a loom. In His eyes shone the light of a hundred suns, with a radiance that betrayed a distant and ancient wisdom. His dark lionesque head went unadorned by crown or braid, His beard falling nearly to His waist in thick waves, and all of it from crown to beard streaked with the glistening silver of age. His powerful body with a chest like a bull and arms as heavy and thick as oak was constantly gowned in rich purple cloth, its fiery weave winking out with its own light and carrying in its heavy folds the scents of myrrh, cinnamon, and olive.

Hidden within a cool grey chamber beside a glassy sea, this Master did not come on this day merely to amuse a fancy, but to shape and form carrying out a particular vision that had begun to haunt His dreams. His site, well chosen for its secrecy and peace, shielded him from the constant attendance of His created spirit companions.

Strands of gleaming thread, endless in variety, were drawn from a pile by His talented hands as He watched a tightly woven piece of fabric begin to take shape before him on a loom.

When He had finished weaving, He pulled the lovely cloth from the frame, His fingers caressing the varied textures of its promising surface. He then sat at a large embroidery frame to which He fastened the weighty fabric. With great care and surety, He began to stitch the story of a world, His language written in the elaborately embroidered figures and scenes.

This tapestry was filled with every creature imaginable, the beauty and variety a testament to His artist's hand. On fields of emerald green silk, four-legged creatures with flowing hair and elegant heads cavorted, their shiny hides sewn in every color. In the secret corners of satiny forests, shy beasts with glowing eyes hid themselves beneath muslin moss and woolen boulders perched as though awaiting the night.

When the last stitch was in place, He saw that what He had made was lovely to behold. The flowers of that woven world curled through every inch of the cloth, some with the promise of tight buds and others the fruit of heavily drooping blossoms. The creatures from the ponds that leapt and swam looked shiny enough to be wet. However, even with such detail, there was neither animation nor warmth to their forms. It was a shame, He decided, that these bright creations should forever remain frozen in the fabric of His making. What was a rose without its perfumed apple scent or the motion of a nodding head? How could one know that a pair of creeping eyes in the grass next to the pond was a frog without hearing his melodic croak? For some time, the Master wistfully traced the lovely design with His fingertips memorizing the expressions and textures of His creations. Then all at once, with His face brightening, He leaned forward calling His world to life both with the warmth of His breath and His spoken word.

He watched then in great delight as the cloth began to undulate and breathe, the creatures and scenes instantly jumping to life. From the folds of the tapestry, came scents of sweet flowers and new green grass drifting up and out as incense. In that fresh breeze, too, was mingled the odors of warm musky earth and salt laden ocean spray that softly misted the master's gladdened cheek. The creatures of the cloth did not know their beginning, and their surprised whimsical expressions caused the Master to chuckle with laughter, especially when they continued on as if they had always possessed movement, sense, and life. Hour after hour was spent watching them. Then all at once, a great desire to rest overcame The Master, for He had been at His loom and frame for six days and six nights without rest during the creation of the tapestry. Lying down upon His pile of thread, the Master drifted off into the secret world of dreams with His head pillowed on soft curls of gold and blue silk thread.

When He arose again, He exchanged His raiment for another garment made of sky blue and silver brocade for His spirit was light and merry. When He was once more clothed, He whispered to the air and suddenly with a sound like thunder, swarms of gleaming spirits, which had been seeking him six days without end, rushed into the room to attend to their master. Grumbling lightly at His lack of consideration for "having gotten lost," they offered him ambrosia to drink from a silver goblet and a golden platter filled with thin slices of honeycomb for His palate. After this sweet refreshment, He bade them all leave, and when the last form has exited His chamber, He stepped into the tapestry as passing through a portal to gently form companionship with the beloved characters of His created world. Each day thereafter, upon His first awakening, He sought out the creatures formed after His form and spoke with them in the most pleasant garden of their world enjoying their wide eyes, endless curiosity, and softness of breath. In all things, they loved to praise Him, and He in return loved to give them every good and lovely thing.

One night when this Lord had left His creation behind in the room of grey stone and had sought again His throne room, a tiny door on the wall of the chamber opened admitting a character dressed in light.

The figure having been assured of no interruption, with the Lord elsewhere occupied, took up in his hands a long black thread made of flax. With the end fastened to his waist, the creature dove into the undulating folds of fabric that still hung from the embroidery frame. The hours passed as cold stars twinkled above the chamber, their light shining in the barely darkened sky of cornflower blue. When the figure finally exited the tapestry at first rosy light, nothing seemed to have been changed in the secret woven world.

This same dawning light brought the Lord from His duties, and as was His wont, He immediately approached His tapestry to see if it was as magnificent as His fancies continued to tell.

For a long while, He gazed at the interwoven threads and delicate embroidery, enjoying the beauty of his work while noting where the fabric had stretched and developed, in keeping with its adaptive nature. Then a small flaw caught His eye. He gazed closer still, and in anger saw that someone had stitched a tiny mess of knots into the lovely garden scene in the east of His created world. The black thread introduced by a hand other than His own had been animated by the breath and word already in the cloth and now found life just as the other original stitching. Tendrils of this black fiber had begun to creep through the cloth covering and outlining, though not destroying, the beauty of the Master's own weave.

When the Lord touched His finger to the black snarl of knots, He instantly recognized the trademark of His exiled and once most prized apprentice, Crynlaird. This creature had been taught the sewing skills of his master that he might be of aid to Him when some new work needed stitching. However, out of raging pride and jealousy, Crynlaird, when he had learned the secrets of his Lord, had declared himself also a lord, though he was created in the same manner as the works he sewed. The apprentice was then banished to the outer darkness beneath the gates and form of paradise. Crynlaird, though he was not physically kept from the land, was so despised by those who remained that he found it unbearable in his pride even to walk the streets. Along with him went an exiled batch of unworthy, self-concerned, greedy, slothful, and petulant spirits who had taken his part against the Master. This made his banishment all the more hateful, for the apprentice considered his sensibilities to be very delicate indeed. Though he had at one time found the banished spirits helpful, he was in no way a peer to them and should have been given his own lands or so he had told his master when his case had been reviewed.

The true Lord, without a moment's hesitation, having recognized the hand of Crynlaird, called him forth again from the outer lands and asked of him the purpose for this intrusion, this further betrayal. The outcast spirit, with greater pride than before (for he had dwelt in his own thoughts long enough to have justified his every action), announced again that the work before them was proof of his own lordship and pointed to the creeping black as if he had animated it himself. He further added, feeling very sorry for himself, that his punishment was unjust and demanded that the Master clear his name and seat him again at the highest place in the courts.

Angrily, the Master sent Crynlaird back to the lands of exile, and then entered His tapestry hoping to find His creations unaffected. However, He could neither see nor hear the creations formed after His form, who usually awaited Him in the middle of the garden. He searched the span of green, and when He found them, He bade them to draw near, but they could not hear His voice and so He approached them instead. When He was very close indeed, He was sickened by a rotten stench rising up from their breath and skin - the scent of death had entered the once eternal land. They looked right through him, their eyes foggy and blind, and when he tried to touch their hearts that they might be comforted by His presence, He found this dwelling full of shame and darkness. They had received and believed in the counterfeit promises given to them by the lovely apprentice (whose only goal was possession of the land) and now no more as a creation knew the true Lord's paradise. With an aching heart, the Master mourned the loss of their close companionship for His creations in having believed and received Crynlaird, had in essence made contract with him. The Master called the damaged world Berynth and returned in sorrow to His own kingdom.

The years passed as the world grew and changed—a garden of roses filled with weeds - while the threads of darkness continued to creep through the weave of its dimension. The inhabitants of the world, seeking asylum from the darkness, cried out for some relief from the hateful and black harassment of the exiled apprentice and his court of fiends.

Crynlaird joyfully bullied and enslaved the creatures of Berynth finding some measure of relief in their pitiful spirits and fearful worship of him. He caused horrible envisionings and dark thoughts to arise in their minds so that they would not remember that somewhere, long ago, they were treasured. He also feared that one day he would be revealed to them, as he truly was, a very small, even comical figure, having no beauty or fullness of soul and no joy or homeland to call his own.

Crynlaird relied on his knowledge of his Master, one who was so pure and true that He would never break any contract that had been made, regardless of His desire to do so. Without the willing and total participation and agreement of His creations, the Master could not again regain Berynth.

It was not that the Master could not hear the cries of Berynth or that He did not mourn their separation from Him, but He would have to cunningly regain that which has been unlawfully stolen less He Himself become a thief and liar.

With their best at heart, the Weaver crafted a plan to redeem the world. This redemption could be bought through the line of a creature called changeling, through a certain woman great in courage and faith. To her, He would reveal His intent, and from her seed, would be borne His plan.

The weaver looked at His world with a heart full of hope, for the story that unfolded held for its creatures a fullness of joy, should they, in faith, see it to its completion.

ORACLE OF THE PROPHET
ISAIUM

BERYNTH, IN THE PROVINCE OF YERUSLA
IN THE DAYS OF THE ANCIENT KING

On hills of green, weeping heart did burst
grown from blood and death's turned curse;
weakness, sorrow both abhorred
crowning the victor with sweet reward.
Bloody ashes suckle victory
—love and tenderness, humility.
From twins, two nations, two nations, two paths;
weaver's web, His unknown plan . . .

CHAPTER ONE

BERYNTH, IN THE PROVINCE OF FALDA

Our story begins, with the seed of a fortunate house, grown up in comfort and bathed in the luxury and security of great love. This seed called by the name Alida, being strong, willful, and given to pride, has yet that certain tenderness and promise, which comes to those borne of a cherished existence. She is cast as our heroine.

Begin then in the cold and cloying darkness, where smoke-filled wind whips by, stinging your eyes and saturating your clothing with its odor. Feel the madness and primal drive of war as the sound of drums pounds deeply in your ears and belly. Chaos reins all around you, and not afar off you see our heroine, her eyes bright with fear and anger, praying for safety from a siege upon her family's heritage lands, lands that she had once thought invincible.

Breathe in, breathe out, suck for air until it burns your lungs, or do not survive. Ignore the shaking of your legs and the pains of hard breath in your side. Don't fall, don't fall–keep on as you've been taught. Alida admonished herself in this way, her legs feeling close to buckling, their normal strength weakening in the unforgiving rush to live. Sobbing out the names of loved ones amidst ghastly echoing screams, she turned yet another corner hoping against hope for the sight of a familiar face. Body after body was turned over and every face examined for familiarity despite the horrors of blood and wounds and defecation done out of fear. The smell of smoke, blood, urine and sweat mingled in the humid air of the castle halls; her first smell and taste of the paralyzing horrors of war. From a dark niche in the wall and in the presence of looming shadows, the sudden merciful grasp of Deive, her mentor, offered the only comfort of the night. With gasping breath, they sought escape from Falda keep. If they could slip through the mass of battling men, they would find freedom in the dells beyond the city walls.

Everything she had learned, every lesson intended to protect her was remembered in those moments as black-eyed warriors grabbed for her flying cloak and tired limbs, their sour breath hissing from between yellow teeth. Their gnarled fingers that grasped at her arms and side were knocked away in fury. For their trouble, more than one felt the ice of her blade slice neatly between their ribs. The sudden presence of her mentor in that hallway had given her strength to collect her senses, and in having done so, her anger as well, for this was her homeland and her family. Fueled by rage, she fought with a hunger that bordered on madness. Her arms throbbed from the constant motion of swordplay and cold sweat washed her already exhausted body, but she would not leave Falda without having made a mark. Taking in another iron-tinted gasp of chalky air, she continued on. Step after step, holding her breath to hide her location, then another few steps and the plunge of her sword through a soldier's tender neck. It was the unique dance of war.

Acting on instinct alone, all reasonable thought long since transformed by the sheer surprise of her overturned world, Alida battled on, not knowing where her sword hilt ended and her arm began. The ache of bone and muscle had long since morphed into the iron of her sword.

When they were finally able to sheath their weapons and had entered the musty dark forest surrounding the back of the city walls, Deive, though she was in great pain from a wound, inquired first after her charge. Her voice had grown hoarse from shouting and breathing in smoke, but she would not be quieted until this young woman before her had been deemed safe.

"Are you injured?"

"Nay, I remain unscathed."

Alida dropped to her knees, the icy wetness of snow soaking through her leggings. Her dark, waist-length hair fell tangled to the snow covered ground. She groaned aloud, the sound grating in the cloaked silence of the forest.

"Please tell me that I dream, Deive, and will soon awaken. For this night is not a possibility." Alida's jaw and shoulders shook as if she chattered with cold. But, it wasn't tears or the winter that caused the shaking, it was coming instead from withholding the hot emotions of hatred and sorrow.

Deive wiped away her own gritty tears, her voice faltering. "This is no dream, Love. Falda is no longer yours. Your house lies slain on its reddened soil, and you are chased from the walls of promise by these . . . these beasts that call themselves men!"

Alida covered her ears, her hands visibly shaking. "You speak lies! They cannot all be dead! For 'twas their arms I fled to for comfort and their eyes which I sought to please just this past eventide. How can this be, that *you,* nothing more than a halfling, should speak *my* family dead?"

Her voice trailed off into the bloody night with a sob.

Deive cringed, the painful words spoken by her ward cutting her to the quick. "Am I not your family, Alida, and are we not both of more than human blood? Look at me! Do you not think my tears apologize, beg, and disbelieve? You think *me* cool in the face of these horrors! I but speak the truth, and though I would wish it otherwise for thee and me, we are not saved the pain of our loved ones' passing. We must believe and hope, as we have always done, and we must clear our minds for what lies ahead." Deive swallowed back the cost that the angry words had meted out.

Alida rose to her feet and crossed the clearing, angrily brushing aside the chill of her tears. "Now is not the time to school me, woman, for I would not hear your words."

Deive, knowing the fear that gripped her charge, spoke no other word, but after having grasped the angry hand intended for her cheek, tenderly pulled the young woman to her breast. In response, Alida's hot tears were loosed, her moaning cries echoing into the dark as her knees collapsed beneath her. Deive felt the pulse of her ward as if it was her own and the vibration of Alida's sobs echoed throughout her own breast.

"O gods of the heavens, why would you end the precious lives of those who sought you the most earnestly of all. Why would you take from me my dwindling heritage and my very blood?"

Deive grasped her tighter, her voice hoarse and soft. Into Alida's soft curls she whispered, "Do not curse the gods, which sent thee thy gift and calling. For though your family lies sleeping, you have been granted life and this for a purpose."

Alida sobbed deeply into the smoky folds of Deive's cloak. "'Tis no comfort that I remain without them, Deive, for they were my all."

The mentor's voice softened still and she drew the young woman's face closer to her neck. "I know."

Alida succumbed to her anguish only for a few moments longer and then brusquely wiped her face clean of tears, pulling away from the violet eyes and tender embrace of her mentor. She would have time later to mourn all that had happened. A part of her was not yet ready to admit the ramifications of all that had transpired, and though she did not know why, she felt yet some small drive to live.

Strangely, the grit-covered hand that she had drawn across her wet cheek was covered with a sticky warmth that had not been present before. Knowledge of her friend's injury dawned clear and sharp as the odor of blood wafted by soon after. Alida immediately grasped Deive's shoulder, turning her so as to see her back in the dim light.

Blood had caked and dried in the cloth of Deive's tunic over much of her left shoulder, but it was a dark, wet hole in the tunic just under the shoulder blade that offered up the wound itself.

Alida, ignoring her sore hands, ripped open the cloth muttering under her breath at Deive's lack of concern for herself. She then tore strips from her own tunic and cloak pressing their tattered folds onto the wound to stem the seeping flow of blood.

When much time had passed and the bleeding had fully ceased, Alida took the cloths and cleaned them as best she could in a frigid nearby stream. When they had been thoroughly rinsed out, she tenderly cleansed the area around Deive's barely seeping wound with the cool, wet rags. Then she took the small medicine bag from Deive's side and applied a sticky, sulfurous substance to the wound as she was instructed. Her inexperienced stitching with a needle and sterilized sinew closed the wound though in a considerably rougher manner than Deive would have done herself. The whole while the nurse, with a thin sheen of pain-induced sweat upon her brow, gasped back moans that each stitch pulled from her. Every line of sinew brought the hot sting of unavoidable pain followed by heat and throbbing. Only after having taken these steps to assure her mentor's removal from harm did Alida take time to stretch her own aching back—tension and pain remaining in every muscle of her body, arms, and hands.

They rested there like that for a while looking at one another without words or defense. It had been a hellish night.

When Alida could no longer stand the silence, she stood and wearily paced away from Deive towards the center of a small snow-dotted clearing staring up at the star-filled sky. Instantly, Deive knew her intent.

"You wish to fly?"

Alida nodded and then with a whisper said, "Yes, for I must know the outcome of the battle."

Deive's voice grew harsh with worry. "There is still great danger, Alida. For though you do not approach in human form, should one of Quirin's warriors see a white falcon flying through the darkness, a shot could be fired out of fear."

Alida was silent and then darkly said, "I need to know, Deive."

The eltar halfling nodded in response. Alida crouched over the earth, her palms and nails pressed into the cold dirt and snow. Presently, she heard the familiar roaring silence and flood of sensation as her body was transformed into the compact form of a white falcon.

Deive disentangled the screaming thrashing bird from the crumpled, heavy confines of the cloak and tunic before whispering protective blue wards around the body. When the task was completed, the falcon was released to the skies.

The bird's wings beat against the cold wind–the frigidity cutting at her joints like an ice pick. Her eyes and mind, cast somewhere between human and beast, stared down into the depths surrounding her desecrated home.

For hours, she circled the walls of the castle and boundaries of the land, careful to avoid large gatherings of Quirin's men.

Then in the distance, she saw a huge pillar of smoke. She turned toward the awful beacon and saw that its source was a huge burning mass of furniture, castle goods, and bodies. Not being able to contain her curiosity and horror, she swept in closer lifted by the hot, malodorous updrafts of air from the blaze and saw the beloved crumpled forms of her mother and father awaiting their cremation along with others she had known from birth.

It was in that moment that vengeful anger, physically hotter than she had ever known, washed through her blood, pleading for the demise of the enemy. The heat of her blood made her neck and eyes burn with a hatred that begged for satisfaction.

A lone warrior, who oversaw the burning mass, looked up with red, smoke-filled eyes just in time to see a screaming white falcon plummeting towards him, its beak and talons stretched forth in glinting vengeance.

The guard's screams bled into the night only half-uttered, as his flesh was torn from his throat in a fiery, stinging mass. In a flurry of soft feathers and steel-like talons, the horrible deed was completed, the omen of his death returning swiftly to the skies. Alida had gone to seek again her refuge among the trees of the forest beyond.

The clearing she had left behind was soon found again with a white-faced Deive staring up into the cold night sky.

Alida landed, her talons inelegantly sinking into the snow. Transformed, her feathers become skin and her hands uncurled from the clench of talons into the powdery ice around her. As soon as she was able, she answered Deive's anxious cries while dressing herself with quivering hands.

"They're all gone, Deive! Even your little Fiona. There is no one left. But for us, they have destroyed everything in our world. You did indeed tell me the truth, but I could not accept what I had not seen!" She lay on the ground curled into a ball, dry sobs racking her already sore, smoke-ravaged throat.

Deive collapsed nearby, crying deeply over the reality of her own loss. How could she lead this young woman when her own dreams had been crushed? They both remained in the clearing sharing the darkness of the night. They did not speak or touch, their unity drifting along on the soft sounds of the other's sobs.

Presently, though it cost her everything, Deive arose and spoke. Her voice wavered with the impossibility of what she asked. "Gather your strength, child. We must settle in for the last few hours of night. For come first light, two warriors of Falda who have been spared will see to our safety. A third was sent on ahead by your father's own hand to secure lodgings and to see to our future when he saw that his own was not so secure."

Alida did not comment but rose wearily to her feet, joining Deive to create a shelter of fir boughs and leaves within the dark folds of the trees. Before dropping into a fitful sleep, Alida whispered a prayer into the heavens. For though she had the will to survive, her heart had been shattered sucked from her breast into the aching depth of her bones. The prayer did not come easily from her lips, for soft gulping sobs and keening drifted towards her from the bed of fir needles beside her own an echo of her deep sorrow.

The next morning dawned too quickly, and Deive and Alida arose with bleary eyes to meet their warrior protectors as planned. They stumbled from their cold makeshift bedrolls with shaking weak legs and mouths full of cotton. Presently, they were stowed away in a rough little drover's cart with damp hay as their only protection against the prying eyes of Quirin's guard.

Neither Alida nor Deive had much desire to talk which served well the purpose of silence. Alida could not even bring herself to ask what their path would be, but quietly took to her place as a thing which had once lived but was now rotting from the roots.

The days went on endlessly within the cramped and itchy confines of the drover's cart. The natural scratch of the musty damp hay and biting fleas that dwelt within, made every moment closer to hell than one could have dreamed. Alida lay dry-eyed and empty, not knowing and not caring overly much about the course of her future. She had never felt so heavy and so tired. She slept darkly with images of the siege ringing through her dreams. More often than not, she dreamt of nothing but a great black void. When they were able to rally and stretch, relieve themselves or eat within some safe cove, she felt unable to speak and rarely finished her allotted portion of cold stale food.

Back at Falda, enemy troops hurried from the main hall out into the frigid burned fields, not wishing to be present before their master if it was not required of them. A handful remained in the courtyard nervously awaiting their orders, cringing at the punishing oaths and bellowing coming from within the great hall. Every word ricocheted off the cobblestones around them.

"Where is she?" If she is not found before dawn tomorrow, the remainder of my guard is to be divided and dispatched directly on the roads both north and south. She and her wench of a nurse are probably hiding in a woodpile outside the castle or in a secret room. Find them before I decide to use one of you as the channel for my anger!" With that, Quirin overturned a nearby trestle table and then smashed a pottery pitcher against the stone floor, his eyes burning brightly within his handsome but twisted face.

His anger somewhat diminished, Quirin Laucher paced toward the dead ashes of last night's fire, silently watching his men scatter before him like chaff. He scowled at the cluttered great hall while sucking in great breaths of foul smelling air, his patrician lips curling in disdain. His forte was battle, not housekeeping, and between the rape and murder of Falda's inhabitants, there were few hands to be found. His mastiffs hulked near the hearth chewing on bones, which suspiciously looked human. Snorting in frustration, he kicked the dogs away with a heavy boot and picked up a frozen pewter tankard from off the floor. Perhaps, with luck, he would find a meal and stout drink in the kitchen below the great hall, for someone was still providing a meager ration to his army.

With elegant hands curling into twisted fists, the tall, slender man strode away from the fire his thin lips pulled into a sneer. He would probably have to use other methods to find the two women, for he had no overt trust in his men's ability to complete the deed satisfactorily.

Many days later, a little drover's cart made its lonely way along a cow path. The main byways had only been skirted for the cart's contents were too precious to risk a quicker but less secure route.

In the bed of the cart, Deive smoothed Alida's hair away from her brow with a newly calloused hand. "Why will you not speak to me, lass? Is it your future you fear, or is it this recent past that has so entangled your tongue?"

When no reply came from the young woman, Deive tried again. "There is no hope for changing the plan. Your father's guard refuses to take you anywhere else. They gave their oaths to him that you would be safe, and they will see it finished."

When still no sound issued from the young woman, Deive continued, "She is honor bound, and generally desires the best for her kinsfolk for it directly reflects on her. You should not lack for necessities while in her care."

Alida's deep blue eyes gazed out from under dark lashes at her companion. Finally, Alida whispered, "Your words do not put me at ease, not that I will ever find ease again. For what has been done and will be done fills me first with horror and then sadness. I do not desire to live with someone I've never met, for necessities will carry me only so far. Love is what stretches between, and I cannot return to my homeland for certainly that place is lost to me. I would rather then make my own way. Am I to have no choice regarding my own fate?" Her voice trembled uncontrollably then, while hot fat tears rolled slowly down her chapped, dirty cheeks. Deive laughed, though not unkindly, for one's fate was never a choice, and she told her ward as much.

Turning away in trepidation, Alida fixed her eyes on the rough-hewn boards of the cart. She now wished that days earlier she had inquired of Deive the exact path of their journey.

It was many hours later that the horizon offered up a city of grey granite rising from snow-covered hills. One of the guards quietly alerted the women that Lyrnne, their final destination, lay just ahead. Alida curled into a tighter ball trying to ward off the fear of what was to come. She had heard very little of this aunt, into whose care she'd been given, and what little she'd heard was not flattering. She didn't feel strong enough to deal with anything, for her sadness sucked at her strength like a leech to blood. She did not want adventure or unknowns, for she had a bellyful to last a lifetime. She had been known for her strength and willfulness growing up, but somehow she could not tap that vein, so heavy was her grief. Without hope, and utterly weak, she whispered another prayer adding it to the hundreds of the preceding days. The air around her remained cool, still and lifeless.

The clattering of a captain's sword belt followed the sounds of his clipped stride as he passed through the massive doors of Falda into the damp, dark interior of the neglected hall.

"Sire, we have not yet found the women. Your warriors have been dispatched, but not a drop of gossip or blood gives us trail to whence they have gone." The captain of Quirin's guard tried not to sneer at his lord's back. One day he would take position where his lord now stood. He was as given to honor and valor as Quirin himself.

The tense back of his lord did not give any acknowledgment that he had heard. Instead, several moments later, in the casual manner of someone who has set aside pure rage for cunning, Quirin said softly, "Very well, I will attend to the matter myself. However, should they be found by you or your guard and either one returned to me with marks of any kind, you'll find you head the ravens and worms rather than my army." A subtle signal to the dogs at Quirin's side caused the lips to draw back from the massive beasts' teeth. The growls issued from those thick, hairy throats led the captain to ease his sneer and return quickly to his duties.

Another soldier then stepped forward, cowardice in every line of his body. "Sire, the guard, Ranald, was found by one of the outlying bonfires this morning with his throat and face torn and his eyes ripped out. 'Tis not the work of war but of a beast, though none can say what beast would cause such marks. The men say that is was a demon. None of them will touch it, and I have other duties to attend to."

Quirin turned smoothly, his elegant voice tight with disdain. "Are we to leave bodies lying around to spread disease?"

Though the guard's face showed how afraid he was of his Master, apparently, his fear of the corpse was worse, and he issued no excuse neither did he give further explanation.

Quirin sighed, "I'll come with you to view the corpse, but then I want it disposed of, and you will be the one to do it!"

Quirin strode from the hall out into the crisp morning air. When they reached the snow-dusted corpse, Quirin crouched near it, examining the wounds and fallen position of the body. Then he drew in a deep draught of air, allowing both his nose and mouth to discern the things that are hidden from sight. He caught a hint of sulfur in the breeze, and the hair at the back of his neck rose stiffly. Only the remains of magic would leave such an odor. His stared at the body until his inner sight took over, revealing the spiritual tint of blue around the torn throat and face. These were the remains of ward power. He also smelled the scent of female around where the body lay. His eyes gleamed softly with an unnatural light.

"On second thought, Nerul, leave me with the corpse for a goodly space. Prevent any others from coming to this area. I need some time—alone."

The soldier saluted crisply, glad to be removed from the horror.

Quirin bent closer to the body and drew in another deep breath, again tasting the air on his tongue for small clues as to the owner–for like spores in the wind, the fragments left behind by souls had their own flavor. The wounds, too, were a clue for they looked the same as that of a bird of prey. He had never heard of falcons or hawks attacking a human other than in instances of a nest being guarded. He was well acquainted with commoner's tales of changelings, but he and other sorcerers believed these creatures to be extinct. This left only the work of magic, for a counterfeit form could be taken under the power of the arts. The remains of such magic hung around the body in wisps and scented aura. It was not Deive's work, though there was a hint of her flavor. That could only mean that the chit, Alida, had used power beyond what he had thought her capable. He worked over the body for an hour or more until he had memorized the scent that would now be Alida's trademark.

A horrible smile found its way to his lips. They were careless, and because of it, he was given a trail.

Far away, the hungry and travel-weary refugees of Falda found entrance to the walls of Lyrnne Keep. The clatter of horses' hooves in the courtyard could be heard to the upper parapets of the castle.

There had been an escort over the snow-covered hills through the city gates and winding streets once the drover cart's contents had been made known to the guard. Now the noise alerted the entire castle to the visitor's arrival. There was no turning back.

Deive and Alida climbed from the cart stretching listlessly, unconcerned about their surroundings. Their shoulders and backs ached from the cramped riding conditions, and their legs wobbled from disuse. Their skin was chapped and bleeding from the frigid cold. Sores caused by the mites and fleas that flocked to the rotting warmth of the straw covered every inch of their once pampered skin. Their hair was oily and tangled, though they had done their best to keep it within their hoods. Alida's hollow eyes brought Deive from her own grief and discomfort. She whispered to the young woman, straightening her cloak and reassuring her softly. Then, as if in silent agreement, they both held themselves proudly, allowing no further sign of their insecurity or weariness to become visible to their escort. They were of a noble house, and as such would behave with dignity.

Two stiff soldiers escorted them to the main hall and then abruptly left for other duties without as much as a word of welcome.

The women's first view of the interior of the castle was magnificent and humbling. The sweep of two stone staircases on either end of the great hall led the eye to majestic tapestries and gleaming clan icons. The feminine influence of Savine, Alida's aunt, could be seen from the fine stitchery on the table linens to the dried flower arrangements flanking the stone ballasts. The hall also gave off the subtle scents of a woman's perfume. No cost had been spared to make the castle a place of beauty. Yet what it had in luxury, it lacked in warmth and welcome. The servants were closed-mouthed and stiff, and the normal sounds of a busy keep were muted. There was also a decided lack of children and tamed creatures, which in any other keep of this size would have abounded within the hall.

Deive's violet gaze slid over the room without interest in the physicality of the space. Her mixed eltar blood gave her an unusual proficiency for the discerning of spiritual presence, both good and evil, but here she found only a void. The castle was cold, though fires blazed at every hearth, and she wrapped an arm protectively around her ward. Had Greyson known that he was sending his daughter to a tomb, a sort of purgatory where life and normality had been suspended?

Deive felt a hardening deep within her spirit. She could not stand with her defenses down if she intended for them to survive this place.

The sounds of whispering linen drew Deive's eye to the furthest stair where a tall woman, attended by two handmaids, descended to the hall. Deive's grip tightened on Alida's shoulder, and she whispered encouragingly to the young woman. After a small reminder and a kiss, Deive, behaving with graceful decorum, stepped forward and began to introduce herself and her charge. "Good tidings to thee wise mistress of Lyrnne, sister by marriage to Greyson of Falda." That was as far as Deive was able to proceed.

Savine cut her off, dismissing her with a pointed glance and wave of a white hand. Lyrnne's mistress then promptly withdrew a delicate handkerchief from her sleeve. Holding it over her nose, she approached and subsequently addressed her niece.

"You must be Alida," said her aunt in a cool, well-modulated tone. "A bit unpresentable aren't we, my dear? One would think you'd desire best impression since we've never made acquaintance, but perhaps the untamed northern influence of your father has left you more lacking in manners than I thought. He always was somewhat of a boor."

Deive, who was already blistering over Savine's stint with the kerchief, frowned at her overtly rude reference to Alida's newly deceased kin. She warningly placed a hand on Alida's arm, knowing her short temper even under the best of circumstances.

Alida's chin came up a notch, but she, unlike her hostess, showed a decided abundance of manners in bowing and apologizing softly for her state, rather than commenting on the obvious lack of hospitality and grace. Deive knew that Alida's decorum most likely stemmed from the deep exhaustion of both her spirit and body.

Savine's gaze over the handkerchief never changed. She softly circled the two women, noting every detail, while keeping her distance.

After peering at them for some time in this manner, Savine turned on her heel and in parting called out to the handmaids who had been left behind, "Clean them up in the troughs outside. I'll not have the linens and tubs of this keep infected with the lice and fleas they are presumably carrying. Erta can then show them to their rooms. Give them clean attire and the other necessities of a lady's toilette. You needn't overly attend them as I am sure they are accustomed to waiting on themselves." Then in mid-stride she paused and addressed Alida over her shoulder, "We will dine somewhat past the setting of the sun. You'll be expected when the call is made; do not be late or your place will not be held. Oh, and your companion may dine alongside us on the dais. From all appearances, she will behave with decorum."

This time it was Alida's hand upon Deive's arm, which doused any retaliation. Deive's eyes had turned a thunderous purple.

The handmaids, with great discomfort, led the pair out of the hall as politely as they could. They secured a stall in the stable and had a large trough brought in by a stable hand. The tub was filled with freezing water and rough servant's soap. One of the maids rolled up her sleeves and was obviously preparing to strip Alida of her garb when a sharp command from the doorway stopped her.

"How dare ye handle a guest in such a manner?"

The girl stuttered out Savine's instructions but was promptly ordered to stand aside by the sturdy, wide-hipped woman with leaf-brown hair and green eyes who had made her presence duly known.

Erta, as they found her name to be, took them to their quarters. There she had gallons of steaming water brought in until the huge copper chamber tubs had been filled. She proceeded to add generous portions of rose and linseed soap until the room was filled with the fragrance. She apologized gruffly for the behavior of her mistress and the handmaids and bid the two women of Falda welcome.

Deive's and Alida's clothes, which they apologized over, were balled up and thrown into huge linen bags that were taken away immediately to be burned. The maids attended to Erta's every word, for they knew that although Savine was the voice of command in the keep, Erta was the hand.

The women were settled into the tubs while Erta herself rolled up her sleeves and gently set to work cleaning their hair and backs. She sang as she worked, lulling the exhausted kin of her mistress to sleep in the sheltering baths.

Smiling, she left them to rest a bit while she ordered up more hot water.

When the baths were complete, the women were coaxed from the tubs by the promising folds of heavy velvet robes. They were then seated in massive oak chairs set before a blazing fire. Erta ordered that their feet be rubbed brusquely with scented sand and then a lotion made with peppermint and cucumber. Their legs also were treated to the rich lotion while another servant was given instruction to comb and braid their hair.

The sores caused by the fleas were soothed with an odorless paste, and their scratches and cuts were covered with ointment. Deive's wound was checked to make sure it was healing properly, and Erta gave her a drink of thick juice that would aid the healing process.

When all these things had been completed, the women were dressed in clean, warm gowns and tucked away into huge velvet and fur-covered pallets. Erta called the serving women out from the room and left the two travelers to their rest.

Many hours later the call for the evening meal was given. As the final notes of the gong died away, two creatures of beauty descended the stairs. No longer were these kinswomen of Falda dirty and tired.

In her kindly way, Erta had awakened them in plenty of time to dress for the meal that they might not present themselves late. As a result, light gleamed from Alida's head like burnished mahogany and from Deive's like a raven's wing. Both were fair, with the black hair, violet eyes, and the exotic features of Deive speaking of something lush and powerful—the demure, untouchable gaze of Alida speaking of promise. The younger woman had purposefully scorned the blood red gown of mourning. She had no wish to remind herself constantly of the painful passing of loved ones. However, this lack of tradition rankled with Savine, already seated upon the dais, who immediately let her unguarded speech lead the way once again when the two had attained their seats next to her.

She stared straight ahead nodding and smiling at arriving dignitaries while her cold voice ripped her young niece to shreds. "What, no scarlet attire? Think you above tradition? But then again, what should I expect from the useless offspring of an uneducated man and his ninny of a wife! You'll wear the color of mourning from now on, for I would have you honor this house. And as for your companion, it may very well do for her to eat at the tables with the soldiers and serving women, but that is something we can discuss later."

Deive ground her teeth over the woman's lack of mercy. She'd not long tolerate the mistress's forked tongue. Deive concentrated on the tables full of warriors and wenches, gentry and keep managers around them, removing her thoughts from their infuriating hostess.

In an attempt to ease relations between all parties concerned, Alida spoke on the first topic to come to mind using a particularly airy, light tone. "The cold makes a fire and heavy clothes feel so welcoming. Thank you for providing your hearth to myself and Deive." She paused, flashing a bright smile at her aunt and then continued. "Perhaps tomorrow I might have a simple riding tunic and pant so that I may explore my new surroundings? It has been several days since I was able to take a ride alone so the time to think and stretch would be the perfect tonic for my restlessness."

Her aunt's politely astonished face showed that never in her experience had a woman of a noble clan made such a request. The ingratiating smile did little to drain the displeasure in her eyes.

"My dear, such a request will obviously not be honored as you are unmarried and vulnerable to any wandering marauder. I shall never permit your unattended ride cross-country. You are well-bred and should know better than to even think that such an atrocity would be allowed."

Alida swallowed her surprise along with a retort to the hypocritical response of being well bred just after having been told she was not. All contrivements towards merriment dissipating she said softly, "But Aunt, I have known such freedom all my life. It is a privilege and one that I hold dear indeed. How shall I be whole if I may not tend to that part of my nature that screams for flight and fancy?"

Savine sniffed delicately. "To where would you flee, Alida? A lady does not need freedom, but the constraints of daily life, which encourage the desirable attributes of patience and modesty. Daring and brashness, though presumably a part of your earlier life, will not be allowed while in my care. I am determined to form you into that perfect tapestry of malleability, constraint, and helplessness that men desire. All you have is your behavior, beauty, and name. Without such character, you'll be next to useless both to me and any future husband."

Alida swallowed the drink that she had lifted to her mouth and nearly choked in her anger, instantly bristling beneath the smooth derisive tone of her aunt. She was, if nothing else, capable and had always considered herself worthy of trust. Did this woman think her so dimwitted that she'd take her own safety for granted? She also was deeply offended that her aunt, into whose care she'd been given, thought of her as nothing more than a broodmare to be bought and sold at will.

Her tone cooled greatly, and she turned to Savine, speaking no louder than could be heard by the two of them and Deive. "I assure you that I am anything but helpless, Aunt. My mother and father encouraged my natural talents for archery and skillful riding, as well as giving me the ability to tend sensibly to my own protection. They also schooled me extensively in the use of a dirk and sword, should I find myself in battle one day."

When Savine sought to speak, Alida held up her hand and continued. "And whatever your opinion on my mother's character and strength, Aunt, she also was neither weak nor submissive. T'was her knife's twist—felt in the ribs of a soldier twice her size—that gave Deive and I the opportunity to slip away when the siege first began. I only wish she had allowed me to stay and fight alongside her. For had she allowed this, Deive and I would have never been separated, and my last view of my mother would not have been of another of Quirin's unwashed followers sending her to her death. She kept me from the impending danger out of great love for me; you keep me "safe" out of concern only for yourself and your future.

And as to my riding unescorted about the countryside, being an 'atrocity' as you called it, a true atrocity is watching your kin's forked tongue slashing away the memory of a beloved sire and dam upon every possible occasion. Even in our 'untamed northern region' as you've so named it, civility and hospitality rein over self-concern. Apparently those of your province consider such honorable traits beneath you."

With those words, Alida gently lay down the crumpled linen napkin, which had been unmercifully squeezed in her hand, and excused herself, slipping out of the great hall into the night for a breath of clean and healing air.

Deive gazed across the broad-polished table, attempting to control her anger at the indelicate manners expressed by her hostess. Her tone was as quiet as had been Alida's, being meant for Savine's ears alone.

"Mistress, it would do you well to remember that Alida is my ward, and to her welfare, I am more than capable of attending. She is young and struggles yet with the pain of having lost her entire family, birthright, and people. You are to be her material guardian, but I was assigned the whole care of her person at birth. I know her capabilities and strength. Into my hands her ultimate safety was given, heed therefore, I pray thee, my counsel. You can only make an enemy of her on your present course."

Savine shifted uncomfortably under the piercing gaze. "Watch your place, Nurse. Well trained you are, but not without the weakness of needing my charity. While under my roof, you and your ward will bear in mind the rules I have set forth. Do not toy with her future or your own."

Deive turned away her voice, very near to a whisper. "Just when I believe your manners have expressed the basest emotion, you stoop lower still. How dare you remind those under your care that they rely solely on your coffers! Giving, if not done from the heart, is the same as taking."

Savine, sneering and indignant, said nothing. When the silence between the women outlasted any hope of bettering relations, Deive returned to her meal. The roasted pheasant and boar with mushrooms, turnips, bread, sauced berries, and strong honey mead spread out on the table before her, its fragrance bidding her to eat. Deive grinned wryly to herself, if nothing else, while here at Castle Lyrnne, they would not starve.

Early the next morning before the sun could rise; Alida awoke and lay quietly for a while, trying to remember where she was. When she realized that she was in her aunt's keep and was now a ward of that holding, she felt an angry tear slide down her cheek. Not normally one to feel sorry for herself, she was surprised at her reaction. It was definitely time for some vigorous exercise, a good tonic for keeping one's mind occupied.

Unable to sleep any longer, she climbed from her warm pallet stretching and yawning in the chilly air of a dark winter morning. She then quickly clothed herself in borrowed leggings and a tunic that Erta had found for her the night before. Little time was spent brushing and braiding her hair and cleaning her teeth before donning a dark cloak and slipping from her chamber. She quietly made her way down the servant's stairs like a shadow and went out through an unguarded side door in the kitchen pantry.

The freezing morning air hit her full force as she rounded the corner on the way to the stables. She leaned against that frigid blast and let it whip her cloak into a frenzy around her ankles, before running silently the rest of the way through the deepest shadows.

When she approached the stable door farthest from the drawbridge, she gathered her senses and quietly glanced about; making sure that no one was nearby before proceeding to open the heavily carved oak door. A sentry approached as she slipped into the enormous low-slung building, but he did not turn to pass by, as she had thought, instead he headed for the very door she was just closing. She quickly let herself into the nearest stall, pleased with the familiar musky scent of horses and fresh hay that enveloped her. She ducked down into a corner of the stall, pressing against the rough boards while praying that the horse would not give away her location. As she huddled there in the dark, she heard the quiet rustle of hay as the owner of the stall moved forward to see who had come to visit. The horse muttered in the dark, and she felt it press against her side, softly blowing on her clothing and hair as he discovered who she was.

The guard paused only a moment and then with a clipped pace made his rounds through the stables. With so many aisles of stalls and storerooms to check, it was quite some time before he had exited out another door on the other end of the stables.

Alida let out a great sigh, thanking the gods that she had not been found out.

Her walk the night before had not only produced the knowledge that the pantry door was unguarded but also the sight of a magnificent stallion being unshod until the next day. When the groom had walked away, she had become acquainted with the beast. Within a matter of moments, the gorgeous, satiny black stallion had relinquished his will under the power of her firm but sweet persuasion. She had watched until the same groom had returned to bed the beast down for the night, putting him into the very stall in which she now stood.

She smiled at the horse's reacquaintance with her, giving him a small apple as a good morning tribute. While he munched on the treat, she wound strips of coarsely woven burlap around his hooves to mute their eventual travel through the cobbled courtyard. The sentry would be in the other half of the yards by now, but she would not risk any echoes.

It wasn't long before she quietly let herself and the horse out, approaching a small door in the side of one of the keep's outer walls. An ear pressed to the wood gave no further reason for caution. She slipped out into the surrounding snowy meadow with the horse in tow his utter trust of her endearing. Then keeping close to the castle wall, she led him round the perimeter until she reached the woods behind.

"If I have to keep this up I'll be more exhausted than free," she whispered in the horse's ear. The response of his soft nicker made her laugh. "One of these days I'll have to learn your true name, until that time, you'll be called Raven. I have need of your services, and you have a feel as broad as my own heart when it is winged."

With that, she had him kneel and mounted him bareback, her arms around his massive neck until he had stood once more. When she had gained her seat and had his reins fully in hand, she gently nudged him to a quick walk, not wanting too much motion or sound to rouse the guards up on the wall behind them.

With the approach of the woods, she was able to give Raven his head, and he proved to be as fleet footed as she had hoped.

When she had come to the next meadow, Alida spurred the giant stallion into a gallop. She was an excellent horsewoman, and though her lithe form seemed inconsequential to his size and power, she controlled him to perfection. She gloried in the closer contact of his bare back, which let her feel Raven's pleasure at this unexpected freedom.

Throughout the ride she absorbed as much of the broad beauty of the countryside around her as was possible in the dim blue light of morning. It was a good deal more rounded than the craggy mountains near her home, but it had its own mystery as well. The birdcalls, with the coming rise of the sun, were alien to her ears, and the scent of the woods and snow were unfamiliar but sweet.

When they reached the middle of a large field, she gathered her muscles and leapt from Raven's back, rolling into the deepest drift she could find. His quizzical expression brought ready laughter to her eyes, then without warning, she burst into tears. He cantered back to her and nuzzled her ear with his poky whiskers. Then blowing on her face, he stood as close to her as he could.

Her tears rolled from her face dripping to the snow in shimmering drops before disappearing. When she began talking to the beast her voice quivered with anguish. "By the gods, Raven, I miss my parents. This is only the seventh dawn since their death. How will it feel to go on day by day with my heart this torn and broken?" She choked down the sobs that rose from her gut, having never felt so alone.

Raven brought his head close to her's, responding to the anxiousness he felt from her. She patted his silky cheek and chuckled through her tears when he blew on her face. "You remind me of Shining. He was a grand dappled grey. My father presented him to me on my last birth celebration. He never gelded my mounts and would have been proud that I handle you so well though you are a strange horse to be so responsive on the first ride. Have I indeed cast such a thorough spell upon you?"

Raven tossed his head and pushed her deeper into the snow. She lay there looking up at the muted colors of dawn. The golden streaks, which had just now begun to show, burned as brightly as her mother's hair. She missed every thing about the woman—her scent, her tenderness, the huskiness of her voice when she sang, and her fire and determination. Her mother hadn't been weak, and she would shame neither her dam nor her sire by being emotionally crippled. However, she also knew that tears and sorrow were a necessary and natural part of her recovery from their deaths.

She settled into the snowy cradle around her, gazing up into the changing sky. It was silent here and beautiful. She let the morning seep down into her, occasionally choking back sobs that were so deep that they hurt her chest.

All at once, she remembered an ancient keening melody she'd heard the warriors of her keep use during funerals for their comrades. Its message of death and rebirth caused the tears to course unbidden down her cheeks, for her sobs could no longer be restrained. When she could, she sang aloud to accompany her memory, the tears choking back some of the most powerful lines. When she finished the first few bars and the last note was dying away in the morning air, two shooting stars slid through the sky's predawn color.

She sat up hugging her knees to her chest, screaming into the skies at the unfairness of having been left very nearly alone to make her own way. Here the world turned as normal, with snow falling and stars making their course, while her and her private world ground to a stop. She was angry, hurt and even fearful. For the burden of all that she had lost, lay with her at night and rose with her each morning. The screams turned into deep sobs that wracked her whole body. The pit of her stomach felt as if it had been wrenched out. When sheer exhaustion caused her sobs to slow, Alida shakily rose to her feet.

Silence spread around her, the cool of the winter air soft on her hot, damp cheeks. She hugged her arms around her middle trying to remember how it felt to be hugged by her father and held by her mother. She resolved silently to not forget their particular smiles or the ways they performed duties throughout the day, as if by keeping these small things, she would somehow keep them.

As the memories became more vivid with recall, she wiped away her tears, collecting her voice. They would not be forgotten. Perhaps one day she would have a bard write a song to commemorate their triumphs. Until that time, she would dedicate her simple warrior's song to all that she had loved about them and her homeland.

Some of the notes that followed were so low and grating that the young woman felt them as deeply as if they had been her own moans of anguish. She sang the song to the finish, swallowing back tears as they rose in her throat, for she felt as if this were her first test of honor and womanhood.

Back at the castle, Deive sat straight up in bed from a deep sleep. She listened to the silence in the castle and then felt her heart stir once again as she listened closer. A sweet sadness shot through her breast and the groggy warmth of her still sleep-filled mind as she absorbed the power of Alida's song and farewells. She gathered up her purple dressing gown and stepped to the window looking far out into the surrounding meadows.

Just a little farther. Her inner sight stretched further than her physical ability ever could.

Opening the windows, she reached forth her arms and a small button of light crept from the tips of her fingers and out through the window. She sent it with messages of hope and empathy, feeling unity with her charge and yet a peculiar singleness as well in her own sorrow.

Alida's mourning had begun her own. She left the window and climbed the stairs outside her room to the uppermost parapets. When she reached the top, she sang the accompanying harmony to Alida's song in low, sweet tones. Her hands wove in and out in magic signs, older than memory, as she symbolically pulled shards of pain from her heart and mind and body. She had lost her adopted daughter, Fiona, as well as dear friends who had been with her much of her life; and all because of the black hatred of Quirin. For even though she had not seen him, she had felt the mad curling tendrils of his anger on the day of the siege. She had known that Fiona was cut down before Alida had told her, for a wound had seeped deep into the flesh of her heart. Now she wept for Fiona, Alida's parents, and her friends amongst the servants. Her keening was silent, making her a strange sight atop the castle with outstretched arms, flying black hair, and purple robes akimbo. Her last, silent tear was for a lifelong love she'd never admitted to Alida and often times not even to herself.

When the stars shot through the sky, she laughed to herself. "What a sign you two have sent me." With those words, she closed the circle of her hands and recognized the strengthening of her place as acting guardian.

She knew that Alida, somewhere out in those fields, still mourned, yet in sharing this small thing they would share more than either could have ever said.

The cold suddenly became very apparent in that moment and Deive left Alida to the privacy of her sorrow, for the warmth of her chambers below.

Out in the fields, Alida tasted the power, as the button of light that had waited for the right moment settled upon her lips. Deive knew. She continued breathing in the morning, and when the sun had risen a little higher in the sky, bringing true dawn, Alida headed back towards the keep. Knowing that her aunt would not arise until noontide, she had stayed as long as possible. The horse would be missed first, but not if she could slip back into the courtyard and stables unnoticed.

With a greater urgency than she had felt earlier, she rode Raven hard until she was once again in the surrounding forest next to the castle. She kept close to the walls, waiting until the sentry moved off and then slipped back through the same side door from which they'd left. She had just removed the burlap strips from his hooves when the sleepy groom opened the stall. She pressed against the wooden wall in the shadows until he had hung a full water bucket and grain bag on the waiting hooks just inside the door.

The nickers of the other horses drew the groom away before he could notice the sweat covering Raven's chest and back. Alida, unable to leave such a fine horse without rubbing it down, set to work as softly as she could. When the job was completed, she slipped out into the courtyard and back towards the pantry door, having again awaited the passing of the sentries.

However, she forgot to listen at the door to the kitchen, and she walked in, nearly colliding with the head cook and Erta, who were already about the business of the day. Erta, with a scowl wreathing her pleasant face, pulled her aside.

The housekeeper waited until Alida looked her fully in the eye, her green gaze piercing and stern. "What are ye doin'? I loaned the clothin' to you with the understandin' that your jaunts would be discreet. Thank the gods, 'twas us you ran into. I'll be able to explain away your behavior this once, but not again!"

"Erta, Love," said Ansel with every conciliatory tone, "there is no need to explain anythin'. You know I'd undermine the grand Savine at any and every chance given." Then turning to Alida, the cook gathered his best stern demeanor, shaking his finger in Alida's face and growling, "Don't think you needn't heed the good Erta's warnin'. For Savine is a cat with many eyes in the mice that serve her!"

"What if I was merely out for a walk in the courtyard this morning," Alida said with a glimmer in her eye and quick wink.

Erta was not amused, "Aye, but what is the purpose of the man's attire then, if you were only walkin'?"

Being duly warned, Alida smiled thankfully and ran back to her rooms.

Erta shook her head, "Poor lass, I'd do anythin' if I could help ease those tears from her lovely cheeks. I'd warrant all I had that she's a good girl with a good heart. May the gods take their pleasure out on the hides of all the beasts what took from her all she's ever known."

Ansel squeezed her shoulders and kissed her softly. "With some attention and a little winkin' when it comes to what we see her do, she'll be right as rain soon enough. I'll take it upon me'self to make sure that the guards and groomsmen know that they might have a missing mount occasionally."

Erta patted his cheek and ordered, "Get ye back to work, before I kiss all the goodness right out o' ye!"

———————————————————————

The next few weeks, Alida spent her days exploring the castle, courtyard, and stables of Lyrnne. Savine had also begrudgingly allowed Alida an escorted exploration of the city with the exception of "the braziers." It was an undesirable part of the city reserved for brothels, gaming houses and a generally uncouth citizenry, which did most of its activity at night, by the light of the coal-filled containers. More secretly of course, when she could, she would slip off in the mornings for rides on Raven outside the city walls.

The stable hand had told her that the horse's name was "Grimace," because from the time he was a foal, he would frown at people that tried to train him. As he grew older that special expression of disdain was saved for those that tried to ride him. She thought the name he had been given was terrible, for he had never looked at her that way; so she continued to call him Raven when they were alone. They made a marvelous pair, and Alida looked forward to her daily public visits with the horse. Other than Ansel, Erta, and a few select guards, no one would have guessed her capabilities as a horsewoman for she acted very naive bringing the beast apples and asking questions that anyone familiar with horses would know.

Alida was not surprised by Savine's response one evening when one of the warriors, over supper, mentioned that he thought the stallion had a special attachment to the girl. Savine had declared that no ungelded mount would ever be appropriate company for the young woman and even ordered that Alida keep her distance from "those high-strung, dangerous beasts." Savine had no taste for equine pursuits and did her best to curb her niece's taste towards the same.

As the days passed within the walls of Lyrnne, amidst the normalcy of common people and common duties, Alida felt a fragile healing begin to take place in her shattered heart. She still mourned, but it only caught her sharply at odd moments now and then when some expression on a friend's face or a scent would remind her of her home and family. Time was proving to be the aid she needed. She did not know how or when it came, but she was beginning to feel assured that perhaps she would overcome the blows fate had dealt her.

Because she was still healing, Alida tried to keep occupied during as many of her waking hours as possible, not just acquainting herself with the physical aspects of the castle but also its inhabitants. She made many friends, but clung most dearly to her relationship with Deive, which now had grown even deeper as they related to one another as peers rather than as nurse and child. When the questions about fate or the world around her would become too deep and heavy to bear alone, she would seek out her mentor and friend for much-needed advice.

The Madame of the castle seethed over the fact that she had no emotional control over her niece. She also felt that the castle had grown somehow louder and perhaps less controlled since their arrival. This, combined with the fact that none of her own people had ever responded to her as they did to these two, greatly pricked her closely held pride.

The people of the keep recognized all too well the bitter jealousy of their mistress, and they sought almost as a whole to protect Deive and Alida from her pettiness. Erta replaced the coarse, prickly undergarments that Savine had ordered for the women with some made of soft cotton. She watched as her mistress dumped an herb into Alida's drink that would cause indigestion and cramps, promptly replacing it herself with a fresh cup of good juice when Savine's back was turned. She laundered Alida's clothes daily so that when she rode Raven and returned to the keep, her rooms would not smell of horse. Erta and Ansel together wrapped little gifts of cake and baubles bought with their own money and placed them under the pillows of the two women, finding with delight similar gifts put in their rooms when they least expected.

There was no real harm to the camaraderie that had arisen beneath Savine's nose. Secretly, however, Erta feared that the dangerously hateful child she had seen in her early years at the castle would somehow return in the woman who was now ruler of the keep. Savine would not see the friendships as being harmless. She wanted every ounce of control for herself.

Spring was fast approaching, despite the petty, silent wars that went on behind the keep walls.

Alida became restless in response both to the occasionally tense atmosphere of the keep and the promising hope of warmer days and green fields. When she grew careless about the length of her morning rides, she was strictly reprimanded by Deive, who had not so admonished her in months.

"Alida, you must beware the rising of the sun! You've been staying out past the time when prudence is your guide. If you are caught, Savine shall not let you ride again, escorted or not, for some time. Moreover, do not forget that you are not the only one involved in this ruse. It has taken many hands to ease the way of your comfort. Do not risk the discipline of those who have faithfully assisted you."

Alida was momentarily quiet, recognizing the truth of what her friend spoke. Then she said softly, "I would find a way, Deive. I'll not let her keep me locked up when there is a world beyond to explore. But, for your peace and the safety of those who have helped me, I will watch the sun more closely and return at the beckoned time." Deive knew that the weight of the responsibility of caring for Savine's people sometimes weighed heavily upon her charge. At the same time, the wise guardian recognized that in order to develop a character proper for a clan chieftess, Alida would need to accept restraints even when they occasionally chafed against her wild nature.

It was not many mornings later when Alida awoke to a different scent and knew that spring had finally appeared. She dressed quietly in soft, grey-colored leggings and a warm, dark blue cotton tunic topped with a lightweight, dark grey woolen cloak. For her feet, she pulled on soft, dark grey kidskin boots with pointed toes, which lacked any solid heel that could give away her stealthy creeping about. The whole ensemble was chosen for its ability to blend in with the shifting grey blues of predawn. Slipping out of the room she shared with Deive, Alida went gliding down the stairs and along her usual path out of the kitchen. Today's ride would be especially exhilarating with the newly warmed breezes and abundant wildlife she expected outside the gates of the keep. The wise warnings of her mentor those few days before were utterly forgotten by the young woman in her excitement to explore.

CHAPTER TWO

BERYNTH, IN THE PROVINCE OF LYRNNE

The smell of warm horseflesh and crisp spring wind flowed in currents around Alida as she gave Raven his head in the fields far beyond the castle. The steed's broad back became quickly heated under the insistent and joyous commands of his mistress. He glimmered in the light of a newly rising sun with shadows of blue and purple dancing in his fine, dark hair beneath Alida's grey-clad legs. He, too, felt the promise inspired by spring and his step was light and swift, nearly that of a dance. Alida was all too aware of his excitement, for it was translated to her through the powerful muscles that bunched and moved beneath her own athletic form.

Then it was as if the wind had become Raven's blood, for he stretched into his fullest speed with Alida bending low over his back. Unable to contain her joy, she whooped loudly in exhilaration, not knowing that a far-off figure had paused to watch their progress.

Ulrich Drachmund, Chieftain of the Heights, sat golden and powerful in the dawning rays of the morning. A rare smile smoothed the lines around his mouth as he watched the young lad on the distant horse career over hill and dell, keeping perfect control of the massive stallion. It wasn't often that so slight a rider could control that much exuberant horseflesh, and he was intrigued. It would pay to have such a talent under one's tutelage.

Most grooms would just be rising to feed and muck out stalls, still sleepily stumbling about and groaning over the weight of their duties. Perhaps, as in the case of this young lad, the love of horses was a stronger force than sleep or a jealous owner. Ulrich was ready to bet a good deal that the true master would be aghast that such a prize mount was being pranced about in plain view of any number of thieves, pack dogs, and marauders.

His curiosity gaining the best of him, Ulrich decided to follow the lad through the morning paces. Perhaps if the youth were not yet set in his loyalty, the lord would ride home with a new equerry. He turned his own mount and rode behind, careful of his distance, so as not to alert the boy to his presence.

========

It wasn't long before both riders were ensconced deeply in the shadows of the forest where dawn had not yet crept. The cool, fragrant branches of cedar and fir swept down from the rich canopy above, caressing the faces of both riders with dew-wet fingers.

Though it was spring, the morning was still brisk, especially beneath the cover of the trees. Alida wrapped her cloak more tightly about her shoulders and laughed when moisture from overhead branches crept down her neck and between her shoulder blades.

The sudden, light sound of laughter that issued from the lad startled Ulrich. He could well imagine that the boy was teased for his feminine tones. The lad's voice must not have yet changed, making it even more incredible that his age was no impediment to his riding.

When Ulrich rounded a corner, thinking to see the rider and mount, he was surprised to find that they had disappeared. He slowed his pace and watched the fuzzy ears of his own mount swivel, catching the muted sounds around them. When his charger snorted, prancing nervously and nearly carrying them off the path, Ulrich stopped and dismounted quietly, every nerve alert to any unusual sound or scent. He had only gone about fifteen paces when he heard someone singing a lively song in a false bass voice. He peaked through the branches of a towering fir, and there before him was a hidden glen, nestled close to a little mossy hill. A hot spring, in the bank of the hill, trickled down into a warm, deep pond whose mist was even now rising softly from the surface of the water in the cool morning air. A woman with long, curly brown hair waded in the water with men's trousers, which she was wearing, bunched up to the middle of her thighs. She was completely at ease singing with great gusto and merriment.

He saw the discarded hooded cloak of the lad he'd been following and had to struggle to keep from chuckling aloud. The slender woman before him, dressed in those ridiculous leggings and a man's tunic, had led him to believe, through her dress, seat, and excellent horsemanship that she was of a different gender.

His delight in the beauty before him turned to puzzlement, for he could imagine none of the noble houses in the area allowing such a prize as this to wander alone outside the protective walls of the city. He assumed, therefore, the creature before him was perhaps of merchant blood, because despite the rough, male clothing and absence of escort, her skin and hair showed a pampering not common amongst laborers.

It was also more than unusual to see a noblewoman display the strength that had been an obvious part of her riding skills. He squatted low to the snow-dappled ground so his perusal of her would go unnoticed. True intrigue was not a daily occurrence. He had been a warrior all of his life and was seldom surprised by anything. To see such a woman under these circumstances warmed his mind to an attractive mystery.

After watching her for the better part of an hour, Ulrich with a great surge of boldness stepped from the cover of the forest and brazenly leaned against the trunk of a cedar tree. It was enough movement to cause her head to come round.

Alida stared at the golden-haired man dressed in dark, well-worn leather, a long, rough cloak, and heavy black boots. The leather chest plate he wore was emblazoned with a galloping red wolf, and his dark blue-green eyes were piercing enough to lend credence to this crest.

She quickly stepped from the water and bent down as if to pick up her cloak, keeping her eye on him the entire time—too late, he realized that she had hidden a sword beneath the cloak. He had just drawn his own as she lunged forward, her blade nipping at his sword arm painfully.

She withdrew only long enough to recover her footing before they began a full-fledged round of well-matched parries and thrusts. There was nothing amateur about her stance or use of her weapon, and Ulrich was disgusted with his underestimation of her. His initial surprise wore off as a rhythm was set in their swordplay.

Each was skilled and competitive, but Alida had never seen some of the techniques that the man before her used. His style was just different enough that she found herself constantly off balance.

Presently Ulrich lunged and caught her on the same arm that he himself had been cut. He only nicked her both because her own skill kept it from being worse and from his purposeful withholding of a deeper wound. He knew the wound she had made on his arm was only superficial, and he had no intent of injuring her worse than she had him.

All at once, he chuckled; the low, warm sound at odds with the situation. "Do you not find it amusing that we've never met and yet we battle?" he said softly.

Alida sneered as her parries quickened. "Would you find it amusing if I were a man?"

Ulrich grinned. "If you were a man we would have had some polite squaring off before jumping into battle with one another. If you were a man, you would have been wearing an emblem by which you'd be instantly recognized. And, my lovely woodland sprite, if you were a man I would have stayed to the forest, going on about my business and avoiding anything unpleasant by doing so."

She didn't respond, for his movements had increased as if in challenge. Rather than giving way, she increased her own offense, but he kept her at bay.

Ulrich watched her, playing off her technique, while constantly looking for ways to overcome her. She was cautious, but not weak, and he didn't relish the thought of another wound. Quickly, he found a hole in her style that would give him the advantage. He watched for the move again, and when he saw it, he stepped in and disarmed her with a single flick of his wrist.

Alida gaped in chagrin as her sword went clattering into the pond. Before she could turn and run, he leaped forward and took her down, slamming her into the soft earth near the pool. They struggled for a moment as he attempted to pin her down, the task difficult with his sword still in hand. It was then that he felt the chilled blade of a small dirk biting into his exposed neck. She was quick and had withdrawn it from her waistband as they fell.

He chuckled again, marveling at her resourcefulness, and with a smooth motion, he quickly moved off her, drawing back just enough to ensure his own safety without relinquishing his threat to her. He didn't move as he watched her with great interest, his blade circling dangerously before him.

Alida was anything but amused as she struggled to her feet, "What do you want, or need I even ask a ruffian and cad such as yourself?"

Ulrich smiled, a wolfish-grin wreathing his face. "If that is what I had come for, I would have taken it already. I was watching you long before I made my presence known."

Alida felt chills crawl up her spine. She warily grasped her dirk, keeping an eye on his rotating blade, which was all too securely held in his grasp.

"If you mean me no harm, why did you not announce your intentions when you stepped from the forest?"

Ulrich didn't respond, but instead lunged forward and disarmed her of the dirk.

Alida's eyes grew wide in fear, for she had no other tricks to employ, and she knew by now that he was not someone to trifle with. She whistled shrilly and turned, quickly gathering up her cloak and boots, praying that Raven was on his way. Her bare feet dug into the cold ground, a desperate energy enlivening their movement. Within moments, she was astride the obedient charger that had answered her call, kicking him towards home, ignoring the pain and splinters in her frozen, abused feet.

Alida continued to glance over her shoulder as she fled the woods, watching the progress of her golden-haired pursuant.

Ulrich, who had mounted his own steed not too long after her hasty exit, laughed under his breath at the retreat of the forest sprite. She was again quicker than his estimation, and he had to use all his own cunning, speed, and talent to keep up with her. He loved a challenge and had found it most unexpectedly this morning in the slim, mounted rider before him.

Alida's headlong flight brought her quickly to the edge of the forest, thankfully coming out near the castle where she would reenter through her usual route. She lost sight of her pursuer and did not see that he had emerged yards down from where she was.

She pause for a moment, quickly taking stock of her torn, soaked garments, praying that she still looked the part of a lad with the cloak hood covering her hair and hooding her features. When her assessment of her apparel proved sufficient and her boots had been hastily pulled on, she wheeled the large beast towards the walls of the keep.

The warlord sat mulling over her behavior as he watched her enter a thicket near the keep. Why would she have to appear to be a lad within the city walls or in the castle keep itself? Was she a prisoner or a kept woman to some warrior or warlord within? Was there some hunger within her fiery breast that caused her to so foolishly risk her life? He could tell from her actions that she was aware of the danger she'd put herself in by wandering outside of the keep alone. Yet there should have been no danger to her within.

The sprite's destination further puzzled him, for the keep belonged to none other than Savine of Lyrnne. The lands had been passed on in her family for ages, and her and her kin were enemies of his own holdings. Her father and mother had held their lands with the lack of respect commonly seen amongst many of noble blood. Tales from those that no longer served within Lyrnne's walls had related incidents of servants being regularly beaten and made examples of to the others. Costly gifts were expected from all the laborers on the land, and very little was given in the way of aid during rough winters or war. He remembered Savine herself as being petty and spoiled, her looks ruined by a mulish mouth and sharp haughty eyes. There had also been rumors of late that due to mismanagement her lands and keep were losing their once abundant wealth.

What was the female that he'd seen and fought with doing in the keep of this sharp-tongued snake? The door the girl had entered would not put her into the city but the castle directly. Apparently, these lands did not breed spiritless women. He resolved to come to the keep the next day to see if this was a pattern of behavior on her part. Eventually, if it was indeed a daily occurrence, the maiden could be trapped and coaxed into giving information should his own investigation fail.

With that, he turned his sweating mount and melted back into the shadows of the forest, his mind alive with the morning's adventure. He grinned to himself. He liked women who were uncommonly spirited and strong. In his experience, females with that nature were nearly nonexistent in his peer group. Women of the clan houses were overly trained and under stimulated from birth, until they fit against one another as spearheads made from a mold. He was often hard pressed to mind his tongue and manners when state affairs brought such insipid but eligible maids from around the province. He was unwilling to seek the hand of anyone who would not match his intensity, for he desired a mate in the truest sense of the word.

At his wandering train of thought, Ulrich shook his golden head. Had his thoughts taken him to wedlock so quickly? He laughed quietly at his foolishness and turned his mount for the little glade. Though it was true that he was intrigued, he did not intend to become unnecessarily wrapped up in this adventure. No maid yet had proved to be what he hoped, and he was unwilling to believe that this one would offer anything different. However, it wouldn't hurt to keep a souvenir of the morning adventure. Alida's sword and dirk were retrieved from where he had disarmed her and taking the treasures with him the chieftain returned to his own lands.

Alida crept up the stairs to her room and donned her normal attire with shaking hands. Her heart was still pounding hard from her jaunt in the forest, and she recognized the need to show even more care than she had promised Deive. With shaky hands, she began to try to brush her hair, which had bits of moss, mud, and twigs caught in its abundant locks. Her arm ached from the cut she'd received during her battle. It had not yet fully dried shut, so she tried to bandage it with a strip of torn linen from a towel. Without warning, she began to cry. What if she had been killed or hurt too badly to return; Deive would have been alone, the last of the women of Falda. She tried to gulp down the hysterical tears that rose up in her throat at that thought. She made another go at getting her self in order, but when she saw that it would do no good without a bath, she simply gave into the tears, frustration, and fright. It was in this state of utter disarray that Deive entered the room behind her.

"Alida, you look like you have been rolling around on the forest floor. What has happened?"

Deive's eyes widened as she caught sight of the bandaged arm and tear-stained cheeks. "Who did this to you? So help me, by the gods, if anyone has harmed you, he will pay!"

Alida struggled to cease her crying and wiped at the muddy tears that streaked her cheeks. "How dare you burst in here and start flinging questions at me! Please leave me alone—I will be all right!" She then promptly burst into tears again.

Deive was beside herself. "What is wrong? You are hysterical and you're frightening me! Please calm yourself and allow me to help you!"

Alida choked out amidst further gales of tears, "Please don't be angry with me. I couldn't handle that right now."

Deive just scowled, so Alida continued, "I took as much care as I could in my morning ride and was preparing to return to the castle, but was tempted beyond control when I came upon the cleverest little cove. I found a little hot spring tucked away in the cove and set myself to have a bath. Without a second thought, I took leave to do just that. I waded in and was in the process of enjoying myself immensely, when I heard a sound. I looked up and saw a man standing against a nearby tree, watching me with great delight."

Deive choked out, "Surely you weren't naked!"

Alida shook her head vigorously. "No! I was still clothed, Deive! How foolish do you think I am?"

Deive just stared at her, and Alida hung her head, finishing the story. "I immediately grabbed my sword and proceeded to fight him, but he disarmed me and toppled me to the ground. I was blessed that I had my dirk available for who knows what would have happened then. He took that from me too, but I escaped and rode like the wind making it to the castle safely."

Deive was quiet for a moment and then stepped forward squeezing the young woman's shoulder with an iron grip.

"Obviously, by your tears and guilty countenance, you realize that you may have been captured and held for a king's ransom, or things much more unmentionable, but most importantly, you could have been lost to me forever."

With that, Alida was again in tears.

Deive all at once realized the true cause of her friend's distress. She hugged her tight and whispered soothingly, "We will not lose each other for a very long time, Dear, for there is too much yet to teach you."

When Erta knocked on the door sometime later, she found the two of them attempting to set Alida in order. Erta in her usual efficient way, without questions, ordered a bath and fresh attire. The trousers and other clothing were bagged, washed, mended and returned to their rightful male owner.

Some rooms away, Savine's smooth voice and sharp clap of summons pushed away the silence in her quiet, darkened chambers. "Lizel, send Erta to me at once and do not delay in helping me dress! I wish to be the first down to break my fast. Your information that my ungrateful niece has been riding unattended about the countryside in the mornings, in obvious rebellion of the discussion we had months ago, has been most useful. I intend to let her know this morning just who exactly holds the keys to her future. When she learns the nature of the punishment she is to receive, as well as the punishment I will meet out to those who aided her she'll not so brazenly ignore my commands."

The glittering gaze that Savine turned on Erta, who had just stepped into the room sent the head servant's stomach into a downward spiral. Surely, it was Savine's intent to make an example of her. Mistress Savine's gaze did not waver as she called in her personal guard to escort Erta out to the prisoners' hold until such time as the meeting out of her punishment. Lizel, the cruel-faced serving woman who had been gathering up her mistress' clothing, made it clear by her manner and cat-like grin that she was anything but sympathetic to Erta's resolute expression. Lizel had fantasies of one day replacing Erta and hoped that the information she had given to Savine would hasten her cause. Some moment's later, in a sweeping flurry of linen and aromatic water, Savine descended to the great hall below to face her rebellious niece and the eltar nursemaid. In Savine's wake, Lizel followed, the servant's weak chin and large nose jutting into the air like greasy rock formations.

The presence of malicious power chased away the light scent of spring that had filtered into the hall through opened doors and windows. Deive almost gagged on the spiteful gloom that had fallen over the morning and turned towards the presence as if it were a living thing. She was not surprised to find that it was emanating from the keep's Mistress.

Savine's voice was low and steely as she approached the table where Alida had come quickly to her feet. "Good morn to thee, Niece. I see by your expression that you find it unusual that I should arrive so early at the table to break my fast, but then unusual circumstances require my immediate attendance."

Deive stood silently, feeling as if the tip of a hungry blade waited for their blood.

Savine took her spot, the silent darkness of her mood chasing away any beauty from her slender patrician face. She was as still as a carved ivory maiden on a crypt. This deathly calm pooled around her for she was the eye in the storm tossed waters of the scuttling servants who nervously arranged her utensils and served her breakfast. Then in the clamor, her voice whispered almost too softly to be heard, "You have been a reckless girl, one whose behavior requires instant and thorough punishment. Do you know of what I speak?"

Alida's startled glance to Deive was full of meaning. How had she been discovered?

Savine turned then with a sharp gaze and pinched Alida's cheeks painfully between her thin elegant fingers. The mistress's voice was low like a snarl. "Answer me, girl! What is your defense for ignoring my demands and pursuing these mad rides upon the plain?"

Alida jerked away from the pincer-like grasp and drew herself up. It took all she had, to fight back the sneer that sought to creep upon her lovely lips from the corners of her mouth. "You desire the truth, Aunt? Then the truth I shall give. I am no *girl* that stands before thee but a young woman having already suffered much and learned much for her time. I loathe you and your lack of grace. I loathe this keep that smacks of your vanity and your wasteful lusts. I abhor your treatment of your servants, and most of all, I hate your control that never seeks to teach, never guides, never loves. You are an empty, cruel woman and your house will fall before your eyes, leaving one that is better to take your place."

Savine's eyes glittered at her niece's retort. There was one master of this keep, and she would remain so or take it with her to the grave. She pushed away from the table as she rose to her feet—her knuckles turning white as she grasped her napkin in her bejeweled hand. "Only once before in my experience has a direct order from my hand been dismissed with such complete ignorance. I had a slave once who had been given to me by my father as a gift. She was honored in our keep for her beauty and skills with song and lyre. She was given the highest seat among the servants and was called to entertain us nearly every evening. This girl fell in love with an eltar halfling from an enemy keep to the north. The little trollop carried out her clandestine romance right beneath my nose for more than a year. When I discovered her disloyalty, I had her title and position stripped from her. A physician was sent to examine her after another servant swore that she was with child. It was indeed discovered that she carried this enemy's tainted seed. She was kept under lock and key until the babe was born. My loyal guard then destroyed this seed borne of her unlawful union with the enemy, and she was set as an example to the whole of the serving class, both with a beating and then in her later demise in our dungeon. The eltar halfling never sought to free her, and it is assumed he disappeared out of cowardice as such of ignoble blood is wont to do."

When her smooth voice had died away in the silence, Savine called her personal guard to her side. "Tremain will escort you to the dungeon, Alida, where you will be stripped of your fine gowning. While in confinement, you'll be allowed no contact with your nursemaid or others within the castle. You'll eat the humble food of a slave and will be required to recite and scribe the attitudes and characteristics of an unspoiled woman as taught to you when you were still in nursery. That is, of course, assuming that your parents had the foresight to teach their little hellion any rules whatsoever. Perhaps some time spent within those cold walls below stairs will remind you of your position and the luxury that my favor offers. In truth, you have no more position or power than that slave of mine so long ago."

Tremain stepped forward to take Alida's arm, his attitude more solicitous than Savine's had been. Deive, who had risen to her feet during Savine's speech, angrily moved from her place advancing on Savine. "This is outrageous! How dare you humiliate your kinswoman! She was given to your safekeeping!"

Savine turned away, a tiny smile on her lips. She had never felt so powerful! With a simple flick of her wrist, Deive was restrained and carried away to her chambers, as Alida was carted down to the dungeon.

The handmaid, Lizel, would be well rewarded for her sharp eyes and tattling tongue. She would be useful in the future as well. Meanwhile, there was the betraying Erta to which she'd attend. This widened the smile on Savine's lips. She would take out her aggression there. It was obvious that the need for extreme measures was at hand. Without the constant evidence of power, the lower castes would begin to rebel and grow slovenly. She refused to run a city or keep whose inhabitants did not fear her.

After a restless night's sleep, Alida awoke early, her muscles cramped and cold. It was just a moment later that the previous day's events came crashing down on her groggy, newly awakened mind. She rushed to the door but was chagrined to find no sentry posted outside that could give her further news of her aunt's madness, for she had been down in the cell since the previous morning. She pounded on the slimy, mildewed door with chilled, chapped hands, crying loudly for a guard to attend her, but no one came. Restless and worried, she strode over to the thinly covered cot in her cell and pushed it beneath the single, high iron-barred window. Shivering from the chilling cold and damp, she shakily climbed on top of the cot and strained to look out of tiny alcove. There, yards from her face, in the center of the courtyard, her eyes beheld a startling sight.

Though it was still very early, she could make out the shape of a platform that was being constructed by Savine's soldiers. Lanterns shone gloomily on the chilling form of a whipping block at its center. Was her punishment worsening? A shiver crept down the column of her spine.

All morning she paced before the window, her anxiety growing. When a guard brought her a bowl of dubious looking porridge, she inquired about her fate and was curtly refused any information. The tankard of mead, left alongside the meal, was gulped down, hastily being imbibed in the hopes that it would help control her worry and warm her bones. When it had been fully swallowed, she instantly regretted the warm bitterness. It turned her stomach sour, and she was hard pressed to ignore the bile that rose in her throat.

The hours passed slowly before she discovered the identity of the whipping block's victim, for as she gazed out through the iron bars of her cell, she caught sight of Erta. Only she did not look composed and well cared for, as was her natural way. Her hair had fallen from its neat braids and the leather thongs that held them were now entangled in its brown mass along with mud and straw. She had been stripped of her well-made tunics, a rough undergarment comprising her only covering against the steep, chilled wind that had come up suddenly as spring weather often has a will to do. Her shame at being so slightly dressed, as well as the cold from the sudden rush of air, was apparent in the blush upon her cheeks. Yet shame had not yet fully rested upon her.

For though she was nearly naked and humiliated and though one or two of the less desirable slaves from the keep threw clods of dung and rotten fruit at her, she carried herself with great dignity.

All at once, the crowd grew silent, and Alida watched as Savine swept through its midst. She climbed the platform, dressed warmly in a cloak and heavy tunic, and addressed the gathered keep with a suitably somber and commanding voice.

"This wretch you see before you is Erta, my once trusted servant. She has betrayed this trust by helping my young, foolish niece in a plot to undermine my authority, and by doing so, she risked my niece's life." Savine paused for a moment allowing her words to sink into the minds of her servants and soldiers.

The crowd murmured, some with assent and some with worry, but none stepped forward to challenge her.

Savine continued, "She is to be beaten, the marks of which will remain as an ever-visible sign of her shame and disloyalty. Guards, bring her forward!"

Two thick soldiers climbed the platform with Erta between them. Alida recognized them as some of the roughest in Savine's entourage of protection.

Savine turned again to the crowd, which now included some noblemen who had been awakened by the racket outside. "Let this just and swift punishment go forth as I have commanded!" She then murmured some instructions to the guards and gracefully descended the platform her chin held high.

The wind grew colder and rain began to fall as the guards roughly ripped the shift from Erta's shoulders baring her chest, arms, and back to the gaping crowd. Tears of shame coursed down Erta's cheeks. She had been a favored and respected member in the keep, and now she had nothing left, including her pride.

The guards then turned her around and hooked her wrists through the manacles of the post, pushing her firmly against the cold, rough sides of the whipping block. A wicked-looking cattails was produced and the lashes began.

Alida's eyes filled at the humiliation Erta was forced to suffer on her behalf. She ground her teeth together as the sound of wet leather on bare skin reverberated around the yard.

Just then, a guard entered and roughly ordered her above at Savine's request.

Alida flew up the steps of the dungeon and out into the yard, jerking away from the control of the guard and completely bypassing the assembly and Savine herself who was seated off on a higher grade than the yard. With Savine and the guards screaming behind her, she proceeded up the steps of the platform and grasped the whip from the guard before he could issue another blow. With quick and vehement force, Alida struck the guard across his face with his own whip, instantly drawing blood.

"Curse you for following the black commands of a lunatic!" She raised her hand for yet another blow. The guard swore and grabbed at the descending cattail, yelling at Savine for direction.

Savine's voice cut through the uproar like a screeching bird. "Leave your hands from the whip, girl! You'll find that your punishment has just increased tenfold . . ."

"As it should, Aunt," Alida interrupted in a steely voice. "For it was I that endangered my own life and it was I that made the choice to wander at will. Erta is a servant and simply did as she was bid." Alida's voiced then caught as if in a sob before she said with strength, "I choose to claim the law of this land that allows any person to take the place of another in punishment!"

The crowd stirred to life. Never before in the collective memory of the gathered keepsmen had anyone claimed that particular law, much less someone of noble birth for a mere servant. The rabble rousers in the crowd called out, "Let her take the punishment; let it be meted out to her in Erta's stead!" The others in the crowd, who felt such action would be shameful, quickly silenced these dissident voices.

The rain poured down over Alida's thinly clothed frame, matting her hair to her head. The silence of the yard was deafening.

Savine's eyes narrowed. "You have no idea the pain you invite with this suggestion, Alida!"

Alida's chest heaved from her action and fear, but she did not step down. Instead, in a clear and resolute voice she shouted, "I *will* stand in Erta's place, because it was my action that caused her plight. No just person would allow another to take their blame!"

Savine turned away and whispered to the maid at her side. As she waited for the girl to reach the platform, she called out to the guards, "Await my command!" Then with dignity, Savine arose and addressed the crowd. "She shall take the punishment by her own choice; let this day be well remembered!"

She then motioned to Lizel who now stood beside Alida on the platform. The gleeful maid, instead of just undoing the fastenings as she had been instructed, ripped away at the piecing of Alida's tunic. In doing so, she left much more skin exposed to the rain and cold as well as to the imminent blows of the whip. She then turned and flounced away, glee clearly written on her cruel features.

Erta, who had nearly fainted, called out weakly to Alida, "Don't do it, girl! I could not bare the guilt of yer hurt as well as m'own pain!" The tears on the maid's face were washed away by the rain as quickly as they could rise but her sobs gave evidence of her great emotion.

Alida leaned close and whispered, "Savine is determined to mete out retribution for her wounded pride, but it was my fault, kind Erta, not yours. I beg your forgiveness for the stripes and humiliation you've already had to bear." Alida saw Erta's teary-eyed forgiveness and quickly reached out, wresting away the keys to the manacles from a nearby guard. Without hesitation and despite the guard's interference, she undid Erta's bonds and gently lay her down. With the keys bundled into her fist, she dealt an unexpected blow to the side of the guard's cheek, her anger at his blind obedience to Savine raging hotly in her breast. Then without a word, she dropped the keys at his feet and spit in his face, stepping into the servant's previous position at the block. The guards, which had been publicly humiliated by her, jerked her wrists tightly into the manacles, clasping them as far apart as her arms would allow.

The whole crowd turned at a piercing scream from the doorway of the great hall. "Do not touch her, you butchers!" Deive darted madly past the crowd and headed for the platform, but was captured by two nearby guards. She was strong enough to cast one aside, but the quick grasp of the second upon her arm drained away any further strength. Her hair cast a wild black halo about her face and her violet eyes looked like daggers. Deive did not cry out again, her rage overcoming all other emotion.

The cattails were lifted into the air repeatedly. Alida did not cry out, though tears cascaded down her face and neck. With each blow, her body tensed, quivering with pain. When ten blows had been meted out, Savine called out to the crowd and guards with a clear voice. "Enough. My niece must be presentable for marriage, and thus I shall not inflict further blows. However, she will remain in the dungeon for the next month, carrying out her original punishment along with this pain she has chosen."

The people stood bunched in silent, horrified groups. They had always known that the nature of their mistress held a streak of cruelty, but never before had they seen its depth. It was madness to demean one's own kinswoman in such a manner.

Deive tried again to start forward towards the two women on the platform, but was cuffed behind the head and restrained. Not being able to withstand the dizziness from the blow, she was unaware of her trip back to the small, windowless room of the night before.

Alida and Erta were roughly pulled from the platform. Erta was taken to a small, dank room in the servant's wing that would act as her permanent quarters; a far cry from the quarters that had once so cheerfully ensconced her. Alida, as her aunt had decreed, was reinstalled in the dungeon. Their backs bled and caked over without a soul to aid them, until guards brought clean rags and water to each. They had to attend to themselves, and the job was miserable and not thorough enough. Erta cried herself to sleep, for she had never felt so much the vial slave as she did at that moment. Though she was bitter over her treatment, her greatest sadness was the pain she had caused Alida.

Alida, without any tears left to shed, hovered between rage and a horrible calm. Her mind envisioned every method imaginable for slaying her aunt. When finally she succumbed to a fitful sleep, her dreams consisted of one plot for revenge after another.

She awoke sometime later to a small scuffling sound and looked up to see Deive rummaging through a purple chamois bag. The pouch contained herbs for remedies as well as tinctures and drawn oils.

Alida gazed quietly at Deive and then squeezed her friend's arm. Then turning her back, she submitted to the older woman's ministrations. Alida stiffened, her knuckles turning white on the arms of the chair when Deive unwound the bandages and gently reopened the wounds with warm water. Alida was given something to drink to lessen the pain as Deive sewed the cuts shut with neat stitches. The pain that could not be removed by the drink was eventually overcome by the soothing salves and clean cloths that were placed on her back, but both women were crying when Deive had finally finished her attendance.

"How did you get to me? They have me guarded on all sides." Alida's voice was weak and tired.

Deive smoothed the younger woman's hair away from her brow. "The people are not happy with today's affair. Many have joined against Savine and her few cohorts. I was easily slipped from my room and brought to you. Erta is next. Our main boon is Savine's own captain of the guard. His men will not rise against him."

"I have also made remedies that are odorless so that Savine cannot suspect your aid. You will feel pain when the salves begin to lessen in strength, but I will leave them with you to use again when needed. They will heal your wounds more quickly, and you will not have to bear fever or the worst forms of scarring from your injury." Then more softly, she whispered, "Oh lass, I wish that somehow I could take all of it away for you."

After gently attending to Alida's final needs, Deive said in a hushed voice, "I will go to Erta now if you are comfortable. She has become my good friend and confidante. I'll not see either of you so badly handled."

Alida smiled softly and drifted off to sleep, trusting in Deive's protection. The potion the older woman had dumped into Alida's ale would soothe the young woman's pain and give her a deep rest. She then gathered her bag and quietly slipped out of the door.

Unlike the gloom and folly of that southern domain, wisdom and justice reigned at the court of The Heights. There in the richly appointed great hall, Ulrich judged the needs and laws of his people. His tribe knew him to be fair and tough; for though his decisions did not always garner friendship, his wisdom was greatly respected and sought from every corner of his land.

He was not easily crossed and had never been known to lose to cunning devises against himself or his domain. Those who tried his sharp intelligence were often brought up short, such as the archer who had just this day been executed for spying on the battlements of the keep and relaying the information to an enemy holding. Ulrich had found that the love and respect, which his people had for him, had served him well by uncovering plots along with the aid of his own observations.

His crest, too, was well deserved. The wolf was a creature of ravenous appetite and power and was known for its loyalty to its portion. Because his family, generations back, had been known for their conquering rule and constancy in battle, the wolf had been given a red hue. The result was a form that demanded respect. There were few in the surrounding country that did not know of his power. However, his position also held its share of drawbacks.

Bejeweled and fragrant women trickled through his memory like bright petals, not a one distinguishing herself to his heart through any tender emotion. They had come to him from the time of his youth, asking for his bed, hoping to gain greater power with him through this channel, seeking to please a father or uncle by obtaining his name, money, and military backing. Those who did not seek the riches of power sought his protection or favors, but never his love. Many rumors had been generated over the years that he was incapable of feeling the softer emotions and even that he favored men over women. Though his allies turned a blind eye to such rumors, many believed they were backed up by his apparent disdain for the affections and attentions of women.

In reality, he had yet to find a woman who could equal him in zeal, innocence, and valor. He had dallied privately with many of the women that had come to him, but he had never claimed to feel love or used its possibility as a draw, for he had jealously and wisely guarded his heart. While he allowed some physical attentions towards women upon occasion, he never consummated the dalliances. His parents had warned him when he was only a boy that the intimacy between a man and woman was best served in the wedding bed alone. They had told him that once a heart was bound it could not be set free, and to bind your heart to many women was to make a slave out of a king. He was always honest about his intentions, and though he spoke the truth, few listened, thinking that they would capture his heart and lands. Though he longed for privacy in these matters, he was hounded day and night by the constant appearance of new, suitable women.

Finally, at the beginning of the new year, after a particularly trying season of festivals and matchmaking, Ulrich issued the order to his household: His name and heart must no longer be pandered to the available daughters of the clan houses in their region. Out of respect, his staff backed away from the duty of providing him with a wife and family.

Nevertheless, there were times, in the early hours of morning or late at night, when his mind would stray to his self-imposed loneliness, but he refused to settle for anything other than the fire and purity he had seen between his own parents. He would not be cut back from the strength that their wisdom had promised him.

As a man of flesh, these passions often threatened to overcome his deepest personal vows, but rather than satiate them with a woman who might make claim upon him, he instead rode furiously, often late into the night, bringing back exhausted mounts in the morning. These were the times when his people whispered amongst themselves that he was touched with lunacy. In truth, he could find no other outlet for his deepest desires.

CHAPTER THREE

BERYNTH, IN THE PROVINCE OF
DRACHMUND HEIGHTS

In the weak light of early morning, Ulrich rolled over and collided with a very pleasant warm body. The furs had been piled high the night before, and though he had entered them alone, he now knew companionship. Opening one lazy eye, he noticed the bright red hair of a familiar maidservant who he had caught shyly glancing his way numerous times. He had turned down her fumbling advances just as he had turned down the advances of much more experienced women.

He gazed at her for a moment, and then gently moved her head off his shoulder. When she murmured in her sleep and nestled closer beneath the covers, he moved away slightly so as not to startle her when her eyes opened. The moment she came awake, he felt her stiffen with the unfamiliarity of her surroundings. She cautiously moved her head until she was looking into his deep blue-green eyes that jointly showed disapproval and humor.

"So the little red bird is determined to make a nest despite the unwillingness of her companion."

She blushed, but determinedly pulled the furs a little lower, nodding in response. She then shyly reached her hand out laying it on his chest, cringing at his down-turned mouth.

Just as he was ready to send her from his bed with a cool dismissal, the door crashed open and in stumbled one of his stockbreeders.

He was a large, quiet lad with spiky hay-colored hair and ruddy cheeks. His cheeks were more flushed than usual, Ulrich noted, and in his hand was a well-worn dirk. The weapon was immediately turned on the couple in the heavily appointed pallet. Ulrich smiled at the boy, but every muscle remained at the ready. He recognized a battle stance when faced with it.

"To what to we owe this pleasure, Kurt? Have you a need for anything?"

"You . . . you beast! You best have not harmed or touched her in any way!" The lad stuttered uncontrollably and could hardly see straight—he was so afraid and angry. Ulrich was amazed at his courage. Not many men, including his own soldiers, would dare face him in such a manner.

Kurt had just moved forward, when the captain of Ulrich's guard rushed through the door behind him. He quickly had a knife to the youth's neck with the dirk laying safely a number of feet away. When he moved to finish the intent his wicked blade showed, Ulrich stopped him with a powerfully commanded, "Hold"!

Then more softly, the lord said, "Let us hear what he has to say for this morning's odd behavior. Mayhap this is his sister whose charge he has been given?"

At a nod from the captain, the lad stuttered his complaint. "She is my betrothed, or will be when her father agrees to give her hand to me. I'll not have her sullied by you or any man! She loves me; I know she does, but we quarreled some days ago. Since then she's been ignoring me, saying she'd come to your bed. I was stubborn and had set my teeth to scorn her. My father, who claims knowledge in the ways of women's hearts, sent me out last night to search for her, saying I was green for not trying to soothe her. He was right and I will . . . well, I'll not lose her to you over a small understanding."

After this tremendous speech, Kurt turned his gaze to the red-haired lass on the pallet. She quietly rose commanding imperiously that all the men look away. She then dressed quickly, glared at the guard until he released the lad, mumbled a quick apology to Ulrich, and rushed out of the room safely tucked beneath Kurt's arm.

Ulrich fell back against the furs and groaned. His guard gave him a sly look and then said with an unmistakable twinkle in his eye, "Difficult to have such an interlude stopped, milord, though by the talk below stairs the whole castle warrants you could use one–your temper is foul of late and could use the softening of a wife to bed." Ulrich ordered the captain to leave and then threw a discarded tunic top at his retreating back.

In truth, his frustration had been over the passion displayed between the two, and the fact that once again the nature of females had not been favorably illuminated. The maid's scent remained on the furs around him, and he swore again under his breath. How could women look and smell like heaven and then unsheathe claws more suited to the pits of hell?

He felt the longing rise again in his chest and loins for a relationship not based on jealousy, power or gain, but instead on passion and friendship and unity of mind.

With great effort, he rolled off the pallet, pushing aside such melancholy thoughts. He'd find distraction in battle training or review of his estate's records or in the choice of numerous other avenues. Fate would have to be entrusted with his desires.

The afternoon sun beat down on Ulrich's bare-chested form, enticing the swarms of gnats that rested during the cooler hours. Ulrich cursed under his breath as they tortured him and the horse that he was putting through its paces. When he could bear it no longer, he called out to his groomsmen, and they took the relieved horse back to the cool stables where refuse fires smoked away the annoying legions. He wiped his chest clean of sweat with a rough cloth and threw on a cool linen tunic top and pants.

All around him were signs that spring had come, for few patches of snow remained to mock its arrival, and lazy-headed flowers had begun their blossoming from the rich soils of The Heights. With the renewal of beauty around him, he regretted that this was not a season of rest.

He had planning yet to do if crops were to be planted and herds bred. With this thought in mind, he hurried off to find Eldridge, the superintendent of his affairs. He found Eldridge with head down turned to a leather-bound ledger. The fresh charcoal tick marks on the pages showed that Eldridge had been to the storehouses to check the remains of winter stockpiling. His puckered forehead caused Ulrich to wonder about the stock's decrease. The powerful lord moved forward in the weak light of the stone-walled room, startling the gentle man before him.

"Oh, 'tis you Ulrich. The ledgers hold me fast. I've not been about the keep all day." With that, the older man stretched, every muscle flexing in his bony arms.

Ulrich smiled and patted his mentor on the shoulder. "I take it the storehouses are not fairing well this year?"

Eldridge shook his head. "We've used a good portion this year, milord, but there is still much available. The wars with Quirin's army and the raids from the north have depleted only our stock of barley. We still have all the rye, oats, dried goods, and furs we'll need, as well as the herbs and onions from the new gardens. When our oldest cows have given their last milk at the weaning time, we'll butcher them and dry the meat for our spring supply. The calving is already being handled by Kurt Grogur's sire and the foaling by Kurt himself." At Ulrich's cringe, Eldridge raised an eyebrow. "You have somewhat against the lad and his sire?"

Ulrich sighed, "No, 'twas just an embarrassing misunderstanding between the lad, his betrothed, and myself." At Eldridge's expectant expression, Ulrich told the advisor the entire morning's adventure. His cheeks stained red when his tale had been fully told.

Eldridge laughed, "I am still the only inhabitant of the keep what can make you rosy, boy. With all that has transpired, do you want to oversee the herds this year yourself, or do you want me to post another manager?"

Ulrich was quiet for a moment as he contemplated the situation and then said, "Have Kurt and his father oversee all the needs of the stock themselves as usual. They can report the news to me or through you as they so choose. We'll go on as if nothing has transpired, for they have well earned the right after so many faithful and productive years to continue in their duties. Do mention, however, my one desire to have them sire Titan with the new chestnut mare. She is clean-lined and spirited. It should produce a smaller but finer animal. I expect the color to be smooth and even, the chest heavy but well matched to the body length and muscling on the legs. I have no designs on the breeding of the cattle, so leave that matter untouched.

Have the burghers of the southern orchards increase the planting of sapling walnut trees and green apple, as well as clearing and turning another field for barley. Have the burghers of the northern orchards cut back the existing planting, and do not allow a new planting. If we are raided again this summer, I want less of our available produce in the forefront. Also, when the crops are rotated, see that the onion and leek fields are rotated north and the oat and rye brought south. Better we have the staples than flavoring alone."

The instructions aided the easement of Ulrich's embarrassment, and he went on, until the sun turned rosy in its descent and the sounds from the great hall could be heard filtering down the passageways to the now-dark anteroom.

The dungeons of Lyrnne fulfilled their purpose, surrounding Alida in a cold, lonely embrace. After the single night of attendance by Deive, Alida saw no one else but the guards, for those who had taken up arms against Savine were cautious. They had food and notes couriered to her, but had warned Deive against further visitation.

The month passed slowly for Alida who was given no other occupation than pacing to suppress her volatile anger. She fought off fevers and chills that thrived in the damp, endlessly musty walls of her cell, the madness that fever brought adding fuel to her regrets. Her dreams were plagued by memories of her flogging and seemed to especially repeat the scenario of Erta's humiliation.

She was greatly changed. Her hair had grown limp and dirty, for she was not given any means with which to groom it. Her clothing hung on her like a sack, for she could not stomach food in her state of anger and anxiety. She was loathe to present herself to the guards, for she was not given any sanitary means of dealing with her physical needs. The only thing that remained unchanged was the fire in her eyes and her indomitable spirit.

Despite the discomfort, filth, and pain from her wounds, she never spoke petulantly or in anger to her guards, always respectfully voicing her questions and needs. It wasn't long before she had garnered the nickname "Bremryth," the common heroine of a local tale that had overcome great odds to lead her people out of slavery.

Then one rainy day, the key sounded in the lock of the cell, and Alida was released, her freedom administered by the same hands that had taken it from her. She made her way with great dignity up the hard, cold stairs of the dungeon and out into the courtyard sucking in the fresh, misty air until she nearly choked.

The guards took her to the servant's quarters where she was given a bath in a small, wooden tub. The warmth and fresh scent of the water seemed like heaven after the conditions of the cell.

Three tubs of water later, she stood before the handmaids, fully bathed, combed, and very wrinkled. They anointed her still-moist skin with soothing oils and rubbed some of the same substance into her hair. She was dressed in a fresh simple tunic and skirt, a warm but light cloak, and stockings and shoes.

She had just begun to grill the servants as to Erta's wellbeing when a stiff guard entered and gruffly requested that she follow him. Alida obediently walked after him, quickly recognizing the path to her aunt's private chambers.

When they reached the doors of the chambers, she paused for a moment, swallowing her bitter pride, almost running back the way she had come. Then she stepped forward, her chin at the level of a queen's.

The heavy door clicked shut quietly behind her, and she stepped into the grim lighting of Savine's bedchamber. Heavy scents of myrrh and lavender clung to the overly rich trimmings. Alida nearly gagged on the odors that were made more pervasive by the stuffy warmth of the space.

"I see by the tilt of your jaw that your spirit goes untamed, girl." Her aunt's voice crushed the calm with all of its expert disdain.

Alida, who had rehearsed several searing lines over the preceding month, remained silent, her anger suddenly gone from her.

How pitiful her aunt seemed in the rainy light. She had no one who cared for her, nor were there any that she adored. Her face was hard and pale, the edges created by a long-lived bitterness and petulance.

Alida shuddered—would she become as her aunt, caught in anger and regret and violence?

"Have you nothing to say, girl?" Savine had risen and bore down on her, the dark tunic she wore billowing about her like crow's wings.

Alida did not lower her gaze, but the hardness in her eyes had gone. "I pity you."

Savine screeched, close enough now that Alida could very nearly feel her breath. "How dare you say such a thing when you know the power I have to punish you? I have been luxuriously ensconced in chambers while you have had to grovel in the filth of the dungeon at my behest, and *you* pity *me!* How is that possible?"

Alida hesitated a moment weighing her words. "Because, Aunt, you are weak. You are weak, cold and utterly alone without comfort or ally. You spit cruelty at all those around you, and you do not know the meaning of mercy."

Savine lunged forward to scratch out her niece's calm, penetrating eyes, but Alida stepped aside. Savine, catching her toe on the edge of the floor tapestry, fell face first, her rage turning into a gurgle of surprise in her throat.

Her advance upon Alida had been so forceful that when she landed there was no mistaking the sickening thud of her face on the floor. Instantly, blood began to trickle from her nose and mouth.

Alida stepped forward quickly to help her, but Savine shook her off, her shoulders and chest heaving in anger. As she wiped away the blood on her face, her voice had turned deadly quiet. "You will pay for tripping me, Wench."

Alida's mouth gaped open. "It was your own action that caused you to fall!"

Savine rose to her feet as majestically as she could under the circumstances and immediately called for the guard, pressing a piece of her tunic to her bloody mouth and nose.

A young, thick guard stepped into the room, and to Alida's surprise, flatly refused his mistress' order to return the young woman to the dungeon. Savine then sent him to gather Tremain, and when the captain had entered the room, he, too, refused her command. He motioned to Alida to leave the chambers.

As the heavy door closed behind her, Alida could hear his soothing tones, though his exact words were muffled from her ears.

Inside the quarters, the captain respectfully addressed Savine. "Be careful, mistress, lest you lose the loyalty of your guard and their protection, for you have committed the unpardonable crime of needlessly humiliating a peer of your station. They are greatly taken with Alida's looks and kindness, for she never neglected to say a good word to them before she was beaten and locked up. Even the guards who administered her punishment and who felt the sting of her anger bore her no ill will, for she has become greatly respected during her detention. A month of watching a young woman who displays the best of character can do wonders for softening a man's heart."

Savine glared at him, and he humbly lowered his head. "Are you or are you not my captain?"

"I am."

"Then do as I have commanded!"

"I will not."

When her fists balled in frustration, Tremain replied softly, "I have been given the place of protecting you, and there are many within the keep who would love to see you lose your station. Save yourself by withholding your hand."

Savine was silent. Then her voice hissed out, "Get you gone!"

He nodded curtly and bowed before exiting the chambers. He knew that the underlying river of resentment and fear towards Alida had not been stemmed, but at least for the time being, Savine's destructiveness had been waylaid.

Alida was that day, restored to her chambers with Deive once again nearby. After checking her charge's wounds for progress, the two of them nested down together in the cozy warmth of the rooms for the rest of the rainy afternoon, pillowed by furs, linen, and tankards of hot tea.

Eventually, after hours of conversation and healing laughter, they fell asleep on Alida's pallet, a picture of restored friendship with their entwined arms and closely nestled heads.

The next morning a well-rested Alida closed the heavy, carved door to her room and listened to the calm around her. She then headed out of the castle towards a room in the worst section of the servant's quarters, where Erta had been moved on the day of her confinement.

Since the flogging, according to Ansel's report, Erta, his precious wife, had remained silent and grey. Her wounds had not healed as well as Deive had hoped, and Deive was sure that Erta's downcast spirits were the reason for the prolonged suffering.

Ansel, who could not bear to be away from his love, had without a second thought moved all their belongings from their old, clean, bright chambers to the new, tiny, dark ones. He was more downhearted than anyone had ever seen him, though for Erta's sake he kept up his spirits as much as possible, not only continuing with his daily kitchen duties, but also cleaning their new chambers and caring for her, all with a tender smile and large, gentle hands.

Alida, determined to face her regret and possibly Erta's retaliatory anger, tapped on the door to these new quarters, and when she was given a weak leave to enter, pushed back the oak planking, allowing the glow from a single, high window to creep past her into the smoky, raucous community hall.

"Erta," she said softly, "I have brought a brew from Deive filled with herbs and well wishes. Please drink it up—I shall wait for you to finish." With that, she handed her a plain stone bowl with a carved stone lid.

Erta weakly removed the lid and sipped from the bowl with little energy. When she finally spoke, the sound crept out into the room in a near whisper.

"Why did she do it? I was 'er companion for years, 'er *only* confidante, and the *only* one that came close to understandin' er in the keep. Though I aided you, still my loyalty was to 'er and should you, even you, 'ave asked for something that would'a harmed her, I would'na done it. She was m' friend, and I think that perhaps I did do 'er great harm by not tendin' after a kin's wellbein'." Her luminous eyes gazed up at Alida, striking her with their hurt innocence and purity. Alida's heart skipped a beat at the sob-like catch in her friend's voice. She dropped to her knees by her friend's side and grasped her cool hand to her breast.

"Some people have hearts that never warm, Erta. Savine is one of those. She has never given nor been given, love. She is by nature selfish and cold; presumably a byproduct of her upbringing. Erta, 'twas not your fault and you mustn't accept that your punishment was a just one. You are mine and Deive's true friend, and are still greatly admired by the rest of the keep. Ansel's heart has been broken because of his love for you, but not even he can bind up your world forever. You must understand that we all need you."

Erta blinked.

All along, people had been telling her how much they loved her and that they were grieved over what had happened. Nevertheless, these comments had just made her feel more guilty and disgraced. She had yet to hear anything that made a difference, until now. She was needed. Here was her chance at redemption and forgiveness. Here was the path back to happiness, a way to begin again.

Erta's sudden smile made Alida more worried than she had been the moment before. She watched as Erta gingerly climbed out of bed and began picking up the room. The woman's slippers rasped against the stone floor, imitating the sound of her slightly labored breathing as she tidied their small chamber. Though she hadn't said anything unusual, a gleam had come to her eye that hadn't been there before. Alida decided to run and fetch Deive. The linen of her tunic was sliding past the door before Erta even knew she was gone.

About a half hour later, Deive and Alida rushed back towards the tiny room worriedly chatting about their friend. Just as they reached the door, Erta came out with a rush broom in hand and a fresh apron over her rumpled clothes.

Deive stopped dead in her tracks and with a falsely light voice said, "What are you doing, Sweet? You'll tear the wounds open anew with all your charging about."

Tears sprang to Erta's eyes, and she dabbed at the flow with a corner of her apron. "I've found the answer friends, or rather been given an answer—redemption for the wrong I've done. You, Alida, come here."

Alida stepped forward and felt the woman's cool, soft hand on her cheek. "Thank you."

Alida was confused. "For what do you thank me? 'Tis I that should have received all the shame and the entire whip's fury. Instead, you bore for me, both the brunt of your mistress' anger and the loss of position."

Erta said simply, "It does'na matter what happened or why, it matters only that I am needed. Don't ya see that?" She embarrassedly wiped at tears again that sprang from her eyes.

Alida's eyes lit with understanding, and Deive swallowed back her own tears, fighting with a lump that had risen painfully in her chest. Erta was not going mad, as they had feared. Deive grasped her friend in a gingerly hug to avoid injuring her still-tender wounds. Then all three proceeded through the hall, rapidly discussing the ways in which the keep had fallen into disrepair since Erta's seclusion. Deive bantered with the two, but her heart ached for Erta who still looked a little pale and shaky. Deive prayed for the speedy recovery of both her friend's mind and body together. She would also watch like a cat from the shadows for any untoward move that Savine might make. She already burned with anger over their treatment, a root of resentment growing firmly beneath the layers of her calm demeanor.

Escape at last!

Alida felt the bunching thrill of Raven's warm, taught muscles beneath her, knowing that his dancing steps were in anticipation of the day. She, too, anticipated a great freedom and adventure after having been contained for so long. Her joy welled to the surface, and because she wanted to savor each moment of the day, she tipped back her face toward the young but already burning sun overhead and drank in the balmy air of summer humming softly to herself.

A couple of months had passed before any progress had been made in loosening her aunt's guard over her. Even now, she was expected to have constant escort by one of the keep's warriors. The one following behind her now had the promise of being less restrictive than Tremain's first suggestion had been.

He was newer to the guard, Glynden by name, and was very taken with her. Though no signs of his infatuation were apparent to Tremain or Savine, he was so enamored of Alida that he had agreed with her in secret to fall back when she so wished, though his instructions had been vehemently to the opposite by Savine. He even helped saddle Raven for her, though another mount, a gentle mare, had been directed for her use.

Knowing that her freedom was safe in Glynden's hands, Alida loosed Raven's energy once outside the city walls and bent over his warm neck, going as fast as she dared over the dells and fields. Her riding was wild, as she recklessly drove Raven over obstacles, his hooves easily clearing walls of brambles and fallen trees. Though her muscles were stretched to their limits as she fought to remain in control of her seat and Raven's head, she was filled with nothing but exhilaration. It was obvious by her mount's reactions that he, too, had not had enough exercise over her months of confinement. When she reached the edge of the forest, out of breath and laughing, she was so full of joyful distraction that she did not see the figure duskily hidden beneath the long boughs of a fir just to her right.

Ulrich drew in a breath of warm air. By the gods, she was beautiful! Here was the wild woman who had haunted his dreams. It had been a long time since he had fought with her, and since then, though his rides had brought him through her lands, he had failed to catch any glimpse of her or her mount.

Ulrich took in every detail of her face and husky laughter, noting that her attire and demeanor were not as before. She came dressed in the folds of a simple green tunic and skirts cut appropriately for a woman this time, rather than her original leggings and top made for a man. It was one of the plainest gowns he had ever seen on a woman; a noblewoman at that. For this time, he was assured of her status, by the far-off proximity of a guard flying Lyrnne colors, and by the heavy but delicately wrought torc about her neck. Her status was also reflected in her silver armbands, each with her family's insignia carved proudly on their width, the sunlight reflecting off their polished faces in flashing joy.

Everything about her spoke of an ancient wildness that was not given to being mastered. The gleam in her eye and her tousled heavy locks had caused a pleasant, slow fire to begin to burn somewhere deep within his belly. While she motioned to her guard and impatiently awaited his arrival, Ulrich drank in the sight of her, catching snatches of her scent that was blown his direction by the breeze.

When the guard arrived at her side, Ulrich frowned. He didn't like the looks of the young man; this woman before him would undoubtedly be better served by someone more her equal. Remembering the prowess she had shown during their fight, he would bet that in a battle she would end up saving the guard who was presumably sent to do the same for her. Ulrich melted back into the trees, watching the foolish grin that spread across the youth's face at her firmly given orders.

"Glynden, please remain here outside of the glen. I plan to bathe and do not want to be disturbed by anyone or anything. Should I need you, I will call for you."

She rode silently into the glen, the early morning drip of dew off the branches and twigs singing a soft melody to her and the flickering ears of her mount. She found the little glade where she had bathed before and where the hot sun of the fields had not yet reached. After having dismounted, she began removing her fine stockings and shoes as she went. Then without the least bit of propriety, which Savine was working overtime to instill in her, Alida hiked up her skirts and waded thigh high into the water.

Ulrich was without breath for a moment. Was he made of stone to have to resist the tempting sight of such limbs all bare and smooth, glistening from the water? She was not a common noblewoman in anything he had seen her do, much less in this present wanton behavior. She was as unsubdued as the glen around her or the broken cliffs of his beloved mountains. No noblewoman would dare display her flesh to the light of day, especially in a relatively unguarded glade. He shook his head to clear away the cobwebs and to calm his rising interest. The shake only made her appear more clearly. He chuckled to himself, turning his mount that had danced away from the lovely view. How easily he had been fetched by her vision. Though he had only seen her the once before, he had returned day after day, until finally he was given this new view of her.

Alida turned in the water and dipped in her bare arm to the shoulder, withdrawing a smooth blue stone from the bottom. She rolled it over in her hand, her silent study a sign of her ignorance to Ulrich's presence.

She then flung the stone out across the pool, laughing out delightedly when it skipped five times across the surface. As her morning progressed, the sun began to grow hot over the pool. Therefore, it wasn't long before she removed her sun-warmed torc. Then, scooping water into her hands, she poured the cool refreshment over her head enjoying the relief it brought. The fall of the dark glistening curls, her bare arms and neck, and her shimmering thighs made Ulrich's groin tighten.

His pleasant perusal of the wood nymph, however, was abruptly cut short by her sudden movement. She had heard a rustling sound off to the right and turned to view the intruder. It was a fair-sized rabbit. Thinking that it had been some time since her last hunt and taste of rabbit stew, she quickly removed her dirk, pitching it expertly towards the very spot where Ulrich sat hidden. His muscles readied for action, just as he caught sight of the rabbit sitting directly in the path of the dirk.

With the rabbit firmly pinned by the knife, Alida rushed forward and finished off the beast with a quick twist of her hand. She now stood close enough to Ulrich that he could smell the light scent of sun and spring water coming off her warm body, as well as seeing how deep a blue her eyes were. He withdrew further into the wood, silently moving so as not to alert her, cursing that he had to remove himself at all. He knew that if he stepped out this time and confronted her, he would also have to fend off the guard.

Just then, a crashing noise from the other end of the clearing drew her view away from his hiding spot. She turned to see Glynden rushing towards her.

"Milady, forgive my intrusion, but I heard much rustling about and came to see what transpired."

Her merry but consoling voice put the youth at ease. "Twas only a rabbit, Glynden. I wanted it for my supper and so have captured it." She proudly held up the downed beast and then casually sat down to pull on her discarded stockings, shoes, and torc.

Her lack of propriety in having been so undressed brought a deep blush to Glynden's cheeks; however, the brash youth did not make a move to turn away from the lovely sight. Ulrich felt a stirring of jealousy that anyone other than himself should see her bared beauty, though he could make no more claim to her than could this pitiful guard.

"Why, Glynden, you are rosier than a Pink ," laughed Alida. "Have you never seen a maiden's legs before? Mine are not so different from the serving girls that coyly draw your attention at the castle, nor do they vary much from the kitchen help that vie for your community at supper." With that, she playfully pinched him on the arm causing the youth's blush to deepen.

At that point, Ulrich would have given anything to have her banter with him. He watched as she walked out of the glade, rabbit in hand, to where Raven awaited her. When she reached for the saddle, Glynden stopped her and offered her his aid. He blushingly grasped her about the waist with shaking hands, lifting her high and setting her gently into the saddle. With the rabbit safely stored in the saddle pouch, he mounted his own steed and awaited her command like a dog awaiting a juicy tidbit.

Alida cockily challenged him to a contest of horsemanship, being somewhat at a loss of how to handle his amorous behavior.

Ulrich watched with open admiration as she dashed off towards the open plain, her body in perfect rhythm and command of her mount. When he felt it safe to leave the glen, he, too, moved off, staying to the protected areas of stone and tree stands that dotted the open fields.

Following their tracks, Ulrich was able to catch up with them a little while later at a well-protected spring that bubbled from a group of boulders. Dismounting, he silently approached the pair watching the little scene before him.

Alida had gutted, skinned, and spitted the fat rabbit, deciding she was too hungry to wait for stew later on. While Ulrich watched, the meat began to brown, sending off a delicious rich aroma. While they waited for the meat to cook, she exchanged stories with Glynden, laughing when he found every occasion to assist her. With blushing concern, he laid his cloak down on the ground muttering that a lady shouldn't have to sit where it was cold and damp. Next, he excused himself and came back presently with some mushrooms, berries, and small, tart apples. He made sure that she received the most fragrant and ripe of the fruits, watching with great delight as she licked away the juice that ran down her fingers as she ate. He then neatly divided the cooked rabbit, giving her the best half and complimenting her on her cooking abilities as he devoured the firm flesh.

Ulrich glowered in the shadows. The only thing missing was lark song and posies. Surely, these tactics were not working on her! The young idiot would never find favor with such a firebrand! How could she sit there so cozily with this hopeless boy?

As if called by his request for lark song and posies, a little bird landed on a nodding flower not far from him and warbled away, his little head cocked in question. Ulrich snorted and made himself comfortable against a rock, trying to ignore the overly pleasant banter below him.

A little over an hour later, when the sun had reached its zenith, Ulrich knew he was unable to find reason any longer to dally about watching the pretty woman and her attentive companion. Feeling greatly disgruntled, Ulrich reluctantly mounted Titan and rode off towards his land.

He felt a bit foolish for finding his heart so entranced and his head so willing to build a picture of good character into a woman he'd met once under poor circumstances. For all he knew, she was selfish and petty. Perhaps a good horsewoman and huntress, but surely not the woman of which he had dreamed. She was just a flesh and blood female, as common as any. These were his private arguments to himself as he spurred his mount on through the fragrant, hot summer fields, though his heart hardly believed a word.

CHAPTER FOUR

The energy of the castle was almost palpable, as Deive and Erta called out instructions to numerous servants and warriors. Occasionally, the two women smiled at one another, sharing their love and talent for organizing everything around them. Deive, knowing the trial that Erta had survived, was still surprised and pleased at her friend's tenfold improvement.

Though Erta was no longer allowed to run the keep, she still had much influence over the daily habits and needs of its people. She had done an excellent job for years, and because of this, the household looked to her for guidance. They came to her secretly in the evenings or when Savine was elsewhere occupied. This event only increased their need for direction.

"Morgan, please attend to freshening the straw throughout the castle. Oh, and dear, don't forget the flowers and herbs in its mix." The young servant moved off quickly at Erta's softly spoken command.

When the servant had left to attend to this duty, Erta pursed her lips in thought, knowing that there was still so much to be done in preparation for the week's worth of celebrations surrounding Summer Solstice. Savine had planned a huge costume feast as the highlight of the festival, and had asked her guests to come specially dressed using forest spirits, creatures and ancient deities as their basis for costuming. In addition, there would be the usual special games, bards prose, acrobatics, and music. Erta, blowing a strand of hair off her hot forehead, ticked another preparation off her list and bustled away to the kitchens, wisely avoiding the more open areas of the common stairwell and hallways. She had no desire to meet up with her nasty mistress.

Deive, playing the eyes and ears of her friend, made her way through the keep, noting that the heavy wood furnishings had been polished and dressed with elaborately woven cushions and fine tapestries as ordered. The floors had been swept clean and the supply of fresh rushes was being prepared ahead of time so that a fresh layer might be spread every morning. Where there were no rushes, the floor would be covered with more tapestries of lesser quality. Most of the tapestries and fine wool pillows had been sent from the weaver's guild in the region, although they were interspersed with others made of blended linens and velvets. The sconces and lanterns in every room had been fitted with new tallow candles and the wicks trimmed. Some of the candles had been dipped in herb oil, giving off fragrant and sometimes heavy scents when lit. Deive's satisfaction over these myriad preparations would be passed along to Erta so that the housekeeper's list could again be shortened.

The kitchen, too, was a constant hive of activity with piles of luscious, fragrant pork pastries, oyster cakes, sugared fruits and nuts, apple and rum pastries, and fresh bread being prepared and stored away or wrapped in cloths for later. The heavy scents of the bread, raspberries steeped in cream, and ripe apples clung deliciously to every corner of the busy nest, interspersed with the stronger odors of the roasted pork and shelled oysters.

The plans for roasted beef and lamb, basted in rosemary and olive oil, stews made with fresh forest vegetables, fried freshwater eels, and sugared whey and cider made every mouth that happened through kitchen, water in anticipation. Add to the list various wild game and cheeses that would be brought in from the smokehouses, and the feasts for the celebration were complete. Like cackling chickens, tasters, brewers, vintners, and cooks rushed about, their loud, piercing voices ringing anxiously about their particular delicacy and its place of honor.

On heavy wooden carts, fresh honey mead, ale, and new wine arrived daily, being quickly stored in a spring cellar next to the kitchens. Specialties like oranges, pomegranates, limes, figs, and dates sent via local merchant couriers were duly given place in the cool, stone caverns so that the spring cellar air was hung with the scents of citrus and desert fruits.

Erta, near laughter or utter frustration at any given moment, was hard pressed to calm her husband the head cook, Ansel, as the time drew near for the coming out of his tasty culinary creations and those of his protégés.

_____

As if in another world, far above all the bustling odors and voices, in the cool, private chambers of the keep, Lizel quietly commanded a bevy of fine seamstresses as to the creation of the designs to be worn by Savine during the celebration. Lizel had refused to give aid to Alida and Deive in their costuming and was gleefully smug at the idea that they may now be less appropriately gowned. She did not realize that a very talented set of hands was even now preparing Deive and Alida's costumes with ease and creativity.

In her chambers, down the hallway from Savine's, Alida occupied herself in making an appearance her parents would be proud of, as well as studying more deeply the ancient powers so much the desire of her heart. Under Deive's tutelage and demands, Alida often stayed up past all others in the castle memorizing the elementals and their corresponding signs, as well as learning the healing arts expected of one with her gifts.

When her studies would become too overwhelming, she would find good company with the bakers in the kitchen who had been quite surprised at her prowess in the culinary arts. She, unlike Savine, had never been taught to disdain the work of commoners. Her mother had insisted that she learn to cook, clean, and dress herself appropriately that she might be of aid to her keep in times of war or want. Alida had found that she had quite a fondness for cooking and baking, and under Ansel's watchful eye, she had increased her talent.

The only one that remained useless during the hustle of the festival's preparation was Savine, whose main occupation drifted alternately between her disturbing obsession with ridding herself of Deive and Alida and her obsession with presenting herself in the best light possible. She had ruled her household with such an iron fist for years that she was well assured of the utter perfection of her servant's domestic results and only had to attend to her own beautifying needs. The already overly busy staff was sent at every hour to collect some new bauble or perfume for her. They were run ragged over her demands to again fill the tub in her chambers after she had bathed twice already the same day.   Finally, the staff sent Tremain to her, who, with a weary and somewhat disgusted voice, begged her to hold off on her grooming lest her skin and hair suffer due to her over-attentions.

Meanwhile, in the neighboring region, Ulrich had heard of the feasting and had determined to include himself in the celebrations. He continued to remain intrigued by the unusual young woman housed within the walls of

Lyrnne. However, because of his status as enemy to the Lyrnne keep, he was not overly hopeful about receiving an invitation. Instead, he planned on quiet and unobtrusive arrivals at varying times throughout the celebration, playing the part of a spy and interloper.

To aid his entrance into Lyrnne's feasting, he had gathered a good collection of commoner's gear and clothing. Additionally, he had procured a vintner's wagon, for a charger as grand as Titan would surely call attention to his status. These preparations and the slight change of his dialect and facial appearance would complete his guise. His court thought nothing of his plans, for they assumed a military rather than personal involvement and were quick to assist him.

The first day of the gala event arrived with the sun blooming a bright red in the east. The bustle of a keep already in full swing rang through the surrounding dells and coveys. The rush of hurrying feet both heeled and smooth bottom soles filled up the empty spaces with their scuffling and clipped resonance. Friendly shouts mixed with the calls of those who were stressed over the upturn of some detail, vied with the sounds of rushing skirts and jingling adornments. The animals, sensing the energy of the day, brayed and cackled, neighed and lowed. The sounds of their bodies with swishing tails and stomping feet added to the growing symphony. The medley of smells including oily cooking and freshly baked goods mixed unexpectedly well with scents of musky perfume, dung carts out in the open courtyard, and the pneumonia smell of cleaning supplies such as lye and salts. Nary could a sleeping form be found for all the inhabitants and guests of Lyrnne found they were unable to remain abed amidst all the sounds, smells, and fresh air of a newborn festival.

In chambers, Savine donned a slashed, scarlet linen sheath with golden belts. The under tunics showing through the sheath were also of a fine, soft linen in colors of spun gold and cerulean blue. On her feet, she wore golden round-toed shoes that were embroidered with scarlet and cerulean blue threads. Her hair was painstakingly braided with inset flowers and jewels, and her face had been colored with fine powders from the apothecary's shop. She had rings on all of her fingers, sporting large perfect stones in every color. Round her wrists were layers of finely wrought bracelets, some with precious gems and some with only twists of fragile, precious metals.

In a room several doors down, Alida arrayed herself in a much simpler, dark green linen tunic with a satin tapestry bodice adorned with soaring falcons and flowers. Her feet were encased in kidskin boots that had been dyed a soft green and embroidered with gold linen thread. The toes of these festive boots were curled over themselves and to make them practical as well as beautiful, she had ordered them with black. hard-tack leather soles. She had placed her family's silver torc around her neck and the matching bands around her bared arms, making sure that each shone to perfection. Disdaining the overly heavy adornment of her aunt's coif, she had decided to wear her curly hair long and undressed, save for two braids on either side of her face, which had been finished off with light silver encasements. She rubbed rose scented oil onto her arms and neck, and after these simple preparations, she sat restlessly awaiting Deive's arrival.

A long hour later, Deive swept into the room, the scent of jasmine following her progress. She was gowned in deep purple linen with the black crest of Falda embroidered on the front of the gown. The wide, pointed sleeves were lined with black linen and left her skin visible from mid-bicep in order to set off ornately etched silver wrist cuffs, with the distinctive craftsmanship of the eastern mines. She was wearing her purple and silver insignia ring as well as a black onyx cuff ring given to her long ago by her own tutor. She was magnificent with her heavy black tresses braided up around a single silver and ruby circlet. Her violet eyes were set off perfectly by the gown, and as always, her strongest attraction was the aura of power that emanated from her.

Together the gorgeous pair swept down the keep stairs into the noise and promise of the day.

They had proceeded through the courtyard en route for the back doors to the kitchen gardens, when Alida felt a firm, cool hand on her arm. She turned to find Savine angrily glaring at her from beneath a furrowed brow.

"Not even on this one occasion can you humor me and adorn yourself as befits a noblewoman of this keep. You would disgrace me, even now that you have felt the sting of my anger."

Alida pulled away, her voice husky and dangerously low, "And you, Aunt, would yet complain and dwell on the unimportant details of appearance rather than busying yourself with the duties required of a keep's mistress."

The two women squared off like spitting cats, and as with other occasions, Savine felt herself unable to stand without flinching before her niece. Out of pride and nervousness, Savine declared in a high-pitched voice, "Attire yourself as I have commanded, or you will enjoy no part of the festivities."

Alida sought to put an end to the inane conversation. Enunciating clearly, as if to a child she said, "I'll stay adorned as I am *and* join in the celebrations, for you have already spread the word about my presence at the festival. Should my presence not be seen, you'd suffer the inquiries of the many Chieftains assembled by your persuasion to sample my beauty and bid for my hand. It seems that you have given yourself no choice, Savine!" Her aunt could summon no reply and turned on her heel, her hands and chin shaking in anger.

Deive took Alida's offered arm, and they continued towards their original point of interest, the kitchen. When she finally did speak, her only comment was "Every day your power grows. Soon Savine will not be able to utter a single word to you, nor stand before you without great humility."

The two women entered the keep's kitchens and sought out Erta, who had gowned herself in a new flowing tunic of light blue muslin, embroidered round the neck with bright folk art. Her nut-brown hair was wrapped beneath a matching muslin kerchief, and by the pride in her eye, they knew that she had found great joy in the results of the intensive preparations of the preceding weeks.

Trumpets sounded at mid-morning, and the feasting and merriment began after the pomp and circumstance of speeches and instructions by Savine. These opening ceremonies were made in an outside court beyond the city walls that had been assembled especially for the occasion. Entourages from neighboring regions had been arriving all week, and some were still making their way to the mown fields where the open-air court had been set up. By the end of Savine's final speech, the open-air court had filled with merrymakers and rowdy reunited servants. Alida and Deive made their way through the masses, amused by the whispers and inquiries that followed in their wake.

"Oo is she?"

"The young'un is Savine's niece sent from a far-off region."

"She has a strange look to her, and such attire be na' appropriate for a decent chieftain's daughter."

"Aye, what of the bared arms and torc, a bit pretentious if ye ask me. Surely, she won't be favored for her manner of dress and demeanor. She's too bold, just look at 'ow she talks wi' the men!"

A third voice piped up, "I think she's lovely! But there's no doubt as to Savine's feelings if you common wenches are passin' judgment!"

Alida's ears caught the gossip, and she smiled softly at Deive. "Thank the powers for your companionship today. I wonder that the people of this land are so predisposed to judge. That is what comes, I suppose, of having no real spiritual leadership. Haven't you noticed the lack of holy places and holy governors in Lyrnne? Falda's traditions were rich and well known once, though now they have died away. Yet this land has not even any memory of traditions. You yourself have taught me that the power of magic must be accompanied by discipline and by those willing to carry the torch from age to age. The only hope for these hopeless masses, I fear, are rumors of the wondrous signs and strength of those who call themselves Yeovite Priests. I have heard that such lowly traveling men believe that an Ancient One abides, abundant in his rein over all, including the powers themselves. They even foretell the arrival of their god in the flesh."

Deive, trying to contain her sudden foreboding, tightened her grip on Alida's arm. "Alida, our ancestors foresaw the coming of a powerful presence, and it was recorded even in the natural inscriptions. Many of our order fought the arrival of such men and women and continue, even with their reduced numbers, to fight this . . . invasion of the Yeovite Priests. Who has been enticing you with such stories?"

Alida was surprised at Deive's worried expression. "Have you not told me that the powers accept all teachings?"

Deive's brow furrowed. "I know only what I have been taught, but if I exclude any thought or way, it is the thought and way of the exclusive. How could there be one Power, one Holy Deity higher than all the rest? What religious poverty, this adoration of one god! I much prefer our four powers of wind, earth, water, and fire and the delightful magic of all the children of

Berynth—forest sprite, eltar and changeling. No, I think this Yeovitess belief is dangerous. I, too, would fight it. Would you have Lyrnne serve a single belief? They are so close-minded already!"

When Deive saw Alida's deeply thoughtful expression, she rubbed her forehead as if to dismiss these troublesome thoughts. "These are nothing but the ramblings of an old woman, Alida. Let us be merry on this day, for your lessons have been intensive of late, and I swore by the powers that they would not have you cloud-faced today!"

Alida nodded somewhat reluctantly. Then all at once, she let go of Deive's arm and spun in the warm light of the summer day ending her spinning waltz with a low comical bow. Laughing with arms akimbo and hair on fire from the warmth of the sun, Alida made an enchanting picture. "Is this frivolous and merry enough?" Deive clapped her hands together enjoying the youthful explosion of energy. All around them, the whispers became somewhat more flattering and many a male turned at the sound of Alida's musical laughter.

Kellen Grost, with special interest, looked on in appreciation at the spirit the young lass showed. She was less fashionable than the maidens he was accustomed to, but her laughing eyes and young figure were attractive enough. He was not one given to great passions when it came to women and had coolly decided before the festival that he would seek out a mate, preferably someone needy and willingly bargained away.

He was in his prime, a magnificent specimen of manhood with heavy red-brown locks and green eyes. He was a favored bachelor, sought by wealthy families who were excited by the prospect of his rich land and army.

Though indifferent to the charms of women, he did not want a woman of small spirit. He preferred the process that taming required. He was determined that along with the attributes of neediness and an unconcerned family, the chosen female would be pleasant enough in demeanor, with a fair face, pure virtue, and enough spirit to break. Though he did not intend to be overly involved with her, he wanted a woman that would bring a certain uniqueness to the name of his house.

With the thought that Alida, as she was called, seemed to fit his needs, he stepped forward and found his place on the raised dais reserved for the nobility. He found his neatly embroidered name on a place setting in close proximity to Savine. He was most amused that she had reserved a spot for him also next to the very object of his interest. Their families had been fast neighbors and comrades over the years, and he knew that a union of their two houses would be very desirable. Shortly after being seated, a pleased Savine turned his way and smiled disarmingly.

"Kellen, son of Braun, what an honor to have you at my little festival. May you find rest and pleasure. I'm sure you'll find that there are a great many diversions to be had." Her gracious countenance and formal address were suitably vague, but Kellen was not without his moment of wit.

With glowing eyes and a jovial smile, Kellen addressed Savine. "Let us speak with candor, dear woman. We both know that diversions of today's proportions are best suited to the game of matchmaking. Do you find your niece to be of that desirable age and demeanor for marriage? It is the sight of her loveliness that at once prompts me to ask."

Savine's finely arched eyebrow rose even higher. "Kellen, I believe you draw quickly to the point, and because she does now approach, I shall quickly answer. She is a very pleasant young woman of good manners and breeding. She would don the wifely character with ease at the time of marriage and remain in all faithfulness to the husband that took her."

"Will she agree to a marriage of your arrangement rather than her choice?"

Savine smiled in a gentle manner that those who knew her would find startling. "Sir, she has no choice but to rely on me. I have kindly taken her under my wing and seek a decent man of noble stock to be her mate. A young woman in her orphaned state has no choice but to depend upon the good will and wisdom of her only remaining family. What is love compared to comfort and long life? I must make the decision for her well-being and future." *Though anyone would do,* thought Savine to herself. A man who was known to beat and then discard his women as soiled leggings would be a fair enough husband for her headstrong niece. Luckily, for Alida, this one was known for his dispassionate nature towards the female of the species.

Savine turned with an overly bright smile at Alida's approach. "Alida, how lovely you look—come and join us. This is Kellen Grost of Kinterden Dell."

Alida's eyes narrowed. Something was amiss. She turned to Deive for an instant and saw the wariness in her friend's eyes as well.

With a graceful movement, Alida seated herself. She then dipped her fingers into the offered water bowl and caught up a corner of the soft napkin placed on her lap by a young, male servant. When she had completed the movement, she offered her hand to Kellen. His kiss to her hand was cool and dry, neither the least bit distasteful nor arousing. When he delayed in ending the contact, she softly withdrew her hand, nothing spoken but a whisper from her clothing.

"And what pleasant topics have the two of you discussed to cause such smiles?" asked Alida politely.

"We have been musing over the availability of many of the attending maidens while trying to guess which suitors are most likely to catch their eye," replied Kellen. "We believe that the son of Gaitlin Browhurst has decided early on to catch the favor of the woman called Hettie. It 'tis the perfect season for matchmaking, and your Aunt and I seem to have a talent for its completion."

Alida felt the personal intent of his dry conversation all too clearly. This was compounded by Kellen's suggestive, slightly arrogant smile.

Alida made do with small talk throughout the meal, but was the first to rise, quickly making the excuse that she wished to see the archery contests being held just out of sight. Deive was about to follow smoothly behind, but was sidetracked by Savine and Kellen.

"Allow me to escort you, my dear," Kellen interjected while taking Alida's arm.

"Oh, yes do, Alida. Kellen is a most agreeable companion. You'll find the day is quite quickly whiled away in his company." Savine smiled innocently at both Alida and Deive. "Deive, do sit and talk with me awhile, as we have not conversed since before the arrangements for the festival had begun."

Deive turned to Alida, gave a poised nod, and said, "Fare thee well, and I will meet you at the creek when the sun has dropped a little. It will not do for you to be alone with an interested suitor come eventide. As your mentor, the protection of your maidenly virtue is my duty."

Savine clamped down on the instant retort that had come to her lips and smiled irritably at the attractive couple before her. "Very well, Alida, you are dismissed."

When Kellen and Alida had progressed a ways from the dais, Savine turned angrily towards Deive. "Where was this great concern for Alida on all the other occasions of unruly behavior? Did you think that your dismissal of Grost was not very transparent? Alida will marry whom I choose, despite your attempts at guile. She is my ward in the truest eye of the common law. You may have been her nurse and mentor for these twenty and two years, but I am her physical guardian and master."

Deive's elegant, cool smile bit into Savine's composure. "As you wish, Savine, but mark that your niece is a woman of deep independence. You have not, nor will you ever, crush and bend her to your will. If she is agreeable to a match, then it shall be done. If she is not, may the gods save your pride! She is most able to make her feelings known."

Savine, unable as usual to make a suitable reply, turned to another less desirable suitor on her right and talked breezily about crops, fashion, the festivities, or anything else to keep her attention turned from Deive.

Two tents down, Kellen and Alida strolled passed a storyteller who had gathered a crowd. They listened to his tale but left before its completion, for Alida was restive in Grost's company. Further on down the line of festival tents, two dark men from the south performed amazing magical tricks—their white teeth flashing from behind full lips and their eyes filled with bright intelligence. While watching the performance and listening to the occasional whoosh of fire that came from their mouths or from prearranged platforms, Alida was delighted to sample figs and dates that had been stewed in cinnamon. She also munched happily away on chewy, bright yellow curried almonds. However, not even such diversions could compensate for her lacking companion.

Kellen, not oblivious to Alida's discomfort and boredom, talked about his lands and wealth. He also referred lightly to his family's connection with the Lyrnne name, as if to coax her trust and admiration. She avoided any commitment by referring to her desire to remain a ward of the Lyrnne keep for as long as possible. She also talked quietly about independence and self-direction, topics that were disturbing to Kellen.

He did his best to entertain her with stories and baubles bought at small booths scattered between the tents, but it wasn't until they approached the gaming fields that he saw anything close to interest spark in her eyes.

When they arrived at a warm, fragrant mowed field set up for races, Alida felt a sudden surge of joy rise up in her at the prospect of a challenge.

She was uncomfortable with pleasantries and was not socially skilled as were other maids her age. She had found it a great effort to remain composed and mannerly in Kellen's presence.

As she looked about, half-heartedly responding to Kellen's monotone voice, she noted that the majority of the riders were mediocre horsemen intent on outdoing one another. She could easily best all of them and, as always, was loathe to let such an opportunity pass. Besides, her sudden un-maidenly behavior would most usefully disarm Kellen's attraction.

A very surprised and blustering Kellen was seen traipsing after her as she called for the charger, Raven. Her quick, light mounting of the unsaddled beast drew cheers and whispers from the surrounding crowd. The cheers were drawn from neighboring regions less known for their civility and the whispers from those regions famed for more courtly behavior.

From the outskirts of the crowd, a bent and quiet burgher watched with admiration as Alida urged a prancing Raven to the starting line. The race had been set with obstacles and pitfalls as well as a long stretch made for pure speed. The burgher assessed the distance needed for a win and threw money down for a wager, his coins clinking as they fell. He was anticipating the defeat of all against the curly-haired beauty. When the keeper of the wagers roared out with laughter at the amount that was cast, the men around him, including Kellen, turned in amazement, quietly dissuading others who dared to bet on a woman. Surely, the burgher was a fool!

When all of the contestants had gathered, they were given a moment to settle themselves. Alida gathered her heavy, fulsome tresses from off her neck where warm strands were beginning to stick to her skin. Carefully gathering her braided dreadlocks as well, she deftly tied all of it up with a rough leather thong. She then pulled up her tunic to her knees and tucked it around and under herself. She did not want any distractions or restrictions when it came to the guidance and protection of herself and her mount.

When she hiked up her skirts to her knees, the women in the crowd turned away with feigned virtuosity, aghast at her lack of modesty. The men drew closer in admiration, and many a hoot and lewd suggestion was heard from those with few manners.

From the sidelines, skin drums began to beat with a sound so deep it reached one's heart, and Raven, recognizing the sound of war, pranced about nervously. A man stepped forward with a raised banner, and the crowd fell silent, save for the drums and the roars from the other gaming arenas. Then with a holler, the call was given and the race was on!

A bold movement against Raven's warm side cast rider and beast into the lead position instantly. Alida leaned forward so close to her mount's hot furry neck that she could feel his wildly racing pulse. She expertly guided the charger through closely set wooden posts and around heavy thistle bushes, ignoring the pain when a wayward branch of thorns would snatch at her legs. The crowd's chanting and hollers startled some of the less-experienced mounts and several riders went down. Hay obstacles set with formidable spears flew away, untouched beneath Raven's pounding hooves, and every pitfall that was avoided added to Alida's sense of accomplishment. When Raven faltered at a wide creek running directly across the field, the crowd held its collective breath. Two contestants passed them during Raven's hesitation. Alida remained inalterably steady, and Raven drew his strength from her. He was able to hop inelegantly across the tributary and was reassured by his rider's soft word. When they reached the open stretch, Alida could feel the joyful bunching of Raven's throbbing muscles beneath her legs in preparation for headlong flight. Alida yelled out a blood-curdling war cry, and with a burst of pure and graceful speed, rider and mount moved ahead of the other two contestants for the win!

The crowd fell silent for a moment. Never before had they seen such beauty and untamable spirit in a woman. Suddenly a chant began from deep within the masses and grew to a throbbing adulation of the young maid. Kellen, with bright red spots upon each cheek, threw his lost wager into the pot and watched with a disgruntled sneer as the wily burgher took a small fortune into his pockets.

When Alida had dismounted, several young maidens from regions far to the east approached her. They all carried spears and wore tunics that were made from strange material that was thin as a butterfly's wing. Alida longingly fingered their serviceable garments, making instant friends with all the girls. Each of the maids congratulated Alida, and her deep smile into each set of eyes was a testament to the shared independence and strength. They chatted about her preferences for controlling and encouraging a charger. Many of the women standing with her had been denied participation in horse races by strict families, but the few that were brave had stepped forward to learn her methods and planned on running in the next few rounds.

It was with a different expression that Kellen approached the group. When he quietly and firmly took Alida's arm to remove her from the scene with an iron like grip, the crowd booed its disapproval. He leaned over and whispered in her ear, "You incite the crowds to disobey the common rules and regulations of the festivities. I thought you more of a gentlewoman, though I cannot say that your spirit displeases me. In fact, I feel quite invigorated by the prospect of taming you."

Alida gently removed her arm from his grasp, and without another word, she turned her back and walked away. Not even the expected "fare thee well" would she bestow upon a man who would tie her wings.

The bent burgher had overheard their conversation and was inflamed over the man's lack of appreciation. Yet there was a place in him that was glad over the displacement of such a rival. Surely, she would not take kindly to being contained. Watching her retreating form, he inquired her name from a nearby smithy. He smiled privately over his findings—Alida—small winged one. The burgher thanked the smithy and hobbled off, following the young woman.

CHAPTER FIVE

Ulrich's eyes glittered from within the burgher's cloak. Pacing himself a good eight yards behind Alida, he was able to follow her without being intrusive or obvious. He noted how a path opened for her through the crowd. It was clear that she was greatly admired among many of the people, especially the commoners.

When Alida had almost reached the dais, he saw a raven-haired woman rise from a seat very near Savine of Lyrnne. With a murmured excuse, she quickly descended the stairs. The two women clasped hands warmly at the bottom of the steps and moved off quickly into the crowds. Ulrich pulled his scratchy hood a little further over his features and hobbled by the dais, turning his face away from Savine's alert, constantly searching eyes. It would not do to be recognized at this early point in the festivities.

When he had hurried by the dais, he lifted his eyes once more and caught sight of someone observing the two women. The fellow was large and crude with greasy hair and large meaty fists. Ulrich quickened his pace and drew a little nearer to the man, his heart skipping a beat in warning.

Completely unaware of Ulrich's presence and with surprising skill, the unwashed commoner continued on trailing Deive and Alida, remaining unnoticed by them, despite his size, as he wove his way through the festivals crowds.

Ulrich noted the strong odor of too much wine and an unwashed body that wafted back from the burly man. The strength of the odors would have dissuaded most from trailing him downwind, but Ulrich's battle training to ignore everything the senses had to offer kept him from drawing back.

They had passed many large tents and an open livestock corral before the heavy commoner signaled to another far-grimmer looking man that had been paralleling the two women at a good ten yards off.

Ulrich instantly grew that much more alert, trying to take in every detail of their faces and body language. When the two men drew closer together, Ulrich heard them earnestly discussing some important matter. The murmurs were too low to be deciphered clearly, and Ulrich was loath to draw too close, lest they discover his presence. He dropped back a little ways when the press of the crowds lessened, just as the two men split off from each other, obviously having come to some agreement. Surprisingly, they also left off following Alida and her companion.

At first, Ulrich thought he must have mistaken the two men's intent, for the second commoner had clambered onto an inconspicuous hay wagon, lazily making his way towards the forest. Then Ulrich turned to see that the burly first commoner had mounted a destrier caked in mud and sweat. The fine charger nickered to the rider and turned instantly beneath his command. When the sinister fellow had taken off at a quick trot towards the north, a piece of burlap under his seat flew up disclosing a glimpse of a very fine blade. The incongruities of a commoner on such a fine horse, which responded with familiarity, and a weapon of such quality, made Ulrich uncomfortable. He knew many of the guards and commoners of this region and some from the visiting regions, but it was still possible that he was unfamiliar with a few. Could these be men of a private force sent to protect the two women?

Ulrich dismissed this thought, trusting his instincts more. Their rush to leave and hooded behavior spoke of something sinister. Ulrich moved off at a quicker pace fingering his own cold blade hung at his side and hidden beneath his clever disguise. He trailed after the women who had become small targets in the dwindling afternoon sun his every sense at alert.

Alida pulled Deive's arm close in hers a wry laugh softening her pensive words. "Deive, I fear that I have passed the age when resisting marriage is permissible. For all intents and purposes, I am now considered an old maid regardless of how far from the truth that may be!" Then more softly in a thoughtful tone she mused, "Except for his blazing ego, Kellen seems harmless enough, but I cannot help feeling choked in his presence and by his words. There is also the matter of love, which I do not comprehend, except as I have seen it in the example of my own parents.

It is clear that Savine will do all she can to marry me off at this festival. She could choose any manner of husband for me, though I am sure that she will not find it in her heart to offer allowances for my individual choice, since her pocket is dependent upon my success. The bride price that she would receive would most likely cover what she has had to pay in her disgruntled charity towards me. I feel the time drawing nearer for me to choose between the lesser of two ills. Either I take this Kellen or some other chieftain to husband or suffer Savine's vile wrath yet again. It seems that I must become a woman in the truest and dreariest sense, that of a mother and wife. Would that I had the strength for this so soon after my parents' absence."

Deive grasped Alida's hand tightly and murmured, "It is time."

Her forehead wrinkled in question. Alida looked to Deive. "Time for what, Deive?"

"I have been saving your initiation into the service of the powers for a time of necessity. Because the night and day are equal tomorrow, it will be a time of great energy. Tomorrow night we will make you a part of all you see and feel; both those things of the physical world and those of the spirit world. You must prepare, in the most secret place of your heart, a pledge. It can be anything you choose. You will give this pledge, and through the release of it, you will be empowered for the decisions necessary to your life and necessary for the good of all you meet. You will give your talent to and humble yourself beneath the powers. Because of this, you will become strong. Remember that only those who maintain a balance between light and dark will remain strong eternally. Those who live in the extremes of either force will remain tortured through all the movements of the abyss for all time, for they are in disagreement with the powers."

Deive looked at Alida and releasing her hand said, "I request of you the following: Do not drink ale or mead overmuch at tonight's feast or throughout the day tomorrow. Today let your thoughts dwell on the pledge you will give along with your talent. Also, adorn yourself as befits the daughter of great warriors and bards. Enjoy the evening's festivities, but be prepared for the sobering of your spirit. I guess that the merriment that I encouraged this day shall have to be held aside for another time."

Beneath the heavy shade of a nearby oak, Ulrich overheard the whole conversation. He recognized immediately the references to the old ways and to a "talent" of Alida's. His grandmother had held sacred many of the old practices and had fought the ways of imbalance for years. He had gained great respect for her and her wisdom, and because of this, he did not fear unseen things. He himself had no great power other than the character imbued by his crest. His grandmother had said he did have a talent, but that it would be hidden until he chose to see it. Her words came back to him now, and he felt a tiny thrill crest above his heart.

He would come again after the great feast on the morrow and would learn of the secrets the two females planned. The one called Deive was obviously a woman of great power. She would hold Alida steady, concentrating on the task before them. He would cloak himself as deeply as the shadows, and neither would know he was there. Perhaps he, too, would learn something of himself in the evening to come.

Because the sun had dropped almost completely, Ulrich headed for the borders of the region that were hosting his countrymen for a similar festival. He would feast and be merry with them, but his mind would remain with the woman who had now found a staunch hold within his blood.

The first evening feast of the festival began after the final horse races and games. Though it was high summer, some of the nights remained cool and misty. Deive and Alida made their way back to the great hall where the festivities had moved. Alida was very quiet after speaking with Deive. She was not prepared to face a great mass of people, but knew her duty therein lay.

The hall was lit with great masses of candles and lanterns. They were seated upon the dais and soon the volume from the music and laughter rose until Alida felt her head would burst. She had been attempting to make conversation with Kellen when a tall, slender man approached the head table. He was very elegant in his dress and manner, and when he requested a dance, Alida agreed. The moment his hand touched hers, however, she felt a threatening shiver caress her neck. He pulled her into the crowd, despite some resistance on her part. The music tinkled madly about them, and Alida felt a bit as if she was drifting. When the dance brought them closer together, he leaned to her ear and whispered, "When next you rip the throat and eyes from one of my men, remember fledgling enchantress that aura is left behind, and through it, you can be traced. You are not so very safe, you see." The world careened around her and a great roaring cascaded through her head. From a long distance away, she could hear Deive calling out instructions.

––––––––––

"Careful! Do not move her too roughly. Lay her here, and then get ye to the kitchens to gather up cool water and salts!"

A hand brushed across her brow, and Alida drifted into the tempting dark that had been grabbing at her.

––––––––––

Some hours later, a pale and quivering Alida found consciousness in an unfamiliar bed. When she bolted upright screaming, Deive rushed to her side and pulled her close. "Hush, Dear, do not fear. You are safe." Deive smoothed Alida's back in rhythmic circles as if to pull the fear and panic from her body. When she had calmed a bit, Deive began to ask questions.

"Do you feel well enough to answer me?"

Alida nodded.

"Do you want something to drink or a blanket to warm you? You are very cold." Deive watched every motion, cataloging the myriad of strange symptoms.

Alida drew in a great gulp of air and said, "Did you catch him? Was he restrained by the guards?"

"Of whom do you speak, Love? No one has been restrained. There has been nothing but merriment and music."

"Quirin. Did they restrain Quirin?"

Deive felt bile rise ever so slightly in her throat, the taste souring her mouth. "What do you mean, Alida? Make your thoughts clear to me. I do not understand."

Alida fought to speak clearly her lips and teeth chattering so badly that her jaw ached. She could not stop her shaking. "He . . . he took my hand. We danced . . . whirling and gliding about the hall. The mad . . . maddening music was all around us, and people laughed and pointed in the dizzying spin of his arms. *We d-danced!*" Alida's eyes were wild and disbelieving.

Deive took her hand. "Alida, you never danced with anyone. You were talking with Kellen, and all at once, you fell into a swoon. Your arms and legs twitched with convulsions. We called to you, and I grasped at your conscious thread with my magic, trying to bring you back, but you remained out of my reach for many hours. There is still a part of you that remains unavailable."

Alida looked utterly bewildered. "He *was* there. He placed his cool hand upon my hand and his other upon my waist when we danced–I felt the weight of it upon my hip. He was tall, elegant and very cruel. He knew that it was at my hand that his sentry died. He said that I was not safe. He has found me, Deive, of this I am sure. Help me! Help me to know how to overcome him."

Deive gently pushed the shivering and teary-eyed Alida down onto the pallet and pulled furs and linens up around her neck. "Sleep, Alida, and do not worry this night. You are in the warmth and safety of my room, and I will stay with you throughout the dark hours. I will keep you this night as I have all others."

"Safe. Safe. Safe." The word rang through Alida's head as she drifted down through sleep. She remained edgy, even when dreams came softly and brightly from the corners of the spreading darkness. Like the motion of waves against a ships' side, Alida felt herself tossing on the warm pallet and could not keep from crying out now and then.

Deive closed off her quarters and took out her tools of discernment and healing from a leather pouch slung at her side. She worked over Alida until the wee hours of the morning when she finally found what she was looking for, a thin line of cosmic red attached to Alida's healthy blue line of consciousness— the small bits of aura creating pathways to the location and health of a person's soul. Quirin had indeed found Alida and had linked himself to her. Deive felt wrath rise within her at the thought that any man had dared to threaten that which was to be pledged to the powers in the close days ahead. Quirin had grown powerful, but he was bitter and overzealous. Deive knew that indeed Alida's time had come. The blessings of the powers would be more needed than ever if Quirin's reign were to be ended. In the meantime, Deive knew his tentative hold must be moved from Alida's mind. Deive began muttering incantations in soft guttural tones and presently reached out her hand, plucking away the offending red strand from off the blue one. Alida jerked in her sleep.

In a misty keep, many regions away, Quirin felt a tiny bloody wound open in his mouth. Startled, he rolled the taste of blood, and more subtly, the scent and flavor of magic left behind, across his tongue and found the flavors familiar. All wards and spells had a taste and all magic carried with it a flavor particularly unique to it's weaver like a signature or seal. It was his nemesis and savior. The sweetest and most wrathful thing he had ever consumed. She had filled his mind to overflowing with her plum sweetness and almond eyes. She was smooth and cool. He licked his lips. She was his Deive. The strange light in his eyes deepened.

———————————

When Alida arose the next morning, she felt drained and earthbound, her limbs like heavy marble columns at her side. However, she no longer felt the deep panic of the night before, and for this, she was thankful. She stood by her window watching the light come up in the east.

Laying her head on the moist, cool windowsill, she whispered a tiny prayer to the powers. Then she gathered her spirits within her and sang sweetly with all her might into the cool dawn, allowing the sounds of low and lovely praise to smooth away her remnants of fear. Her voice was sweet and soft enough that it was carried away by the wind, no ears catching its melody save the ears of the powers.

———————————

The next morning, although bright and beautiful, could not dispel the darkness of Falda. Hard, guttural, male voices echoed out into the hallways of the keep. "Now that we know where she lies, we may take the city at any time. The lands of Lyrnne are not as well guarded as Savine would have them, especially during this time of celebration. It would be so easy to approach, infiltrate, and conquer." Quirin's captain of the guard restlessly went over his well-laid plans of attack, his excitement barely contained. They had received from the two spies at Lyrnne a message that had arrived via the back of it's pigeon carrier. Quirin, however, remained unmoved, staring off into space, his eyes fixed on something far away.

"You believe this to be as simple as any other skirmish on weak lands. You do not realize the great value of what we are seeking nor the power behind it. We will not attack the Lyrnne keep yet. I have other plans in mind." Quirin waved his hand and his bewildered captain left the anteroom with a slow-clipped stride, his heels echoing on the thick stone floor.

Quirin stared into the fire. Its warmth was the only thing keeping away the pervasive chill that followed him continuously. The flames before him turned into swirling images, tinged in hateful red. He would not make a simple pillage on the castle Lyrnne. He would wait and torture, caress, and entice. He would bring fear and then wait to realize its end. His grin was soft and malicious as he devised his perfect revenge on a charge most hateful to him and the only woman he had ever loved.

_____

After a full day of festivities amongst his own people in the hot sun of Drachmund Heights, Ulrich walked solemnly down to a hovel where the old woman preparing his evening costume awaited him. His feet tread softly upon a carpet of fragrant pine needles, and the air grew cooler the lower he descended. All about him, the rustle of the wind in the boughs and the stirrings of small animals beckoned his peace, but peace eluded him.

He had thought his preparations for the Lyrnne feast would be enjoyable and light. Instead, he felt strangely agitated. A great deal was anticipation, but there was also a sense that something was coming of an unknown quantity—for good or for bad.

He shook his head to clear away the disturbing thoughts. He just hadn't had enough sleep the night before. His dreams had been filled with the thrashing wings of a beautiful white falcon that was caught in a patch of briars. A snake approached, and from where Ulrich stood, he was unable to assist the bird or kill the snake. The image had been repeated several times, for he would awaken with a start and then fall back into slumber. Finally, when dawn had peeked through the grooves in the castle walls, he had seen the snake strike the falcon until the fowl's breast had run red—its scream into the mists of the dream covering his body with goose bumps.

This evening's diversions surely will mend my unease, he thought to himself. He looked forward to the great merriment of the feast and a woman of unsurpassed beauty. He made his step a little lighter and straightened his shoulders with determination, for it was not often that he was able to crash his enemy's festivities.

The Lyrnne keep rattled with activity as Erta, Deive, Alida, Ansel, and many others added the final touches to fat-dipped torchiers and festive decorations. The hall was strewn with fragrant hay, laden with fresh herbs, including mint and lavender and with green cut rushes and rose petals. The walls had been adorned with swags of powerfully scented wild flowers and bright ribbons. All was in readiness for the evening feast. Because the feast was to be the main activity of the day, many of the visitors and castle inhabitants allowed themselves to sleep off the ale and mead from the night before, knowing that they would not be needed until later. Bolts of smooth linens and fabrics from far off lands had been secreted about all morning by the nobility's attendants. Many a sleepy servant, who had been unwise enough to keep longer hours than their lords and ladies, could be seen wandering through the hall with bits of fabric and ribbons trailing from their fingertips–their dazed expressions belying their attempts to look busy.

In the great hall, Deive and Alida would glance at each other, exchanging a few excited whispers, their eyes shining with anticipation. Their costumes lay in readiness in a secret room. Many hours had been spent with the seamstress and her aides. The results were exquisite.

When the first hours of the day past with its myriad preparations, and all lay in readiness for the afternoon and eventide, Deive and Alida retired separately to their quarters.

Alida sat upon her pallet, reciting the elemental charts and basic incantations until all shadows had been chased away by the bright afternoon sun. She then pored over the leather scrolls that held ancient runic inscriptions regarding associations to the elemental chart and its properties. She remembered the stories passed down from Deive's eltar relatives and the history of her own bloodline passed through her parents. These helped to make her dry studies more bearable. There was also the matter of deciding upon a pledge to give to the powers. Her forehead creased in thought as she anxiously jumped from one reflection to another, her worried hands moving over the soft creases of the leather scrolls.

Her musings were eventually overcome by a loud knock on the outer door of her chambers. Deive's smooth voice called out, "I know that you are studying, Alida, but you must allow your mind some time to rest."

"Come in, Deive!" She stretched languorously, enjoying the prospect of having her studies diverted. Her muscles were glad for the movement prickling with new blood flow.

The rustle of a sweeping cloak of deep blue followed the stately Deive into the room. "Pray put away your inscriptions and heavy thoughts. I am having a tub brought up, and the little maid, Hattie, should soon be here to help you with your preparations. Do not ponder your training any longer; neither consider your calling. Let your mind and heart rest. You will find strength in doing so." Deive's crisp voice followed her about the room as she laid out scents in bright glass and crystal bottles with a clink on the great, wooden dressing table. Her presence stretched like wind around the room as she fussed here and there picking up the whispering folds of Alida's discarded clothing.

Thus spoken, a tub was brought in—a great resounding thud echoing through the room as two strong serving women dropped it to the floor. The merry tinkling of water and scented mineral spirits were poured into the oval container accenting the merry chatter of the women. Eventually, they left her to soak. After her time had been taken in her luxurious bath, crushed lavender and rose petals were rubbed all over Alida's body and scented oil was sprinkled in her curling locks. The heat from the day intensified the sweet scents - their lovely tones being languorously fanned away from her body by lengths of willow branch. Her feet were massaged with linen strips and chamomile paste. For refreshment of her breath, she was given parsley sprigs, cucumber slices, and linseed twigs on which to chew. Then with a final rinse of rose water over her body and in her mouth, she was ready. When the shadows had lengthened in the outer court, a much refreshed and glowing Alida shooed away all the attendants.

Her skin was a light honey color from the sun she so adored and her hair hung to her mid-back. Her long legs stretched before her, soft and relaxed, and her feet tingled from the attention they had received. She felt sensuous and alert all at the same time. Wouldn't Kellen be enamored at the results? She chuckled to herself over his cool mannerisms, doubting that he would be anything but cordial, even after the vows of marriage had been given. She sighed at the thought of having to take his hand at some point in the future and lazed back onto her fur-covered pallet, letting her musings dispel the disturbing thoughts of the looming possibility of a marriage without love.

For in her private thoughts, from the time of adolescence, she had envisioned a tall and muscular husband with wheat-colored hair and blue eyes. He would be fervent and insatiable–the kiss of his bearded face a constant in her days. There would be no cool demeanor beneath the furs when once their vows had been given, and they would whisper quietly about the deep secret thoughts each possessed. He would delight in her spirit and strength and would be able to best her occasionally in horsemanship and archery. He would be widely respected, and most importantly of all, she would be unable to resist his power, intelligence, and friendship. She did not care for a man of simple mind and intent. She wanted one of deep passions. She longed to be overwhelmed and to overwhelm.

It would have been of great surprise to her, had she known that her thoughts were noted by the bright spirits that crowded her quarters.

This time it was a quiet knock that interrupted her musings, and upon her salutation, a young woman entered with her costume. It was time.

CHAPTER SIX

Savine shifted uncomfortably in her chair and cast a fourth glance at the two empty seats beside her. The merrymaking had been increasing for the last hour, and there was still no sign of Deive and Alida. Kellen had asked twice for the maiden and was beginning to look slighted. Savine primped and fussed, distracting those who were too intent on the arrival of her niece. Her smug smile to herself was evidence that she believed her costuming to be the finest at the feast.

She was dressed as a white stag. Her chestnut hair had been wired into tight crescents high upon her head and out of the centers of each, the light antlers of a young buck had been fastened. Her deep brown eyes had been heavily outlined in kohl, and her eyelashes had been darkened to accentuate their length. Her pouty lips had been stained with berry juice and her skin glowed in the candlelight. Her tunic was pure white hide, and it flowed down to matching tiny slippers, upon each of which diamonds, like dewdrops, glistened. She fanned herself with an assortment of delicate and fragrant branches. She was the embodiment of the elusive spirit of the forest. She was that mythical beast that many had sought throughout the ages.

Savine turned to a dinner companion and flirted outrageously, enjoying her status as the most alluring of the attendees. Her pride was quickly crushed however, when Deive and Alida finally descended the steps.

Deive was dressed in unusually dark blue linen, which had been covered in an exotic shimmering fabric of spun metals. Light cascaded from bits of silver and diamonds that had been woven into the cloth. Her lower face was coated in a fine translucent blue tinted powder that also sported tiny flecks of the silver. Her black shiny hair had been left long, lightly covered by the same shimmering transparent fabric of her gown and held aloft by a beautifully wrought crown of highly polished silver. The crown was encircled by cresting tides at the center of which was a water sprite whose chest had just broken the waves. The sprite's long hair flowing into the waves that surrounded her, framed her perfect face that was tilted towards some far off sun. The brilliant violet hue of Deive's unusual eyes were accentuated by a black half mask encrusted with tiny amethyst and sapphires and by black kohl used to lightly outline the eyes' shape. Her lips had been painted a deep blue and the startling sight of deep purple eyes, blue lips, and translucent skin made many an attendee shiver with delight. She was the figure of the goddess of the deep; the soul of the heavy blue water that gave drink to forest inhabitants. Everyone recognized her character by the symbol emblazoned on the front of her tunic and by fingers encased in silver claws encrusted with amethyst and sapphire. Many a wide-eyed child had been told the tale of the goddess, which out of a lack of heirs of her own, would snatch away human children who came to bathe at her banks, her magic turning them into web-footed creatures of the deep.

Directly to Deive's right descended a figure dressed so brilliantly that Savine's gown was put to shame. Alida had adorned herself as a rare white falcon, sporting a robe and tunic of trailing delicate feathers and bits of fabric designed to look light and airy enough to lift her into the air. Through small slashes in the lacing at the sides, neck, and thighs of her tunic, her warm honey-toned skin showed through. It was a tempting sight that drew many an appreciative glance from the men who bordered her ascent on the dais. Her eyes, too, were lined in kohl as Deive's and Savine's, but her lips had been painted a brilliant red. Her hair had been fashioned into hundreds of tiny braids that gave her the sleek and startling look of a falcon's feathered and elegant head. The costume was accentuated by a half mask complete with a gold-dusted beak and encrusted with pure white feathers and a diamond at the outside corner of each eye. The final touch was sharp gold tapers encasing the end of each finger—an impression of talons. She was as ancient and beautiful as a falcon's scream.

The music did not come to a halt, but much of the talking and laughter died down as the two approached the dais. They were stunning. Masks were generally associated with commoners or foreigners who frequently used them in the miming prose and games of the day. They were not generally used as an elegant form of costuming such as was displayed by the two women. Their bold use of the unusual costumes made them instant favorites.

On a sturdy, rough oak bench lining the walkway to the dais, Ulrich, in his tree deity costume, sucked in a deep breath at the appearance of Alida. He had been playing the part of a jovial commoner very well, but at this moment, he wished himself an escort equal to this woman of beauty. When she passed by him, he breathed in and tasted the roses and lavender that emanated softly from her skin and costuming. That strange possessiveness felt on other occasions welled up fulsome and aggressive. The wolf's blood within his veins growled deeply, and he found himself balefully eyeing the man who took Alida's hand to guide her to her place.

Kellen was greatly pleased by Alida's appearance. Though he had been agitated awaiting her arrival, he was now puffed up like a bantam rooster because of his status as the most desirable suitor for the lass. He catered to her every need throughout the night and made light conversation, pointing out the many diversions and feeding her delicacies from his fingertips—his romantic gestures a far cry from the lack of emotion he felt inside. By his actions, Kellen constantly reminded everyone around them that he was interested in Alida. When he leaned over and whispered some bawdy joke into her ear, Alida rolled her eyes at Deive, for he had also taken that opportunity to nuzzle and kiss her hand, a gesture that did more to annoy her than it did to elicit any feeling.

Though Ulrich appeared to be involved with a rambunctious serving maid, he did not miss any of Kellen's behavior. He playfully warded off the unwanted advancement of the wench who wanted to see the face beneath his humorous mask knowing that although pretty she could never be distraction enough from the glorious sight upon the dais. Nothing could remove his attention from Alida's beauty. He had already decided that he did not approve of Kellen's overly cocky attitude and unwanted familiarity towards Alida. He watched and waited throughout the dinner courses until finally Alida excused herself to take a walk around the outer yards. At nearly the same time, he rose and crudely asserted a need to pass water and to find a barrel in which to dunk his inebriated head. This was met with bawdy laughter, for his dinner companions had grown rowdy and unmannered with ale and the strong new wines of the region.

A breathtakingly clear night greeted Ulrich with a welcome freshness as he passed into the courtyard. Up above him, the stars and full moon shimmered brightly. He was able to catch sight of Alida as she passed into the broad garden by the kitchen. No sound was made as he followed her and slipped behind her into the bushes and silky caress of the overhanging trees. He watched silently as she gracefully sunk to the ground beneath the overhanging boughs of a weeping willow. Ulrich quelled the strong desires that came over him at the sight of her moonlit shoulders and thinly covered décolletage. She leaned forward, and a single braid fell into that delicious cleft. Ulrich decided to wait no longer.

Remaining deep in the whispering trees, his approach was subtle for he caressed her only with his voice. "Have you ever known love?"

The smooth male voice startled Alida's absentminded perusal of the garden. "Who is it? Who is watching from the trees?" She gracefully rose to her feet and stepped forward trying to see who was concealed by the shadows.

"That was not the reply I sought, fair one. Shall I ask again?" He silently moved to another spot beside her, also concealed by shrubbery.

"I would never relate such an intimate detail to someone I could not see. If you wish a response, you must first tell me who you are." Alida prepared for a confrontation and fingered the dirk that was always strapped within her stocking, her heart beating rapidly in her breast and goose bumps covering her skin.

Ulrich's deep voice whispered from beside her, "Why a falcon? Why that crested and regal beast?"

Alida jumped again, realizing that the positioning of the voice had changed. "If you do not tell me who you are, I shall attack you where you stand."

Ulrich's rich laughter wafted towards her through the still warm air. "I am the forest. Now—what about my questions?"

Ignoring all that he had asked, Alida said, "I am dissatisfied by your identity, Forest. Show yourself!" She stared more sharply into the shadowy bushes.

"If you want more answers, then answer me."

She said softly, "Your queries are foolish."

"If they are foolish then their reply should come easily."

Alida glared at the shadows. "Whether I have known love is not the concern of a shadow, and I made this choice of costuming for . . . for reasons of my own."

With the aid of the moonlight, Ulrich could see her high color. He chuckled deeply and left the safety of the bushes.

"I did not ask these questions to offend you nor to make you uneasy, but rather to incite a rise in your strength. You are glorious when your pride is under full sail."

Alida gaped at the strange figure that had stepped out before her. He was an odd humorous character, appearing ages old and very wise. He was the spirit of the oak. She gazed more piercingly at Ulrich as though she could discern what his features were beneath the mask. Ulrich drew in air to calm his heart. Her eyes and features were even more powerful beneath the full moon. She was beautiful and magical in the pale costume, her form glowing like a beacon.

"I ask again, Shadowy Forest, who are you?"

"I am Wolf."

The guttural intonation of his voice made this announcement very realistic. Alida could almost hear the growl deep in his chest. She shifted uncomfortably.

Ulrich chuckled deeply at her discomfiture. "If you turn your back to me, I will remove my mask so that my voice is not muffled, and you can ask any question you want."

Alida pondered the wisdom of such a move. If he were a stranger intent on kidnapping her or hurting her, would she not have felt those emanations of evil already? Would she not have felt more afraid? As it was, her heart pounded out of something closer to anticipation and wariness.

He whispered, "You are curious. I can almost hear your thoughts. Turn your back and satisfy your curiosity."

She was interested but was reluctant to open herself to danger. Ulrich stepped forward again his voice strangely warm. "If I wanted to harm you, Alida, I would have done so already."

She shivered at his declaration. There was something about his voice— she would love to hear it more clearly.

"How do you know my name, Wolf?"

"Everyone within the region and even beyond its borders knows your name. Now turn your back."

Alida slowly rotated away from him, her hand tightening again around the stock of the dirk.

She heard a rustle as he removed his mask and a soft whisper as it was cast to the ground.

"Ask me a question."

He had moved closer. Alida shivered again. His voice was clearer without the mask, deeper and more alive.

"From where do you come, Curious Oak?"

"From the home of my family."

"And from where does your family hail?"

"They come from the stars and the earth and the air."

She sighed, agitated over the game. "You do not help me with your answers. Shall we try again? What is your purpose here?"

"You."

Alida felt him approach another few steps and shivered at his answer. "What do you want of me?"

"Thyself."

She swallowed and whispered, "You do not know me. Why do you have such interest in me?"

"But you are wrong, Fair Falcon, for I know thee from the glade and from the field and from the back of a spirited mount. You are ripe for picking, but not any harvester can claim thee."

Regally, she replied, "Aptly spoken, for I am not yours to take, Wolf. Why do you seek that which you cannot have? Do you not know that a suitor has claimed his right to court me on this very night and that my aunt approves?"

"Yes, Fair One, I do know of your suitor, but I also know that you like him little enough to leave him in the hall and come wandering about beneath the stars, alone. Would you leave any other suitor in whom you had interest?"

Alida jumped when she felt him gently place a hand upon her waist. The contact, even through the cloth of her tunic, was startlingly alive. She felt his spirit command presence within her space. The air between them was very alive. His touch was not soothing and indifferent as was Kellen's. He leaned very close to her ear.

"I believe I saw your handsome suitor whisper, as I am whispering, right before he did this . . ." Ulrich ran his hand down her arm and gently lifted and nuzzled her soft, scented hand, his kisses falling upon the tip of each slender finger.

Alida almost crumbled as a trail of sensations trickled to her chest and stomach. In response, Ulrich felt as if he had too much wine. He forced his voice to come alive, but it was gravelly with the chemistry he felt.

"Did you experience pleasure when he did this to you? Did you desire for him to do more than hold your hand, say . . . in giving thy sweet mouth a kiss? It is really very simple, Alida. You are a woman of deep passions, and you deserve fervency in return. This is why I inquired of thee regarding love."

Alida swallowed and found her voice. "If you are so inclined to provide this fervency, why do you not ask my aunt for permission to court me? I can tell from your voice and manner that you are well-born, are you not an appropriate choice for a suitor?"

Ulrich gently pulled her against his chest and stomach. "Hardly, milady, for I am an enemy of the Lyrnne keep."

A myriad of emotions assailed Alida. She pictured Quirin and his power over her the night before, she felt Ulrich's strong chest against her back, and she could see the stars spinning overhead. Her stomach dropped at the vision of a rabid wolf at her neck.

"You are an aid to Quirin, then." There was resignation in her voice.

Ulrich tightened his grip on her and rasped out, "By the gods, you are wrong. I am an enemy of the Lyrnne keep, but I am an enemy to others as well. Never would I find an ally with a beast such as Quirin."

Alida breathed a little easier until Ulrich had gently nestled her once more against his chest and thighs. Alida was not accustomed to being held by a man nor playing the games of seduction and courtship. She responded elementally, from the deepest part of her being. She arched back against him, and unleashing her arms from his grip, she put them behind her head to his face as if to discover his appearance from her touch.

Ulrich had expected her to call out to the guards on the walls above, to kick him or slap him away as any other noble daughter should have done. Instead, she had behaved as though she was familiar with him. His stomach did a flip, and he groaned at her touch. "I do not think my proximity to you and your explorations is a good idea."

"But your closeness does feel right, and your face holds so much strength," said Alida truthfully without any coyness.

Ulrich chuckled and pulled her hands from his beard where her fingers had come to rest. "Do not tempt me further, maid. There is something within me that calls out to treat you fairly and without too much intimacy. I want you to know me first."

Alida laughed and said, "Then why did you caress me? And why do you hide your identity from me." When he did not answer immediately, she said softly, "Very well then, answer my first question."

He released her fully, commanding that she not turn around, and pulled the mask back on over his head. "As much as I would like to answer thee, I must leave, for it grows late. You, too, should return to the merrymaking. Your entourage will wonder where you have disappeared."

She turned in time to see his retreating back slide into the shadows.

A flushed and bemused Alida returned to the rowdy merrymaking in the hall. She felt light headed and curious. Every face and costume seen was examined as if she could discern from the expressions what the shadowy man of the garden looked like. Her ears were sensitive to voice intonations and characteristics. She pinched her arm to try to make herself come out of the dreamlike state into which she had ascended.

From a dark corner at the back of the hall, Ulrich watched in amusement as Alida's glance darted here and there. He noted with pleasure how absentmindedly she meandered along pausing now and then to gaze into someone's face. Thankfully, most of the attendees of the feast were drunk and were not paying enough attention to her to think she was making advancements upon them.

When she reached the dais, Alida sank into the chair next to Deive and refused to meet the eyes of her friend. She feigned curiosity in the gaming and prose going on below her, but was too much of a novice at lying. Deive gently took her arm and whispered, "I expect to know what happened to you out in the gardens before we proceed to the sacred grove this night."

Alida blushed deeply. She had completely forgotten about this eventide's sacred rites. Gathering her wits, she concentrated on the solemnity of spirit that was required for the upcoming ritual. She was able to fend off Kellen's drunken caresses as well as responding appropriately to Savine's queries and light banter, but she forced the greatest part of her musings around the charts and signs and healing techniques that she had been taught. She cleansed her mind of further, fanciful contemplation of the mysterious visitor in the garden. She would talk about him later to Deive and rinse away any further queries of her heart and mind into his identity. The time had come for her to behave as a woman and put away such childish fascinations.

When the time was appropriate, Deive and Alida made their excuses to Savine. They kissed Erta goodnight and made their "fare thee wells" to the other attendees though there was little response from the rowdy gathering.

Pretending to be tired, both women called for handmaids to aid them in the removal of their costuming and then shooed them away, feigning to proceed with preparations for bed. When they were assured of their privacy, they dressed instead in simple dark tunics and cloaks and slipped off together through a small passage and out of the keep.

Ulrich had watched them slip away to the upstairs chambers. He allotted them some time to change and make good their ruse, then he, too, left the hall quietly, knowing that they intended on meeting in the cove. He changed out of his costume and into his darkest cloak, tunic, and leggings and then patrolled the outside walls, his eyes alert for two dark figures. He knew that they would not want the keep's guards or inhabitants to see them leave for they would have to explain their errand, not something desirable under the circumstances.

His deductions and patience paid off when two diminutive figures slipped from a grove of elder trees next to the keep's wall. He made a mental note to explore the little grove on another day in the assurance that a secret door would be found.

Deive and Alida walked quickly and quietly away from the walled court, and it wasn't until they were positive of their isolation that they felt free to talk quietly.

"What were you out doing for so long, Alida? Kellen drove me mad with questions as to your whereabouts. He almost came looking for you." Deive peered into Alida's eyes. "'Twas no normal walk to make you so flushed and awkward."

Alida looked at the ground in front of her concentrating on the footing. "I met a man, or at least I think he was a man rather than a wood spirit."

Deive stopped mid-stride. "What do you mean, *a man?* 'Twas not Quirin again?"

"Nay 'twas not the same aura. Moreover, he adamantly denied association with Quirin and called him a beast when I asked the stranger if he was one of Quirin's men. He claims to be an enemy of the Lyrnne keep but also of Quirin."

Deive stared at Alida. "And you did not immediately alert the keep guards to his presence? Are you mad? You could have been carried off, raped, or killed. Or worse still, the rest of the keep may have been attacked." Deive began walking again her pace quicker as a sign of her distress.

Alida blushed but steadfastly defended her actions her pace rapid until she was abreast again with Deive. "Deive, he was *not there* to attack the keep—he was there for me. He knew my name and recent activities. He was gentle, cleverly spoken, and seductive, though only far enough to tempt my interest."

Deive stopped again and gasped. "Seductive? Alida, listen to yourself! A man who is the enemy of *our home* tried to seduce you! Do not flatter yourself overmuch that he was merely there to entice your interest. Suitors are less devious about such things. An enemy of Lyrnne is an enemy of yours."

Alida pulled Deive's hand dragging her along. "I said the same thing in my mind, Deive, but something was not right about his lack of interest in the castle and the city. He was there for me. I am sure of it! He only discussed things of a personal nature. *Not once* did he try to gather information from me regarding anything to do with Lyrnne itself!"

The voices of the two women did not carry far in the still night air, but Ulrich was following close enough to hear every word. He was hard pressed not to laugh outright.

Deive released a long sigh. "Give him time," she snorted and then conceded. "I don't know why I trust your judgment, Alida, but I will settle myself to do so. This trust I now feel in you and your decisions is one of the reasons we proceed to your sacred rites. I know you to be a woman of common sense and deliberate direction."

Alida wisely kept the memory of her sudden, knee-buckling weakness to herself. They spoke no more along the way to the grove, each keeping their thoughts to themselves. Alida concentrated again on the task at hand.

Ulrich heard the ensuing silence and hushed his own progression even more. He also felt inclined to pull his black cloak around him more fully.

CHAPTER SEVEN

Deive and Alida reached the beautiful, circular grove of oak trees that Deive had found on an excursion of the surrounding area.

When they stepped into the moonlit grove with soft grass beneath their kid boots, Alida felt a hushed reverence rise from the surrounding trees as if they knew her purpose. She turned slowly in a circle counting the trees, noting that they stood seven in number. Deive smiled at the wonder in her eyes.

"Aye, Alida, it is one of the sacred ancient oak groves. It is not as well known as Falda's grove, but it is holy just the same. Look carefully at the largest tree."

Alida walked silently to an ancient bent oak and noted that it had something standing at its base. She brushed away leaves, dirt, and twigs and found a sorcerer's stone clearly inscribed with the direction that each tree faced as well as the stellar configurations found above its sacred circle. When Alida had finished reading the stone, she made connections between it, and all she had learned under Deive's tutelage. She was given a few moments to worship and reflect before Deive stepped forward with her leather pouch.

"Go and lie in the center of the grove with your face towards the stars, Alida, and await my further command."

After Alida had done what was asked of her, Deive walked around the grove using her most powerful wards to encapsulate the grove with protection. When she had finished, she began to chant and sing the ancient words to the initiation rites while circling Alida's supine form. Her beautiful, searing voice echoed beneath the trees and carried with it a strange power.

Alida listened closely to the ancient language and followed the rites in her mind and heart. She watched the gestures being woven by Deive barely able to withhold her own fluid motions.

After some time went by, Alida was instructed to arise and undress down to her snowy white undergarments while Deive spread a special clothe upon the ground.

Alida knelt on the cloth at Deive's instruction and was given a drink of herbs and water made from the contents of Deive's pouch and a nearby spring. Her throat burned from the drink, and when it had entered her system, she felt her body become weightless with its suffusing warmth.

Ulrich knelt hiding in the shadows just outside of the circle. Before him appeared Alida, gloriously bathed in moonlight with her hair falling to her waist and her eyes strangely glowing. She had the aura of the woodland sprite he had imagined her to be. Her form was pleasing, and he longed to approach her position and tell her of his presence and protection.

Though she was exceedingly beautiful, there was a reverence in her pose that touched and calmed Ulrich. He forced himself to concentrate on things of the spirit over things of the flesh, his own early schooling in the ways of the gods drawing him into participation with the religious rites.

He heard Deive utter a few more phrases before she pointed at Alida, giving her a quiet command. Ulrich watched fascinated as Alida lifted her hands to the heavens and made a spoken pledge. Her voice was mellow and strong and compelled him to give homage as well to the powers. As she finished speaking, her lightly clothed form was infused with a bright light, as of her own volition she changed into the brilliant creature that was her crest. The scream that was hurdled from her bright throat into the surrounding air raised the hackles of both Deive and Ulrich. There was a new power to her voice.

From the glade below, Ulrich watched in awe as the falcon streamed into the waiting heavens calling out to the air, the earth, the water, and the fire and all the things that they worshiped from ancestor to ancestor. Her wings flashed like gossamer beneath the lunar rays. He had never before witnessed such an event.

Though many whispers had been handed down over the years about shape changers, he knew how truly rare a gift it was. He quivered now at the unearthly sight, watching to see if it was of magic or make that she was able to transform into the body of a beast.

The cosmic ripples that emanated from the new initiate reached Castle Falda and a very restless Quirin. He had foreseen Alida's growing power, and with his distasteful sorcery, he had tried detaining the inevitable. Some of the slithering evils sent by the sorcerer to harm Deive and Alida had been warded off by a stronger and more benevolent variety of the watchers. These creations made their way silently through the veils of the worlds doing only good or evil while knowing little of the machinations of the ones who had sent them.

Quirin sat stewing beneath the rays of the full moon. It was a time of madness for the powers he served. Surely, there was a way to tap those powers and injure the untouchable spirit of Alida. His hands roved over his faced tiredly, and when his frustrated senses could no longer be contained, he drifted deeply into himself, allowing his spirit to sift out silently over the countryside.

He saw the commoners' hovels and silent herds. He could smell the sulfurous entities of other spiritual beings and watched with his usual fascination as they darted back and forth about his body. Some were maleficently gleeful, while others shimmered with purity. He swiped at a little flash that had been inalterably bright. His mood was anything but charitable.

The cosmic plane was strangely empty of the larger evil entities that were now roaming Berynth in search of calamity. He spied a few malevolent beings below him inciting a drunken fool to murder a helpless beggar. Quirin grinned and sped faster toward the grove. Perhaps he could collect a few of the entities and bring them to his aid.

When he had reached the grove, the growling menace of six such entities crowded about him.

They recognized the taste of evil that emanated from him and had followed him to whatever mischief he'd create. They landed softly in a horrid bunch and crept towards the circle of light.

The wolf within Ulrich stiffened at some disturbing presence. Though he could not see anything, his senses detected a malevolent force. He peered around blindly, not realizing how great the danger. Though he remained unseen, as his inner spirit had the particular habit of sliding easily into both physical and cosmic shadow, Deive was brighter than a lantern in the blue evening mists, an easy target for the prowling spirits. The magical rites had opened a portal in the thin veil between the physical and spiritual realms.

From up above, Alida, as the white falcon, could see the forms creeping up to the grove of trees where Deive stood captivated and reverent. Alida's rage and panic at the audacity of such an attack swept through her, and she dropped from the sky with talons extended and eyes a piercing red.

Her screams of attack echoed in the minds of Quirin and his dark aides. Three of the grisly spirits disappeared in fear, returning to the dimension from which they had come. The last three twisted their hands with glee at the anticipated battle.

The surprised faces of the slimy creatures lent credence to Alida's unexpected strength. Her talons ripped limbs and soul strands from the sullen apparitions. Her powerful flailing wings beat at Quirin's face confusing his vision, and her beak pecked at his glowing red link to the physical world. When he screamed in pain at the piercing intrusion of his linkage, the remaining apparitions deserted him completely. In a blind rage, he struck out at the only object he could feel—Deive.

The eltar halfling crumpled at the unexpected attack. For though she had placed the wards about the grove, they could not withstand Quirin's magical wrath. He dug deep into her chest tugging at her life force, cackling gleefully over her demise.

Then all at once, into the melee, a great force unknown by all, save the suddenly fearful apparitions, burst in with a searing power. A humming sound like the song and speech of congregations made its way through the cove destroying Quirin's putrid companions and sending Quirin's sorcered spirit back to his body.

"ENOUGH!"

The presence knocked Alida from the air and pulled all the breath from Ulrich's body, the cove a thousand times hotter and brighter than the core of a wood fire. The booming voice that they believed to be audible, though only of spirit, pounded through their breasts with the deep bass of eternity.

"Children of Berynth, you involve yourselves in things forbidden! The laws governing the dimensions were placed for your own safety and for the safety of the worlds. The black arts are the scent of apple before the taste of worm, for what can your small hands do but unravel things too great for you to know. Magic is the practice of pride and self-will. I am the commander of the obedient and the servant–I have no interest in those who seek their own godhead. Listen well to what is said this night, for you shall know the meaning of true power. No thing above or below, in the deep or the heights, in the pit or the heavens is greater than I. There are no powers to worship save my own. For you stand in the presence of *I AM*."

Alida, having transformed back to her human state burst into tears and fell face first to the ground, her hands hiding her face from the view of God. She could not breathe, and she could not feel anything but heat and presence. Every wrong attitude and every seed of hate or rebellion or pride was brought to light before her eyes. She was stripped down to the merits of spirit alone and was disgusted by what she saw. Then, too, she saw how foolish she had been to think that she could control the powers and courses around her with foolish incantations, rituals, and amulets. Even with her changeling blood, she was incapable of understanding the depth, height, and length of the other worlds that she had attempted to manipulate. She saw the level of danger in which she had placed herself and the humans around her by opening a door to things that she could never fully know or understand.

Behind the closed doors of her eyelids, she saw and heard the name of the great I AM as a song, a rite, a power all its own. She was all at once no more worthy than the lowliest of beasts and as uncomprehending as the grasses of the fields. She knew his mighty power then as if caught in the rush of white rapids and knew that even the powers of the air were under his command. Fire, wind, water, and earth were his creation as was everything around her. The stars, too, in all their glory, the very ordering of the universe—these were nothing compared to the fire in his eyes and the throbbing presence of knowing him that echoed in the deepest parts her belly.

She had always thought of herself as unique because of her lineage, and yet now she saw how much this Ancient of Days had treasured all of his creation. She was merely another key another joint in the great body of his works.

With a great sob, she begged his forgiveness for her ignorance and pride and then offered up the only gifts that she had - the gift of soul and spirit, the willingness to follow her fate, and then the gift of a new pledge, a secret in the ear of Creator. The offerings were fragrant and humble, most beautiful to behold. Alida, not being able to look or move, did not see how the waif-thin watchers that attended I AM rejoiced at her gift. There in her silence, God laid a straight path for her, commanding her to worship Him with the use of sacrifices and offerings of her land's bounty. He gave her detailed instructions for how these were to be performed. There in the grove, she learned that her greatest communion with Him could only come on a regular basis through her obedience to the laws He laid forth.

From the edge of the clearing, Ulrich, too, did not go unaffected. He had tried to live his entire life wisely and with passion. He had tried to rule with a just hand and had tried to know his place. Yet there, in that instance, he saw how truly frail and inadequate these had been, but he was also given the joint knowledge that through this presence his world would be opened and his questions answered. He, too, paid heed to the instruction of I AM that he and his people might prosper. In two of the hearts encapsulated within the grove, the same words and instructions rang clear, and the same voice, all in all, changed the things in them that were unlovely and hidden.

Creator stayed within the circle for a very small amount of time. Yet the wisdom that was imparted to its inhabitants was worth all of time and essence to them and was almost more than they could handle. Before leaving them, Creator issued a command that they rid their lands of the ancient arts and of the sorcerers who saw themselves as masters of all. He also commanded that their lives remain in submission to him through the regular offerings and sacrifice that he had instructed in order that they might approach the holiest of holies. No mere person of their own merit could stand in that place–the light and heat too great to understand. Even during His instruction, it was His back that they saw and not His great face.

Alida lay trembling long after I AM had left her. She was spent and hollowed out. Her body was unable to comprehend what had taken place. Nevertheless, her spirit knew, and from this joy, she was able to draw strength, for His instructions had been clear and she would be faithful.

When she finally opened wet and bright eyes, she saw Deive only a couple yards away, lying very pale and shaken. Alida walked trembling to her friend and mentor's side, still unable to absorb all that had transpired. Cradling Deive's head in her lap, Alida, instead of the elaborate incantations she had learned, whispered a prayer for her friend, the new childlike utterances strange to her. Then the watchers sent by Creator in response to the simple prayer came and attended the two women. As they both were revived, Alida began to sing softly, trying to comfort and soothe both herself and Deive. She did not know that her songs were heard by Ulrich, which allowed his own comfort to be attended to by the presence of the one who had heard what he had heard and seen what he had seen.

As Deive was attended to, Alida made herself rise, and she tore down the headstone from the circle. She destroyed all the other markers of the cove as well, smashing them against each other until they were a fine dust upon her hands. Then after having cleansed her hands with running water from a nearby stream and a torn bit of cloth, she took three plain, flat, round stones and lifted them one upon another, making a small altar to commemorate her newfound faith. She dedicated the cove and land surrounding the cove to the way of The One True ruler of the heavens.

Eventually, Deive's eyes fluttered open, and she hoarsely thanked Alida, for she did not know all that had happened.

The two women, weary from the night's adventure, straggled home from the grove. Ulrich followed warily behind, seeing them back to the safety of the castle, his own heart full of what he had seen, understood and the myriad of new unanswered questions that now filled his mind.

The next morning dawned with a clarity that can only follow such a night of terror and awe.

Alida awoke later than usual, but still at an early time compared to many of the inhabitants of the castle. She stretched and was amazed at how fit and energized she felt.

Lying on her pallet, she again felt the presence of Creator, only gentler than before. She could not help the joyous tears that trickled from her eyes at the guidance he imbued.

When some time had passed and she had fully spoken with the Ancient of Days partly in silence and partly in prayer, Alida dressed herself in a soft white kirtle and tunic and bound up her hair with leather thongs. Then with energy, she took off through the castle surprised at the lack of human activity. How could the castle and its inhabitants appear so common after the events of the night before? How could it be that the experience had only touched her?

A quick perusal of the kitchen, great hall, and outer courtyard produced no sign of her one companion in the event. Somewhat troubled, Alida tracked down Erta and asked her to look in on Deive. Alida explained her inability to do so herself, due to the need for an early morning ride and setting of arrangements with the keep's archers for a contest later that day. She told Erta not to be overly concerned; Deive was probably just suffering the effects of too late a night. She knew that if Deive had seen and felt the same things as she that Erta would know soon enough what else had transpired.

Erta complied, briskly taking the stairs to the upper chambers where she gently shook Deive awake. When Deive opened her eyes and smiled shakily at Erta, asking for some tea to be brought up, Erta responded immediately to the request. It seemed only moments before she came with the hot sweet tea, bringing also a thick, fragrant slice of buttered bread and fresh berries covered with cream.

Deive, however, left the bread and fruit untouched slipping back into a deep sleep. Erta covered the sorceress' exhausted body and drew the curtains round the pallet to ensure a deeper rest. The serving woman's puckered brow was the only sign of her concern for her usually vigorous companion.

In a chamber, several doors down the hallway from Deive, Savine awoke feeling fretful and peevish despite the flawless execution of her plan to have Alida married off. For one, the keep's mistress had imbibed too much ale and new wine the night before, causing a heavy ache behind her eyes. Second, she could hear a voice that sounded like Erta calling out instructions in the hall below. Savine gently rocked her head, trying to clear away the cobwebs and pain clouding her groggy mind.

When she heard the voice a second and third time, Savine decided to quietly investigate the cause. She slipped open the door to her chamber, witnessing a most disagreeable sight.

Erta stood with pride and assurance in the midst of a circle of servants calling out plans for the day's activities. Savine was at first surprised before anger began to burn with a coal-like softness deep in her belly. How dare the wench attempt to commandeer the keeper of the house's position once again as if nothing had happened? Savine closed her door softly and swept towards her pallet where she lay with an arm over her eyes. She screamed out for Lizel, and when the groggy maid entered, Savine snapped out commands with blistering derision. At one point during the ablutions, the mistress even slapped the unsuspecting young woman for poking her with a decorative pin.

When Savine had dismissed the sniffling female, she turned to her dressing mirror, smoothing the tunic with restless hands and reassuring herself regarding her position as keep's mistress. She donned a light cloak to ward off the morning chill and glided down the stairs to the hall below.

She would let her anger build until the festival had ended and her guests had left. Then she would teach Erta the final lesson. A maddened gleam lit her eye.

Alida rode for a few miles keeping Raven at a quick and unstrained pace. She did not give him his head until they had passed out of the city and past the last tent reaching the open fields. After her performance a few days before in the riding tournament, Alida no longer felt a need to hide her identity. Whereas she had feared attacks and advancements before, now her fear of what could assail her had lessened, for she knew that nothing could occur that Creator did not allow. She had viewed the powers as being uninvolved in her day-to-day existence. Now she knew about a presence greater than the powers that was not only available, but also very much interested in her and her path.

She saw the day spread before her and was awed at the new eyes she had been given. She saw Creator's abundance and was invigorated at the day's activities to come. Ulrich had sought to hunt and ride alone that morning as well. As had become his wont, his trail had led him towards her lands. He, too, viewed the world through different eyes.

When he saw Alida afar off, something prompted him to go to her. For though she was not aware of what they now shared, he felt it all too deeply.

Sitting alert on Raven's back with archery cuffs already around her wrists and a bow and arrow upon her back, Alida was the embodiment of a confident huntress. She rode towards the spot where he lay awaiting her behind an outcropping of boulders. In that instant, he realized how much he admired everything the woman before him represented and felt a thrill of interest at seeing her again. Yet on this morn, he saw her also as so much more. For now, he knew without any doubt that they both shared a knowledge of something greater.

He followed her throughout the morning, watching as she warmed and honed her archery skills. Then as she and Raven loped deep into the forest for a quick hunt, he was close behind her, riding quietly with great appreciation for the view before him.

When she stopped her mount at a clearing and gazed off into the bracken, Ulrich realized that she must have spotted a quarry. Her back stiffened imperceptibly, and she softly dismounted Raven, dropping to the earth in a crouch with a graceful thud. Her bow was pulled from her back and strung in readiness. The bushes to her left where she had been gazing suddenly shook with a crisp rattle and she raised her weapon, every muscle tense for the kill.

The screech of a fleeing bird set her back on her heels as it rustled out of the heavy undergrowth. Alida started and then laughed at her reaction, kicking herself for not recognizing the sounds of a mere bird. The rustle had seemed so profoundly huge, as if bigger quarry awaited her bow.

She had just lowered the sights of the arrow when abruptly a boar erupted from the bracken. His stiff mane bristled over his hunched shoulders and his tiny black eyes gleamed in the dim shadows surrounding Alida. His snorts and squeals showed him to be highly irritated, as did the unsure flickering of his leathery ears. The agitated beast lowered its head in a charge, its hoof beats ringing a cacophony in the silent forest air. Alida raised the bow again and released its deadly course into the boar's throat, knowing that she only had moments in which to dispatch the formidable beast.

The arrow reached its mark in a timely manner, but the momentum of the boar's charge and the rush of adrenaline in its hairy body kept it on course directly at a grim and prepared Alida.

She continued to crouch low on her haunches, bringing herself close to eye level with the boar. When he reached her position, her dagger lay in readiness having been pulled from her boot in an instant. The heavy slash at the boar's tough throat and Alida's sharp, coordinated leap to the side were testaments to her athletic prowess and agile reflexes.

From the shadows, Ulrich, too, had dismounted and stood watching the entire scene, his own muscles prepared to aid the woman before him should some mishap befall her. It was due to his readiness and position that he was the first to see the approaching cat. Its ears rotated, gathering every sound around it as its muscles banded tightly for the pounce. Alida had dispatched the cat's quarry, and the cat was now prepared to gain back its meal. Her back was turned, for the cat had come from a circular and opposing direction, seeking to cut off the boar from its path of flight. The cat, seeing her vulnerability, pounced with claws spread in readiness and a low, hair-raising growl.

Ulrich, too, leapt from the shadows into the clearing, a dirk in each hand, landing squarely upon the beast's back. He drove one blade into the ribs of the cat just behind the front leg and slashed the other across its throat. Both beast and man crashed into Alida's oblivious back. The mess of creatures tumbled into a heap, and Alida found herself gazing into the most captivating and compelling blue eyes she had ever seen.

Ulrich blinked and then grinned lazily into Alida's eyes. "This morning has no chance of matching your beauty, Fair One."

Alida started at the smooth tone and manner. There was something about the voice.

"I always enjoy a good adventure first thing. 'Tis what makes the day so fair," she rejoined cockily.

She rolled off the smelly boar whose rank hide also now reeked of the iron smell of blood while pushing the limp, golden claw of the cat off her leg. Then standing gracefully, she caught her wild hair back into its thong. She grinned back at him, and the sight of her unaffected smile warmed Ulrich from his toes to the crown of his golden head.

He stood as well and brushed leaves and twigs from his leggings and tunic top. He was an excellent figure, tall and heavily muscled throughout his shoulders and thighs. His hair was worn long, and he brushed a wayward lock from off his brow.

Alida gazed thoughtfully at his features then memories assailed her. It was the owner of the voice she had heard in the garden. Embarrassment stained her cheeks berry red. She stalked forward; her eyes flashing with amusement and a bit of wariness.

"You followed me into the forest, Wolf. This has been the game you have played to know my every move, and not only then, but also when I first arrived at Lyrnne. You have long played the voyeur!"

Ulrich's grin grew broader at her recognition of his voice. "Aye, I would have continued my game and gone unnoticed were you more attentive to your surroundings. You were fortunate to have had my unknown company."

His words were tinged with arrogance but more out of playfulness than true ego. Alida bowed low, her stance mimicking warriors who had been bested at the tournaments.

Her flamboyant stance and elegant features were undeniably attractive. He looked away lest his admiration glow too apparent in his eyes. He wanted to play a cool suitor to this woman of fire.

Alida would have none of it. She walked up and clasped him on the shoulder, congratulating him boisterously over his prowess in the kill. Her behavior astounded him, and he was reminded of the sight of her with her languorous warrior, the second time he had watched her in the forest. She behaved as no other woman he had ever known.

When she struggled to lift the heavy cat, he stepped forward giving her aid. Together they gutted the creature then lifted it onto his charger's back securing the prone body with leather thongs and a rope made of flax. Next, the two did the same with the boar. Raven side danced at the bloody musky smell of the fresh kill and an unfamiliar man. However, the steed was instantly gentled by Alida's ready soft words and caresses. Ulrich glanced jealously at the favors the horse received.

When they had buried the steaming entrails and had erased signs of the struggle, the two stood facing each other. Ulrich reached out and wiped a smudge of dirt off Alida's cheek with his thumb. The contact was electric, and both parties were stunned by its power. Suddenly, the mood went from playful camaraderie to an uneasy silence.

Alida looked at the ground, unable to make eye contact any longer with the beautiful male before her. Though she had behaved in a mockingly masculine manner, she was very aware of her femininity. His touch, soft and rough, had been all that was needed to fully remind her of their emotion the night before.

Ulrich's deep voice growled into the silence of the clearing. "You are imbued with power this morn. You dispatched the boar more skillfully than many men I have seen. There is something different about your capabilities and manner that reflect a new knowledge. May I admit an imperfection about my own nature to you?"

Alida nodded in response, her brow creased.

"I witnessed your initiation in the glade last night without your invitation, a continuance of my game that was ignoble." His voice was calm and low, belying the embarrassment he felt for spying on her and Deive.

"What did you see?"

"The deepest of the deep, a falcon and a snake." His words rang in her ears.

"And what did you think and feel when you watched silently from the shadows, Wolf-voyeur?"

"I felt honor."

"Nothing else?"

Ulrich hesitated. "Fear of the unknown."

Alida continued to look expectant.

Ulrich looked deep into her eyes. "I also felt a power that I have never before experienced. I knew us all for what we are and felt an understanding of the order of God's world."

Alida thoughtfully raised her hand and massaged the muscles of her neck. "I did feel another presence, noble in nature. It was at the time when we were attacked by the loathsome Quirin and his band of fiends and before the appearance of Creator. You must have been the benevolence I perceived. Odd though, that you would be imbued with a power and nature that is the kin of wolf, for it is not a very benevolent nor nurturing crest."

"Aye, but it is to its own kind, just as your crest is powerful to those you call family. The wolf is known to be protective of its interests."

Alida blushed at the reference to herself as an interest of this powerful man.

"How fairs Deive?" His eyes reflected a great concern. "And what will you tell her about the cove, Alida? You have destroyed that which was not only precious to her but sacred in her mind as well."

Alida's color instantly deepened, and she breathed a heavy sigh. "It is an issue that has given me much worry since last night. Though I know 'twas the right thing to do, and though I perceive that Creator will aid Deive's understanding, I fear her ire and most of all her withdrawal from me and the way that is right. He commanded us to remove the arts *and* the sorcerers, Ulrich. How am I to remove someone that is as close to kin as I have remaining, should the time come that she refuses The One?"

Ulrich longed to touch her arm or face to comfort her, for he had seen how close the two women were. Instead, he allowed the soft tones of his voice to encourage her. "God would not ask of you what you were not capable of giving, and would you withhold anything after knowing that He *is* the ALL. You have no right to disobey even when you do not understand. She is not unreasonable either, for she has much in the way of wisdom about her. Pray for further guidance, and I will join my requests with yours."

He saw further worry on her face and merely listened this time, praying for her. "You asked how she fairs, but I do not know how her health is this morning, though I intend to find out first thing after I have made some arrangements for the afternoon's archery contest. Unfortunately, she was still asleep when I left. Will you be present again as you were at the feast in some costume or disguise?"

Her frank interest, anticipation, and even need glowed clearly in her eyes. He bowed mockingly, a stray wave of hair flopping down over his bright eyes. "I will do my best."

With a backward glance over her shoulder and pleasant thanks for his aid in the hunt, Alida bid him goodbye. She was mounted and off before he could utter another word from beneath his thick beard.

The abruptly ended contact filled him with a yawning ache. He desired above all else to possess her in both mind and body as his wife. He shook away the thought. He doubted Alida would ever succumb to being possessed by anyone.

Later that day, Alida spoke quietly with the master of the archery contest, her voice barely audible above the growing noise of the crowds. He was an older man of much wisdom and humor, having seen many fine warriors come and go. His nodded assent to her requests filled Alida with pride. This day the women would be allowed their own contest. After wrapping up details with the man, she strode off towards the keep, her short tunic flapping in her haste.

When she had entered the walls of the city and then the castle, she slowed her pace and glanced about looking for Erta or Deive. Neither was readily apparent.

She took the steps hurriedly two at a time to the upper chambers and then hushed her stride when she came to Deive's door. She pushed the heavy-hinged planks open until the pallet was visible. The curtains were still drawn about the pallet, though early afternoon light poured through the window case-ments.

She approached the curtained bed cautiously and pulled back the fabric quietly peering into the darkness. Deive stirred beneath the furs and linens that covered the bed. "Who is it?"

"It's Alida."

"What is the time, child?"

"Early noon. The company is drawing together for the contests. Do you feel well?"

"Aye, though the slightest bit shaky. Quirin took a piece of my soul. He probably gloats over it at this very moment. I have never felt so cold, as if a shard of ice presses into my heart."

Alida frowned, her new distaste for magic repelling her away from her old friend. She gathered herself together and then whispered, "Do you need more rest?"

"No, the cold abates as I have worked all morning sewing together the strands of soul that were disturbed. Would you like my companionship at the tournament?"

In those moments, Alida realized that her friend knew nothing of Creator's presence or of the power that saved her.

She hesitated, and a small voice within whispered, "You must tell her."

Alida, without a sound, sank down upon the pallet caressing Deive's cheek. "Creator visited us in the cove last night, Deive, while you were passed out." Her voice cracked with tension, though her touch remained gentle.

Deive raised herself up a little on her pillows, a wariness at Alida's tone showing on her face. She waited quietly and expectantly, her breath the only sound in the room.

Alida swallowed. "He said that we are to rid the land of the arts and sorcerers for these are displeasing to Him. He also told us that it was He who created the forces around us, and that they do not have any special power of their own that was not given to them. It is the highest blasphemy to worship that, which is created, over its creator. His final instruction was that we begin to offer sacrifices as He has instructed, and that by doing so, we will purify ourselves in His sight."

Deive pushed Alida's hand away shocked and struggling with the beginnings of anger. "Did you test this 'appearance' Alida? Did you question and defend? Did you expound upon your knowledge and the knowledge of the ages? Did you do anything at all but listen like a lost lamb?" Deive was breathing hard now, her chest heaving with the rise of her emotion, her face feeling as if it were on fire.

Alida tried to console her. "There was no testing necessary, Deive, for He broke every spell and every ward in the cove, replacing them with His own guardians and power. He shattered my secret knowledge that I had indwelling, which no magician or power known to us could have dominion over. You have taught me the most powerful spells ever known, and our magic has been more than sufficient to fight the likes of Quirin and others, though not to take dominion over them. In His presence, the presence of the Almighty, nothing else *was*. Please try to understand."

Deive was crying now, her anger mixing with a great fear that what she had known was being lost to something greater. The grief over the potential loss of everything she had built her life upon squeezed like tangible hands at her breast. "Your betrayal is complete then, Alida, for there is no give in your voice and your actions. You show only a sad resolution to make me believe the same."

Alida longed to reach out and touch her friend, but Deive sat stiffly on her pallet, an invisible wall of distance and anger creating a chasm between them. "There is more . . ."

Deive stiffened more, her eyes large, wary, and overflowing with hot tears at her ward's betrayal and resolute progression into this frightening topic. "Don't tell me—you were also ordered to sacrifice me as your next offering since I am a sorceress! Oh, and before this can be done, you are to rip my heart from my ribs since this is the seat of my 'sin'!" The last of her bitter words soured the air around them.

Alida had begun to cry as well, her tears falling more silently than Deive's, in an unsteady stream. "No, Deive, but I cannot suffer magic any longer in my life. I can no longer be intimate with that which offends my Maker. I will love you forever and will hold you dear, but if you do not change your ways, our ways as intimates must part. There is no fine grey line between our past ways and His desires, Deive. He drew the lines in blackest coal, and I will not cross them, though I love you and though my own heart breaks. In addition, you must know that I have destroyed the sacred cove's artifacts and inscription stones. They are thoroughly shattered beyond repair, in their place I have made an altar to God. Though I understand little of this with my reasoning, my spirit complies and is satisfied, Deive. These acts were my first steps of obedience."

Deive covered her mouth as if she were going to vomit, her stomach heaving and her eyes frantic. "Get away from me! You are surely possessed! Such degrees of turning are impossible without sorcery!"

Alida then dropped her head a great weariness and sadness filling her bones. A voice whispered, "Pray." And so she did. She turned her back and with her lips moving silently, she cried out to Creator.

The room that had been filled with light from the sun grew brighter still, and a fog-like air began to rise from the edges of the room covering first the rugs, then the legs of the furniture, then the pallet and finally all sight of anything tangible. Deive cried out, her hands waving in front of her blindly, as she screamed out spells to no avail. Alida's eyes were tightly closed, her focus on her Maker so complete that even these cries seemed like mere whispers themselves.

The fog grew thicker and warmer until there was nothing but light, and then Deive was given the knowing just as had Alida and Ulrich, and Deive suffered at the folly of her past. She groaned at the utter foolishness of controlling bits and pieces of the spirit world while the rest had been advancing upon her at her eventual death. She saw the impurity of her own nature and was disgusted that she should have presented such filthy rags before God who was nothing but purity, light, and truth. She fell back at the force of His power and love and was cleansed by her tears and submission, joyful hope replacing the lack of knowing that had plagued the edges of her existence since birth. Then as silently as it had come, the fog dissipated, and the women were once again alone.

Alida cautiously opened her eyes. For all she had known, Deive had been staring at her while she sat motionless, neither feeling nor hearing God herself. Nevertheless, the light remained on the face of her friend so brightly that Alida almost felt the need to close her eyes again.

Deive reached out for Alida. Deive's body and soul were exhausted and invigorated all at once. The hug between the women was warm and tight, and Alida began to laugh aloud, her guffaws bouncing off the stone walls. Fearing for Deive's sense of hearing, she moved away from her friend and danced with all her might in the midst of the room. There was a new world to know, and she and her friend would take it with gusto and joy, together.

Deive smiled softly and then chuckled. "Dance away, Daughter, for I will not be joining thee, Creator has sapped me momentarily of any desire for movement of any kind! And here I had planned on joining the crowds at the games!"

Alida came to a stop and then skipped to her friend's side, placing a warm calloused hand on her cheek. She tried to sound stern, but her voice was still filled with merriment. "You may only go if you are sure you are well enough. The warm summer air would do well for thee, and you would be refreshed by the normalcy of the congregated merrymakers."

Deive summoned the remaining strength she had, wiping away the remains of tears that had gone from bitter to healing. "Very well, help me into a tunic; something simple and light will do. I do not wish to lie abed all day."

The two women worked together dressing Deive in a light violet linen tunic then stopped for a moment to place her jewels on her fingers. When they looked in the mirror, Deive started at Alida's appearance.

"Your white tunic is covered in earth and blood. What have you been doing?"

"I was out riding and hunting this morning." She averted her eyes.

This time Deive did not directly ask her about her avoidance. "You had better change before the beauteous Savine discovers your forest trysts."

Alida rolled her eyes, and leaving Deive upon a comfortable cushioned chair, went to change in her own chambers.

The view that greeted her in her own mirror was distasteful at best.

"Aren't I just the picture of beauty personified?" Alida mumbled to herself. "He'll be enraptured over the changes from last night until now."

It suddenly occurred to her that he had seen her on two occasions the night before—once in the garden, but more importantly in the grove. She flushed deeply, and then turning slowly back and forth before the mirror, she tried to look at herself with a stranger's eyes. She noted the light in her eyes and the perfection of dainty facial features. She saw how her hair hung in lustrous locks to her lower back and how she was firm and athletic in build. She nodded to herself. If he could keep that image of the night before in his mind, she need not fear other appearances. Then she blushed ashamed at the train of her thoughts, for he was interested in her, but surely not romantically.

She dressed in a serviceable green and blue wool tunic and donned her torc and armbands. She did not remove the protective wrist guards, for she was prepared to participate in the afternoon archery contest. Her last preparation was fixing her hair tightly into a long, smooth braid.

Then she and Deive went down together, as always, the perfect pair.

They crossed the now trampled fragrant hay fields to the raised dais where Savine and Kellen already sat amidst the normal collections of nobility and servants. They took their places and Savine turned to them, a cool, little smile affixed to her lips.

"Something odd is taking place. Apparently, it has just been announced that any women who are willing may participate in their own archery contest. I never authorized any such thing." She peered at Alida with barely concealed contempt, her pointer finger flicking at an annoying buzzing fly near the rim of her goblet.

Alida with neither apology nor aggression said, "It was I, Aunt. I felt that the women should enjoy the games as much as the attending men."

Savine turned in exasperation to Kellen. "Do you feel it befits a woman to participate in such manly affairs, drawing gossip and ill-used attention?"

Kellen thoughtfully pondered her question. He decided that the politics of siding with Savine were greater than those of siding with Alida, especially since Savine's nails were digging painfully into his forearm. "You speak the truth, lady. I find that women who are overly rebellious and given to unflattering pastimes are best suited as the worst kind of commoners."

Alida's cheeks glowed at the thinly veiled assertion that she herself was no better than a harlot from the brothels. She rose majestically, making some polite excuse and then exited the dais stiffly to walk away her anger. In keeping with her custom, Deive arose as well, not being easily dissuaded from attending to Alida.

When they were out of earshot, Alida said in a taught, angry voice, "They treat women as if they were no better than brood cows. Grost will take me as a possession, never caring that I have a mind, will and deep emotion. He will get me with child, consign its care to me, and leave me to the patronizing pastimes of embroidery and music, locked away in some back room." She turned to Deive. "I truly do not mind the pursuits of weaving and music. However, to have these pastimes employ my complete attention without any diversions such as hunting, archery, riding, and the tending and management of our lands seems so restrictive. I further do not ken why some believe it is healthy to bring up children under such beliefs." Her hands balled stiffly by her sides, punctuating her rapid flow of words occasionally with an angry thrust.

Deive smiled and put her arm around the younger woman. "Do not fret about that which has not yet happened. Do you not think that those who care for you will help you to arrange matters that concern your life, especially something as big as marriage?"

"Are you in favor of a marriage match between myself one such as Kellen?" Alida had stopped walking, her eyes piercing into her friend's, waiting silently for an answer as a warm summer breeze flattened her tunic about her shins.

Deive shook her head negatively and then brushed away a stray bit of dandelion fluff that had landed on Alida's sun warmed head. "I want for you to have the life you want, and to have the life that Creator has called you to, in whatever form that takes." Her voice dropped a level and a wisp of a tear slid coolly down her cheek. "I never understood fully before what words like that could mean, but now I understand the Creator Himself, and I am at a loss before Him." She brushed the tear away and took her friend's arm urging to walk once again. "To tell you the truth, I have a very bad feeling about Savine and Grost," Deive said softly. "I don't like their equal conspiracy and their arrogant ways. There was a time when I had begun to toy with plans to murder Savine for what she did to you or to torture her with any number of spells, but now I know I must leave her to Creator. This doesn't make me rest any easier with her nature though."

Alida squeezed her friend's arm all the tighter, thankful that this tragedy had not come to murder. She knew that such retaliation would have greatly angered God. Alida, too, felt uneasy about the quiet laughter and knowing eyes of Grost and her aunt. In her heart, she could only picture a set of perfect blue eyes that had laughed into hers that very morning. When she thought of marrying a man such as Kellen, she had to shrug off the chill.

CHAPTER EIGHT

Beside an inconspicuous pavilion, Ulrich watched fascinated as each archer released their deadly arrows into markers and targets. In Alida, he recognized a continuation of the expertise he had seen earlier in the forest. *Today she is my favorite, not that I am partial,* he thought with a smile. She was magnificent, and many of the archers found it difficult to outdo her on the field. He was so sure of her skill that he made a pretty wager and won enough money to purchase a fine falcon or hunting dog.

When Alida walked by later that day, deep in conversation with a tall, powerful archer from Savine's keep, Ulrich slid jealously into the shadows. He had attended the festival but did not want his presence known by her until the right moment, even though he longed to break up the animated discussion between her and the handsome man at her side.

As for Alida, the day wore on in perpetual boredom once the archery competition had ended. She had yet to see any sign of the wolf, and even when she was in the midst of diverting conversations, her mind was partially on the dashing and mysterious stranger with whom she now had an even greater bond.

The continuous stream of southern nobility that Savine paraded before her increased her boredom. Alida, growing restless with the social niceties of the festival, had to quell the urge to run into the forest in search of a more palatable diversion.

When evening came blushingly over the hills, the entire company once again moved indoors for a late feast. The fare was simpler than the first gatherings of the week, for people craved wholesome and hearty food after the myriad delicacies consumed on other days. Alida found that even though the hearty stews were fragrant with sage and rosemary and the bread was very fine—she had no appetite. Even baked apples and salty ham could not tempt her appetite. She restlessly fiddled with her goblet and napkin and when spoken to, had to force her smile's appearance.

She blamed her lack of hunger on Kellen's unstimulating company.

It was not that he was the worst dinner companion she'd had to endure, but she was not in the least interested in the things he had to say. Everything he spoke of centered on gossip or his own self-interests. She also did not care for his strong wayward hands, which had several times grasped her leg beneath the table's cover, one time edging up higher on her thigh than she had ever permitted a man. It never occurred to her that she was unfairly comparing him to the witty, admirable, and deep-voiced stranger she had met on two other occasions.

When Alida could bear no more of the inane conversation and grasping claws, she slipped outside for a breath of fresh air. She meant only to stand beneath the stars just outside of the door for a moment, but when she had exited, she heard a coarse whisper.

"Alida, come to the herb garden where first I met you."

She whirled to where the voice had come, but could see nothing in the dimly starlit shadows. She hesitated for a moment, and taking up a lantern, she headed for the garden.

When she had entered into the fragrant boundary of the herb garden, she saw a figure off to the side with an oddly stooped back turned to where she stood. She was a bit confused, expecting the strong tall figure of Ulrich, and so she did not make an immediate move forward, all the while listening and looking for clues to his identity. Because she could see clearly for a few feet in front of her with the aid of the lantern, she called out to him to turn and come to her.

The figure straightened, and reaching inside his tunic with a rustling whoosh, removed a pack of rags that had given the impression of a hump. He approached Alida, straightening his bent back as he walked, while sighing in relief. Feeling greatly amused at her look of surprise a warm chuckle escaped his perfect mouth.

"What is wrong, Alida?"

"I knew your voice, but your face and figure were very odd. I was beginning to wonder if I had mistaken the sound of your speech."

He laughed merrily, and with a grand bow he said, "A humble burgher at your service, ma'am. I will always need to disguise myself while on these lands, and I find with time that I am becoming cleverer at the costumes I choose. I bought hair from a maid in the village who offered the overly long locks for a price. I then had a weaver turn it into a beard. When that was completed, the whole of it was attached with honey and paste. I also darkened my brows and made my hood deeply concealing. Don't you think me very fair?"

Laughing in delight, she blew him a kiss. "You are the most handsome of burghers."

His sudden levity and grave voice altered her mood. "Were that your kiss was real, and the words you say true."

She swallowed at his suddenly piercing eyes and prowling advancement. "You never know what a maiden may think. Can you read my mind, Wolf? Perhaps the words I say are true."

He was very near to her now, and she could smell his good scent carried on the warm evening breeze. "And what of the kiss?"

"Only a rogue would demand a reply on something so intimate." She backed up a step, his advancement beginning to encroach upon her space.

She could feel the warmth of his presence. "Come now, Alida, you are not the cold nobleman's daughter you pretend to be. Your response this night is a learned one, not one from your true nature, for I well remember the way you responded to a mere embrace the other evening and the way we were branded when we touched each other."

She swallowed again, the sound loud in her own ears. "You are right. Such coyness does not suit me." Then she said honestly, "I would like to try another kiss, but not now and not with a hairy burgher." Her genuine smile and suddenly relaxed stance eased his advancement.

"Then meet me tomorrow in the woods at your glade. We can exchange words and perhaps even a kiss if I appeal to your senses then. I am sure at the moment, however, that the group on the dais eagerly seeks your return. I just couldn't wait any longer to see you. It would not have been safe to show myself to you earlier in the bright light of day." Though he had waylaid his advancement towards her, he was close enough to touch her and did so gently, running the back of his hand down her cheek and under her chin.

She shivered slightly at his touch and then reluctantly turned to go. His voice had grown oddly husky. "By the by, I did watch you at archery and found the other females to be lacking. You are an amazing creature!"

She smiled to herself, his praise warming her to her toes, and called back over her shoulder, "When next it 'tis kisses and words I shoot, I need to know the real name of the man that is my prey. If I am so admired by you, then trust me with your name."

He called out his name in a low voice, amazed that he would be so free with information she could use against him.

She smiled to herself, *Ulrich*. The manly figure of her daydreams now had a name.

When Alida entered the stuffy, loud hall, her aunt motioned irritably at her from the dais. Savine had yet to recover any semblance of good spirits towards her niece and was always on the edge of an outburst with her. Alida made her way softly and quickly to her aunt's side, her back stiff and her face resolute. She was wary after having spent the day enduring her aunt's tongue-lashings.

"Yes?"

Savine's pinching, long-nailed grasp bit into Alida's soft wrist. Her aunt's smile was anything but natural; her white teeth pressed together in a grind. Her voice hissed out only loud enough to be heard by Alida, "Sit down and behave yourself properly for once! You must stop your meaningless wanderings. I have an announcement to make, and I wish for the hall to see us all upon this dais as a unified company."

Alida sunk gracefully into her chair and moved a few inches away from Kellen who immediately reached for her hand. Now that she had taken fresh air, she could smell the sour scent of alcohol on his breath.

Savine rose and clapping her hands loudly called out to the attendees of the banquet. "Quiet! Quiet, everyone! I have something to tell thee."

The crowd fell into a rustling murmuring silence as Savine smiled benevolently from her place.

"We all know that the festivals that mark the seasons and solstices are a time of merriment and passion. We also recognize the desire of many families to use such opportunities to make appropriate matches for the children of their house. The gods have made it a time of great fruitfulness."

When the crowd murmured in accord, Savine turned to Kellen. "I have been no stranger to the passion and matchmaking of this festival, and

Kellen Grost, fair neighbor and friend, has also been an avid companion to the feast's goodwill and merry behavior. We have aided the matchmaking of at least two couples, at the thanks of their families, and it is out of this spirit that we are pleased to give yet another announcement of betrothal. However, unlike the other arrangements, this one is of a more personal nature to milord and myself.

"I can hear your questioning murmurs, and so it is without further adieu that I announce the betrothal of my niece, Alida, daughter of Castle Falda, to Kellen Grost of Kinterden Dell. Together they will make a most stunning and passionate pair. I hope that you will accept this betrothal with all the gaiety and the best of wishes you have."

A roaring applause echoed around the hall and many cheers were heard from Kellen's gathered kinsmen. The echo that roared through Alida's mind was not from the crowd, for she had expected a match, but not so soon and not in the aftermath of meeting as interesting and promising a mate as Ulrich. She was not disagreeable to marriage, for she knew that in Savine's care such things were inevitable, but she had hoped for a love match or at least one of good companionship and genuine passion. She had not expected to feel the budding emotion that welled up in her now for the enemy of her aunt's keep and her utter opposing distaste for the chieftain seated at her side. What was she to do?

Then with sudden horror, she realized that Ulrich might have heard the announcement. A burning flush crept up her neck, for he would think her the worst of teases. No honorable woman would have behaved as she did in the garden knowing that in a few minutes her betrothal to another was going to be announced. She licked her suddenly dry lips and prayed that he would give her the benefit of the doubt.

The well wishes and toasts to the most unexpected betrothal of the festival lasted well until the sun was moments away from rising.

Ulrich had left long before, fury and disappointment raging in his breast. As he mounted the warm back of his steed, he muttered aloud angrily to himself, *I don't know what I expected to gain from a liaison between Alida and myself. Creator knows that her aunt would never authorize such a match. But 'tis the added insult of her being taken by one such as Kellen that angers me the most. Savine should have chosen a more decent companion!*

As he kicked his horse into motion, he made the stubborn decision to go to the glade tomorrow. Perhaps there was still a chance that Alida would come to him; for he would in no way believe that she had made the promise to him, while knowing of her eminent betrothal to Grost. Besides, betrothals had been broken before, perhaps he could persuade . . . , but perhaps was a word that came too easily to mind. He rode his mount hard to the borders of his land trying to work off the anger and fear of loss that were eating at the edges of his heart.

Back in the halls of Lyrnne, when Alida was finally able to exit gracefully from the merrymakers, Kellen decided to accompany her from the dais to the long, stone staircase. He kissed her lightly upon the hand and cheek in farewell, bursting with pride at the match that had been made.

As before, she was struck by how unpleasant his kisses were. His lips were too cool and moist for her liking. To worsen the unwanted contact, there wasn't even the slightest thrill of natural physical interaction. He might as well have been a statue with bad breath. His eyes gazed deeply into hers, obviously ignorant of how stiff she had become when he ran a hard palm along her jaw. His caresses all seemed so calculated. Someone from the crowd behind them called out, "Kellen makes love to the lass in anticipation of an early bedding!" Everyone laughed and then returned quickly to their merrymaking, allowing the embarrassed couple an undisturbed moment.

Kellen leaned to her ear, leering at her while continuing his caresses. "Will you take a ride with me on the morrow? We can leave as early or late as you like. I can have a small repast packed, and you and I can ramble about the countryside. It is what lovers do, and I have officially become your lover."

Alida gazed at the ground. She was to meet Ulrich the next morning and would have to find a way to dissuade Kellen until her meeting was through. Looking up at her betrothed with large, innocent eyes Alida said, "The night grows late, warrior Grost. I would like to sleep until noontide tomorrow, and then we'll see if I am up to a ramble after such an exhausting night. It has been eventful, has it not?"

He winked at her and pressed closer to her side, his alcohol tinted breath washing over her face. "Call me, Kellen. I will be delighted to escort you at any beck or call you give, sweet lady. I understand the fragility of a maid and her need for her beauty rest." He smiled benevolently at her, and kissing her once more upon the cheek, he made his fare thee well.

Alida walked silently up to her overly warm room and sat gazing at the crisp flames of the fire in her fireplace. It irritated her that Kellen had fallen so easily for her overly bright smile. She doubted that Ulrich would have been so easily duped. How could she have gotten into this disagreeable situation? A chill ran up her arms.

Deive let herself in through the open door without disturbing the troubled young woman, leaving it slightly ajar for her anticipated exit later on.

"If you stare too long at the flames you will consume them and the room will go dark."

Alida laughed, irony ringing in her voice. "I'm dark enough inside over this whole mess as it is; perhaps I should darken the room to match."

Deive, desperate to comfort her ward, said hesitantly, "You know it could be less distasteful than you think, dear one. Perhaps he could become a great love after some time has past."

Alida frowned and gave her a look that spoke volumes. "Such hopeful words are far from the reality of the situation Deive. Even with your gift of creativity, you cannot make it any brighter a situation. It is what it is, and your initial unease over Kellen and Savine earlier is proven more and more as time does pass."

Deive replied quickly, explaining herself. "Each must make his or her own path, Alida. In many ways, what we become is what we make it to be. Though I would wish you a love match, it does not eliminate the fact that you are in a very tenuous situation. Your future is in your aunt's hands. To give up this place and her provision to escape from a marriage match would leave you without attachment or protection. Your family's land has been emptied of the warriors and keepsmen necessary to run a province—there is nothing for you there. I hate that you are being placed in such a position, but unfortunately, all I can offer at this point is hope that something good can come of the match.

If nothing else, your homeland will continue to have a future at being retaken under your husband's army."

Alida wearily rubbed her brow. "I do not begrudge this man's need for a mate, but he could have found someone more to his airy taste. The Dulmont wench would serve him well. She is concerned mainly with looks, gossip, and festivities. Why of every potential suitor would Savine choose him? I don't even like him, Deive, and though I know of the potential benefit to me in terms of wealth and protection, I become more of a slave once married than I am now under my aunt's care. Kellen will assume my lands as his own, and I will be nothing more than chattel."

Deive was silent for a while, and then with a sarcastic tinge to her voice said, "But don't you see, Alida, though Kellen is not deep and fiery himself, he desires that in someone else. The man has fine taste!"

Alida chuckled, "Aye, I just wish someone else had suited his palate!" Her jest was grim. Alida then turned earnestly towards her friend. "I saw him again this evening, Deive. He has given me his name. He is Ulrich of Drachmund Heights."

Deive grew very still, her eyes not moving from Alida's face. "Ahh, here is the crux of the matter! Be careful with the game you play, Alida. I cannot stop its momentum, but I can challenge your conscience and beg your wisdom!"

Alida hung her head and sighed deeply. "There seems to be no easy answer, Deive. I feel so drawn to Ulrich, as if I have always known him and was intended for him!"

Deive approached her and hugged her shoulders. "We must take some rest love, perhaps I'll read your fortune in the bones tomorrow. . . ." Her voice drifted off for a moment and Alida heard her sigh. "I mean I will pray a little prayer tonight, and we'll see what comes on the morrow." Then even more softly, Deive said, "The old ways have held me in their grasp for so long that every little habit and every thought must be turned."

From the shadows outside the slightly open chamber door, Savine leaned against the wall barely holding her tongue. Ulrich Drachmund! By the gods, would the chit's rebellion grow deeper? She had come up to instruct Alida to act appropriately the following day and had not expected to hear such startling news. She stole away from the door, the now familiar feeling of inadequacy in her dealings with Alida causing raw rage to bloom fully in her chest.

Alida awoke early the next morning after only a few hours' rest. Her heart was pounding lightly with anticipation over her meeting with Ulrich, and she decided to dress a little more carefully than was her usual wont.

She donned a soft shortened tunic woven in blue and burgundy stripes and shot through with silver. Then she adorned herself with her heavy silver torc and armbands, leaving her hair long with only two thin braids on either side of her face. She tinted her eyes with a little kohl and put some berry dust on her lips to darken them a little.

The reflection that stared back from the mirror was tall and graceful. She looked very noble though not aloof. Her lips were full and bright. She ran her fingers over them wondering how a kiss from Ulrich would taste and feel. She had not much experience with such things—her only kiss having come from a servant boy when she was but five years. The thrill then had been over the covert nature in which the kiss had been taken. However, she was no longer a child. She knew that her woman's body would respond to the kiss itself regardless of the surroundings or circumstances. She knew that a kiss between a man and a woman like her and Ulrich could set fire to the dampest of kindling. She smiled at her musings over an, as of yet, unsealed and simple affectionate exchange.

When she had completed her toilette, Alida slipped out into the morning by her usual route of hidden passages. She had never been a vain person and her attention to looks lately disturbed the usually composed and confident young woman. She snorted to herself over her own vanity. The sun's inevitable rising was already apparent just at the horizon. She would have to hurry.

Raven nickered softly when she took him from the stall. As usual, the grooms were all snoring in their soft hay beds. She mounted the warm back of the black destrier only after they had exited the keep walls, not wanting her added weight to make his footfall louder.

She rode as quickly and smoothly as possible through the city exiting through her favorite hidden passage. Once beyond the city walls, she rode carefully over the dew-covered shadowy dells, barely noting the beauty of the morning and tinge of coolness that had finally come with the lingering mists around her. She could concentrate on one thing and one thing alone, the blue eyes and handsome visage of her land's enemy and her first infatuation.

Ulrich arrived in the cool dampness of the glade first and was disappointed that Alida had not yet made an appearance. He scowled at the thought that she might not show. The end to last night's evening had not been a promising one. He could not keep the marriage from taking place without declaring war, but perhaps Alida herself, if she were interested enough, would take steps in halting the unwanted union.

He stayed mounted for a while, his steed growing restless with the wait. When he could deny his own thirst no longer, he climbed irritably from Titan's broad, smooth back and drank from the refreshing nearby pond. He was just raising his hand to his mouth for a second cool drink when a soft feminine voice called out, "Look, Raven, a fair man on a fair day. His thirst easily quenched in yon clear pond."

Ulrich turned towards the voice, his square firm mouth still glistening from the drink. Alida swallowed back the desire she felt at the obvious sensuousness of his lips. He nonchalantly rose to his feet while wiping away drops from his lips as he walked to where she sat on her mount.

He did not touch her immediately, but his voice reached out as if it were itself a hand. "There are thirsts, my lady, that are not so easily quenched in a pond, clear though it may be."

Alida's sudden nervousness was covered promptly by her jaunty dismount from Raven's back. She proceeded to the pond with a ladylike swagger, acting as if she owned the glade. "I'll drink of the water and be quenched, good sir. 'Tis a desire most easily remedied."

He laughed softly and purposefully avoided the tempting opening left by her. He could think of many desires and their immediate remedies.

As she drank, he lazily leaned against a rough tree trunk watching her with lively interest. "I am surprised and gladdened that you came to meet me. I was afraid that you would scorn our tryst now that you are most publicly and properly betrothed."

"Is that what we are doing, Ulrich, participating in a tryst? I could still denounce you and tell you that I have only come to tell you of the end to these meetings." She did not look at him, her back and even tone giving no indication of her demeanor.

Ulrich swallowed in alarm—her light comments creating a ball of fear in his gut. Though it cost him everything he continued on playfully as if he was completely untouched by her threat. "We are indeed trysting, fair maiden, for you are unescorted, and I am your enemy. I would say that this creates a compromising situation. Include with this the fire felt between you and I, and the tryst blooms."

Alida stiffened a bit at his retort, the hair on her neck rising in small prickles. Her breath came a little faster, and when she heard his footfall approach where she knelt, she had to swallow so that her voice was clear and strong. "You assume much, my lord, to think that there is a liaison between us after so few meetings."

Ulrich could take no more of the teasing comments. He swept forward, grasping her arm, and pulled her body towards him, turning her as he went until she faced him. He wrapped one arm tightly about her waist and the other about her shoulders and took her mouth into possession with heated, firm lips. He was careful not to touch her too intimately, for he was moving quickly with her as it was. Nevertheless, she inflamed him as no other woman he had ever met. She was special and fiery, and now he tasted the sweet flavors of tart apples and dandelion wine from her full lips.

He drank fully from her mouth, feeling his body rebel against restrictions and good intentions. She was delicate and robust all at the same time. He groaned as she met him kiss for kiss, her moist kiss-swollen mouth matching his similar demands.

When she made a soft sound low in her throat, Ulrich felt the wolf inside his skin rear its head. They sank to the ground together as he pressed his lips closer to hers, enjoying their closeness. The scent of crushed rose that came from her hair and skin pulled him closer until he thought his senses would be drowned. He responded vocally to her little purring noises with a deep growl of his own.

Suddenly, he tore his hungry lips away from hers, for he realized how free she and he both were being with their passions. The delay in contact was enough to bring her to her senses as well, and she pushed him away from her, giving him a withering look as if the sole blame for the physical contact lay with him. Inside she was groaning with the war between pleasure, and embarrassment over her own participation.

Ulrich reclined lazily on his side, propped up on one elbow. His piercing eyes turned her way, and despite her frown, he caressed her cheek with a gentle hand. "Have I, in the depths of dreaming both day and night, conjured an unrealistic passion between us? Your lips and body did not reject my affections; they were, in fact, eager participants."

Her eyes felt heavy and her bruised and throbbing lips felt warm from his ardor. She did not answer immediately.

Ulrich continued to touch her, caressing her cheek here and a strand of hair there, for her face was still turned towards him. He found it astounding that in spite of the obvious latent effects of passion, he had never seen a clearer or deeper gaze. She swallowed once, twice, and then presumably decided to ignore his question.

Her voice asked instead a simple and unrelated question. "Is your mother or father the fair one?" She had removed his hand and had risen, walking away to where Raven stood grazing, his teeth loudly clipping at the fragrant green grass around his feet. She feigned nonchalance, turning her back while acting fascinated with an adjustment to the saddle.

Ulrich continued in suit, his voice somewhat amused. "My mother was the fair one. She had hair that was almost white and deep violet eyes. My father had hair as black as midnight and blue eyes. He says it was this startling combination of their looks together that settled their families into letting them marry. No more stunning couple could be found in the region. I always nodded when they told me the story, but knew 'twas their undying passion and respect for each other that made them a true couple. Looks as a bond have no merit when enough time has passed."

Alida gazed thoughtfully out over the water. "'Twas the same with my parents. Their passion was very apparent. It was rumored round the castle that twenty children should have been born from such a powerful union."

"You were the only one?"

"Aye. And you?"

"I was the only child born to our house as well. My parents never sorrowed over this, though they were protective of me. If my mother were alive today, she would tremble at the exploits I have had since then. I tried my best to never give her cause to worry." His intimate comments about his parents gave Alida another chance to respect him, for she, too, had loved her parents and was proud to boast as she had of them.

She turned to him and cocking her head asked, "You are athletic and brave. Why have you not sought to marry a timid maid that would benefit from your strength?"

Ulrich grinned lazily. "I prefer fiery kisses to fainting. Would you want a man of tepid character? I like your strength and beauty, Alida. You have fervor for life. I have never before seen a maid hurl arrows, mount steeds, and converse with such dexterity. I will not have a fretful wife, for I intend to marry a woman of character and direction. Fretfulness and timidity are signs of lazy intent and weakness."

Alida was thoughtful at his words and did not comment immediately, her hands smoothing her ruffled curls absentmindedly.

"You disagree, fair one?"

Alida grinned. "Nay, I was just trying to picture you with a woman who was lazy and lacking intent. You would drive her mad and she you! You need someone to take you in hand."

She turned to the pond intending to gather another drink and saw his impish smirk from the corner of her eye. He said softly, "Will you volunteer for the job, Alida?"

She grinned largely at his gaze, her cheeks stained at the same time with deep, hot color. As she had at other times, she wisely avoided comment. Choosing to clear her throat loudly was the best she would do.

The morning proceeded, and they talked of many things together, comparing the paths their lives had already taken and prospects of things to come. They strolled through the forest side by side, and Ulrich was very impressed with Alida's intelligence, noting as well small clues she gave regarding her character. She, too, was more and more impressed with this strong, tall man at her side who was all at once gruff and warrior like and the next smooth and droll. Though those two qualities were fascinating when taken alone, Alida found that in Ulrich's pleasant company there was no end to her absorption in his person—for he was also wise, knowledgeable, physically attractive, and blazed with deep, unfed hungers that were relayed time to time in his burning gazes. Neither were humans of light intent or shallow nature, and they had found an equal in the eyes and words and untested passions of one another. There were moments in the dappled light of the forest, amidst the cheerful calls of birds and other small creatures, when each of them was almost afraid of the depth their companion exhibited. It is not easy to be struck with eternity and completion in a single moment.

CHAPTER NINE

Alida left the cove midmorning and headed off reluctantly for the castle, feeling as if she were leaving paradise behind. She and Raven reentered Lyrnne by the massive front gates where her charm and occasional penny kept the city gatekeeper amiable. Once inside she pulled her hood closer about her face and slumped slightly so as not to call attention to her well-born carriage.

She had grown gravely cautious after the incident with Savine and Erta and took very few folks into her confidence. Savine was now a Pandora's box in Alida's mind, for she never knew the mood or tantrum that might strike her aunt. Loyalty within the keep had swung to Alida and Erta's favor, but there were still a few that would gleefully report every misdeed.

When she had rubbed down Raven's hot, glistening coat, Alida went silently up to her quarters via the cool back passages. Though she suspected that few servants were about the keep, she wanted to be able to back her improvised story of sleeping late.

She reached her room, undressed in the shadows that had escaped the morning light, and carefully folded her tunic into the trunk at the end of her pallet. Before she closed the lid, she breathed in deeply, smelling the scents of the moss and soil and more importantly of Ulrich. She reached into the folds of cloth one last time where his scent had become imprinted, and smoothing their length, she closed the trunk.

When she had risen, she reached absentmindedly for a clever gem clip that Ulrich had given her. She relived his carefree passion as he had hooked the clip to the cloth over her chest that peeked from her over tunic. He had tried to pass it off as if it were a simple bauble meant to charm, but when questioned, Alida discovered that the origins of the pin showed it to be a valuable gift of most unusual lineage.

He said that the pin had once belonged to an ancestor of his by the name of Roushti. She was an exotic and silent creature who had been taken by force from her cold northeastern country by Ulrich's forefather, Gambin. Roushti was a woman of magic in her village, and though she had been forced to leave behind all belongings, she had refused to give up an amulet bag that she'd grasped in Gambin's haste to leave the pillaged glen. Those of her village claimed that the pin held amongst her other amulets was refuted to have powers of protection for its wearer. It was a stylized wolf that encircled a red ruby. The gem was clear and had an odd cast that almost made it purple. Gambin had considered the pin fate's approval of their liaison, for his crest was a red wolf. The two had eventually fallen in love as time went by, and many strong children had been born into the family from their union. On her deathbed, Roushti gave it to her eldest female child in the hopes that it would make her daughter strong and invincible. It had passed thus from generation to generation until Ulrich had received it by default, being the only child born to his own parents.

Alida thoughtfully turned the gem over in her hand and made the decision to hide the cold jewel beneath her shift rather than putting it away. She felt honored to be given such a gift. Ulrich had said she would be connected with his family forever now, whether or not she was so connected by blood or marriage. The gem was a sign of fast friendship.

When she had secured the jewel within her shift, Alida sank down upon her inviting pallet, hoping to catch a few more hours of sleep that had been lost to the morning. She wandered off into the comfort of sleep, content in a world of laughing blue eyes and deep voices, her head cradled by her fluffy, cool pillows. Yet not only Ulrich drifted with her in sleep's womb, for as soon as Ulrich had fastened the pin to her bosom that afternoon, Alida had felt as if she had been given his family as well. She had been curiously infused with confidence that her path would be protected and strangely assured of sharing some part of that path with Ulrich–a confidence that she attributed to Creator. Her rest was deep, for she had enjoyed her exercise and companionship that morning. She refused to think of the upcoming afternoon.

When Deive came to awaken Alida at the suns mid-height, she was pleased by the deep peace that the sleeping woman portrayed. Perhaps her charge and friend was not as worried about the betrothal as Deive had thought.

She sat on the pallet by Alida's side for a moment studying the flickering eyelids and warm smile. It had been a long time since Deive had simply watched Alida sleep. Deive reached out and gently smoothed away a curl that had fallen over the young woman's cheek. She almost jerked back her hand, for a power flowed from beside the sleeping form with a strength that Deive had never felt surrounding Alida.

Troubled, but curious as well, Deive remained where she. Presently a voice softly whispered through the room, and it was separate from anything she could see. She called out in an even voice, "Who goes there?"

"I am called Lordifyn."

"Why do you stand alongside this young woman? What is your purpose and place?"

"Deive, you and I have much in common, for I have been assigned her care since her birth."

Deive trembled at the use of her name, peering about her and hoping that a figure would appear. "How do you know me?"

"In the same way you know me. Search your heart. Have you not had a sense of her safety that exceeded the facts of the moment? I was assigned by God Himself. You see, each of you are given a watcher for his or her own care."

Deive stroked Alida's cheek thoughtfully mulling over the conversation.

"I know that I have never been alone as I know that Alida has never been alone. I used to think it was a magical sense of the powers."

"There is no magic, only a sense of power, power that originates from Him."

"Why is my own watcher not revealed to me?"

"I am the captain of the watchers. Alida's path is a special one, and Creator entrusted her to me as a special honor. She is key to a mystery that has yet to be revealed."

"Are you a human that has passed on to the netherworld?"

The wave shimmered, and Deive felt as though it had laughed. "Nay, I am a spirit created separately from humans to minister and serve in whatever capacity called by God. Once a human spirit enters the afterlife, it does not return. As watchers, we are given leave to move between this plane and that.

But we run out of time for further questions, for look, your child awakes."

Deive looked down and saw Alida stir. She came awake most luxuriously, stretching and flexing almost as if some warm draft were lifting her from slumber. Deive shook her head to clear it from the astounding conversation that had preceded Alida's awakening.

Alida turned and smiled some secret still hidden upon her sleep-ridden lips.

"You grin with a contentment that has no root in this day's coming adventure, sweet one."

Alida giggled. "Not all days have a single adventure, Deive." Alida slowly climbed from her warm pallet and walked with lazy strides to the window.

Deive blinked, Alida's feet were not touching the ground. "Alida, wake up!"

Alida stopped and her feet came to rest on the rich floor covering that stretched from her pallet to the window. "I thought I was awake."

"Dreams can sometimes stretch between, Alida. You were floating, presumably somewhere between this form and that of the bird."

"Don't all young maids in love, float?" Her husky laughter echoed off the chamber walls.

Deive frowned and walked forward turning the young woman so that they faced each other.

"Your heart has changed that much toward Kellen since last night's announcement?"

Alida just smiled, not willing to answer further questions about her heart.

"I met your watcher today."

"Who, Deive?"

"The one that strives with you. The one that has been given your care by Creator Himself."

Alida was thoughtful running her bare foot over the woven floor covering. "The Creator has a passion for us. He delights in the many forms that our love and lives take and would see each aspect completed and protected to perfection."

Deive blinked, and with Kellen in mind said, "Again you reference a deep love, though last night you could not stand the one man, and I assume you've not had enough time to bring to maturity a relationship with the other. But you talk in such a way that one would believe the stars were ready to fall and the earth tremble on its axis with such a gift being given."

Alida ran and jumped onto the pallet next to her friend, embracing her closely in a warm hug. "Stars have fallen, Deive, and the earth has been shaken to its very foundation. Just not in a way you believe and not when you were present to feel it." She smiled mysteriously once more. Then turning to dress for the day, she said, "I am confident as I have never been before, Deive, for I know that fulfillment comes when we least expect it. It is not our timeline to follow, but The Divine Creator's. He has sent aid in his presence."

Kellen had been in the castle for several hours impatiently awaiting word from Alida. He was dressed in a purple velvet tunic woven throughout with gold strands, and his deep auburn hair had been brushed until it hung in a perfect fall to his shoulders. His warriors' brow was high and fair, and he thought very well of the reflection that looked back at him from the polished silver in the hall of Castle Lyrnne. He had also taken care that his during his toilette he had been lightly sprayed with pine scented water, which he thought would be a pleasant scent to any maid.

When the time drew nearer for her appearance, he made the conscious decision to walk with measured and manly steps about the hall so that when Alida came down she would see how well-muscled his calves were. Sitting had been discarded, for his clothes would be wrinkled, and he would look lazy.

Such mediocre and useless thoughts tumbled through his brain until he heard a pleasant and detached voice over the clicking of his heels say, "Good noontide to thee, Kellen."

He turned and in his most charismatic voice said, "Good noontide to thee, as well, my little betrothed flower."

Alida stifled a bubble of laughter that tumbled up through her throat. He had meant to be dashing and affectionate, but instead had managed to be pompous and overly groomed. Instead of laughing, however, she merely nodded looking at the floor rather than at his eyes.

He took this to be a sign of modesty, and pleased with her demure and virtuous looks, he stepped forward and grasped her arm, pulling her alongside him breathing in her fresh scent of roses and cucumber all the while controlling her by the soft, firm flesh of her bicep. He prattled on about a good many things, again none of which interested Alida. Nevertheless, she was in good spirits and decided to concentrate on thoughts of Ulrich rather than listening to this swaggering rooster at her side, a man that she had every intention of turning down.

When she could bear no more of his prattle, she politely explained that she wasn't up for a ride, and that he would have to find another companion for the day. She could imagine nothing worse than spending such a bright and glorious day with someone like Kellen whose forced companionship had already ruined portions of the festival for her. For one, the scent of pine that permeated his clothing was watery and overpowering all at once, not bearing much resemblance to the actual scents in the forests she loved. He was also just as stuffy as ever trying to put in order anything she said that he did not think was ladylike.

She had just turned to go when Savine, who had that particular gleam in her eye, which showed she bore a foul mood, descended grandly into the hall. She grasped Alida's arm and painfully pulled her close, her ever-sharp nails cutting Alida's tender skin. Though she was smiling in order that Kellen not know of her displeasure, her whisper was harsh and angry. "Don't think to leave so quickly, Niece. Whether you feel like it or not, you will accompany Kellen today, and you will marry him when I command. Don't think that I am foolish concerning your whims and tastes, for it is clear to me you do not think well of the match. Whatever your tastes and whatever you think you will do, I am here to tell you that you will do as I order, for your fates were no longer your own when Falda and all within perished. You and your body and all you represent belong to me!"

A fleck of cool spittle born of Savine's vehemence and rapid discourse landed on Alida's cheek. Alida wiped it away quickly and pulling her arm from her aunt's grasp said with her own ingratiating smile and hissing voice, "Your wish is my command, aunt!" A beautifully performed curtsy completed her sarcastic modesty. She saw Savine's fist clench, as if a slap had been barely restrained, but then the socially adept woman swept away in a stately glide.

After fawning on Kellen for a few moments, she erased any worries that he would be unaccompanied by saying, "Alida really is up for a ride, but it must be a gentle mount, for she has an occasional panic regarding horses. None of us is ever certain whether bravery regarding riding will occur or this sensitive fear, but in general, she seems more apt to experience the latter. She will gladly act as your mate today as long as you both ride gently."

She could have made the situation no worse for Alida. Although Kellen was slightly bemused over the fact that the woman he'd seen racing along without a care would ever fear riding, he took it all in stride and gladly gained the opportunity to spend more time with his wife to be.

They began their outing with Kellen choosing ladies' tack and a dainty mare for Alida. Not wanting to anger Savine or make things any worse, Alida refrained from any comments about her true taste in mounts. Secretly frustrated with the day to come and seething with anger at her aunt's control, Alida mounted the calm little mare and groaned quietly, adjusting to the tiny squeaky sidesaddle of a noblewoman.

Kellen's idealistic imaging of all noblewomen as faint and fragile made the day pass slowly. They did not raise their pace above a canter and stayed only to the sunny and pleasant dells rather than the wild and interesting play of shadow and light that beckoned from the forest. He raised an eyebrow at one point, quelling a comment from Alida on her love of the hunt by reminding her in a sarcastic voice of the panic that could overtake her and cause her injury, or worse, her death. He would not allow her to dismount alone and was most disagreeable when she removed her hot, sticky stockings at one point to cool her feet in a delightful little creek by commenting with great sternness that noblewomen, especially one which would be his wife, did not show their flesh in the presence of day.

By the end of the afternoon, Alida could think of nothing but returning to the silence and autonomy of her chambers and the keep stables. The only thing that had amused her at all was Kellen's discomfort in the hot sun—his velvet tunic having long ago become a thing of annoyance. Only a fool would wear velvet in the midst of summer.

Throughout the day, she tried to dismiss images of Ulrich that floated unbidden through her mind at the oddest moments, but could never quite rid herself of his cocky and handsome grin and adventuresome manner. There was something about him that made him difficult to forget.

The last feasts of the week passed slowly, for Alida could not rid herself of Kellen's sticky presence. He dogged her steps and constantly offered advice on how to be more ladylike or docile, all at the behest and accompaniment of her aunt. After the final night of the feasting, Alida dragged up to her chambers, glad that she should have some space from him.

Deive found her before her fire, staring at the remaining coals with her feet up and a light blanket across her lap.

"This seems to have become a favorite spot, Alida. Are you feeling well?"

Alida muttered sarcastically, "Do not walk so briskly, Alida. Do not sit so sprawled, Alida Could you not speak more virtuously, Alida? Of course I don't feel well, Deive. How could I with such refrains constantly playing in my mind! He is much worse than Savine! And I now officially have a pounding headache from which there seems to be no reprieve."

Deive came to the fireside and gently rubbed Alida's rock-hard shoulders. She did not speak, allowing Alida to vent instead.

"He may have good taste as you so stated earlier, but he takes something that is acting out its nature and tries to change it into that very thing that did not attract him. I will not be molded by that vain peacock's hand! He chose me, as I was - wild and uncommon. Now he tames me and douses that fire until only a sodden ember remains. He tells me to wear my hair elaborately woven and wants me to gown myself in heavy, cumbersome cloth that cannot even be worn for the gentlest of riding excursions. I would have to be carted around in some over-adorned wagon. I can only imagine the ridicule of the archers whom I have befriended and mockery of the spear maids, though they would probably feel more pity than disdain. I have some sense of dignity, and I wonder at his audacious handling. Have I not the mind and heart of a falcon? I will not to be trained!"

After her tirade, Alida sat smoldering, her last words echoing off the rock fireplace. Her emotions had never leant themselves to being suppressed and overcome. Deive continued to massage her friend's neck and arms, not once offering advice, for she wholeheartedly agreed with her fiery charge.

Alida went out riding early the next morning, eager to be out of the castle and far away from Lord Grost's attentions.

She rode like one chased by fiends, her anger at her confinement and joy of freedom spurring her on. Her hair flew behind her completely unrestrained, and her eyes were wild and filled with emotion. Across the dells, she rode until Raven was covered in flecks of white foam and her own breath came in hard bursts.

When she realized what she was doing to her mount, she slowed and caressed his silky damp coat, taking in a deep breath of his warm horseflesh and the fresh morning air.

"Raven, you are blessed to be a horse. There is only so much a man can do to you. You must consent only as much as it takes to be trained for riding. You are even highly prized for having spirit, yet I, a mere woman, must bend and cajole and that only to gain a sad counterfeit of freedom." Raven snorted and tossed his fine head dancing to the side.

After walking her mount for a while and soaking up the sounds of the squeaking leather and birdcalls of early morning, Alida dismounted and pulled out soft clothes from her pack to rub him down. She would let him graze and drink from a stream before mounting him again and returning to the keep. It was then that she realized that they had somehow made their way to an unfamiliar place far from the keep and cursed herself for not having paid better attention.

"I didn't realize I had driven you so far, Raven. I wonder where we have ended up?"

She looked up to where the new day's sun had risen and then searched the horizon for high mountain peaks and landmarks. She then knelt on the ground and drew a rough map in the dirt with a stick. She estimated that she must have gone two or three leagues from the castle, for she had tested Raven's speed many times and had been riding for several hours. She should be close to the perimeter of Grost's property.

A thought quickly formed into a plan. Alida decided she would mount up into the air as a falcon and review her exact location. Her plan would provide for her steed's rest as well. Besides, it would give her some breathing room, for she had not had given herself the pleasure of flight for a while.

She drew Raven to the shelter of a cove and left him untied should he need to defend himself while she was away. These forests were full of ravenous beasts, and it was wise to allow a trained mount their head.

She then nervously contemplated how she was to fly without opening up herself unwisely to danger. She looked about carefully and found a little, fir-fragrant hollow beneath the bracken. It looked like a Roe deer had bedded here with her young, and there was no better or safer place than the bed of these fleet-footed creatures. She could do without protection if her place for transformation remained undisturbed. Deive in the past had protected her life by powerful magic. However, she would be safe here, for now she believed in a power greater than Deive's. She knelt on the spongy ground and silently allowed her body to morph into the beautiful winged animal cradled by the smells of earth and woody bracken. She took to the sky screaming and free as she felt the waves of warm air from the new sun lifting her high into the clouds.

Down below she could see Raven patiently awaiting her return, and so she flew on to explore a little. She flew north adrift on the warm air hearing all her benevolent watchers whispering at her wing tips and above her sleek head. After her experience with Creator, they had become known to her, and she had soon become accustomed to their constant presence. She watched as Grost's lands dropped away, leaving only the rugged hills that separated his lands from the lands of a nearby city. She kept herself high on the draft of air so that she would be less visible from the ground and swept ahead to the high turrets of the unknown keep. It was then that her sharp eyes saw the emblem of a red wolf. 'Twas Ulrich's keep!

Her falcon mind and heart did not think of him in human form, but in the form of a scarlet predator stalking through the forests. She had begun to believe that he and he alone could provide the satisfaction for those peculiar deep desires that her human and falcon forms shared and understood. Even the form of wolf was strong and sleek like her and given both to raging passions and deep loyalty.

She screamed aloud, her cry of joy flowing from her appreciation of freedom and the increasing warmth from the sun. There was something more blessed about this keep than Grost's. Her strange eyes blinked and peered around, her noble head swiveling at the new sounds and sights, while her delicate wingtips caressed the air.

All at once, a silver-eyed watcher appeared before her. This one was not small as the others had been and had a powerful form and visage. His hair was white and cascaded down over massive shoulders. Alida peered closely at the watcher and her heart asked, "What are you called presence which follows me? You are not as the others!"

"The watcher filled the air before her even more and whispered I am Lordifyn, little winged one. You know my presence. I am your appointed watcher."

"You accompany me now?"

"Aye, as I have and always will. And soon you will know another too, that will keep you in safety."

The presence smiled and disappeared amidst the clamoring masses of little golden and silver watchers who peered first at the closing space around Lordifyn and then at Alida, the smell of warm myrrh scented smoke surrounding her.

Ulrich was riding Titan through a fern-covered glade below his castle when he saw the flash high above his tallest turret. He squinted up into the sky until the sun made his eyes water. He knew that form. He turned his mount in a tight circle until his back was to the sun and then looked up once more, controlling the twist and pull of the reigns in one hand. 'Twas Alida!

He watched the gleaming bird as it circled his castle, a small smile forming on his lips. She was viewing his home! When she veered off south, her scream punctuating her departure, he wheeled Titan and followed behind. Every moment rang through his heart as he rode fast enjoying the muffled thud of hooves on the thick forest floor whose tempo now matched his rapidly beating heart.

His mount was hard pressed to keep up with the falcon, though she flew lazily through the warm air, but the advantage of knowing the territory, as well as Ulrich's expert guidance, made the trip smoother and faster.

He followed the bright unmistakable form until Titan was thoroughly lathered, and they had crossed into Grost's domain. When he thought he could ride at such a pace no longer, the falcon dropped into the shadows of the forest up ahead.

He spurred Titan forward into the cool silence of the forest with a squeeze of his thighs, and the charger graced him with a last burst of speed. They pounded up to a glade where he could see Alida's black mount restlessly awaiting his mistress.

Ulrich and Titan were able to approach Raven, for he recognized the scent of the man and beast before him as they had been with his mistress on other occasions.

Ulrich dismounted Titan and quietly crept through the forest, his footfall nearly silent. His eyes took in everything, noting a broken twig here and soft footprint there. He came suddenly upon the roe's bed just as Alida morphed back into human form.

Ulrich's heartbeat quickened once again against his ribs, and he felt joy leap within his breast at the sight of his beloved encircled by numerous bright watchers. Their beautiful forms cavorted playfully, shining luminescent in the shadows of the bracken and trees. They were there to watch over her vulnerable position at the behest of their Master.

She lay curled in a fetal position. Her nakedness was hidden from his sight, allowing her body to rest from the exertion of transformation. While she slept, Ulrich watched over her as well and worried at the increasing climb of the sun. They both would be expected back at their castles. Was such rest normal for a changeling?

All thoughts became filmy in light of his appreciation of the form lying before him. Her hair cascaded over the leaves around her—its mahogany richness glowing in the dim light. From out of the circle of watchers, one delicately arched foot and shapely calf protruded. He crept forward to get a better view, thirsting for just a glimpse of her face. He said softly to no one in particular, "Never before have I felt so much passion for a woman!"

He saw her shiver, and as he stepped in closer, removing his cloak to cover her, a stern, deep voice commanded softly, "No further! She is not yours to behold!"

He gently stepped back, fastening his cloak back over his shoulders. He then bent down and picked up her cloak from the ground, lightly tossing it into the air while watching in bemusement as the shimmering forms took it to their midst. Presently, the folds of the cloak covered even the bare foot.

He sat down beside the nest, and after a little while, he again glanced up at the sun's climb and decided that she must awaken and return home.

He backed away and thrashed the bracken with a huge stick, awakening her instantly with the racket. He watched as she clambered up from her nest with the cloak clutched about her. Then realizing that she was preparing to attire herself, he retreated fully from the nest turning his back.

When she had fully dressed, she wandered out softly treading the bracken. Her eyes were alert for Raven and wide from the noise that had awakened for she feared that the sound was some predator. Ulrich repaired deeper into the forest without making a sound. He had already removed Titan, realizing that she was leaving. He watched as she agilely mounted Raven, straightening her shoulders and supposedly readying herself for the ride home, though she looked yet a little weary.

He felt his stomach clench as it always did when her beautiful form was removed from his sight. Then, he wheeled Titan away silently, taking an unseen path through the wood, eventually disappearing completely into the shadows. His chest felt empty where a heart had been, and he assumed the disloyal organ had followed the young woman with the curly hair and fiery spirit.

Alida was forced to spur on Raven once again at top speed the whole way back to Castle Lyrnne, keeping her eyes open for people who would relay her whereabouts to Savine. She approached the city's back gate much later than she had intended, her heart pounding at being caught. The gatekeeper let her in, but shook his head in exasperation for the stables had been in an uproar over the missing destrier. Alida would have to face Savine and conjure some excuse for her absence.

The groom's mouth dropped in astonishment as Alida walked an exhausted and lathered Raven into the wide stall. He walked all around the horse and asked, "How far'd ya take 'im, miss? We've been in an uproar looking for 'im. He's a favorite of the head groom!"

Alida ignored the chastising tone of the groom and straightened her cloak. "He has been ridden hard. We came in through the back so none of the guards could have seen my exercise of him, regardless of our location." She stared hard at him and offered him a penny cementing the fact that she wished no further conversation.

The groom frowned and thinking better than to ask further, especially at the cost of losing his coin, proceeded to rub down and curry the fatigued animal. Hopefully, Savine was ignorant of this minor adventure, for she would be suspicious of the distance ridden.

Alida avoided as many other people as possible, hurrying back to her chambers via the servant's streets and stairs. Once she arrived in her room, she dressed in a fresh cool tunic, combing her sun-warmed hair as she went that she might be presentable for her difficult aunt and anyone else that should happen through the door.

She hurried down just as deep afternoon approached and was dismayed when Savine greeted her with a smoldering, "You've broken my rules again, chit!" The screeching diatribe continued, "Out and about while unprotected without any notice to anyone in the keep or city for that matter that you were leaving! You will remain in your chambers again for the next fortnight and will not communicate with your precious nurse and friends during the entire banishment."

The last line of Savine's tirade broke at almost a screech. She was completely out of control in her own castle and would have no more of it.

During the blistering scolding, Kellen walked in, having decided to say goodbye before returning to his own lands with his traveling companions. He quickly walked to Savine's side after her shrieking voice had died away in the hall. "There, there, fair woman. She'll be off your hands soon enough, and I daresay that wifely duties shall occupy all her wild ways once she's is given unto my control." His ingratiating smile and quick order to a maid for wine calmed the peevish Savine.

She sat down, her anger smoldering in waves about her, all the while observing Alida with pursed lips and daggers in her eyes. Then a gleam slowly infused its way into the depths of her pupils, and she grinned at Alida. Her voice was soft when she said, "Be on your merry way, Kellen. My niece is well in hand. I had but a moment of vapors."

Kellen kissed the mistress's cheek and said, "Let me have a moment with your niece, and then I shall do your bidding and be on my way."

He took Alida's arm and led her firmly out into the aging sunshine. His smile belied the cold tone within his voice. "You are a grown woman of sharp enough intelligence. Mind the words that your aunt gives, for she is a very great gentlewoman and you nothing more than a pitiful orphan. I'll not allow you to damage the pact between her and me regarding our betrothal. I intend to see our lands married. Up to this point, the woman mattered not who would increase my holdings, but now I have given my word and intend to keep you to that end." He emphasized his last point by firmly shaking Alida, a bit of nasty temper and ego showing through.

She was in no way injured, but her pride stung from his actions. She pulled her arms from out of his grasp and looked him straight in the eye. "Do not ever shake nor impose your person upon me again. In fact, don't ever appear before me or expect my presence. For as of this moment, I myself am drawing an end to this wedding pact." Her voice had been very quiet when she spoke, but there was no mistaking her firm intent.

Kellen laughed then swallowed, for her cold expression had not changed. He immediately tried to undo what had been done. "Understand me, little one," he whined. "I am caught between two immovable stones, yourself and your aunt. Be biddable and do not cause her further strain. You shall be a very great woman once you have my name and wealth to back you. You'll also have more freedom, but you must be docile and accepting of her word."

Alida looked away and said softly, "I meant it, Kellen. It's over with as of this moment. Though you and my aunt are too proud to dissolve this ridiculous farce of a betrothment, I am not! I will not marry you–God giving me strength– nor will I have anything further to do with you!"

Unsure of how to further proceed, Kellen chose the safe route, returning Alida none too gently to her aunt. Then gruffly making his "fare thee well" the offended warlord walked quickly out into the fresh air, calling his captain to his side immediately, while snarling an order that some missive be written.

When he had exited the courtyard with his entourage, Savine with shaking angry shoulders commanded Alida's attention. "You have made the mistake of crossing me for a second time! For even within the few moments you spent with Kellen, you have managed to offend him. You had best seek your gods if you value your freedom for only they will be able to wrest it away from me you ungrateful little cow!" Savine, with the back of her thin hand, wiped away the spots of spittle that had flown from her mouth in her fury. Unable to remain in the same room with Alida, she rose and retired to her chambers calling Lizel, who had stood casually by, to attend her. She had no real need of the maid, but felt the sudden urge to give a command that would be obeyed.

CHAPTER TEN

The next few days were nerve racking for Alida. She had been immediately escorted by iron hands and rapid steps up to her chambers following her run in with Kellen; and had been cooped up in the stuffy, small space since then without a soul to talk to. Even her serving girls would not speak to her for they feared Savine's wrath. The gigantic guards posted outside her door would not move, even with her pleas and offered coins. Savine had chosen her henchmen well this time around.

Meanwhile, Savine gleefully made use of Alida's absence to goad Deive at every occasion and secretly followed Erta about her duties. Savine discovered that Erta had indeed fully ensconced herself back into a position of power and was very favored and respected by all the castle inhabitants and by many within the city. It surprised and infuriated Savine that Erta was even more beloved now than she had been before her humiliation upon the platform. Then to Savine's further dismay, she received a blistering missive from Kellen telling her of Alida's denouncement and his own displeasure at having been taken for a portion of the bride price, which Savine had insisted upon early.

Therefore, with great cunning, Savine began to devise two separate plans for bringing Alida and Erta to their knees. Neither of the two women meant anything to her, for one was nothing but an orphaned chit and the other nothing more than a beast of burden. Alida would easily be disposed of via her upcoming marriage, which was easily repaired with a reply missive and gifts, and the other would be a pleasure to dispatch by means less common. Savine's eyes gleamed with malice.

A week later Alida could be found brooding over piles of soft, shimmering clothes that were brought to her in cartloads to view and choose from. The mistress of Lyrnne had decided to suspend Alida's punishment just enough, in order that servants and seamstresses could proceed uninhibited with the wedding plans while coming and going in a steady stream to and from Alida's chambers. The state of solitary confinement had become anything but solitary. However, this merely served to make Alida's life more difficult. For though she had steeled herself against any union with Kellen, it did nothing to dissuade Savine's momentum and mulish insistence. Like a donkey braying after a carrot, Savine would not let the sight and smell of money and title vanish away when it was needed the most.

Skillful seamstresses and nervous handmaids poked and prodded Alida, making decisions over the top of her head as if she weren't alive, for they had learned at the beginning of the fiasco that she would give them no clue as to her desires and tastes. They worked instead at Savine's behest, taking the castle mistress' visions and creating them into masterpieces of wedding finery. It should have been a time filled with the gossip of friends and the fun and excitement of a new season in life. Yet there, in the close confines of her chambers, friendly banter and girlish delights were trapped away behind pinched lips and sullen kerchiefs whose normally starched lines had long before given way to the unbearable heat.

Alida had never been so miserable, for her room was directly in the path of the relentless summer sun, whose scorching waves were only added to by the constant press of bodies that refused her any good conversation. As instructed by Savine, everyone that swept through her room was completely focused on the wedding, all the while remaining stony-faced to her inquiries about the outside world and the keep inhabitants. Any servant or artist that dared make conversation with the young woman was whisked from the room with blistering denouncements accompanied by fisted blows and humiliating kicks.

Alida felt her muscles ache with their lack of use, and she rarely slept soundly anymore, for there was not enough activity and exercise in the chambers to tire her normally energetic body. It was to her further discontent that she was not allowed to see Deive, Erta, or any familiar faces other than one or two of her own handmaids, for Savine insisted that she continue to abide by that part of the punishment, enforcing her commands with the over-paid guards. Further, there had been none of the simple hugs and encouragement that was normal between friends and Alida was feeling adrift.

Alida was not alone in her misery, for Deive was also restless, worrying about her charge and languishing over the growing gloom that was ensconcing the keep. Deive was not overreacting, for the keep inhabitants were indeed fretful and sullen. Savine crept about the castle showing up in the oddest places using the advantage of surprise to wreak havoc on the nerves of servants and warriors as well. Nothing was done well enough for the exacting mistress of the Lyrnne castle. Where there was perfection, she would find fault. There were also the increasing groups of angry merchants and shopkeepers to deal with whose services had not been reimbursed due to the quick rate in which Savine had bled the coffers of the bride price. Every breathing body in the castle had been faced with some collector come to gather their coin. Savine, true to her nature, had bought the most elaborate adornment for herself and the keep, for she intended this wedding to be an unheard of tribute to her power, beauty, and fashion regardless the cost. Though the castle glowed with refinement and smelled of crushed oranges and mint and fresh roses, there was an underlying stench of poverty.

Erta, in her friendly quiet way, tried to shore up humor and goodwill in the servants and merchants, but Savine constantly undermined her valiant efforts. When Erta made a sound decision regarding this cut of beef or that length of broadcloth, her judgment was immediately undone by the jealous mistress just as soon as her back was turned.

The servants began ignoring Erta's commands altogether, even though they knew that Savine's decisions lacked wisdom. To a man, the keep inhabitants began to peck at each other fighting even with the closest of companions that they would normally love and trust. There was a sense of fear for one's station and livelihood–a smell of self-concern. There was the prickly growth of defensiveness and recriminations. The struggle of power dampened everyone's spirits and made a ripe bed for the burgeoning growth of evil.

The twelfth night of Alida's banishment dawned with a full moon slung low in the late summer sky. Its round face illuminated strange shadows in the corners of the keep, while cobweb-like clouds crept over its surface. There were no softly singing birds to wrap up the evening and no cool breeze in the muggy heat. The only night sounds that could be heard echoing through the keep were the chilling screech of a mouse caught in the paws of a predator and the horrid caterwauling of felines in battle. The whole of the castle held its collective breath–a moment of reluctant peace before the plunge of a knife.

A slim figure dressed in a black cloak, no features visible beneath the heavy hood, skulked through the courtyard. The whispering footsteps of the figure seemed to be swallowed up by the sodden air as if the night were collecting memories for some horrid volume. Myriad evils cavorted about the figure grinning maleficently at the keep and at the servants who slept on the hard courtyard cobbles trying to escape the late summer's heat. Periodically one or two of the spirits would break away to whisper nightmares into the ears of the humans that lay all about them. Their craggy maws were filled with the stench of fear and the odorous slime of hell. They pinched, pulled and whispered to the evil figure in their midst, using their sharp claws and glowing eyes to incite further an already deeply evil intent.

The figure silently opened the door to the stables and slipped unseen through the heavy oak stalls. The horses snorted and sidestepped at the sulfurous evil that poured by them–trumpeting their alarm into the night. Their racket, however, went unheard by the grooms, whose deep sleep had been ensured earlier by a potion that had been slipped into the servants' kegs of sweet cider beer. This also accounted for the undisturbed rest of the courtyard inhabitants and the warriors on watch.

The figure crept to the stall that held a most magnificent steed. With a creek of the wooden stall door, the cloaked creature entered the warm hay-filled enclosure pulling the gate closed with a muffled click. The ensuing scream of the stallion that followed on the heels of the unlawful entry shook the stables to its foundations. Then there was a sickly silence.

The figure slipped back out from the stalls and hurriedly rushed to the kitchens where further duty had yet to be carried out. Just as believed, the particular servant required of the cloaked figure was awake and moving about to a quietly sung tune. This servant never imbibed the ales and wine of the castle, preferring instead the thirst-quenching droughts of honeyed whey and water. She was, therefore, the only alert body in the lower parts of the castle.

When the servant turned and saw the figure, the scream that had instantly filled her mouth died away in a ghastly gurgle. For in one smooth motion, the figure had inflicted a deep crimson slash beneath her chin laughing maniacally as her warm life's flow ebbed down her neck and stained the front of her neatly kept tunic. The stench of burned flesh quickly followed and then there was nothing but silence and the porcelain presence of death.

The next morning a very groggy guard made his way to the kitchen. His head pounded unmercifully and an herb essence from Erta would provide the much-needed cure. He felt very odd for he was the only one awake, and the ensuing silence left in the midst of such slumber was all encompassing. It was even more unusual that he had found many of his cohorts, who were supposed to have been on watch in the castle keep, sleeping as well. They would surely be beaten for their lazy handling of the keep's protection. Savine, understandably, did not take such lapses patiently. He shook his head gingerly; perhaps the ale of the night before had been a very strong batch. The guard still wondered in amazement that not even vigorous shaking had roused Tremain, his captain, from his deep slumber.

He stumbled up to the main cutting block that stretched a good fourteen feet across the middle of the kitchen, then wound around the block to the shelves full of potions, keeping his head down the whole way to lessen the unbearable throbbing and bright stars that shot across his vision. His excellent view of the floor afforded him the sudden horrific sight of the castle goodwife lying inert in a congealed pool of blood. She was staring glassily at the ceiling and was stiff enough to have been dead for hours. She was the one to whom he had come seeking aid. No other could ease a headache, toothache, or other various maladies like this woman, Erta.

The sight of her made him a little dizzy and nauseous, for though it was a common enough sight on the battlefield, on this day he had come, defenses down, to a place that had always been safe and welcoming. He dropped down on the cold stone floor beside her and tried to shake her awake, lest it be his drugged imagination that pictured her dead. Her lack of response and the stiff chill of her flesh awarded him the truth. Another rush of nausea assailed him, and he was hard pressed to rise and rally the castle - though after some moments had passed, his training got the better of his sluggish flesh.

Eventually, he was able to rouse one or two other guards who had come sluggishly awake. They decided amongst themselves to seek out Deive, for she would go easier on them than would Savine. There was also the chance that Deive would be an ally in the onslaught of Savine's ensuing wrath.

They rallied the dark-haired woman amidst urgent whispers and admonitions. She came awake easily, a sign that only the lower strata of the castle had been drugged. She arose quickly from her warm, soft bed without complaint, a quickening in her spirit telling her that indeed something was amiss. When they reached the body, an unprepared Deive nearly collapsed at the sight, her only boon to consciousness being the strong forearm of one of the guards who caught her. As he grabbed her, he cried out for her to catch her breath. She drew in great sobbing gasps of the air around her, before something in the boyish uncertainty of the guards around her caused her to pull herself together. With the training that nursing and maturity had brought, Deive, like a mother, gathered up her shattered heart and tucked it away turning instead to the bawling misery of her responsibility and station. It was her swift movements, that got her and the warriors into some semblance of order before an unusually early rising Savine who made her way like a pin-prick into their midst.

They had just laid the body, linen wrapped, on a long trenching table in the hall when Savine's elegant form rounded the corner. As usual, her heavily perfumed scent traveled ahead of her.

She took in the scene very quickly and advanced like a mini whirlwind, her speech a clutter of commands and questions sounding for the entire world like a chattering chicken.

"What is the meaning of this? What dead vagrant do you place on my polished tables? Remove that body at once. Who gave you permission to do what you have done? Wrapping up a corpse in that way! Who is it, anyway? How did someone come to death without a great crowd cackling on about it? Never mind, just get it out of my sight!"

Deive stood immobile before the approaching harpy, her violet eyes a deep steely backdrop for her sorrow. With a low angry snarl, Deive commanded, "Stop where you are, you prattling witch! This is no vagrant, but our own Erta, and I would ask you the same question of how her beloved form came to so ghastly an end. All within this castle know of your animosity towards her!"

Savine faltered then and demanded to see the body at once, completely ignoring Deive's query. Deive watched in wrathful silence as Savine lifted a piece of soft linen from off Erta's face letting the piece of light material drift back down as a blessed covering when her horror could take in the sight no longer.

Though her words were flippant, Savine's voice and hands quivered, "She is indeed slaughtered. Oh my . . . but . . . well, no mind–pay it no mind. A servant was all she was, truth be told. So now come, and remove the body, you dolts, and find some wench to clean off this sullied table." Savine during her speech had grown very pale and wrung her hands unceasingly stopping only to tap her nails nervously on the table whose bench she had sunk down upon. Her sick mind would not loose its grasp from the unpleasant sight before her. She mused over the images like pale vapors that tricked her even now to wonder if Erta were alive with breath beneath the linen for Savine swore that the wrappings had moved.

The warriors' jaws grew steely and more set than they had been a moment before. Laid out in front of them was of the most beloved and respected members of the keep, and Savine was ordering a dismissal of the whole affair as if she had been naught but a diseased beggar found on the roads outside the city. They did not immediately step forward to follow her command, a sullen disobedience overcoming their training.

"I said remove the body!" Savine rose and screeched her command advancing on the nearest guard like a spoiled child.

"Nay, you cold-hearted vixen!" Deive stepped forward. "You'll not strip from her the respect that was due her. There will be a proper period of mourning and a burial. Then we will look into the events that were a part of this horrid affair."

"You dare defy me and my commands in my own keep? You are nothing more than a friend to the unworthy and a wet nurse who has not loosened her hold on a babe much grown! This abomination will be removed from my sight and thrown into the beggar's trench to be pecked at by every raven that passes!"

Still not one guard advanced, for now they looked to Deive. It seemed that she was the only one present who could render proper advice.

"Did you hear me?" screamed Savine. "I said remove the body!"

Deive stepped forward and slapped Savine across the cheek as hard as she could, knocking the horrid woman to her backside and leaving an angry red mark on the pale skin. Deive managed to control herself enough to grind out quietly, "Get out of my sight!"

Savine was so stunned that she could do nothing but rise to her feet, turning and fleeing from the ravenous gleam in Deive's eye, her retreat less than dignified. In her heightened state, she fancied that the linen wrapped creature on the table had risen and was chasing her along with the purple-eyed eltar halfling.

The guards stood at attention awaiting Deive's command. There was a vaguely uncomfortable feeling at having defied their mistress, but they had been present to see the madness and hate that poured from her. One did not treat the dead in such a manner, and they agreed that they would rather deal with an angered mistress than wrathful gods.

When Savine had fled and Deive had calmed the group somewhat, the little entourage gathered herbs for embalming. With the aid of a few heavily wakened servant girls, Deive set to creating an elixir to eliminate the heavy side effects of the drug that had overcome the castle. This was dispensed as quickly as it could be made.

She asked that the empty kegs of the night before be brought to her. Then she asked that she be left alone for a bit with the body of her friend. Out of respect, the guards and serving maids departed. Then amongst themselves, the party agreed to gather up Alida and bring her down. Surely, her internment would be suspended for this affair.

After the group had left her, Deive silently gazed the body of her dear friend. She had an odd feeling about the whole happening. Something was greatly amiss, for there was no reason that her friend should have been killed. There was no sign of struggle, no theft from the great walls, no alarm or other injury that would point to some ignoble purpose.

She felt a single wet tear trail down her face and dashed it away with the back of her hand. There was much to be done before she would allow her eyes to weep away the sorrow.

She knelt shakily on a bench beside the table and prayed for discernment as she began the grim work of an alchemist. First, she took a little powder in the leather bag at her side and dumped it into a half-full cup of ale from the night before. She watched the yellow foaming reaction of the mixture, and then frowning, she turned towards the corpse. She carefully unwrapped the linen sheath and began to study the body, noting the length of the gash. It must have been made with a very sharp blade for the edges of the flesh at her throat were not jagged. It also was of interest to her that the cut was so precise, surely made by someone with battle experience, for the cut had been made directly down the length of the artery. Next with some difficulty, she turned the stiff body onto its side, lifting up long strands that had escaped Erta's usually neat bun. It was then that she noticed some kind of a mark just at the base of the head below the hairline. She looked closer, pushing away the surrounding hair and saw that the mark was the symbol of the sorcerer's guild with the addition of a serpent surrounding its perimeter. She sat down hard on the bench beside the table, all the air leaving her lungs with a whoosh. She could have not been more shocked by her findings. What did Quirin gain by murdering this unsuspecting woman? Surely, her findings had been addled by her sorrow. She leaned in again, closely studying the mark.

She was so concentrated on the discovery at hand that she did not hear Alida slip up behind her. The fluttering touch on her shoulder startled the willowy, older woman. She spun with a gasp, rising to her feet and then smiled wobbly when she saw that it was her greatly missed friend. They hugged each other, tightly squeezing the air from each other's lungs with the firmness of their grasp. Then in a rush, they both began to cry with disbelieving half-sobs. They stood in that embrace for a long unguarded moment as the flow of tears made its journey from their hearts bringing with its salty flow a horrible touch of the reality of what they faced.

Then Alida's voice, soft and confused, said, "I was released to come and be with you, Deive. The guards told me the whole story or rather the part that they know. Will you be all right?"

Deive sank to the bench beside the trenching table, her voice coming back once more in a sob. "Sorrow requires time to smooth its brow, Alida. I loved her very much. Never would I have thought to have found a friend in so simple and kindly a person. She was true and whole and I loved her for it."

"She calmed you, and you stoked something fiery in her. Everyone knew how close the two of you were." Alida was quiet and then clearing her throat she wiped Deive's tears with a soft hand saying as she did so, "Something I don't understand though is why she was singled out and then murdered so . . . so brutally."

Deive wiped hot tears from her cheek, trying desperately to stem their flow. Her voice stubbornly persisted in its shaking. "I don't either, but I've made a discovery that may help us find answers. Her murderer was Quirin. His mark is on her neck. In his arrogance, he would not let an opportunity to boast pass him by for anonymity is his greatest fear. However, dear girl, it is a mystery to me how he was able to create such precise mischief. He had no way of knowing that I was close to Erta, nor was there any attack on the keep last night to make tampering with the ale warranted. I know in this also that his hand was present. There are very few plants that would have had the desired effect, and there are ways to test for all of them. I took some of the remaining ale and mixed it with the powdered Eelroot I keep on hand. It bubbled and then turned yellow. Such results reveal that only one of two types of plants could have been used in the actual drugging, for they have the only oils in them that would cause a reaction from the harmless Eelroot. Hog's Tooth and Glad Lily are available only to the sorcerer's guild. No one else has the knowledge for harvesting the parts of them that create so strong an intoxicant."

Alida struggled with the rush of information that was so different from anything she could have suspected. Just then, a breathless groom burst in on the two women. He was in such a state of agitation that he did not even apologize for interrupting them. "Miss Alida, oh miss, there's somethin' terrible that 'as 'appened in the stables." The lad's cheeks were stained with color and tears, and his hands were shaking badly.

Deive looked curiously at the riled lad and reached for his shoulder with a firm calming hand. "What do you need her for, boy?"

"It's about Raven. . . ." His voice trailed off as Alida rushed passed him on her way to the stables, her boots rasping against the cold stone of the hall.

The sight that greeted the worried Alida was ghastly and unbelievable—for the magnificent stallion, Raven, had been beheaded. She immediately ran from the gore and warm bloody stench of the stall. Then falling to her knees just outside the stall door, she retched onto the cobblestones. Her shoulders shook with the effort of vomiting as well as the emotional horror at having witnessed such a sight.

When the waves of nausea began to subside, Alida wiped her mouth with a corner of a scented handkerchief she kept tucked in her tunic. Tears that had come to her eyes from the pressure of the retching were wiped away on her sleeve. The bitter taste of the vomit in her mouth and the cutting pain of the stones of the courtyard against her knees made a situation that seemed like nothing more than a nightmare, sickeningly real. What brutal work was this? That Quirin could dismember an innocent and incredible animal was beyond understanding. She could imagine that no other hand would have been party to such nasty work.

Alida, with a heavy heart, gave instructions to the still shaky groom that now stood by her side. He would burn the carcass of Raven and clean out his stall once she had gathered enough strength to return to the sight and look over the body of the beast.

He nodded and then waited somewhat impatiently until she had risen to her feet. He then followed her at a clipped dogtrot into the stall, covering his own mouth with a corner of his tunic top at the stench that surrounded them.

She looked over the carcass for a while and then moved on to the more difficult sight of the head. Quirin, with his own particular brand of diseased humor, had stuffed an apple into the beast's mouth and had braided the fore-lock, as cook would do to a wild hog that was to be presented at a meal. This furthered sickened Alida. Her only recourse to keep from being overcome by the horror of the night's events was to allow a good hot angry flame to grow within her breast.

In her chambers, Savine paced the floor, breathing heavily from her encounter with Deive. She screamed to the rafters, "What were you thinking! How brazen was your intrusion and how complete. I only asked for the nettling of Erta and the disfigurement of that grand beast, not their demise!"

Just then, a laughing sulfurous cloud appeared in the darkest corner of her room.

"You are welcome." Quirin's face appeared amidst the smoky mass.

"You did not tell me your claim would be so great," whined Savine. "What am I to do or say now, for that purple harlot from below stairs is more wrathful than I have ever seen her."

Quirin's face went from laughing to enraged in the beat of a heart. "Do not dare to call Deive such a name, or you'll find your fate to be the same as the servant girl, Erta. You are the mistress of this keep, are you not? Behave as one, and take back that which is yours! Never mind the dark duties of last night, concentrate on the glory that will now be your sole desire! But remember that Deive is mine and mine alone to do with as I please. You have no further claim upon her."

Savine stepped back from his devious glare, her hands quivering with fear for her own life and of the magic she saw displayed. "You are mad!"

Quirin cackled, "While you, my dear, are the picture of sanity!"

She turned away, straightening her tunic and said, "Leave me. I will attend to this mess!"

Quirin's presence laughed gleefully again and then was gone.

Down in the hall, Deive felt a shiver caress her neck. She knew that Quirin's presence had been about, but had very little idea whom he had come to see. The only thing obvious to her was that he could not resist passing her and touching her, presumably on his way out.

Beneath towering walls, Quirin came back to his own body, feeling the continuing tingle in his hands at having touched Deive. His fists curled and opened like maddened claws, and he moaned aloud at the sensations the witch had made him feel.

After opening his chamber door, his wild and piercing green eyes looked around for the nearest serving girl and caught sight of a young one emerging from the barely cracked door of the next chamber. Stumbling over his own feet, he hurried to the door and pulled the struggling girl inside his rooms. Moving quickly, he sacrificed her to Lund, the god of virgins, amidst gruesome incantations, while vision after vision of his dear, sweet Deive ran like a stream through his mind. Surely, Lund would answer his prayer–for the hungry god was never fully satiated by human flesh and blood. Lund's grinning face with its sharp teeth and elongated tongue graced a toad-like statue that was placed centrally to the chamber—a private, craven image that Quirin lovingly caressed while his maddened eyes burned almost red in his sweating face.

Hours later, disgusted with the inert body lying across Lund's altar, he bellowed for his guards to come and take the mess away. The furtive guards did so without a qualm. This was the fourth girl within the week, but it mattered none to them for they all worshipped Lund–a bloodthirsty god that mercenary warriors could relate to.

Quirin washed away the blood in a tub full of hot water and allowed his thoughts to dwell on possession of the purple witch. A little later, after drying himself impatiently, he had a full cask of fragrant new wine and a cut of cold meat brought up to him, carrying on with the normal habits of the evening as if nothing were amiss. Nevertheless, inside he trembled with anticipation, for he could not hold out much longer for the woman who had betrayed him, and now haunted his every waking hour. He was filled with a seeping madness, whose only elixir was the woman herself.

A dark, cold mist that had come with the murders hung over Lyrnne and did not lessen with time. A power had taken dominion in the walls of the now unholy keep. In the midst of murder, jealousy, anger, and strife reigned a gleeful ambivalence, which sought to dampen the small, remaining light of the city's only righteous inhabitants.

Deive and Alida sat quietly in Alida's chambers awaiting a simple meal of cheese and bread that was being brought up by the castle maids. The events of the weeks past necessitated their companionship as never before.

Alida stroked Deive's soft hair away from her brow and sighed at the deep grooves that marred her friend's fair brow.

"We could leave in the dark of this night, Deive, and give you some much needed respite from the duties you have taken over in the last few weeks. You have not mourned, and I feel the great tension within you. Let us take this night for your grieving."

Deive did not look at Alida. She was soul weary. This whole mess was her fault, for she should have never brought Alida to this cursed place. There had been trial after trial in the walls of this keep, which never should have touched the purity of her charge. She wearily rose from the fur-laden chair set before the fire and spoke softly to Alida. "Tonight it shall be."

She donned a scratchy brown cloak and headed for the door. She would take some rest before their trek. Alida gazed at the closed door long after Deive had exited. She sighed and rose, crossing to her pallet for a bit of sleep herself, praying as usual that the darkness would be kept at bay while she slept.

Some chambers down the hallway, Deive sought the comfort of her pallet, and when she had lain down amidst the nest of furs and had closed her weary eyes, dreams came to her in a flood.

She saw a black snake striking at the heels of a gentle doe. When the quivering creature had been felled, the beastly serpent fed on the carcass growing in girth and length until it had slithered away greatly fattened into the brush, its form now the size of a horse. In the dream, Deive pursued the snake, never quite capturing it, and when she had entered a dark cove, the snake turned and struck her throat with a mighty and piercing blow. Then the edges of the dream softened, and Deive felt she was floating high in air. It was a most distasteful feeling, for she was not a creature of the air. Then as suddenly as her fear of heights had come, it faded, for a gilded falcon flew beneath her, and there was peace in the air. A great spirit of joy and freedom could be seen in the sleek body of the bird of prey. All about them a presence of love and vibrancy could be felt. Deive felt her voice call out to Alida, but Alida never responded. Deive felt the air itself answer instead, and she was afraid as dark clouds surrounded her, sucking her into their midst and hiding the beloved form of her ward.

Just as Deive was encased in clouds, she saw far below her and Alida, the loping form of a red wolf with its ears pricked forward as it followed Alida's shadow.

Deive sat upright on her pallet, her heart pounding in the silent and inky blackness of her room. The furs around her were soaked with her perspiration, and her cheeks were flushed a hot red. Absentmindedly rubbing her throat, she rose and donned heavy boots and a darker cloak than the one she had been wearing earlier. All she could do was pray, for the meaning of the dream had been all too clear.

CHAPTER ELEVEN

The evening unfolded its dark arms as Deive and Alida quietly made their way from the city, slipping easily through the crisp, dark dells, and following the same path to the grove that they had followed before.

When they reached the silent ring where the altar to Creator had been erected, the two women turned from each other. With a whispered admonition and silent prayer, Alida turned back from the ring to give Deive much needed time alone with their Maker. Her retreating steps through the frost-crisp grass were the only sounds in the cove.

Deive stood very still in the shadows of the great circle, her heart a lump of granite in her breast. Then without a sound, she fell prostrate upon the ground. She wept hot tears into the musky earth of the grove, her fingers curling like a baby's into the soft folds of moss and leaves as she felt the weeks of agony rise in shuddering gasps past her ribs and throat. She screamed inwardly at the pain of so many lives lost within that year and for the folly that was hers and hers alone.

Into the deep night sky, Deive lifted her clenched fist and face, calling out in an anguished voice, "Why was I foolish enough to follow this path? You have spared me no sorrow! I am as wretched and lowly as my spirit will allow. I would that the very earth could swallow me and my terror! For I have seen my impending death and the heavy weight this knowledge casts upon me is almost too much to bear. Who will care for Alida? When shall I be redeemed? I have made a great mess of the duty with which I was entrusted. Even my past that I had thought long buried now betrays me!"

The silence of the ring grew more silent still, and Deive collapsed once more upon her face, the cold earth soothing away the heat of her tears. She was weary that she should not hear an answer in her greatest time of need.

Because she did not have her eyes raised some moments later, she did not see the light surrounded by figures that had come into the circle. She remained inert upon the ground until a gentle and powerful force reached down to where she lay.

Deive was infused instantly with warmth. The light and peace of the air was so heavy that Deive could not raise her eyes though she desired to do so, more than she had ever desired anything.

"Is not Alida my child?" said the breath that had entered the cove. "Did I not form her with my own two hands and cast her upon the earth? You have grown to believe that she is yours and yours alone. Alida's sire and dam, Erta, Fiona, and all the others that have been lost to you have been harvested by the destroyer. Your human hands could have never protected them nor could the deaf and mute gods that this land serves. You have no burden, dear Deive, but to continue to seek the truth with eyes now opened regardless of your remaining time. You were not called to be the defender of those who have always had the greatest of warriors and friends as their allies. Where they were powerless I was their strength, and my salvation will not be lost hence to them though the grave still holds them fast. I have planted again a seed that all may know of me and hide within my walls. You are but one. I AM."

Deive trembled at the Creator's voice. Again, she was struck that this was not the presence of an inept and uninvolved deity of man's making. This was a force that no human could describe whether he or she be mage or priest or sorcerer. This was and ever would be the touch of The All and the voice of the Great Deep.

Deive could not hear any sound but His voice. His gentle true hands drew from her heart all bitterness, pain, pride and darkness. Through His eyes, all ignorance fell away and she had true sight. On her tongue was the flavor of peace.

She lay inert on the ground and smelled the odors of the earth and the purity of the sky. She was burned by his fire and washed in a different kind of water. She understood once again how the elements she had served had been created to serve his purpose. They were not meant to be worshiped. Everything in creation held his mark, but only as a signature, not as things of power themselves.

Deive trembled as her spirit was quickened from the sole of her foot to the dark crown of her head. Then, all at once, God was gone from her, that portion of extra spirit removed as softly as a sigh leaving only the quick bright figures, which had attended His presence.

Deive sobbed into the fragrant earth as terror and pain were robbed of their power to harm her. She whispered softly, "It is You, I adore." All at once, the attendants to Bright Face swept about her body in a single mass. They gave her refreshment of spirit, smoothed her hair, and patted her cheeks with warm hands, whispering contentment all the while in singsong voices.

Deive sighed and gave herself to their attention. She understood now Alida's love of the air. For though the air had no power of its own, the air carried His essence, His peace.

Alida waited outside the circle, her keen ears and senses having heard The All and the singsong hums of the light watchers.

She did not turn her face to the cove. For though she loved the sight and presence of The All, she would not intrude upon Deive's moment of comfort with Him. She quietly laid her head upon her folded arms and started when a warm, heavy hand grasped her shoulder. She looked up distressed at the intrusion upon her and Deive and was surprised to see the gentle, handsome features of Ulrich.

He sat down beside her, wrapping his arm about her air-cooled shoulders and did not say a word for he had felt the weight of the moment. He had come at the beckoning of Creator himself.

The bright lessons of the cove that had been added to her initial knowledge of God were treasured away in Deive's heart, and as a team, she and Alida set out together to teach others of the light—a new hope binding them together.

They were faithful in the offering of sacrifices and worship of God. They did all He commanded them to do and lived according to his law, though it was difficult at times to avoid Savine and her cohorts.

Still, even with interference, little by little, the shadows of Lyrnne lifted and many eyes were opened to the truth–a strenuous process that could not take place instantly. Their boon was the relationship they had made with the keep inhabitants.

Few in the castle listened to their mistress any longer. In her outrageous handling of castle affairs, she had totally removed herself from their respect. Even within the city, rumors and knowledge of castle affairs caused her shame. Few could see in her anything to be admired or emulated.

Savine's hold on her niece as well was released for a time for Kellen had taken himself and his warriors off to defend his lands to the south, putting aside his plans for marriage for the moment. Alida could feel nothing but joy having been given the freedom to roam the keep and lands at her own desire.

So it was with great joy that some weeks later, Alida and Deive were found taking time together to stroll across the soft earth of the castle's herb gardens. The sun was warm in the cool autumn air, and the two women were enlivened by the goodness of the day.

Deive slowed suddenly at the rough, lower wall of the garden and gazed at Alida. "This was the first place you met Ulrich."

Alida stopped abruptly and looked at Deive grinning and nervous. "How did you come to this knowledge? I only told you I met him in the garden, but I did not state the exact spot?" She gently shoved her friend and laughed.

Deive grinned. "I do not only listen to your voice. There is another that has more to say!" Then all at once, her countenance became grave and her voice serious. "Alida, you must make a choice for the path your life will take. Your heart obviously does not belong to Kellen, but I am not sure that it belongs to Ulrich either, for I know your bent towards common sense. You do realize, I'm sure, that though the keep's inhabitants respect you and have waned in their loyalty to Savine, they still feel a great attachment to the land and crest. They would not support your marriage to a sworn enemy."

Alida gazed at the plants around her, her sight not really on them and her brow marred by deep thought. "I feel that Ulrich could be mine and I am intrigued by the prospect, more so than I am toward any other offer of marriage, for he and I have become friends and share our belief in Creator. However, love cannot always make our path. I have a duty to my kin and their land. If I marry Kellen, it will be because Lyrnne will benefit from the rule of a wealthy chieftain, not because of any order of Savine's and certainly not out of any emotional attachment."

Deive puzzled over Alida's reasoning. She did not feel right in questioning her decisions, but she had felt sure that her ward would have chosen another way outside of these two men. She was disturbed that Alida seemed almost resigned, as if she had been given no other paths to walk. In the reply, there had been no mention of Creator other than to state that she and Ulrich shared belief in Him.

Deive took her arm once more, and they finished their stroll. As they came back towards the heavy doors to the hall, Deive whispered, "You learned life's greatest lesson even before I did, yet you are still young in the knowledge. Do not forget God. May He aid you in your journey and give you wisdom."

The Lyrnne hall was awash in the glow of candles and scents of fresh hay and flowers. Soft strumming from a group of traveling minstrels added peace and propriety to the gathering. The inhabitants from the keeps of Lyrnne and Kinterden Dells alike had come together for a celebration of Kellen's success to the south. The Kinterden host, who saw the feast as a double celebration, was sober but hopeful over the prospect of a continuance of a coming union between their lands and those of Lyrnne. Most of the inhabitants of Lyrnne knew of Alida's distaste towards the union but also counted upon her loyalty to the protection of their way of life whatever the cost may be to her personally, and so they too added to the undercurrent of a dual purpose.

This feast had been prepared with great care at Deive's instruction. She had only cursorily employed Savine's ideas, for Savine's function had been decreased to that of a figurehead. And though Savine did not oversee the preparations, every bit of linen that was laid down and every dish that was made was done so with flair and loving attention. For all preparations were made in memory of Erta. She had become their symbol of a warm and prosperous community, and this was the first major feast since her death.

In the midst of the genteel calm, Kellen sat upon the dais with Savine and Alida to either side of him. His arrogant gaze and cocky stance let all know that he was confident in the upcoming bond between the keeps, though he knew of Alida's further cooling towards any thought of marriage to him.

He had, in the deep recesses of his mind, a pleasant image of an abject and docile Alida. She would rely upon him for all her needs and those of the keep. She would be subject to his command and his holdings would double because of their union—a man could ask for no more.

Beside him, gowned in heavy satin and velvet, Savine continued to burn with the tilted madness that had taken such a deep root within her breast. She valued power and aggression above all other things and was frustrated now by the dimming of her importance in the keep. She had given up any remaining warmth and redemption when she had gone to Quirin for aid. His dark power and insanity had infected her already diseased heart. Even now in the midst of this beautiful celebration, she gleefully envisioned lurking emanations that would rise up and devour Alida and Deive. These visions and daydreams were more real than she imagined, and Quirin fed off the hatred in his pawn. Though Savine fancied herself in control of the situation, Quirin was the real puppeteer needing her for nothing more than the torture of Alida and the entrapment of Deive. Eventually, when Savine had become useless to him, her own demise would bring him great pleasure for hatred is a monster whose belly is never fed.

Unlike her two dinner companions, whose thoughts were less than worthy, Alida's musings stemmed to the weighty matters of diplomacy and decorum in her temporary role as Lyrnne's mistress. She would be a primary facilitator in the comfortable relations between the two keeps regardless of any marriage union. Though she felt prepared for her upcoming role in matters of administration and state, she did not allow her mind to wander to thoughts of a wedding bed and love. She had made up her mind to publicly denounce a marriage to Kellen and privately to cool any ardor between her and Ulrich, for she knew her attachment to him and desire for marriage was growing daily. With the sweetness of love, however, came the knowledge that such personal gain could destroy her already unsettled lands. Savine would be asked to step down and Alida would govern Lyrnne. She had the training and blood to take over what her aunt was no longer capable of keeping.

Across the great hall, a silent figure viewed those gathered upon the dais and unobtrusively as possible made his way up the servant's staircase to Alida's room.

———————————————————————————————

Back at Castle Falda, Quirin held a curling leather map down upon a trestle table as he spoke with his captain of the guard. "We will amass our units here and here. The flanking horsemen will be dressed all in black with soot to hide their features, and I want the darkest mounts possible beneath them. Have them in the woods here, awaiting the signal to advance. The darkening light of sunset and outright surprise of such an attack will make our plan a success. Also, saddle my white mount as a beacon for the forefront. It will draw the eyes of both our warriors and theirs. Such a distraction will be very useful during the first advance."

The warriors roving about in Castle Falda's great hall discussed the attack plan and made individual plans for weaponry and armor. They rubbed their blades until the hall glowed with the deadly intent of the weapons. Piles of chest plates, shoulder caps, shin plates, and wrist guards made of heavy, hardened leather, lay about in readiness. Cowed maids and timid pages helped load up wagons of provisions and prepared the mounts for their masters. Quirin's army would march within the next few days.

Ulrich had no news or sense of Quirin's upcoming invasion. He, instead, was focused completely on the matter at hand, waiting patiently in the shadows for his love, Alida. Within his breast, he had chosen to fan a flame of belief that the ceremonies and unspoken wedding preparations below would disappear beneath his constant attention to the object of his love.

From a secret cove near the hearth, Deive watched as the tall, handsome stranger spread something upon Alida's pallet, finding a nearby hiding place when the task was complete. His soft movements were not easily heard over the crackling of the fire. Deive had been collecting a bauble for her charge when he had entered the chambers, unaware of her presence.

She had immediately recognized him but wanted to search out his intentions, and so she remained quiet until he had settled fully into the darkness. Then with a soft commanding voice, she called out, "Who are you?"

Ulrich jumped at the sound of the low, feminine voice—his heart suddenly beating in double time. Rising with his elegant head turned towards the sound, he approached her position, his animal-like movements quieter than before and more dangerous.

"That's far enough," Deive uttered, her own heart now pounding in her throat. "I'll not have you approach me further. You do not belong in this place, and I would know of your business here."

"Who is it?" Ulrich could not see her countenance, since he had the glare from the fire to overcome. Added to this was his inability to recognize her voice since she had spoken so quietly.

Deive remained silent and watched the play of his muscles beneath his tunic top as he readied himself for an attack. She removed a small, plain dirk from her cloak in preparation. Ulrich, not knowing beforehand how keenly she observed her surroundings, lunged toward the shadowy figure and saw a knife flash dangerously close to his neck before stemming his advance.

"My apologies, dear lady," his deep voice crooned sarcastically. Nevertheless, it was only moments later that Deive found herself disarmed and at his mercy. At her croak of dismay, Ulrich drew her closer to the fire to observe her features.

"Deive?" His puzzled frown gazed down into her wary eyes.

"Aye, and you are Ulrich."

"Why did you ask my identity if you knew my name?"

"I wanted to see your reaction."

"I won't hurt her, Deive."

"There are more ways to hurt a woman than physically, Ulrich," she said sighing softly the fight having gone out of her.

With a firm tone he replied, "I would not hurt her."

"Then to save the both of you, you must leave, now."

"I'll not go."

Deive sighed again and broke away from his loosened grasp. "You are more naive than I thought. Do you realize that she will lose the loyalty of all who know her, save myself, for they will not allow her marriage to an enemy! Can you fathom how deeply she will question her choice should your union succeed? Alida has responsibilities of which she is all too well aware! Savine has grown too mad to govern this clan any longer."

Ulrich quietly stepped back into the shadows refusing to be dissuaded. "She greatly respects you and your guidance. I would not have her break her loyalty to you, but you may well hold her from the only happiness she will ever have. Surely you have heard the rumors and musings surrounding that oaf she is being pushed to marry?"

Deive did not immediately jump at his implication that Kellen had serious flaws. She instead paced away from him towards the window, her stiff tunic rustling crisply against her ankles.

He said coolly, "I do not know whether to take your silence as acquiescence or denial."

Deive gazed out the window. "I have heard no rumors."

"Do you wish to know some of the choicest?"

She was silent again for a moment, then rubbing her brow wearily pushed aside any curiosity she may have had. "Nay. One way or another, Alida will be cared for and to my knowledge the celebration below is nothing more than joy over a warrior's victory despite the murmurings of Lyrnne and Kinterden inhabitants that it is a prenuptial celebration."

He stood there utterly frustrated, for he put stock in some of what he had heard, knowing the sources to be genuine. Nevertheless, for all his knowledge, he was ultimately powerless to change the situation and could only pray that Deive herself was not favorable towards a union with Kellen.

With her back still turned, Deive said, "Alida must make her own choices. I will not alert the guards to your presence, but you should be warned in advance that the feast might go late. Though she is not given to much wine, she may be accompanied back to her chamber by any serving maid or . . . other party." Her voice died away guiltily on the last note.

Ulrich went from elation that Deive was permitting him to stay to revulsion over her implication that Kellen may accompany Alida to her room.

"They are not yet wed," he growled out dangerously into the too lengthy silence.

Deive turned and approached Ulrich, and with a soft squeeze to his arm, she said, "She would not bed him before their nuptials 'tis true, but she may allow him in for a bit of lover's play if that is the decision she has made. As all young lovers, he especially awaits the rewards of the marriage bed, and it would not surprise me if he pushes some rights early. Beware you do not find yourself cornered by an angry husband-to-be."

Ulrich rejoined softly, "I *am* an angry husband-to-be." With great patience and something close to sadness, she again squeezed his arm and then departed.

In the silence and dark warmth of the room, he regained his hiding spot hunkering down against the cold stone walls. With somewhat dampened spirits, he settled in for the duration of the evening.

Quirin sat by the fireside lovingly polishing a great, gleaming sword that lay across his lap. The firelight danced maniacally over the figures of entwined serpents that coiled life-like round the grip.

Tomorrow the coming of dawn would bring a march of his forces to the gates of a walled city that had never been conquered. He would set up his slaves and warriors within the fallen walls of Drachmund Heights thereby gaining position to exact his revenge upon nearby Lyrnne.

When his battle gear was readied to his satisfaction. Quirin lay down upon his pallet and gazing up into the canopy, allowed his spirit to seep from his body and join with spirits whose forms seethed with hatred and maliciousness.

He then flew out into the night and allowed his presence to settle within a dark corner of the Lyrnne hall. Below him, he could see revelers drunk from the evening's wine and mead as well many overworked servants. He peered about for some time before realizing that the object of his desire was nowhere to be found. With whispered orders, he sent out grotesque scouts to locate her whereabouts and then began his own search.

He had only been looking for a few moments when Deive felt the chill in the presence of the castle. She closed her eyes and whispered a prayer into the darkened halls. The frantic and dismayed little faces of the watchers who attended to her and her safety immediately surrounded her. At the prompting of The All through his small creations, Deive fled the passageways of the keep for a grove of weeping willows just outside of the walls.

Awaiting her and her attendants stood a ring of bright-eyed warriors of the spirit realm. She heard them whisper amongst themselves and then watched as they were released silently to glide into the maze of Lyrnne's passageways. There they slaughtered the dark abominations that had had begun to follow Deive and were even now setting up residence within the keep.

With a swirl of her own purple robes, Deive began to recite the names of protectors that were whispered to her by The Creator, and within moments, the keep itself was inundated with these powerful figures. Soon every corner of the keep had been swept clear of all maleficent spirits, including Quirin.

He came back to his body and found he was very weak and disoriented. Rising on unsteady legs, he made it over to his washbowl and there saw a grinning spirit of discernment. The little beast rose on its legs and hissed, "You'll not succeed in the attempt to route Ulrich in these next days. Beware that you do not lose your own life in the attempt."

Quirin fell to his knees and groaned—all his plans and preparations, all the work built into this siege. He rolled unto his back on the cold stone floor and gazed up at the spirit who looked over the edge of the washbowl at him. "Go away." The little shadow flitted out the window into the night. Quirin lay like that for some time before he realized that the time for subtlety had ended. They would go directly to Lyrnne.

Despite the cheerful presence of merrymaking, Alida had felt the disturbance in the peaceful continuity of the keep. She was not surprised several moments later to see Deive furtively slip into the hall through a side door.

Making a pretty excuse to Kellen, Alida rose from her seat quickly, catching the heavy folds of her tunic from around her chair and sought out the retreating form of her friend.

When she caught up to Deive, Alida quietly stopped her with an urgently whispered, "Wait." Deive turned and grasped her arm painfully as they proceeded to Deive's chamber where the door was barred to prevent any interruption. The two women then found seats by the warmth of the fire.

"What happened?" Alida asked nervously rubbing her arm where her friend had just grasped her.

"Quirin has grown very bold and strong. He is after me, and everything within me believes that soon we will see his last and greatest attempt." Deive then proceeded to tell Alida of the dream she had. She explained that the doe had been Erta, who had already died at Quirin's hand. Now it was her turn according to the prophetic nature of the dream.

Alida frowned. "Don't you think he is after me? It was my family's holdings that were overtaken. What is his interest in you?"

Deive was very quiet for a moment. "It is not an easy tale, Alida, and I could spare you its knowledge."

Naive to the tale that was about to unfold, Alida took her hand and said, "I do not fear anything you have to tell me."

Deive rose and began to pace. She did not speak until she had collected her thoughts. It had been years since she allowed her mind to review the details of that long ago era. "Did I ever tell you who taught me the arts?"

Alida shook her head and Deive began. "Unlike you and most other women of your line, I was not taught by a grandmother, mother, sister, aunt, or other female relation as was the tradition. I was the orphan of an eltar enchantress and human prince, who had resided in a holding near your grandfather's keep. I was taken under your grandfather's wing after their deaths when I was only five years old at the behest of that holding's inhabitants. Apparently, my family's keepsmen did not believe in a daughter's inheritance. The line had to be passed on through a male heir of which there was none, for I was the sole heir to the lands. The holding was taken over by a non-related party who felt his interest could be undermined if I were to remain in the land.

"Your father, myself, his two brothers and sister, and another orphan, a boy, all grew up together. The boy and I were blessed with the same privileges as your grandfather's own kin for your grandfather had a very ample fortune and giving heart. We were taught to read and write and given the same lessons in diplomacy and statesmanship.

"When we reached our youth, your grandfather sent your aunt, uncles, and father out to other keeps for their adult tutelage, as was the custom. It was the first time that any diversity in our education was noticeably apparent. I was heartbroken; for within a fortnight, all of my companions were gone from me. The orphaned boy who had been a part of the group, rather than remaining in the keep, was determined to make up for the "oversight" of your grandfather and had left to find his own further education. It was several years before I saw all of them again.

"Your aunt Orisa had become poised and beautiful. She no longer was interested in gallivanting about the countryside, but instead desired to find a suitable marriage match. Your uncles were strong, self-centered, and fascinated by battle as well as by the fortune they expected to inherit. Only your father, always your grandfather's favorite, had become a mature, thoughtful man, more interested in others than himself. It's not that battle held no allure for him, or that he lacked a desire to inherit the keep, but he had, as well as those desires, genuine concern for those things of true value, such as family and integrity.

"Some years passed with all of us living together in the keep again, but they were less than ideal. Orisa was very concerned with her looks and with festivals and gaming instead of tending to the needs of the keep. It was natural, therefore, that I step in. Orisa loathed me for gaining more admiration in her father's eye than she had.

"Larkin in parallel nature was constantly into mischief and spent much more money than was suitable. He also ignored the instruction given him by his father and married the vain and selfish Savine of Lyrnne without his father's blessing. Torren was fretful and aggressive. Several times our keep came close to battle because of his folly. Your grandfather was so angered at the petty malicious ways of his children that he disinherited them all, save your father. Your grandfather would not listen to any of their pleas and continued in his plans to give the keep and all its lands to your father.

"After these events, Orisa was married off almost immediately to the son of a neighboring warlord, and Torren left to make his own fortune elsewhere. Within months of their departure, Castle Falda received word that Orisa, her new husband, Torren, and her brother Larkin had all been killed, for it took some time for each separate word to reach us. Apparently, Larkin had fought in and lost a battle for control of the seized lands of Savine's mother, though Lyrnne was kept safe. The brothers of a wronged maiden had murdered Torren, and Orisa and her husband had fallen sick from a fever carried in by the filthy game masters whose pastimes they preferred.

"Your grandfather was so overwrought by the loss of almost his entire family so close together that he fell ill from a malady incurable by all my herbs and limited knowledge. Now, looking back, I believe 'twas more from grief than any physical disease.

"It was then that the orphaned boy from our childhood returned. Quirin had grown very strong and handsome. He was not only beautiful to look at, but had gained wisdom as well. He had learned all the ways of wizardry from a reclusive sorcerer in a neighboring region."

Alida's eyebrows went up at the knowledge that her friend and father had grown up with her archenemy. The news caused her physically to recoil from her friend. Deive faltered at her ward's horrified expression, but then continued. "It was upon his arrival back in the keep that I learned of his attachment to me. He had been in love with me from childhood, and I had never known. I was intrigued by his attachment to me and allowed him the chase.

"Quirin, in an attempt to gain my deepest passions and affection, coaxed me into spending time with him, learning the magical arts under his tutelage. We spent many hours a day together, pouring over scrolls and potions. I learned well from him, for at that time his intent was pure if misdirected. He had the ability to be very charming and a good teacher, and as a token of his love and friendship, as well as a testament to my growing devotion to the arts, he gave me the ring that you see always upon my left hand.

"It was at this time that your grandfather, pleased to have some of his little flock still gathered around him, declared, against the counsel of his advisors, that Quirin and I should have a portion of the inheritance.

"Quirin was filled to overflowing, for now he would have enough wealth to take me to wife. Your father, too, was greatly pleased, even in sharing his inheritance, for he considered Quirin and me to be his adopted siblings.

"However, the peace did not last long. Your grandfather's weakened state allowed a deep fever to settle into his body, and within a couple days of the fever's arrival, he was ranting and raving about his dead children. He called all of his advisor's to his bedside, and they, being men and women of tradition, demanded that he bequeath all of his wealth and lands back to his only remaining son. It was with these proceedings that Quirin and I were cut from the will before the death of your grandfather despite his good word to us.

"Quirin, although upset that his plans had been ruined, was not yet bitter, for he made a good living advising the keep inhabitants on spiritual matters as well as aiding them with potions and medicines. It was also assumed that he would one day become advisor to your father.

"The real trouble began when your father took a notice of me and found me comely. After a time, he sought my advice in keep affairs, and more time began to be spent with him than with Quirin. It was not long before I began to return your father's affections, which had more of a hold on me than Quirin's ever had. Though I no longer encouraged Quirin's pursuit, he could not relinquish his love for me.

"One day Quirin caught us in the keep gardens kissing and embracing one another and was so enraged that he immediately lunged at your father. We were able to calm him after a few moments of reasoning, but Quirin was never the same. He became bitter and suspicious, and he haunted us day and night, allowing us no privacy in which to build our relationship. Everything your father did, Quirin tried to best him.

"When the keep advisors caught wind of the romance between your father and me, they demanded that he seek someone with wealth or name to bring to the union. This only strengthened your father's attachment to me, which in turn fanned the flames of Quirin's jealousy.

"The passion between your father and I could not be quenched, and on one fateful night, he and I were able to slip away from all the watchful eyes in the keep. We rode wildly into the hills near Falda and spent the entire night together in courtship. Unbeknownst to us, Quirin located our trysting place by following the footprints of our horses. Rather than disturbing us, however, he listened to our conversation and watched our affectionate exchanges, for your father on that night had proposed his hand in marriage. In an intense argument some days later, Quirin recited the entire episode to us detail by detail and threatened to go to the advisors with the story.

"Your father was infuriated that Quirin should have gone so far. He demanded that Quirin resign himself to the circumstance and seek out some other maid to court. Quirin stated that he had never loved another, nor would he ever love anyone else. This was the first time his madness became apparent, for that night he destroyed all of my most beautiful tunics shredding them to bits. Then later, he cornered me in one of the keep gardens. There he tried repeatedly to kiss me despite my refusals. When he hit me, I knew that he had become violent and that his madness was complete. Upon hearing my screams, your father came to my aid and Quirin was banished from the borders of Falda.

"I was torn with guilt and feared that no blessing would come to the union with your father. Therefore, with great sadness, I broke all manner of relations with him and chose the path of a celibate advisor. For out of all my childhood companions, only your father remained. I was deeply afraid that something else would happen to take him from me. I loved him the best and knew I'd never survive his death or some other calamity for I was certain that the fates had not appointed us for one another. Your father was very distressed, but because he loved me so completely, he allowed me to choose my lot without an ongoing fight. We had two big arguments with crying and incriminations and never did come to an agreement and so the bones were left where they lay. He turned all his energies towards the command of the land and people who had become his own. We never spoke again of our attachment to each other, but our lives would forever be entwined.

"Just about the time that I had made the decision to leave the keep and seek my way elsewhere, your father and mother met and were married. Theirs was a good match designed specifically to better each of their holdings, but fate smiled on them, and they found as well an unexpected love in each other.

"She and I became very great friends, and somewhere along the way she guessed our past love. She would not let me leave and declared me your godmother at your birth. They were the dearest people I have ever known, and because my love was so given to them, Quirin decided to enact his rage over the loss of me through the siege on their castle. I know that he must have planned and waited for all those years until the siege.

I cannot believe that he will stop in his pursuit of me, for there is nothing more, save you, standing in his way."

Deive took a deep breath and sank into her chair. She could not look at Alida, for she feared that she would see betrayal, disgust or anger in the lass's eyes.

"Why do you still wear Quirin's ring?" Alida's voice was very soft.

"To remind me to never give my affections lightly."

Alida remained quiet for some time, and the only sound in the room came from the popping warmth of the fire.

Finally, she spoke with some difficulty. "I cannot believe how much pain has been created from the foolish decisions of foolish people. I pity you the loss of love, friendship, and family. I pity him the love he could have had, though different in nature from what he wanted. I pity myself as well. Yet Quirin will not regain you, for 'tis true that I am all that remains between you. He will attempt to remove me as he has my family and your friends, but he will not succeed. I will not relinquish my new role as your protector. It seems our places have switched. Creator will lead us both and bring us to the end of this madness." She rose from her chair and crossed to where Deive sat.

Kneeling before her friend, Alida laid her head upon her violet-scented lap. Some time went by with peaceful silence passing between them before Alida rose and bid Deive good night, kissing her lips softly before retiring to her room. Her head was full of all she had learned and all that was ahead of her, and she needed time to digest its magnitude.

Deive sat alone in the empty chamber, scarcely moving in her great oak chair and felt the prick of tears behind her eyelids and a tightening around her heart. She prayed softly to Creator out of resolution and desperation, not knowing where else to turn, for she did not perceive that her ward was right. She knew that one day she would have to face Quirin on her own.

CHAPTER TWELVE

On the way back to her chambers, Alida caught sight of a mildly drunk Kellen holding the hand of a serving man from the keep. To her surprise, it looked almost as if they were flirting with one another, for they were whispering to one another and laughing foolishly picking imaginary pieces of lint from each other's tunics. Suddenly, he caught sight of Alida and sent the serving man scurrying away. She tried to hurry by him, and when he did not allow her to pass, laughing at her frustration, Alida paused impatiently staring into his eyes. He used this lapse to reach out for her, pulling her tightly to him and ambushed her mouth with wet disgusting kisses. She pushed at him trying to turn her face away for though he was not dead drunk he reeked of ale.

"Let me take you to my bed, Alida," Kellen whined, "We're to be married, you know. 'Tis no shame in it."

"You're right; there is no shame in lovemaking. That is, there is no shame in lovemaking between *man* and *wife*." She bit off the last two words, her eyes gleaming and angry. The double entendre of her words hit like a slap to his face. "I will see you on the morrow when you are more in your right mind, and we'll have a little discussion with my aunt."

"Alida, you mistake my relationship with the serving man. He is the brother of my finest warrior, and we were laughing about a conquest of his this very evening. Boldly Kellen ran his hand up her body, his eyes more calculated than aroused. Turning her face heavily with his hand, he proceeded to kiss her deeply, but it was against her will, and he could not make her hold still. He used his other rough hand to grasp her tunic and thought nothing of it when the material ripped in his meaty fist. Reaching up, he intended to grasp the bared flesh of her shoulders, still believing that she was accepting of his explanation. When his grasp slackened on her clothing, Alida took the chance to escape.

She bolted towards her chambers with him calling after her, her feet padding softly on the stone pavers of the hallway. She did not stop, turn, or acknowledge his cries.

When she was within the confines of her room, she slammed and firmly locked the door and then lay heavily against it, feeling hot tears roll from her eyes. Why hadn't she kneed him squarely and run like the wind to begin with? She sighed to herself, slamming her fist against the rough splintery wood. Why hadn't she? Because she had not yet broken the betrothment, because a total dismissal of him without cause would bring shame to Lyrnne, and because she had been so horrified that she could barely think.

From the corner, a cool, well-modulated tone called out, "Tears and heavy sighs do not suit you, Princess."

Alida was instantly alert, gazing into the darkness of her chamber. She wiped hastily at her tears for she would not show such weakness to any intruder. "Who goes there?"

"You still do not recognize my voice, lovely one?"

"Ulrich?" She choked on his name, relief at his presence and embarrassment over not having recognized him winning out equally.

"Aye, 'tis the very same," he said. Then in a mocking tone, "Why the tears and sighing? Are you that much in love with the fool?"

She turned away and bathed her face with water from a nearby crockery of cooled water. Ulrich finally moved from the shadows and approached her calmly, his tread familiar to her ears. It was then that he saw the tears in her tunic. Swallowing a great lump that had formed in his throat, he scoffed, "Surely you did not give yourself to that swine out in the hallway!"

Alida becoming annoyed with his tone and still fighting the fear Kellen's attack had caused said, "T'would be none of your business if I had!"

Ulrich came closer and reached out his hand to her cheek to turn her face to him. He was bewildered at her sudden icy demeanor. "I thought friends made one another their business."

She swallowed the last of her tears and turned away with embarrassment, her cheeks a heated red. "Forgive me. As my friend you are welcome to all the questions you could ask." Then with a cocky smile, she said, "Though I may or may not choose to answer."

He gazed into her eyes, and troubled by the turmoil there, he pulled her into a hug. "Forgive me as well for my sarcastic comments. 'Tis not common to see tears upon your cheek."

Alida did not expect such gestures, but once she was within his arms, she did not have any desire to break the contact. *How easy it would be to love this man,* she thought to herself. His broad shoulders had no need of the padding Kellen used, nor was he roughly inexperienced with his embraces. This brought a wry smile to her face. Experienced indeed! How many trysts had it taken to make his embraces so warm and tempting? Using this as her focus for control, she pulled away from him reluctantly and moved towards the window.

Ulrich groaned inwardly at the emptiness left by her absence. He watched her glide to the window and said softly, "Would you like to tell me what is on your mind?"

Alida took a deep breath, "Only if you promise not to be angry."

Ulrich agreed, his face an unreadable mask.

"Kellen stopped me in the hallway and made a very bad attempt to bed me. I did struggle against his embrace, but I might as well have just stood there immobile for all the notice he took of my resistance. It was disgusting, humiliating, and strangely fitting. Would it be too much to ask the fates for a match I loved? It follows my luck that I would be paired with a vain, uncontrolled swine, who knows nothing of love, valor, or women." Almost guiltily, she realized that she had left out the most important information in her relation of the tale, for she could scarcely believe what she had seen and was fearful of being mistaken.

Ulrich swallowed his desire to comment. So the rumors were true. Kellen was known for his botched bedding of wenches. Many stories had been circulated of his rough use of women as well as his inability to hold anyone's attention for long, something that Alida would have yet to learn. Ulrich, as Alida had predicted, was indeed angry over the fool's handling of her. He concentrated on Alida's words in an attempt to keep his thoughts to himself.

"I have long desired a passionate, insatiable love for a man of magnificent valor and beauty. I cannot settle myself with Kellen's lame version of devotion."

Ulrich gazed at her, feeling his own emotion well within him over her words. Could she not see him standing there before her? He wanted to cry out that he was just such a man. They fired passion within each other, and they would be a good match mentally and physically. His fists clenched at the thought of them sharing the furs together and then taking time to talk late into the morning when keep business should be their only concern. He envisioned her belly growing round and smooth with his children, for he knew that she would be a good mother. She was meant for that which she desired, but the decision must be hers.

"Ulrich, have you ever desired to marry?" Her scent of rose still clung to the front of his tunic top.

Yes, you, he said silently in his mind. Then aloud, "I was never interested in the maids that were deemed appropriate by my keep."

"So you were interested in inappropriate maids," she said, jesting with him.

He smiled at her, but his heart was breaking. If ever so inappropriate a maid had been chosen, it was she. Her expectant face brought words from his closed throat. "I have had my share of romances, and yes, some were inappropriate. When I was five, I made the grave mistake of kissing a serving girl from the kitchens that had the brightest red hair you have ever seen."

She chuckled, but then grew quiet when the silence stretched out too long. Then leaning her face on the coolness of the windowsill, she murmured out at the moon, "I can see babies and lovemaking, adventures, family, and friends. I can see a love so deep that I shiver with its passion, too consumed to look at another." Then she, too, said silently to herself, *And I often picture you.*

Ulrich walked up behind her and clasped her close to his chest, whispering into her fragrant hair, "You'll have all you desire one day, Sweetness, and more." He inhaled her scent and allowed her body to melt up against his. What a temptation she was! How could he claim only friendship when the wolf inside his skin growled at the thought of losing her affections to anyone else!

After some moments had passed, he gently kissed the softness of her hair and cheek and bid her farewell, the nearness of her causing his hands to quiver. Though he was loath to leave her, the night had grown very dark, and he would be missed at his own keep that had noticed his long absences of late.

Alida turned to watch him slip from her chamber via the private passageways. His presence here was so dangerous and exhilarating. She should be unnerved at his knowledge of the keep, but she was instead strangely gentled by it.

She undressed slowly after he had left, feeling the places at her waist and back where he had touched her as if they were imprinted on her skin. She then made her way to her pallet and was surprised at the hide laid out upon the warm coverlet. It was the skin of the animal he'd killed when they had been together in the woods.

She lifted the cat hide and marveled at the expertise with which it had been tanned. It had a buttery softness to it, and had been perfumed with crushed rose petals, her signature scent. She held it to her chest as if it would offer up some portion of the handsome man whom she had just seen.

Sleep did not come easily at first that night, for disturbing snatches of her day tumbled through her mind. She thought of Quirin's evil, Deive's sad remembrances, the mystery that Kellen represented, and Ulrich's warm eyes and embrace. She felt unequal to the task of becoming a clan chieftess and was unsure of how to break the match that Savine had made with Kellen. When she could take no more, she lifted her face to the ceiling and softly whispered, "I need wisdom." Moments later, she grasped the pin on her shift and fell into deep, warm dreams with Creator's hand resting gently on her head.

Alida arose the next day determined to seek out Kellen. She had eaten a hearty apple gruel and fragrant slice of smoked ham having then intended to accomplish some chores when she saw him pass through the main hall. His red sleep-rimmed eyes did not bode well for her, but rather than waiting any longer, she ran up to him and lightly touched his sleeve. He turned and mustered a pitiful version of a smile, and it was obvious that he had imbibed more after the incident in the hallway. She knew all too well the signs of a massive hangover. She once again rethought her confrontation and then decided to approach it with a little more grace.

She motioned to a nearby servant and had them bring him a cup of drink that was prepared for just such discomforts after a large feast. It tasted terrible, but she could see his relief within moments of drinking the awful stuff. She then had portions of the same breakfast she had eaten brought to him and warned the servants towards silence, knowing that his head would take a little longer to cease its pounding.

When it seemed he had been refreshed by her attentions, she delicately cleared her throat and launched into the speech she had prepared. "I know that you and my aunt arranged a marriage between our two houses, and that arrangement had progressed quite to your liking and hers. However, during the past fortnight, we have discovered that my aunt has slipped into a mental state that is not conducive to running a keep. She is unfit for her office at this time, and as such, I am calling off the wedding. We must set these lands and authority in order before any union can be sought."

Kellen was silent, his eyes narrowing with her pretty speech. He leaned close to her as if he had understood and agreed with her argument, but then in a most patronizing tone stated, "To me, it would seem that this would be the very time for a union, young one, considering that you and your people are more vulnerable now than when we began. I cannot in good conscience, put stock in the word of the pretty, but young ward of my closest and oldest friend, knowing that such accusations would benefit that ward and damage a pact that is set and necessary. Who claims, beside yourself, that your aunt is unfit? I found her company most engaging last night, and she seemed normal in both spirit and wit. No—I think that you yourself desire to end this union on your own, but you will not succeed even when questioning a harmless moment between myself and another good man. You thwarted my attempts to bed you last night pretending that you do not like men, and you have always disdained my company, but you will not escape so easily. The deal is done. Do not speak of it again." Thus said, he squeezed her hand until she thought the bones would break.

She abruptly pulled her hand out of his rough grasp and said with coldness, "As you will. I sought to end this with honor and propriety, but you may as well know the truth. I find that I dislike you more every day as I see your true character coming forth. You are no gentleman, sir, and now I know thee for a fool. Savine has had no hand in the operation of this keep for well over two moons. She will be removed from power, and I will take her place. I will not marry you, and as my consent is necessary for the completion of the nuptials, it seems as if this conversation is at an end. I'd rather be a pauper than find any union whatsoever with a man that no only offends my person but whose assumed practices in love (at this she cleared her throat) offend my God!"

Kellen smiled coolly, and then pushing his chair away from the table with a screech, he bowed to her with a flourish and left the hall, his boots clicking on the stones and his shoulders tense with anger.

Alida thought about seeking out Deive and then changed her mind. This was her problem. She would approach Savine directly. She would wait for a little while until she was sure her aunt had risen, and then she declare her intentions. She left for the stables thinking that a ride would ease her tension.

Alida entered the dark, sweet-smelling stall of a beautiful mare that had caught her eye the week before. Her vision had not yet adjusted to the dark when she realized that the mare was pressed up against the far wall muttering anxiously. Alida shuffled forward, her feet finding purchase in the hay-covered floor to calm the beast when she was knocked painfully on the head from behind. Her assailant remained anonymous as the darkness of the stall was exchanged for the inky blackness of unconsciousness.

The wedding day came a couple weeks later. It passed uneventfully for most of the guests with everyone making merry and many well wishes made for the couple.

As at all the feasts, costuming of the guests was elaborate and rich. Many of the warriors wore their emblems proudly displayed on their tunics, and their wives wore clothes of matching tint and texture. All of the guests and food had been assembled outside on dark trestle tables. For the day, although windy and cool, was a beautiful example of autumn's glory. Wafting hints of honeyed mutton and spicy, fire-roasted beef were carried as prettily along on the wind as was the more fragile scent of cinnamon baked apples and roasted yams.

Kellen himself looked handsome, but many of the attendant's wondered about the bride. Alida, although gowned in shimmering white wedding garments and veiled with soft folds of blended linen, seemed barely able to stand, her normally proud stature slightly disoriented and somehow mussed. Deive was allowed nowhere near the bride and was beginning to feel almost frantic about the situation.

Deive thought back to when she had awoken on the morning of Alida and Kellen's confrontation. Unknowingly, it was the same morning that she was told the surprising news that Alida, with a change of heart, had gone to live with Kellen's household until the plans for the wedding could be made complete. This "change of heart" had been deemed by Kellen's manservant to have originated with a great and clever act of courtship that his lord had employed just that morning along with the more private matter of a growing knowledge of her aunt's instability. Apparently, Kellen had removed his bride from a "volatile" situation seeking to keep her safe. Deive, since that time, had received bright but vague notes penned in Alida's own hand about the whirlwind wedding plans and her own undying love for the warlord. Deive, unsure of how to proceed, had even ridden to Kinterden Dell only to be told that she just missed Alida's entourage who had left for a neighboring noble's home for an overnight stay and party.

Deive had returned to Lyrnne resolving that she would not let the wedding pass without speaking to her ward. Nevertheless, as in the weeks before, she was stopped at every attempt to see Alida by one attendant or another. Their excuses seemed valid, and they were all so helpful and hurried that she gave up, seeking instead to continue communication with a note here and there. Now in the rush of the day she fought panic over the bride's behavior for it was almost as if Alida were drunk. She was never without Kellen or Savine at her side, and no guests were allowed any length of time for speaking with her. Even the guards seemed unwilling to help Deive get close to Alida.

From a shady grove, Ulrich once again became the voyeur watching his beloved as she moved through the rituals of the day—rituals that would keep her from him until death should take her spouse or her own life. He shuddered painfully that another man should be given the gift of her lifetime.

When Kellen leaned in for a kiss at the end of the ceremony, Ulrich felt his blood boil. Not only would Kellen have the rights to her kisses now, marriage also meant the wedding bed and all of its implications. Ulrich could not imagine her satisfaction beneath the wiles of the fool before him, and though he knew many wealthy warlords' wives took lovers, it was impossible to imagine Alida doing the same. She was bound by honor to the ways of Creator, and it would forever dishonor her to practice a liaison outside of her initial union. His fists clenched and unclenched again, the sign of agitation a clear indication of his thoughts. He was frustrated and angry over her change in heart from when they had spoken until now. It made him sick watching her swoon against Kellen several times, as if she were weak with love for him. Even the whisper of her veil being brushed away from her feminine shoulders by Kellen's massive hand grated on Ulrich's nerves. Moreover, the general murmur (as if it were some great love story) of the women in the crowd at the close of the nuptials made him nauseous.

It was all too easy to picture her with her dark hair spread out over the furs and her creamy skin barely covered by some flimsy garment intended for the wedding night. Surely Kellen would never be worthy of such a vision. He shook his head to clear away the thoughts for they drew too near to adultery and to the poison of bitterness that worked off his anger and sadness.

As the day grew longer and the sight of her dressed in gleaming wedding clothes became too hard to bear, Ulrich moved away to the concealing walls of the kitchen gardens. He was surprised that tears had come to his eyes threatening to overflow. The smell of the wedding lilies, roses, carnations, and lady's slipper mixed with the scent of delicate wedding cakes and wine soured in his nostrils as rotten to him as any refuse could ever be.

Alida and Kellen, sometime later, walked by greeting guests with their wedding party en towe. Over the branches and milling crowd, Ulrich tried to catch her eye motioning to her but her gaze seemed to go right through him.

He muttered painfully to the air around him, "Remember what the burning of our kisses felt like, Alida, for it may be even yet that Creator has planned one day for me to claim you. I cannot believe that he would create this passion without intending its completion." With that, he turned and disappeared into the gathering shadows of evening, the rustle of autumn leaves attending his departure.

The wedding celebration continued as guests feasted from platters full of fragrant roasted meats and poached fruit. As the evening progressed, the crowd grew rowdier and more joyful spurred on by savory wines and the merriment of a good match. Every attempt was made to give the couple time with one another. Though more than one dance was sought with one partner or the other, they were laughingly dismissed.

Even during the feasting, the couple was displayed alone upon their own dais, again thwarting any plans Deive had of gaining purchase of her friend. When it came time to tuck the couple in bed, Deive felt sorrow and joy mix in her throat for her ward. This night Alida would become a wife in the truest sense of the word.

Upon the shoulders of their celebrating kinsmen, Alida and Kellen were taken up to the bedchamber that Savine's host of servants had prepared for them. All about them bawdy comments and suggestions flew by. It was done out of the merriest intentions, but Deive wondered at Alida's occasionally defiant glances.

Alida was set down within the warm chamber, and her clothes were discarded behind a screen with a bevy of maids redressing her in a fine wedding night garment. She was then brought out before the eyes of all Kellen's kinsmen and her own. The maids placed her upon the giant sleeping pallet piled with elegant furs and warm linen and velvet covers. Her hair was spread out upon the pillow as was called for by tradition, and flowers and scented leaves were sprinkled about her head halo fashion as well as around the silhouette of her body, their soft, papery sound hitting the covers like a moth against glass.

From the shoulders of his men, Kellen's face beamed down on her, his eyes presumably and groggily happy at the vision she made. He was brought to the pallet as well and laid beside her, then their hands were folded over each other's and a wreath of herbs and flowers was placed between their heads. A huge jug of tasty mead had been brought up and placed beside their bed along with a tray of sweet meats, dried figs, and cheese. Many a joke was bantered about over the benefit of having a refreshment area so close to the bed.

Finally, the last well wishes were made, and the door was closed behind the obnoxious crowd.

Kellen's hand tightened on her own, and in a drink-slurred voice he boomed out, "Welcome to your first night of loneliness you foolish pauper. All you own and even your person are now mine. I am your lord."

Without further adieu, he sat up and began clumsily bunching up her gown until one pure white thigh was exposed. He pulled a wicked looking dagger from his own thigh, normally meant for looks only, and proceeded to pierce the skin of her thigh until a little blood dripped out upon the sheets. Then laughing quietly, he flopped off her onto his side and promptly began to snore, the sound filling up the tense silence of the room.

Alida could not move for the spinning of her head the whole day passing dreamlike before her eyes. Her tongue would not work, and so silently she entreated, "Please God! Let this all be some nightmare that will pass with first light." Her mouth feeling as if it were stuffed with cotton would not even afford the relief of a sob or curse. Alida closed her eyes trying to envision something peaceful and familiar. When she could take no more, she gracelessly fell from the bed woozily gathering up her clothing, dressing as best she could. She continued to fight the scents of the room she was leaving, praying for the cool clarity of the air in a passageway hidden behind a carved chest and tapestry in their room.

When she had entered the passageway and had pulled the heavy door shut, she slumped against the cool stone of the wall, breathing in great gulps of the fresh air. She took some time giving her head a chance to clear. The knowledge that she had been drugged was beginning to seep through the layers of her discomfort and hazy vision. She felt that if she could escape the castle and city for a little while she could clear her head and make order of the day's happenings. She made her way to the stables and saddled up a fine destrier, the grooms all being elsewhere occupied with the celebration at hand. She then headed for the gates of the city shrouded by the heavy fog of an autumn night. She rode for quite a ways watching as the silent countryside slipped by covered in shadow and deep peace. The tumultuous feelings that ripped through her did not match the hushed night. She was remembering the entire day more clearly now and knew that this was no horrid dream but a reality that had been imposed upon her. *How blessed I would be if I could slip into the shadows forever,* she thought silently for there was no way to undo the responses that she had verbally made before the gathered throngs of both clans.

After riding furiously for a ways, she all at once realized she was within a fragrant and familiar glade. She had headed unerringly towards Ulrich's keep without realizing it. Alida ignored the lateness of the hour and her unaccompanied state for her continuing need of movement drove all other thoughts away. Her path drove her onwards towards the imposing walls of Drachmund Heights.

Deep in the shadows of the woods surrounding her, a figure watched her progress, and when it had noted her direction, hastily darted towards the walls that contained a sleeping Ulrich. This figure that deftly wound its way through the woods had come from the hand of Creator and intended that Alida should be briefly detained.

Within the walls of Drachmund Keep, Ulrich sat upright not knowing what had awakened him.

Thinking that it was simply more of the restlessness that had resulted from Alida's wedding, he rose and walked to the window.

He started when he distinctly felt the pull of a hand against his arm urging him away from the window towards the place his clothes were kept. Oddly disconcerted by this otherworldly interference, Ulrich backed towards the hearth gazing intently into the shadows. Feeling foolish that nothing had appeared, he prepared to return to bed, but again he felt a pull against his arm.

"What do you want?" Ulrich spoke aloud, not knowing if he would receive a response.

A whisper along his neck increased to a hum and then a soft voice spoke into the silence. "Mount your horse and ride quickly to your southern-most field."

Without knowing why, Ulrich acknowledged and then obeyed the command. He had felt no maleficence from the presence and intended to understand the mystery whispering a prayer to Creator as he quickly dressed.

Saddling his own mount, he rode silently and swiftly out of his keep and presently the city walls, watching the shadows slip by the warm sides of his horse until up ahead he noted a faint diminutive figure nearly swallowed by the fog. Not knowing who approached, he veered towards the cover of a cove and watched as Alida materialized in front of him. He wanted to call out softly to her for he needed comfort from the immediate turmoil her appearance had caused.

Alida moved forward being unaware of anything other than the fog and her own grogginess and nearly ran into him. She started at his sudden appearance and pulled her mount just out of his reach. Brushing her arms vigorously in the cool air, she tried not to acknowledge the fact that the bumps along her arm were from his presence and not the temperature of the night air. Ulrich made a daunting and dashing figure in the curling mist, his face devoid of expression and his hair and beard mussed from sleep.

"What are you doing here on my land, Alida?" There was no welcome in his voice.

She looked at him uncertainly, wondering if she should have turned back. "Is there a crime against such an appearance?"

"Your keep, kinsman, and new husband would no doubt find it unacceptable." He circled her in a predatory manner, his eyes disconcerting and strange in the misty darkness, the only sound other than his voice coming from the fall of his horses' hooves.

"They have never, nor will they ever be able to control me," she said willfully, her voice shaking ever so slightly. "I ride where I wish and will continue to do so. Don't you think I'll be safer now that many, far and sundry, are aware of my union?" *Lord, he must be drawing closer,* she thought to herself, for suddenly she caught his warm manly scent carried on the circling mists.

"If you could call it a union," Ulrich scoffed. "Surely you would find no communion with one such as Kellen, though I warrant that at such a late hour, a union of sorts has been made!" He fought the hunger her scent caused, swearing to remain hard and unyielding.

Alida blushed hotly and looked away glad of the shroud the fog provided. His voice rang out coldly into the air. "Do not come here again. You will not be welcomed. I do not wish to be reminded at every turn of what could have been. You will always be in my care, for I would not see you harmed, but I will not be forced to see you when naught is at stake." He turned his mount and was preparing to leave when her soft, angry voice stopped him.

"You had as much choice to fight for me as I had to choose you. I thought you a friend, but I guess I was much mistaken. I had perhaps even fancied a greater attachment from your tender caresses and voice. Apparently much was assumed."

Ulrich turned in his saddle and his eyes burned into her with a greater sadness than she had ever seen. Then she too turned away, but her remorse at her comments halted her leave. From deep in her heart, she summoned the only thing she could think of. "I never got a chance to thank you for the lovely hide." When no response was forthcoming from Ulrich, she departed completely the staccato of her horses' hooves ringing in the night air.

Ulrich felt the cloying grasp of the fog close in around him, and his throat constricted painfully. She could not guess how much he felt for her, but as it stood now, they had left on uneasy terms. He no longer had any stake in her or her happiness, and even friendship would be deemed dangerous for she had been made a wife by her own vows this day and by her husband on this night.

His shoulders slumped and he rode back through the enveloping mist. The presence that had watched the exchange from the woods silently hummed with energy and then left for the land of the watchers.

CHAPTER THIRTEEN

BERYNTH, IN THE PROVINCE OF KINTERDEN DELLS

Alida sighed as she looked out on the white landscape below, her face pressed against the frigid windowpane. It had been coming down steadily for the past few days without any sign of decreasing. She loved the snow, but had been ordered by her new husband to remain indoors. She snorted and turned, pressing her face to the cool stone wall instead, not wanting to torture herself any longer with the beauty of the white expanse outside.

It wasn't the first time she'd obeyed a direct order from Kellen. His intent notice of her location through posted guards and tattling servants made it hard for her to roam about. She had no desire to undermine her new husband's authority nor her own protection until she knew the politics of Kinterden better, and so she had decided it prudent to remain under Kellen's rule for the time being.

Without her normal activities to occupy her time, Alida turned to exploration of the castle of Kinterden Dell more thoroughly, for she wasn't even allowed exploration of the city without being escorted by a full guard. So on that day as on many others, she haunted the great hall, the servant's quarters, the wintry gardens, and the deep silent corridors trying to discover the secrets of her new home.

Her exploration eventually brought her round to the kitchens where Kellen's cook, Drichten, was stirring a cauldron of stew. The bustle and warmth of the huge area was comforting to Alida who had not been allowed to continue, upon her marriage to Kellen, her companionship with Deive. He viewed Deive and her powerful presence as a threat to the well-being of his keep and his relationship with Alida. It was because of this severed friendship that Alida was spurred even more to make a connection with other humans. She did not want to find herself uncared for and unmourned at the end of her life. Nor, with every beat of her heart, did she want loneliness in the midst of this portion she'd been forced into knowing. It would undoubtedly span a great many years if her own health and her husband's were any indication.

Alida breathed in the scent of the stew and was pleased to smell sage in its mix, an herb that they seldom used at Falda. After smiling brightly at the cook's hearty wife, Bretta, and asking her permission, she picked up a small, sharp knife and began helping with the preparations for the evening meal. The hearty laughter and stories of the kitchen crew helped the time to disappear and Alida relaxed, surrounded and safe in the midst of these good people.

Later that night as Alida dressed for bed in a soft undergarment of brushed cotton, she turned to find Kellen gazing at her from his huge fireside chair with a peculiar gleam to his eye, though as usual, his eye being devoid of interest in her person. At her raised eyebrows, his voice smoothly echoed out into the room.

"I was informed of how you spent your day, Alida."

"You say that with some distaste, milord. Were you dissatisfied with my occupation? After all, I remained within the keep walls as ordered." She busied herself with folding her clothes, letting the smooth flow of the material beneath her hands soothe her suddenly jangled nerves.

"I don't want you to be so involved with the servants, Alida. The interaction between those of class and training and those no better than slaves is not something desirable at any time, and especially not in the case of my spouse."

At this pronouncement, Alida's mouth turned down and her stance stiffened. "You do not allow me the company of my oldest companion and only living close relative, you restrict my activities indoors, and you disallow my connection with your servants and kinsmen. What exactly do you expect me to do with my time and energy?" She fought to keep the last note of voice even though she felt like screeching at him.

"First, my dear, I don't disallow your interaction with my kinsmen, only your interaction with my servants. Second, you are a woman, and one of sound enough mind. Can you not occupy yourself with the wifely duties of overseeing the keep maids in waiting, sewing, attending to my comfort, and planning festivities? Oh, and let us not forget the most important pursuit, that of becoming a mother." He gazed intently at her.

Alida suppressed a shudder at being reminded of the farce of their intimacies. "Milord, I cannot attend to your comfort, the keep, or to the planning of events without interacting with and having the complete cooperation of the servants. In addition, I have found that your keep managers are unwilling to take orders from me as they continually speak of what you yourself have already directed. Similarly, I find no common ground with your kinsmen and kinswomen for they sneer and laugh constantly over my mannerisms."

"And as to the last occupation, Alida? What is your answer for that?" His gaze sharpened. "It's only appropriate that you grow fat with my seed." He rose and approached her, acting as if her arguments over her interactions with the servants had never existed.

He roughly pulled her into the iron circle of his arms, pressing her against his still-clothed body.

The restriction and discomfort of the last few weeks boiled up suddenly within Alida. She'd had enough to last a lifetime. "How can you claim that we are anywhere near producing a child! How could you be so blind! Not once have you visited my bed!" Then seeing his expression, she sighed, forcing back her anger as well as making herself relax in his tight grip. "You prefer the company of men, and I find your absolute denial of this fact as well as the banal assumptions of your kinsfolk about our "passionate love" exhausting. How can I become fat with your offspring when your attentions do not belong to me but to your own captain of the guard!"

The flushed look of embarrassment upon his visage immediately turned into rage, and he pushed her from him like a distasteful piece of refuse. "You wench! Do not ever mention such accusations to me again. You think yourself above me? I am not a fool, Alida! I have seen your look of distaste over everything that represents me and my domain. I have seen you blush deeply when you've overheard the servants sniggering at your viability as a woman, for no one knows that each night, I come to your room but then occupy myself with other activities while here. They assume the lack of a child is the fault of the foreign woman with the "odd mannerisms". I will not worry myself over the rumors and misinformation of vassals that only aid me at this time, and I will not tolerate my own wife spitting her venom at me from her glorious throne!" With that, his hand came down across her face with such force that she was knocked to the ground.

Infuriated, Alida was immediately in a crouching attack position, her eyes fixed on her abuser. Unaware of her vulnerability in her nearly naked state, Alida snatched up the nearest weapon and lunged at him nicking his arm with the tip of the knife blade. His own anger became his weapon, and he nimbly sidestepped her second lunge, casting her down again with a fist to her midsection. His boot then was sent into her ribs, and he fisted her upside her head once again before desisting.

Alida lay on the ground, her breath coming in shallow puffs as she concentrated on staying conscious. Somewhere in the haze above her, she saw Kellen's face float into sight. He leaned very close to her ear and whispered. "I am not as lame as you have thought me, Alida. You threatened once to kill me if I ever mishandled you again. It was a mistake, for you were overly brave and I much too consoling, thinking you to be a delicate little thing. The truth is this, if you ever mention this topic again to my face or to my servants and kinsmen, *I* will kill *you*. Women are weak; 'tis no wonder that I prefer the company of men!" With those words, his hand came across her face again, and she felt the blackness fight her continuing attempt to remain awake.

After some time had passed, Alida gingerly sat up feeling consciousness return. Her stomach was throbbing and sore and her head was roundly covered in bruises, but thankfully, there were no broken bones. She gradually made her way to the pallet where her partially folded clothes lay in a discarded pile having been ignored in the heat of their argument. She was able to dress, although somewhat wobbly and then rose, cleaning out blood from her mouth with a cloth and pitcher of water, fighting down the urge to vomit when her hand bumped against a loosened tooth. When she could stand no longer, she carefully lay down upon her bed falling into a deep, dreamless bout of sleep, her body curled in a fetal position.

When the night was in its coldest, darkest hour, Alida awoke feeling the sharp, wintry chill of the room pervade her senses. She groggily snuggled down under the available furs and linens pushing something from her mind. A whisper caressed her ear immediately chasing away the lingering cobwebs of sleep. The night's events came back to her in sharp detail, and she felt a rush of tears rise from deep within her gut.

Quietly, with as little movement as possible, she arose and tread softly to the window. Her room was far above the snow-covered streets of the city and had a good view of the dells beyond the walls, where a huge winter moon cast its cold white light.

As she had earlier that day, she laid her head on the smooth stone and began to pray softly. "Creator, why have I been brought to such a place? There is much I have had to suffer and none of it without its purpose. So with that belief, to what is the purpose of this new insanity? What do you expect me to learn? Why do you not simply save me from the hand of the wicked, from those who despise your law?"

She breathed softly, allowing her prayer to be diffused in the silence. Then she felt the same caress that had brought her into wakefulness moments before.

In a breath of light that came softly from the corners of the room, Lordifyn, her guardian spirit, stood before her smiling tenderly. "Creator says that you have endured much, though not of His choosing. The evil that walks about this land remains because of the choice of the weak and lustful humans around you. You were able to direct your path and may still do so, as may all who follow Him by obeying His will. Do not be afraid of loneliness or of making your own way. You are a gift, Alida. Kellen is small and not a part of the greater plan. Trust in this."

Alida reached out with everything within herself, seeking reassurance and searching for grains of faith within her spirit that might yet still glow with the fire of Truth. Then the calming warm fingers of Lordifyn brushed across her face instantly dissipating any fears she had, for he was comprised of the same light and joy that infused his master.

The next morning, Kellen smugly strode up to the head trestle table expecting a docile and meek wife. Shock registered on his face, for Alida, despite the bruised discoloration of her features, sat looking more vibrant and strong than ever before. Her level gaze into his eyes shook him more deeply than any argument or hateful behavior she may have employed.

Alida upon seeing his discomfiture had a revelation. This man before her could control neither his desire nor his rage for he was utterly consumed by his wickedness. She regretted in some part her angry words to him if only for the bruises left behind on her body and confidence, but she also realized that no matter her words or lack thereof, at some point he would have become enraged at some petty thing making her his target. This was in part a game of strategy and bluff between them. She saw his intent to overcome her with her own fear that he might somehow be more assured of his own strength.

The nights following found Alida cool and watchful beneath the forceful attempts of her husband to tame her by disparaging words, mocking imitation, and bullying. She gave him no further cause for violence, and in doing so, proved her own dominance. For despite the grave difficulty of it, she had mastered her own tongue, seldom saying anything to him except for the mundane things of "Could you pass me the platter?" or "Would you be so kind as to hand me the salt?" When his attempts at stirring up her anger failed, like a dog with its tail between its legs, he crawled away in shame leaving her to her own devices for the better part of a month.

Glad of her freedom from him and with little cajoling to his guard, Alida began to once again trek out into the city and upon the open plain, a borrowed and fine destrier beneath her. She had won the game for the time being, and victory was sweet, for she obeyed him by never venturing out alone nor becoming overly involved with any one keepsman; and yet her freedom she had gained. In crunching notes of triumph that matched her joy, the horses' hooves on the snow beneath her merrily danced out the very rhythm of her heart from day to day.

━━━━━━━━━━━━━━━━━━━━━━━━━━━━━

Ulrich saw this confident and wiser woman while he hunted in the woods adjoining his and Kellen's property. He had not seen her in such a long while that he was breathless when he realized it was her before him. He proceeded to flank her, unobtrusively watching her go about the duties of a much-privileged wife. Though he was concealed from her view, he felt stripped naked by her presence.

At one point, her visage was turned his direction as she spoke to a herdsman between the two of them. He was astounded at the depth of maturity and growth he saw in her eyes. He was also greatly saddened, for now he saw how completely she'd been removed from his realm. If he had seen some of the girl still in her stance or expressions, he would have been relieved, but the woman that he saw before him lacked any of the flirtatious spontaneity he remembered.

His irritation and sadness were sharpened when Kellen rode up behind

Alida, startling her mount and nearly causing the beast to throw her. There was a perverse pleasure displayed boldly in the man's eyes at the discomfiture of his wife. *Surely,* thought Ulrich, she *couldn't be happy with this man. What a waste to give such a glorious prize to such a fiend.* Regardless of the happiness or lack thereof in their marriage, she was bound to him now.

In a show of further belligerence, Kellen deliberately placed the heaving warm sides of his mount in between Alida and the herdsman, cutting her off from any conversation. With a small salute and sardonic smile, Alida bid the herdsman goodbye, her horse springing back from the contact with Kellen's mount before prancing forward to her whistled command. Kellen could interfere all he liked, for her business with the herdsman had been nearly complete. Her orders to the man had long since been carried out and this was a confirmation meeting only.

All day long beneath the bright but weak warmth of the sun, Alida and her mount made their way through deep drifts and snowy fields conversing with those who made their living regardless of the weather. Despite the cold that sought to invade her bones and the damp chill of her boots that were soaked from the snow kicked up by her mount, she queried about the strength of stock holdings through trade and was surprised that, although vain and selfish, Kellen was a frugal manager. All the villagers, herdsman, and farmers near Kinterden would be cared for during the long winter ahead. She was quiet, strong, and organized and because good word of her had come from the city and castle help, many were willing to answer her softly directed inquiries.

Kellen was always one step behind her and eventually at mid-morning gave up that day's chase and annoyance of her for a rowdy pre-planned hunt with his warriors. Calling Alida's guard to his side Kellen excitedly told the man of the upcoming hunt and then gave Alida strict instructions to finish her rounds as soon as possible and return to the city walls before sunset. He feared little for her life. Actually, if the truth be known, he was hoping somewhere in his dark heart that she would die and leave him to his life and the new fortunes represented by the desirable alliances that had come with her. The guard was placed with her on all occasions merely for the sake of propriety and as a display of Kellen's power. It served as well, the joint purpose of annoying her for he knew how much she valued an unfettered freedom. Besides, he reasoned to himself, the villages that she visited were always within view of the guards on the city walls.

Ulrich haunted Alida's trail all day, watching as she made the rounds with ease and confidence. She was so beautiful in her heavy woolen tunic and soft white fur boots that he could not keep his eyes from her for more than a moment.

As the day lengthened and as duties were completed, Alida felt a need for the comfort of a warm bath. Between the strenuous ride through the snow and her handling of various livestock to check their health, her woolen undergarments had begun to stick to her skin the chill of her sweat making the cold even worse. She rode away from the last group of farmers and headed for the line along the woods, which would lead her back to the impressive facade of Kinterden proper.

It was then, that she recalled a story amongst the keep inhabitants of a series of hot springs hidden somewhere within the fragrant fir groves surrounding the keep. With a glimmer of a smile on her face, Alida decided that a little exploration would be the perfect end to the day. Her discomfort was shortly forgotten, and she patted her horse's neck encouraging his play in the snow.

Ulrich watched as she kicked her steed into a canter, while veering off sharply into the ice-jeweled firs of the surrounding forest. All around them, the snow twinkled from the strong boughs of magnificent old trees while frost choked streams tinkled out lyrical tunes. Ulrich did not take in the sights or sounds of the winter laden forests for he was more focused upon the greater beauty that rode just ahead of him.

Alida was also intent on her path and mission, gazing piercingly into the glades and coves, keeping alert for the sounds of water or abundant wildlife. The soft clipped hoofbeats of her mount on the frozen ground was a particularly merry sound to her ears, which had not heard the music of any wild places in months.

All at once, she came upon a wall of steely grey granite that rose impressively from the ground of the forest. This gave her the choice only of heading left or right. She paused in uncertainty for a moment and headed left.

Behind her, Ulrich had dropped back enough to remain unobtrusive and did not see that she headed left. Therefore, when he approached the granite, he decided to turn right for the way was more noticeably cleared.

Alida followed the wall of granite as the woods closed in around her. Presently, she came to a dead end where the bracken and granite closed off any further hope of continuing. She turned her mount and sat for a moment deciding what to do next. Just then, with a popping crack, a small hare ran helter-skelter from the bracken at the base of the granite.

Alida calmed her horse that had danced forward nervously with muscles bunching at the furry creature's intrusion. It was soon after she had quieted her fractious destrier, that she heard it—the soft bubbling music of running water. She smiled to herself thinking that a spring nearby would be inaccessible. Apparently, the rumors of hot springs did not include the little detail that they were unreachable beneath stone and bracken. She dismounted easily, finding purchase in the snow-crisp grass around her mount's feet, holding out little hope that she could see the source of the spring.

After a bit of frustrated searching, she noticed a section of bracken that rose up the wall of granite. She disengaged her dirk from its holster and carelessly whacked away at the edges of the thick growth, all the while breathing in the smell of cold stone and winter laden vegetation. It was then that a blast of balmy warm air rushed out at her. She crossed over to her mount and retrieved some heavy gloves from the saddlebags hurriedly pulling on the stiff leather before moving back into position near the wall of bracken.

From the opposite direction, a very frustrated Ulrich rode on looking intently at the ground finding it sadly devoid of any footprints or sign of disturbance. He soon gave up the path knowing that even with her skills Alida could not leave so light a trail. He turned his horse and rode back the way he had come deciding he would take the left branch after all, as it might divulge her whereabouts.

He passed the junction once again heading left this time and was pleased to see hoofprints and activity along the way. When he reached the same wall of bracken that Alida had come upon, he was dismayed, for the rider and horse he'd been following had apparently disappeared. He ran his hands through his heavy golden hair, agitation clear in his bunched muscles. Surely, she had not the time to head back down the path and out of the forest before he had come to this place. He had not passed her, did not see retreating hoofprints, nor heard the sound of her leaving.

He dismounted and searched around the path, his eyes detecting no sign that she had dared to make her way through the choking underbrush. Then he noticed some markings along the granite wall where chips had been struck from the smooth moss covered surface. He ran his bare hand over the cold, rough stone puzzling that the marks were like those from a knife blade.

Back at the castle, a returning Kellen searched high and low for Alida, having heard from the villagers and farmers that they'd seen her head back for the high imposing walls of the city. When his search came up empty, he called for his hunting companions. His orders were clear.

"Search the city and all corners of the keep. If we cannot find her and if no one divulges her whereabouts, we will search the surrounding fields. She's bound to be somewhere nearby, for too little time has transpired for her to have gotten far or for some mishap to have befallen her." With that, his companions were dismissed, along with their questions about why he was so anxious to find her.

That little wench, he thought to himself. He'd not put up with her treating him as she had her aunt. He was not so very tame. Then a horrid thought occurred to him. Perhaps she was dallying with one of his kinsmen or warriors. His mouth turned down at the thought, for nothing was more precious than his ego. Her lack of ardor for him could easily be the result of a well-satisfied appetite. If she were in love with someone else, the natural result would also be resentment towards her spouse. He assumed that however odious his behavior as a man, women around him would swoon nonetheless. He did not have a need for a woman's passion but it usefully stoked his needy ego confirming his position as lord.

He paced the floor endlessly until his men returned, all of them innocently unaware of her location. He dismissed the lot of them with no outward sign of his agitation having ever been visible in the guards' presence and then decided to wait out her return. She would be back under his surveillance after this escapade. This time he really did wish her dead for it was troublesome to have to keep track of her.

Blissfully unaware of the commotion she had caused, Alida explored the little, warm green glade she had found. It was surrounded on all sides by granite, and she suspected that over time the warm springs and their resulting streams had worn down the rock until a valley of sorts was formed. The resulting granite bowl had filled with dirt and debris from the forest until windblown seeds could find a place of rest and take root in the rich topsoil.

She was charmed, too, by the carpet of soft, fragrant green grass, which was nourished by the mineral rich springs and balmy warmth trapped within the glade by the bowl-shaped walls of granite. All of it amounted to a beautiful place where chortling birds and creatures had remained untouched for a long time. She would keep it to herself.

She took off her damp boots and dipped her feet into the water, relishing in its bubbling warmth.

From across the cove, Ulrich cautiously intruded, his eyes and ears alert for signs of Alida. It had taken very little time to pull back the loosened bracken from the wide crevice in the granite and enter the small bowl-like valley.

He halted his progression when he caught sight of her mount clipping away at the delicious grass around the pools, not wanting to alert the steed to his presence. Movement of any kind, however, not only halted but became impossible when he caught sight of his forest sprite with her hair innocently unbound while sitting on the bank of the largest pool. She had removed her outer tunics as well leaving only her under tunics in place and was washing her bared arms and shoulders with the hot water of the pools. He forced movement back into his legs, turning away and fleeing the clearing, his cheeks flaming at the forbidden desire that her wonderful tresses and bared limbs had stirred in his gut.

He mounted his horse quickly and rode away, for his temptation to stay was alarmingly strong. As he rode, he whispered a prayer to Creator. In response, a soft voice whispered, "Patience."

He snorted. T'was not a matter of patience, for who knew when he would have a wife of his own. He could not picture marrying anyone except Alida, but this gave him no cause to covet another man's glory. He knew the sight of her and the sound of her as he knew his own breath. Saddened by a desire he could not fulfill and by his own peculiar loneliness, he rode like the wind back to the place where he could mindlessly occupy his time, his breath coming in great gulps at the exertion of controlling his spirited mount to which he'd given leeway after exiting the forest. He would do well to continue in self-imposed oblivion rather than torture himself with the sights and sounds of his neighbor's wife.

After soaking her feet for far too short a time, Alida clothed herself and replaced the natural door to the valley, heading back to the harsh reality of her husband and his keep, innocently unaware that she had been the disruption to more than one man that day.

When Alida breezed through the castle doors shortly after the sun had begun its final descent, Kellen was there to meet her. He sat at the head of the main trestle table before the crackling fire with one leg casually thrown over the arm of his massive oak chair.

His eyes looked piercingly into hers as though he could read her thoughts. Then in one fluid movement, he rose and took her arm in a tight grasp pulling her none too gently towards their quarters, his booted heels clicking on the pavers of the castle stairs.

After stalking through their door and slamming it forcefully behind them with his boots continuing to ring out his agitation, he stalked to their pallet with Alida firmly in tow. He then proceeded to pin her down, strip her, and silence her, all without one single uttered word, his bulk and strength far exceeding hers.

Alida thought she knew what was coming. He surprised her, however, when he let her loose and went for her discarded clothes. She stared at him with questioning eyes, watching as he brought her clothes, both outer and under tunics and subsequently her cloak to his nose. He seemed disappointed by whatever findings he'd garnished.

Alida shivering in the chill of the room ground out through nearly closed teeth. "What on earth are you doing, Kellen? You are acting insane."

He pointed at her with a stout finger, his voice barely on the edge of control. "I am going to ask you a question and by the gods you'd better give me a truthful answer!" Then he grasped her arm, pulling her to him until they could feel one another's breath. "Are you someone's mistress?"

Alida's jaw dropped. "What are you talking about?"

"Answer me, you wench! Where were you this afternoon? I mean it all follows, because why else would you think me so far beneath thee! I can figure only one possible answer!"

Alida shut her mouth tight, her lips burning with the pressure she put on them and her gaze locked with his. All the good intentions and progress of her tight-lipped mouth failed her in that moment. She pulled back from him as far as she was able and then slapped him as hard as she could across his cheek, the air ringing with the sound of the slap. "You are a paranoid fiend. I was out riding after having been contained within these walls for the last few months by *you* and *your* insanity. I even returned by the time *you* appointed if you'll take the time to remember our parting conversation! I am bound by our vows and would not seek out anyone else, though only Creator knows how many times I've been tempted to do just that! For as many hindrances have come against this union, I would keep myself to you and you alone as vowed. As to my disdain, I thought I already made my feelings known! Once again, however, it seems you are determined to place all the fault of this farce of a union at my feet!"

The bellow that rose from his throat drowned out anything else she would have said. Months of his maddening relationship with her, her power and calm and his contrived loss of face with family and the people of his domain rose like a beast within him. All of the wrongs he'd imagined of her and every excuse he could pin to her existence mocked at him as things living and real. He grabbed her arms, and pinning them to her sides, he slammed his head into her jaw.

He then proceeded, like an animal, to beat his wife once again with his meaty fists. He had just grasped her by her hair, ready to rip it from its roots, when his courier burst through the door.

"Milord, forgive my intrusion, but you must come at once! Castle Lyrnne has been attacked and is almost overcome! A dispatch from within their walls has been sent with a desperate plea for aid."

The raging light in Kellen's eyes died down and releasing his battered wife, he slipped into the role of commanding officer with coolly spoken orders as if nothing amiss had just occurred.

CHAPTER FOURTEEN

Deive, thinking about Alida, stood with her face toward the rays of the setting sun, when she saw the first wave of darkly clothed soldiers pour over the dells towards the walls of the city. From her height, they looked like a length of black linen held taut and then shaken in the hands of a brisk breeze. Even the sound of the army was like the crisp snapping of newly washed and starched fabric at the mercy of a fierce breeze.

Within moments, the advancing warriors shouting outside of the walls had gained on the fleeing forms of badly trained foot soldiers and villagers who had been caught unprotected outside of Lyrnne, the gates of the city not yet having fully closed. Deive's horror moved her legs into motion, and from the corner of her eye, she saw the screaming inhabitants of Lyrnne cut down in their tracks.

With her purple robes rising like wings behind her, Deive rushed down into the halls of the keep. She veered off to her quarters, gathering up a small dirk and her bag of healing herbs. Many other times in her life, under similar situations, Deive had gathered up her amulet bag as well as the other two, but she had learned from Alida that there was a greater power to be tapped. Such power did not require useless stones and idle gods but went directly to the source that was available through simple prayer and faith.

So pray she did, with all faith, as she helped warriors and servants alike in barring the doors to the castle and lighting the emergency lamps with a roar of fuel and fire. Nervously, the good men and women of Lyrnne attended to other necessities such as secreting away castle treasures, but their jobs were done out of duty alone. Though she encouraged all of them to rally to the task, she could feel their lack of optimism for they had seen the insignia of the circling serpent and knew that Quirin's deadly army was upon them.

While helping to secure the keep, Deive had the presence of mind to send out a courier to Kinterden Dell. They would need reinforcements against such a raid, for the Father knew that the true mistress of the keep was in no mind to handle such preparations herself.

It was probably for the best, that in the midst of her preparations Deive was unable to see the hordes of malevolent spirits that had been poured out amongst the city and keep inhabitants and the battling forces of the two armies. They had been sent to induce their victims to greater destruction and had she been given spiritual insight, she, too, may have quavered in her faith even as her comrades were now tempted to do. The nasty fiends bit already agitated beasts causing the steeds of Quirin's army to lash out with flailing hooves and teeth. Quirin himself smiled maliciously as he watched a particularly slimy creation lap up the anger pouring from one of his men for he had spent many years learning to conjure sight for the greater spiritual battle that raged about them. After slashing at some heavily armed keepsmen around him, while thoroughly enjoying their screams of death, he returned focus on seeking out Deive. With the aid of his magic, he was once again able to watch her as if through a portal while she scurried about securing the keep and commanding a smaller band of warriors.

His blood leapt hotly at the sight of Deive. He would not be overcome before wresting her away from the safety of this keep. The smells of raging fires being set throughout the city and the more sickly sweet scent of blood spurred his insane intent all the more, for this hell in the making was as close to paradise as he could dream.

From between the cracks of the slowly closing doors and windows, Deive observed the sinister, rage-filled faces of his lustful followers for his was no ordinary army. She unexpectedly shivered knowing the cause of this raid. It was Quirin's mad lust for her. Seeking to chase away the chill, she continued in her stream of urgent prayers not knowing that with each word an army of hungry protectors from Creator himself was amassing to swallow their spiritual counterparts from Quirin's mass. Unlike the night of the prenuptial party for Alida, she was not given any special word from Creator in order to call forth His warriors, for she was praying within faith alone, having only her belief in her God above that they would be saved.

─────────────────────────────

At Kinterden Dell, Alida remained on the floor only long enough for Kellen to gather his clothes and leave. When the door had closed behind him and his men, Alida rose, and with haste she dressed her throbbing, battered body in a man's tunic, leggings, and cloak, caring only about Deive and the safety of the other Lyrnne inhabitants. She had not been privy to the details from the courier having only overheard the portion of the dispatch uttered in the room and now feared that too much time was passing since the original message.

She took a series of cold, dark hallways and coves keeping out of Kellen's sight, should he linger to make more preparations. The iron taste of blood seeped into her mouth for he had managed at one point to split her lip, but she chose to ignore it along with the occasional flux of bile that threatened to overtake her from the sickening pain in her bones. When she finally entered the courtyard, she was relieved that the majority of the Kinterden warriors, along with their leader, had left. The remaining guard was so preoccupied that they failed to notice her light form as it slipped along in the shadows to the outer yards and busy stables.

As was usual in war, the servants and guard that were left behind busied themselves with securing the massive keep against intruders. It was understood that if one was close enough to be considered an ally, one was also close enough to be attacked. Amidst the flurry of activity, she collected an already saddled steed, which was left behind with others for the use of a messenger or other such necessity. Alida took the animal without conscience, for she considered her mission most urgent. She was on her way to aid the last person she considered family. The beast went quietly along with her, the clink of his bridle and stirrups soothing to her jangled nerves. The hood of her cloak hid enough of her features that she could be any servant leading the gelding's stamping bulk out of the keep and into the city.

Though she could have followed the trail of the Kinterden warriors, Alida veered off taking a quicker and more secretive route a little to the south once she was free of the city walls.

Much later, in the nearby forests of Lyrnne, a frothing steed and his sturdy rider darted through rain-scented cove and bracken, the rapidly moving form like a wraith in the darkness. The hooded creature on horseback was an intense and dangerous intrusion upon the perimeter guard set by Quirin. These sentries were of spirit not of flesh and knew power when they smelled it. They, unlike their human allies, were more aware of her indomitable spirit than her physical size, for she was a force to be reckoned with. Her knowledgeable eyes glared straight into theirs—a most unexpected advantage for her—for they had not been warned of any sorceress or conjurer that may know of their presence other than Quirin. Too late several of the little guards watched as spears of silver spirit flowed from her mouth and shot them through with the painful burning light of Creator—the spears formed of God's own Word.

Alida, now accompanied by Lordifyn, continued to strike down the unaware spirits she came upon with her whispered prayers, for she knew that each conquered evil was a boon to their cause. The particularly powerful spirit allies that formed under Lordifyn's command performed independently without her request, following the orders of their higher command. Quirin remained unaware of her approach, for not one of his sentries from that sector survived to bring him a message.

Meanwhile, human defenders of Lyrnne fought valiantly against Quirin's voracious army. Their weapons flashed in the light of raging fires, the maddening clangs echoing out into the dark chaotic streets of the city. Occasionally, a warrior of Lyrnne would gain purchase cutting down Quirin's men, but he could not outdo the angry tirade of greedy, skillful swords and hungry, dominant eyes, for they had been long without training. Savine had been greatly disinterested in the military needs of her lands.

Had this same mistress been in her right mind, she would not have so easily dismissed the sight of a slim man making his way through the secret passage in which she now stood. The passage lay near her chamber, and as had become her wont, she was more preoccupied with talking to herself and preening over the dim reflection that came from a shield hung on the hallway wall than in focusing on the world around her. All thoughts of the trouble raging beyond the walls of the castle were driven from her mind by vanity and insanity alike.

All over the city and around the keep walls, battles raged between flesh and spirit warriors. Bodies were hewn asunder, great pools of blood spreading out from them over the trampled ground like oil from broken pitchers. Alida made her way through a hidden door outside the walls, sickened that the warfare had found its way so far into the battlements of the city compound, having encroached to the castle itself. She was buoyed by adrenaline alone, the screams and guttural calls of war her battle song.

Adroitly avoiding skewered bodies, Alida crept up to an open side door of the keep walls, knowing Quirin's men had used it. She leaned over a slain guardsman, feeling his flesh for warmth. He had been dead for over an hour judging by the lukewarm touch of his sweat-slicked skin. Alida mentally shook away the guilt she felt at not having been more help, for she had responded as quickly as possible, but the messenger sent from Lyrnne had not reached them until well past sundown. Adding together distance as well as the delays necessary for gathering men and battle-gear to the total time needed for Quirin's encroachment equaled the grim calculation that the survival of interior keepsmen and women was slim, if even existent. With a great intake of breath, Alida preceded into the darkened hallway, her heart pounding against her ribs with every step.

The farther into the keep she ventured, the dimmer the sounds of the battle outside became. She concentrated more deeply on the small sounds around her that were growing distinct in the relative silence and musky gloom. Here and there, she could hear a shout or cry but the most noticeable sound was that of hurried feet and rustling garments. She also used her inner sight given by Creator to peruse the spiritual condition of the keep, and in doing so, she caught sight of a tiny silver spirit that whisked by her with worried, little eyes frowning into hers. Alida recognized it as one of Deive's escorts.

Suddenly, Alida ducked as a whistling blade cut the air above her head. The hairs atop her head fluttered back into place as she instinctively unsheathed her own weapon and struck out in the dark. Lordifyn, at the order of Creator, made her strike more sure, and she felt flesh close in around her blade, a curse being drawn from her victim. Withdrawing her sword, she again struck out, this time thrusting forward with her feet well planted. She did not know if her first blow had been enough to bring down her enemy, for her physical sight was impaired by the darkness. This time her blade met the sucking constraints of flesh, and as a testament to the deadliness of her strike, she felt a warm cascade of blood over her hand. The sword had impaled the enemy to its hilt and did not come free easily. Alida grunted and strained, pulling with all her might. As she struggled, her muscles complaining at the force, a man approached with a dimly lit torch, his face a mask of fury in the cold, flickering shadows.

Alida gave one more try, but her sword remained partially encased by the corpse. She was forced to abandon it when Quirin's approaching warrior swung his own weapon in a mighty arch meant to decapitate her.

Rolling off to the side and retrieving the slain warrior's heavier blade, she made herself ready for battle. She continued to be greatly hampered by the shadows, the torch of the warrior causing no steady light. What light was given by his meager torch, soon went out all together as the beastly lamp lacked fuel. Alida prayed that the darkness would be overcome by light. A score of tiny spirit beings answered her call. Then with blessing's kiss, no further effort was needed, for Alida watched as the man with the torch crumpled to his knees, a great sword stuck into his bony back and a look of surprise on his face at the sudden illumination of the hall behind him. A winded servant of the keep reached around the slain bodies for her hand. Then together the two of them removed her blade from Quirin's man.

Alida briefly inspected her weapon while the servant next to her insisted that they leave at once. Alida, intent on her blade, cleaned the blood channel of its blockage of entrails and blood. The servant paled at the sight and swallowed back bile at her cool handling of the sword and the choking stench of death that lay heavily around them. He shifted nervously from foot to foot as he began to realize that she was not intending to leave. His voice cracked in argument as she calmly instructed him to take her horse outside of the walls. When she stepped forward, pressing the point of her sword to his chest, he agreed to ride hard to let her husband's keep know that the battle had progressed to the stages of encroachment and that the interior had been compromised. He would allow guilt to overcome him later at having left the next heir of Lyrnne to her own devices.

With a wobbly salute, the servant darted off towards the side exit, and Alida grimly proceeded with her search. When she had begun to ascend the steeply cut staircase leading to the private chambers, she happened upon a few wounded soldiers of Quirin's army. She was enraged when the men begged for her mercy, when they had given none to others. In response, she cleanly removed their heads from their bodies while Lordifyn dispatched their unclean spirits.

When she had rounded the last bend of the staircase, her neck began to prickle for the heavy odor of smoke had filled the halls of the private quarters. She fought her way down the corridor, and through the thick shield of smoke, and saw Savine weaving down the hallway with the back of her tunic and hair on fire. She was babbling madly about shadows creeping up the staircase and evil perched on her windowsill, all the while thrashing at her wild hair with frantic hands. Alida ran to her and threw her to the ground trying to put out the fire by rolling her aunt's thrashing body. Suddenly, Savine sat up with her back stiff and struck out with claw like hands at Alida's face, her sharp nails drawing a stinging payment from Alida's cheek.

"You little wench, you have destroyed everything I have! You are nothing but the misbegotten offspring of a weak line. The child of a worthless fool who could not keep himself from between the legs of your cursed witch mother. I shall destroy you."

Rising to her knees, she lunged towards Alida with a horribly triumphant grimace, then as suddenly as she had raged, she grew very still and a ghastly little smile slithered over her features. "I shan't be the one to punish you after all, for here comes your demise now. See the little black darlings as they come for you?"

Alida swiftly turned her head, and through a flash of falcon's inner sight, saw a crawling mass of black-red fiends covering the walls and floor while approaching rapidly. However, instead of harming Alida, they covered Savine moving through her mouth, burnt head, and chest like she was made of water. The attack was complete, for as Alida stood by in horror, the writhing mass ripped Savine's soul from her chest and carried it screaming into the night. Savine's empty body lay staring up into the swirling fumes never to move again.

Alida vomited at the dark sight of her aunt's final demise, the sickly smell of burnt flesh and hair adding to her nausea. Lordifyn, knowing that Alida must gather her wits or be destroyed, touched her shoulder, bringing her to her senses with a hot flow of adrenaline. Alida, wiping her mouth and brushing away tears that had sprung to her eyes at the horror before her, forced her eyes off her dead aunt, while trying to concentrate once again on the task before her. By now, the smoke was so thick that Alida could not see more than a foot in front of her. How would she find Deive? Which way should she go? Despite Lordifyn's protection, a rush of fiends descended on Alida and a tiny fiend of fear slipped through the whistle of his blade along with two companions. Alida tried to shake off the sudden chilling anxiety that the fiend had brought, while making a halfhearted attempt to decipher her location. When she began to feel despair and loneliness seep into her marrow, she cried out, all of her being searching for God. Then as a soft reply, the familiar form of Lordifyn appeared to her, for her inner sight came only in times of stress or when bidden by her falcon form. Lordifyn plucked away the offending fiends and took Alida's hand, leading her from the engulfed corridor and back down into the main hall.

Alida fell to her knees on the warm, stone floor and coughed violently at the burn that had entered her lungs from the smoke and fumes. While her head was downcast, Lordifyn disappeared and Alida was once again alone her momentary discernment gone. Though she wanted desperately to lie awhile upon the ground, Alida struggled to her feet, and on wobbly legs headed for the shattered, oaken entry doors knowing that the blazing keep could soon crash down around her.

As she made her way through the portal, wiping sweat and soot from her forehead, she caught sight of a strip of purple cloth caught on the jagged, oaken edge. Alida snatched it from its perch, and when she was safe out in the cool air of the yard, she fingered the soft, singed edges of the cloth, for it was indeed a bit of Deive's cloak. Alida's head came up searching the grounds with bloodshot eyes as if she could see her friend who by all rights was probably long gone.

Deeply ensconced in wintry fog, Drachmund Heights was safe from the carnage that took place not far from its borders. In the dark center of the castle, Ulrich lay in heavy slumber.

Somewhere into the midst of his dreams, a beautiful figure called his name. The form was raven-haired with dark, almond-shaped eyes and moved with the grace of the ancients. The fact that he wore the costume of those gone before confirmed Ulrich's assumption of the being's age.

In the smoky silence of his dream, he watched fascinated as the figure approached him. At first his beauty and carriage mesmerized Ulrich, but when he saw the warning in the dark eyes, he broke out into a sweat. Something was wrong, and this was more than a dream. The figure whispered to him with a voice weighty in urgency then instantly disappeared. Left in his wake was an image of the screaming visage of Alida and Deive.

Ulrich came fully awake, his moist skin cooling slowly in the crisp air. He jumped from his pallet and dressed as quickly and quietly as possible, shivering from the sweat that still rolled down his back. There was something deep in his gut that told him he would not forgive himself any inactivity on this night, despite the fact that his only prod to leave was a hazy illusion and an old bond to two women of an enemy keep.

He mounted the broad, warm back of Titan quickly, without the sleepy groom so much as asking a wayward question. His stable hands had learned not to inquire overly much of their master.

Once out of the fog and away from the dangerous crevices of Drachmund Heights' craggy sides, Ulrich whipped Titan into a steady gallop. He would not waste any time. His stomach churned at the thought that Alida could be harmed, for far in the distance he could see a strange, red-orange glow.

He rode furiously over the snow-covered dells, his mount lathering beneath him from the exertion. The closer he came to his destination, the more the hair at the back of his neck prickled and danced. All at once he was close enough to see that Lyrnne as a whole was being eaten by a huge blaze. He could barely discern dark shapes that were escaping from the heat, the light from the fire tricking his normally piercing vision. He watched as the figures headed for the open dells, when all at once the intruding sounds of war rang out from the plain below him. It came as a deluge carried on the throbbing heartbeat of drums, screams, and bugling of war chargers.

He pulled out his blade as he paused a moment on the crest of the hill readying himself for the crazed sights, smells, and vigor of battle. By the bunching of his steed's sinews, Titan was also readying himself.

He had just settled more fully into the wooden saddle when a blade came whistling by his ear, an instinct born of battles past causing him to jerk away just in time. He sprang into action, responding with a swiping blow, all at once disappointed when his blade caught nothing but air. The mounted rider that had engaged him in battle rode down upon him once again, the stringy hair and red eyes oddly appropriate in the nasty glow of the fallen city below.

Ulrich raised his own blade and his tired foe was soon easily dispatched, for though there was fury in the other man's eyes, his body could not match Ulrich's practiced strength.

Soon Ulrich found himself in the patterned song of battle, his muscles heaving and buckling as he hacked his way through a mob of sweating warriors. He represented a pure magnificence in the eerie glow of the burning keep and the stranger glow of the supernatural. He was metallic and immovable, with golden hair glowing like a beacon in the night.

It was the sight of Ulrich's glorious aura that caught Quirin's eye as the sorcerer easily carried Deive's limp form into the dark shadows of the Lyrnne's forests. Quirin ordered the specters, which were his personal guard, into action against this new and dangerous force. He would protect himself with his strongest wards and power, for he did not trust the bright light of the mounted warrior.

Alida, having escaped first the keep and then the city when she saw that the blaze was spreading, found her strength renewed by the purple cloth she grasped in her grimy fist. She had to get to Deive no matter the cost. She allowed herself to begin the change into falcon form stopping her progression when the sight came, and then whispered softly to her bright-faced scouts watching as they slipped easily through Quirin's forces. Almost as quickly as they were sent out, one returned with his little visage singed and raw. Ward power! Alida touched him and smiled, sending him to safety, his duty done even as his singed face healed instantly. She thanked Creator again for the inner sight, and running as fast as her tired legs could muster, she headed for the black forest ahead.

The forest was not far for a mounted rider to cover, but for her there was a sea of men, bodies, and animals to wade through before she could reach Deive. At this thought, Alida grasped her own familiar blade that she had regained, and with deftness and speed, she began to dispatch members of Quirin's army back to Hades where they belonged.

When she had hacked through several surprised warriors, Alida found herself with somewhat more of an open road to the forest. She took the break in the mass to leap upon the mount of a fallen warrior, the steed instantly gentled by her touch. Within no time, she was free to pursue Deive into the depths of the woods.

The boughs closed in around her eagerly, and Alida advanced unaware that she was being flanked.

When she had gone far into the fragrant growth of the forest, Alida suddenly realized that she was circling back on herself. She cursed mildly and paused, shutting her eyes and mind to her surroundings. It had to be Quirin's wards that were confusing and misdirecting her. With a silent prayer and deep breath, Alida reopened her eyes, and there before her a path opened through what had been an illusory tangle of branches.

She proceeded with greater caution, for Quirin could not have entranced the entire forest but only the area in which his spells and evil would be worked. Then as though she had trod through the lightness of a cloud, Alida suddenly found herself within a secluded glade. The spectacle that was before her made her stomach drop and her palms sweat.

There on the forest floor lay Deive, gowned only in a filmy violet sheath of blended linen that was her sleeping gown, her heavier over robe having been removed. The material of the sleeping gown was so thin that Deive's outline could be seen clearly through its surface.

There was no sign of Quirin nor was there any sign of violence upon Deive's form. She was alive, but breathing deeply as in sleep. Alida dismounted quietly and approached. When she had drawn nigh to her friend's still form, Alida saw that what at first appeared as embroidered vines and flowers upon the gown shifted into a horrible vision of intertwined serpents with jewel-colored eyes. All around her in the glade, evil shimmered as a real thing.

Without any breath, movement, or sign, Quirin appeared menacingly by Alida's side, his eyes glittering in the cool silence of the forest. Alida's mount unable to bear the evil of the glade turned and fled trumpeting its terror into the night. Alida instinctively lashed out, but she was exhausted from the night's events. Within moments, she lay pinned beneath his powerful body. For though Quirin was slender, his strength was steely and abundant.

Quirin proceeded quickly to wrap Alida's hands and feet with both physical and supernatural restraints. Her bonds complete, he carried her to a position near Deive without allowing the two women to touch. Then he rose and began to chant into the night air, his eyes glowingly pleased at his success.

He wove spells with his hands in time to the chanting, and after some moments had passed, he grew completely quiet.

Then suddenly he shouted out to the night skies, "Greyson, I have won! Your only offspring and your lover lay here upon *my* altar! This night your child will join you in your tormented bastion, but I have assured that you will *never* again see the one that we *both* craved, for I have assured that she will follow me into eternity! I will have her, Greyson, her and all you have loved, and in doing so, you will have lost!"

Alida shivered uncontrollably, for she was helpless before his madness and his incomprehensible evil. She turned her head until she could see Deive and willed the beautiful woman to open her eyes.

Deive did indeed open her eyes, but it was sluggishly and with great difficulty. She called out, "Quirin . . . ," and then her voice faded away, any intent to talk taken from her.

Quirin moved to her side, and with burning eyes as if in a dream, he sat slowly on the ground lifting her onto his lap. Alida screamed at him in horror for she feared the intent that she saw in his eye.

Moving softly, Quirin, with a deep laugh, pulled her body close to his.

"You may be cold now, Love, but within a few moments we'll both be very warm." Deive shivered yet again, her eyes still closed from the drugs and wards he had used against her. Deive felt as if his voice were leagues away from her, for her soul and spirit had retreated somewhere deep within.

Quirin rose slightly with Deive still held in arms. He then spread his wool cloak out over the ground so they would have a warm place to lie. He had become completely focused on her and her alone. He no longer registered Alida or his fiends or the dark cold night.

Alida watched Quirin's sick worship of her friend, completely shocked by his madness. She cried out towards the sky in frustration. With tears pouring down her face, she screamed out at the sky, watching as a black power filled the glade.

Quirin continued to gaze at Deive, running his hands over her ivory face, her flesh still taut and soft despite her age. Within her inert form, Deive stretched and struggled against the bonds of Quirin's spells, all the while her spirit crying out at his weak bonds. Then, all at once, Deive surfaced, feeling her flesh and the tears that poured from her eyes and down her cheeks.

Quirin wiped away the tears, and when she opened her eyes, he grinned down into her face. "Welcome back, my love. We will be as we should have been those long years ago."

Deive, still groggy from the potion and the toll the night had taken on her body, could not speak. So instead, as her reply to his madness, she weakly spit in his face.

He laughingly wiped away her spittle and pinned her arms to the ground. He said something, but she did not hear. For in that instant, Deive felt herself come free of her over-drugged body, and she floated up above the entire sordid scene. It took her a moment to adjust. Then suddenly, she realized what had happened. Creator had pulled her away, and it was for good. *Why?* her mind cried out. *Why was I taken? I must return to Alida; she needs my help! It cannot be time! I would bear the shame of his presence to continue in my duty towards the child. Please, please!*

Yet even as she said it, Deive knew that they were only words and that her desire to be gone was stronger than her desire to stay. Creator had taken her to Himself, for Quirin's drugs had been too strong and had destroyed the life of her body. All at once, she was the most at peace that she had ever been. She was warm, happy and devoid of the filth of fear, pain, and anger. She didn't really want to return, but her love for Alida could not be contained. Down below her, she watched as a tall golden man moved with the grace and stealth of a wolf towards that fated glade. Her vision had been fulfilled.

"Take good care of her," she called out to Ulrich, Creator, and anyone else who would listen. The air around her rippled, and she was fully taken into the otherworldly plain where joy and comfort awaited her.

In the glade, Quirin did not know he caressed a shell. For in his deceived state, he believed that the paltry spells he had woven would hold her forever to his side. Creator laughed humorlessly at the frustration of darkness. For it had been pushed back and denied one more soul.

Alida lay upon the cold ground with tears dripping down her face, her eyes closed against the horrid scene, when she suddenly felt Deive's presence leave the glade. A feeling of joy and peace rushed through her, for she knew Deive would not return, for Deive had gone on into the arms of The Ancient of Days.

From behind the shadow and safety of the trees, Ulrich watched Quirin move over the form of Deive as he chanted his dark incantations. He could not tell from his position whether or not Deive was still alive and whether or not Alida was safe.

He had made his way through the wood uninhibited. His keen senses had not been distracted by the magic and by the strange sounds of fiends. He had one directive and one directive only, to save these two women who had become a part of his existence. At his side strode Lordifyn, hacking at Quirin's fiends who were deigned to stop the warrior.

Softly with the greatest flow, he moved into closer proximity of Quirin and withdrew his weapon, encrusted already with the night's blood. In one fluid movement, the sharp blade was thrust through the ribs and entrails of the snake.

Quirin, enraptured by the night's activity and carried on his own adrenaline, did not die immediately, but instead, with his last few breaths, he turned on the wolf with glittering, angry eyes. He pulled a twisted dirk from his boot and lashed out, catching Ulrich across the chest, and then with a twist of his hand plunged the dirk into Deive's breast, laughing and believing the sacrifice of her complete.

Foiled in his attempt to do real damage to Ulrich and smug with his quick dispatch of Deive, Quirin lunged instead at Alida, for she was now the closest target, and he was soon to the grave whether by Ulrich's hand or his own.

Ulrich in a snarling rage moved faster than the wizard and brought his own dirk up through the demon mage's throat. Joined in the blood and phlegm that raged from Quirin's neck was a host of screaming spirits all clamoring to leave the mangled shell in which they'd taken residence. In their midst, Quirin's small, shriveled spirit called out in anguish, for it realized the lonely state in which it departed. Deive, even in death, was not his. Alida shuddered at the unholy appearance and stench of the escaping fiends as well as the pitiful and twisted being that Quirin's spirit had become.

After he had pulled the blade from Quirin's cold form, Ulrich wiped away the gore and moved to Deive's body, gently covering the beautiful, still face and wrapping her in her own cloak that he had found outside the glade. He then kneeled by Alida's side, carefully removing her bonds and avoiding her eyes. He could lose himself too easily within the depths of those orbs—for the horror of the past moments bade him seek solace. In all his years of battle, he had never seen the movements of the spirit world, but this time he had witnessed the powers at work at the time of Quirin's death. He shook his head slightly to clear it of the images that replayed behind his eyes. This woman at his side had been present at several of his first encounters.

When he had loosed her and had made sure that she was safe, he gingerly rose to his feet and made his way to Titan who had been standing restlessly in the bracken. He would see Alida to the boundaries of her husband's land and then would retire quietly back to his own keep.

"Gather up anything that belongs to you, Alida. I will take you and Deive back to Kinterden Dell. You will be safe and free to deal with the death rites of your friend." He turned and adjusted Titan's saddle so that he could place Deive across the steed's withers. Alida would ride behind him.

Alida did not speak, but instead did as he bade. Gathering up her weapon and cloak, she soon joined Ulrich by his mount's side. She could not hold her tongue, however, when he told her how she was to ride.

"I cannot sit behind you, Ulrich. I'll slide straight off the rump. Could we not place Deive behind. I shall sit in front of the saddle."

Ulrich frowned. "Your back will be broken by the time we touch Kellen's land."

"Then I'll just have to walk," she said with forced calm, her mind uneasily grasping the only alternative should she ride.

His frown deepened, and then without a word, he grasped her hand and lifted her onto his lap. The moment she had settled in, his attempt at remaining detached evaporated. She was warm and her scent drifted through the headier smells of smoke, wind and glade that clung to her clothes. He felt an unbearable desire to keep her safe like this for always. The word "fated" drifted through his mind, and he shook it away. So much for the fates, for they had allowed her to become another man's wife. He no longer believed in fate. He had chosen instead to follow the power of God, and now his faith would have to carry his frustrated flesh.

He angrily grasped Titan's reins, and holding Alida closely to prevent her fall, he wheeled out of the glade and into the waning night. All around them the occasional sounds of a dying battle could be heard. The air smelled of smoke and bodies, but the two on the great mount's back remained in some other place together. Their grim camaraderie had once again opened that place within that neither could deny.

CHAPTER FIFTEEN

As Alida and Ulrich rode through the night in the silence and warmth of each other, the forms of their relieved and tired escort spirits flocked around them, breathing a little softness into the harsh wintry air. Nevertheless, when they had come to the borders of Kellen's land, the little protectors disappeared. Alida would be left to Lordifyn and Ulrich's care.

The arrival at the border lands instantly created two opposing reactions within Ulrich, relief and yearning. Here he would once again lose the companionship of Alida, but he was also glad of this, for her form and rumpled beauty had been the cause of mild torment the whole ride. Unable to put any other name to his desire, Ulrich decided that the tragedy of the night's events were the cause for his search for comfort, a comfort that he would gladly take in her arms. He took a deep breath and slowed Titan for their dismount, shaking away his thoughts again for the hundredth time that night.

Alida, too, was silent with her own tumultuous thoughts. Her blood raced at Ulrich's nearness and at the events she had survived. Though her body was bone weary, she felt the deep awareness of what being alive meant. All her senses had sharpened so that she felt the night seep through her with a startling clarity. The air had smells that she had never noticed, and her eyes could see the outline of each needle on the firs around them. Through her heavy winter clothes, she could feel Ulrich's strength and was soothed by his presence. Alida leaned forward slightly and touched Deive as Titan slowed. How she wished her friend were here to counsel her. Her eyes stung and a tear ran down her nose, dripping off the end and onto Ulrich's strong hand.

Ulrich felt it as he nudged Alida to dismount. His intent to move her from his lap changed into a grasp around her waist. The intimacy of his touch and silence of the moment caused a full flood of tears to release from the pent-up place within Alida, and turning her head to him, she took solace against his chest.

While the tears flowed, Ulrich rocked her gently, touching her face and hair and shoulders, breathing her in and breathing in the night. He felt his own sorrow rise behind his eyes, and his tears, though fewer, were witness to the night's events. Unlike Alida, however, he stubbornly tried to wipe them away. Yet Alida, her own sobbing somewhat diverted by the feel of his tears on her hand and by the telltale intake of his breath, lifted her face.

"Why do you cry, Wolf?"

"Because I see the sorrow and loss that is mirrored in your eyes, and because watching the heartbreak of my little bird causes my own to be torn." His face, so bleak in the night, showed the truth of the statement.

"Why do you wipe them away?"

"You need my strength not my tears."

Alida then reached up and softly ran her hand along his cheek. "Tears do not show weakness." Then it suddenly occurred to Alida that something else had been revealed in his words. She twisted more fully in his lap and looked at him with wary eyes. "Why did you just call me your 'little bird'?"

Ulrich took his time, his hand restless against her side and in her hair. "You are fragile and free-spirited."

Her gaze was steady into his eyes, showing her distrust of his response. "I have hewn asunder both men and beasts, and you call me fragile?"

"Aye, as a bird of prey, which is fierce but can be brought down by a rain of arrows."

Alida was silent, processing his words. Then she did not side step the obvious any longer. "You have seen me fly. You told me this after the night that you came to know of Creator. Yet what puzzles me is your use of the word 'my.' "

He wiped away the remnants of her tears that still lay glistening on her cheeks and whispered. "Because you are mine to protect if not in any other way." She stared at him and he remained unwavering beneath her gaze. "You were beautiful and deadly. The greatest vision I have seen, and I have seen you twice. Thus I am kissed by fortune twice." Then he leaned forward and brushed the top of her head with his lips.

Alida started softly and pulled away. "We must dismount and see to Deive. I am married, and you will be my rain of arrows."

Alida, her cheeks suddenly flushed, slid to the ground, hiding her face from him. "You said you saw me fly twice. Once was when I was with Deive on my christening, so when was the other?"

"It was when you took flight over my castle. I still do not know why you were there that day. It bothered me that you were alone and most vulnerable."

Alida's hands shook slightly as she tried to wrest Deive from Titan's back. "By what do you mean vulnerable?"

Ulrich stepped forward and leaned in so that his breath was only inches from her cheek, a mischievous glint lighting his eye. "You lay naked in the midst of your gloriously discarded clothes."

She turned to him, her cheeks flaming red, and she lifted her hand to slap him. He raised his hands and begged mockingly, "Do not strike me, most powerful warrior!" Then with more gravity said, "Creator hid you from my sight. For it was not my place to see you thus."

He felt her sigh of relief. Then she softly told him how Deive had been cast as her protector and keeper and how she would always feel vulnerable now without her friend. It would not be easy to live when she lacked Deive's presence, even though she had been without her the past months of her marriage.

Ulrich turned her around so that she faced him fully. His eyes were so piercing she could barely gaze into them. "Though I know not why, I have been kept from you as a husband, but that does not keep me from acting as your protector."

Alida shook her head. "Nay. We are equally as weak. I was not able to answer you the night of my wedding when you said that you would always look after me. Had I responded, I would have said that I could never feel comfortable with you though you have aided me greatly. I fear that I am tempted by what you represent."

"Then think on becoming only my friend again," he said softly, and when she did not answer immediately, he stepped away from her with a sudden crispness and began looking for stones beneath the winter snow.

They worked together in silence for some time building a cairn to serve as Deive's grave. Alida had told him earlier on in their ride that she did not want a public burial of her friend. Soon a secure enough place was formed, and they both sank to the ground in exhaustion.

Ulrich glanced at her and then looked away. "I must leave, my keep will be awakening and will be anxious at my disappearance."

Alida looked up at the dawn colors, which were seeping into the sky, and she knew a sudden weariness not born of physical exertion. "I, too, must return—to my husband's keep."

"And to his arms, no doubt." The words slipped from Ulrich's lips before he could stem their flow.

Alida's back stiffened and a small oath came from her lips. She gingerly rose from her position and the cold look in her eye told him he had gone far enough. "Fare thee well."

He ignored his instinct to leave her alone and stubbornly stepped forward. "Nay, Alida." Seconds later, he had her in his arms, and he gazed down into her angry face, swallowing back his emotion while trying to explain. "I hate him for the opportunities he's given to caress you and make love to you. I hate him being there when you laugh and shout and take risks. I hate myself for coveting another man's wife and for feeling that Creator has wronged me. I bring up the sensitive subject of his place in your arms because it will not leave my mind, and it boils in my blood."

She drew herself up and with a very soft voice said, "Then I cannot even be your friend. Beware, Ulrich, for such was the path that Quirin took when he lusted after Deive. Your jealousy will grow and become bitterness until you are separated from the side of Creator."

Ulrich's low voice was tinged with anger as he growled, "How could you choose him, Alida? How could you choose someone so alien to your nature?" Alida, her own frustration at her current state rising like a beast within her, reared back and slapped him as hard as she could. Then without a backward glance, she began the trek across the snow to her husband's keep.

The sting of the blow was less humiliating than her retreating back. Ulrich growled low, and with a blind lunge, he tackled her so powerfully that they both went sprawling into the wet snow, their cheeks brushing against the hard rasp of ice as they tumbled over one another. Then the pent up emotion of each exploded, and they both became a flurry of arms and legs.

Ulrich was surprised at her vehemence and strength. She used all the power behind her fists and legs to punish him for reminding her of how much she was missing. Hot tears rolled down her cheeks into the corners of her mouth bringing the taste of salt, and her eyes blazed so brightly Ulrich thought he would be burned. However, he did not give into her painful blows to his chest and arms.

Soon he had her pinned beneath him, and she was surprised to see that tears of frustration and anger marred his cheeks as well, sliding down into his full winter beard. His hot breath came hard and fast from the exertion, and every inch of his muscled body showed how much she affected him and how emotional he was over the loss of her.

"This cannot go on forever, Alida. Though I do not know how, the path that has kept me from you thus far has also intended you for me. It must. I long for you, but I'll wait until God himself delivers you to me in whatever capacity that may be. When he does, I will not be gentled, and you will know that you have never been safer or more thoroughly loved. Until that time, I will forget you. I will do as you have bid, for you are right. I cannot seek what, as yet, is not clearly given, and I cannot in good conscience remain with you when I desire you so. I will flee from you as from a fire and set my sights on God, for He is to be our solace."

Alida shivered from the dampening snow beneath her back and from the deep burn in his gaze. To be given to this man would be a thing of power and beauty, the likes of which she had never known. He firmly and slowly placed one more heavy kiss upon her cheek, his manly scent intruding against her anger, and she was left with no doubt as to his passion for her.

Then as suddenly as the altercation had begun, Ulrich was off her, striding towards his horse—fury, exhaustion, and desire apparent in his gait. Alida drifted back into the snow, and as she gazed up into the sky with tears drying on her cheeks, she heard the pounding hoofbeats of his steed in the crisp snow blend into the birdcalls of the bleak morning air.

After some time had passed, Alida rose and brushed the snow off her clothing. Then Deive's cairn caught her eye. A fresh bought of tears cascaded over her face, and she hiccupped with the force it took to hold back the sob that had lodged itself painfully in the back of her throat.

"Why?!" Her shout rang in the air. "When I think all my tears have been spent and my troubles are at their greatest, I lose another." She shook her fist at the sky and screamed, "You cannot allow me the turn of any cruelty for joy, can You? What is it, God? Do you now seek to destroy me even as you have comforted me in times past?"

The sky was silent and cold. She spat in the snow and then crumpled to her knees for her anger could not outlast her anguish. "Not Deive," she moaned. "Oh God, she was the dearest to me, even more so than my own kin!"

Then before she could move or cry out again, a force pounded through her chest knocking her back flat onto the snow, her face skyward once again. She whispered, "Forgive me, 'tis not thee I hate, but my own lack of control over my fate and will."

Then The Ancient One's finger pressed into her heart, and she thought she'd die from the heat and the knowing. However, the press lasted only a moment, and instead of feeling drained, Alida felt a rush of power.

"Arise," a singsong voice whispered. "You have not angered The All, but you must leave this place for Deive no longer rests here. Arise and walk strong." Then in front of her, on the glistening snow, a gleaming figure about ten feet tall hovered. The figure glowed brightly, and the smile was almost too much to gaze upon. The form was dressed in gossamer threads, and the hair looked to be spun of the same, moving in time to some heavenly breeze. Alida shielded her eyes.

"Arise."

Alida cast her eyes down. "What is there to desire in life, and what do I have to walk strongly for?"

The figure shimmered, "Your children and the fates that will be wrought by them."

Alida trembled.

The figure smiled brilliantly. "More I cannot tell you, for your walk must be one of faith." Alida hung her head, feeling the burden of *just believing*. The figure smiled again. "I must leave. Dry thy tears, arise, and walk strongly." Then the form faded away.

Alida trembled and as she began to rise, Lordifyn appeared at her side. The beautiful spirit covered her with a blanket of power, and his soothing caress along Alida's brow quieted the young woman's senses. It was obvious how powerful a force The All had sent her and how deep the light of this his newest messenger.

Alida didn't say anything but simply allowed herself to be ministered to by the bright beings. Then she wearily bid her guardian goodbye, arose, wiped away the remaining tears, and walked purposefully towards Kinterden, hiding in her breast the words that had been spoken to her.

Back in the lands of Lyrnne, bands of Kinterden warriors gathered up the dead and finished off the few of Quirin's men who survived. Caked blood covered the warriors' arms and filled the valley and dells with the stench of death. Kellen's men shook their heads, weary at the destruction of the lands and keep. They did not know at this point whether Savine and Kellen were alive, for neither had been seen for some time. Knowing that their wounded needed attending to, as well as gaining rest for themselves, they turned with great reluctance towards Kinterden Dell through the lowered clouds and the sounds of moaning and pain. They could not waste too many men on a search for their leader when there were dying men to attend to, but perhaps the few left behind would have luck. Whatever the fates willed, Kellen would turn up eventually, be it dead or alive, as would the mistress of Lyrnne keep.

However, when they reached the rim of the cold, smoky forest, a rider came dashing through the trees, the sounds of crashing branches and bracken following his wake.

"Our master has been found down on a lower field. He is injured but alive!"

A great shout went up amongst the men, and several rushed away to aid their leader.

That evening at the keep, as Kellen's servants nursed the masses of weary and war-torn refugees from Lyrnne, Alida herself oversaw the bulk of the work. Her scraped hands winced when the hot water from cleansing cloths touched the raw flesh of her knuckles, and she fought to keep from swooning while breathing in the steamy heat from bodies and tubs of hot water alike. She was beyond exhausted.

When she was finally able to excuse her presence in the hall, her feet could barely support her, and her hands when she tried to make a fist were like a rusted hinge devoid of grease. The women around her shook their heads and wondered if she was carrying Kellen's child. They all assumed she'd been bound to her quarters from the time the men had left for battle until their arrival home. The warm water of her secret cove as well as soap and fresh clothes had aided her appearance enough that none knew of her exhausting misadventure during the battle nor her stubborn instincts for survival. Most assumed that the bruises and small cuts on her body and cheeks had come at her husband's hand.

―――――――――――――――――――――――

For weeks following the battle, Alida kept to herself spurning activities that would pique Kellen's interest and that of the keepsmen. She did not even come down for the main meals hovering instead on the edges of the kitchen when she was hungry and retiring to lesser-known rooms in the castle during the day.

The servants whispered that she had become a ghost over the loss of too many relatives. Kellen did not care about what she had become or what his people thought of her as long as she was available to him when he called. For he had tested his people's devotion to him and had found it smugly true. The men had never mentioned his rough handling of his wife and had only sung songs and dealt tales of his valor in war the weeks following the battle, for what business was it of their's if he mistreated Alida. He took care of his own and was as wise a land manager as any they had known. Likewise, the women of the keep remained close-mouthed fearing their lord's fierce temper, deigning instead to remain uninvolved.

On an unusually quiet morning, Alida sought the heights of the castle walls. She was unprepared for the hunger for flight that suddenly welled up in her chest when the whistling frigid winds atop the castle, tinted with the smell of castle fires, caught away her breath. Then in bravery, she descended quickly through the belly of the castle and used the morning's darkness as a cover to sneak out from the protective city walls into the cold dells beyond. When she had come to her hidden cove, she lay down on the warm earth and watched for the sun. Eventually, its face rose over the rim of her enchanted refuge. She let the thin winter sunlight seep into the marrow of her bones and listened to the birds who called out mysterious songs and requests, their warbling resonant in her own heart.

She then stripped away her clothing and stretched into the air. It took her longer than normal to transform, for there was an edge of sadness still from Deive's death the stress of her sorrow fighting against her transformation into her second skin. Then wings took form, the trembling of feathers brushing against and out of her flesh. Exhilarated and screaming in freedom, she broke away from the grasp of the earth into the welcoming air of the sky.

She gazed about in wonder at the landscape below and at the lack of restriction placed on her at such a height. Her delicately tipped wings caressed the wind, and she rode the thermal waves of air that rose in the morning light. She flew miles farther than she had in a long time, and within a short amount of time, she hovered over Ulrich's keep, her falcon's heart recognizing the place with some detachment as a useful landmark. Soon she continued on, charged by a need to return to her childhood fields and rivers. What took days on foot, took much less time by wing.

Her falcon's cry echoed out in a fading scream at her homecoming as she crested the last barrier hill and saw the city and castles of Falda glimmering silently below—the grandeur only somewhat diminished by its deserted state. After Quirin had departed for battle with his warriors, the captured people of Falda and slaves from other lands had fled one by one, the lord of their misery absent and therefore unable to keep them well in hand with only a small contingency of paid soldiers watching over them. Last to flee, had been the warriors themselves and their supporting bevies of cooks, servants, and slaves that had comprised Quirin's following, for they were mercenaries without true loyalty to any name. They had no desire to risk their lives when news of Quirin's defeat had reached the walls of Falda via more of the winged messengers. A sort of gleeful bliss flooded her heart that the barren city would be hers for as many hours or days as she wanted it.

Folding her wings over her back, she plummeted into the depths of the open courtyard in the castle. After having found a perch, her falcon eyes gazed coldly about noting the fine snow and dried leaves that had blown into open doors and windows, her ears alive with their sound and the smell of cold stone and damp. She determined with finality that indeed no creature save her was about, and she slowly transformed back into a human female. Though she was exhausted from the unaccustomed exercise of flight, she rose to find cover for her bare skin. With a little rapid exploration, she discovered a cloak that had been discarded in the haste of the exodus. She slung it around her shoulders and almost swooned when she caught a faint remnant of the incense that her mother had placed in all the clothes chests of the castle. The scent of mulberry and lavender and lilac were there just beneath the layers of other human smells.

She sat down hard upon a cold, stone bench and stared up into the bright, wintry sky. It had been so many months since she had dwelt upon the memory of her parents.

She rose quietly and worked her way up a back staircase with heavy footsteps until she entered onto her favorite walkway with a westerly view of their lands. Her only company there on the walkway was the lonely sound of whistling wind and dry leaves. She sat huddled in the fragrant cloak and sang old songs to herself, ones that had been favorites of her mother's. She allowed herself no tears and forced her memories far back in time to when her life had been carefree and warm. Regardless of her present unhappiness, she decided her parents would be proud of her and her ability to survive. She spent the day lost in memories and sleep, her body tired from the emotional wear of the day and from flight.

When the sun had set, she transformed and hunted for small rabbits, her strange eyes flickering in the moonlight. It felt wonderful to be free of enemies, and she flew and gathered in graceful abandon, satisfying her hunger and thirst from the bodies of the beasts she captured.

It wasn't until the night carried on into the dawn of the next day that she decided to make her way home. Though she was loathe to return to the cheerless halls of Kellen's keep, she knew that her future happiness depended on her day-to-day anonymity. She did not want to be missed, for if she was careful this time, she could make quiet forays out alone at other times in the future. Her silence after the battle and lack of response from the keepsmen was proof of this. She would wait for the time when she could leave Kinterden for good and return to Falda where her daily actions were not a cause for a beating. She would return to happiness.

With her mind full of her flight and liberty, Alida lay curled on her side before the stone hearth in her quarters at Kinterden, her cheek softly pillowed on her arm. Her pallet had been drawn close to the fire, and she reveled in the warmth and cheery cackle of the flames. Not a single person had missed her in the day and half that she'd been gone. The choking sadness of that fact only further strengthened her resolve to leave.

She stretched and sat up reaching for a rough, hair-covered satchel in which she had a store of parchment and sticks of coal for writing. She reminded herself again that what she needed was a home. Falda was her first and only choice, and she carefully began to write out a plan to gain it for her future use. She knew she would need to secure the property with more than her name. For although she had been firm with Kellen that the lands were not a part of her dowry, she was wise enough to know that true property holdings, should her's be regained, took the backing of a vigilant staff and army—neither of which she had.

She searched for options until the fire's glow became nothing but near embers, its warmth thinning in the onslaught of cool night air. Crawling from her cozy perch on the bed, she drifted to the window deep in thought. She gazed out far into the night with the aid of the full moon's cheery face, as an astounding and dangerous idea began to grow in her tired mind.

Ulrich had an army, and he had once asked to protect her. Would not the keeping of her lands fall under such a need for protection? Or, as he had seemed so firmly resolved to do, would he refuse what he had once promised?

She prayed that her last refusal of his friendship and his resolve to stay away from her would be nullified with a well-placed plea, for now all she wanted was her own life–an impossibility under her current circumstances. She was wise to fear the next encounter with her husband along with all the future encounters that would doubtlessly cross her path, for his nature seemed to be growing increasingly sinister and cold. She could not imagine him ever releasing her from her union.

Common sense and self-preservation had demanded some sort of plan. Now that she had a fully formed idea, an urgency to convert the plan to action overcame the thought of anything else. She found an empty balcony off a room down the hall from hers and allowed her body to slip into falcon form. She then made her way through the night air to Drachmund Heights. Her flight was apropos of her life now, for there were no warm updrafts to carry her gently to her destination. The cold air around her sang through the forceful beating of her wings, each whistling beat like an ice shard falling to hardened snow.

CHAPTER SIXTEEN

Alida stood shivering from the damp night air and her lack of cover just within his window. His casement had been found instinctively for it was filled with his special scent and even more ephemerally his presence that she could feel to the depth of her own soul as something real and physical. She had not yet fully transformed, and momentary blindness added to her already great vulnerability.

It was the sound of the dry rustle of her feathers and then hair and skin against the window casement that brought Ulrich from sleep.

As before in the glade, Alida stood surrounded by Creator's brightness so that her form was hidden from him. Ulrich watched silently from his pallet, the cobwebs of sleep drifting away from him to be replaced by the weight of his rapidly pounding heart. He arose uncertainly, covering himself as he crossed to where she stood. Impatient with having to wait through her transformation and concealment, short though the time was, he busied himself with lighting candles and torches around the room. Soon the space glowed brightly, dispelling any intimate darkness that might tint the mood. The honest odor of the unscented candles' hissing flames and thin, curling smoke filled the room with warmth. He chose a chair that while proximal to her put yet some necessary distance between them. He could contain himself behind the mass of the large trestle table in his room. The security of the table plus the size of the carved oak arms and high back of his chair, leant credence to his ownership of the room.

When she had fully transformed, the attending spirits gathered up one of Ulrich's large robes and wrapped her in its folds, their bright light continuing to conceal her until the folds of the blanket rested fully upon her shoulders.

"To what do I owe this honor, fair Siren?" Ulrich's smooth voice held little welcome, the boundaries between them having already been too clearly established.

She wiped at a strand of hair that brushed her cheek, her movements jerky and nervous. She shook her head slightly, embarrassment staining her cheeks a hot red.

His harsh chuckle died away, engulfed by the silence of the night. He murmured, "Alida, you are as confounding a woman as I have yet met. Here you come to me unbidden in the dead of night and then hesitate in revealing your purpose. You stand there obviously vulnerable, fighting off what could be presumably a sudden questioning of whatever it was you came to tell me. Don't keep me waiting—I'm breathless with anticipation." His voice trailed off in amusement.

Alida's color deepened, and she could not hold his gaze, her defenses rising higher still and her voice dripping with disdain. "It was hard enough coming here without being mocked by someone who obviously holds himself above such things as needing aid." When he remained quiet she said, "Your lanky posture and studied aloofness are also revealing, you know. For the hot-blooded male that I left as close to a stranger as not would find such a sudden transformation from his previous disposition to the one you now display nearly impossible, unless he was a master of duplicity!" Her voice was sharp with embarrassment, the barb of her tongue cutting away at his composure.

He laughed again, but this time the sound was reflected by a bright twinkle in his eye. The low resonance seeped into her bones, warming her and somehow providing reassurance. "There is nothing duplicitous about me. It was, in fact, my frankness that caused you to roundly chastise me, and not without cause to be fair to you–for I did outstep any decent boundaries that would have kept us friends. And I never would think you a stranger, but simply someone to be avoided in the future."

She straightened her back and turned to gaze out the window, trickles of cool air that escaped around the glass dispelling the heat of her cheeks. "If that is some form of a twisted apology, then I accept." Clearing her throat, she swallowed deeply before continuing. "My purpose for coming to you *is* one of great import. I would not travel to you in the middle of night for something trivial, for I know that the nature of our acquaintance if far too strained already."

He nodded gravely and held his hand out in acquiescence. "Let us call a truce, fair lady. Do speak, and I shall listen, for I would be loath to keep you from your important task, whatever it might be." This time there was no sarcasm or impatience to mark his words.

She turned her head slightly as if weighing his sincerity, and then meeting his eye, she softly touched his warm palm for only a moment before beginning to pace, her voice holding all the excitement of an idea newly born. "I need the covering of your men. I want them to safekeep my parent's land until such time as I can rally my own force and keep it for my name." She struggled to remain focused, the vague distraction of his male scent seeking to impede her purpose.

"Is that not one of the duties your husband would have been obliged to oversee?" His quietly drawled response did not dwell on the word "husband" as it had on previous occasions, his good intentions to remain helpful taking over any latent covetousness he may have harbored.

Her voice lacked strength, some of her earlier nervousness peeking out. "Under normal circumstances, yes, he would be the protector and keeper."

"And these circumstances are unusual?"

"Aye. I rescinded on Savine's agreement to grant him the property as a part of my dowry. I kept it under my own family name and crest, for I refused to sign the deeds over to him when the adjudicator came some days after our wedding. Because of this choice, there is now no military backing for my claim, and he or anyone else could easily take the lands themselves."

Ulrich sat up running his fingers through his thick mane in thought. He was surprised that Alida would keep her property from her spouse. There was much love to be shown in joining two properties and two lives. Though he was curious about the discrepancy, he held his tongue and continued within the train of their conversation. "What do I get in return for my protection?"

"There is a price? But you said that you would protect and help me!" Alida's disappointment helped her to focus her mind away from the vulnerability she continued to feel in his uniquely male presence.

He was quiet for a moment before responding, "Aye, that I did. Command me then as you would your soldier. I am your humble servant and my own strength I will give to thee."

She stared at him, her mouth slightly open and took in a quick breath. "A lone soldier is in no position to aid me."

He looked away for a moment, then thoughtfully gazed back at her once again with an equal mix of regret and resolve. "Think, Alida. Think carefully, for then you will see that I cannot risk the lives of my men who have put their trust in me as their liege on the whim of someone with whom I should have no association."

She whirled away from him, her back a rigid embarrassed wall. When she spoke again, she forced herself to keep the whine of disappointment from her voice. "You have sworn your protection, and because it was most earnestly stated these few weeks past, I have in all honesty accepted it. Now you seek recompense for the whole of your strength, and I question your intent in doing so. For now that I find myself in serious need, what else is there for me to do but agree to any notion you would put forth?"

He laughed outright this time, the sound hard, and then he leapt to his feet. A low growl in his throat told of his approach, and she turned in time to see a sudden spark of anger flare behind his eyes, his grasp firm without causing her pain as he turned her towards him. "Serious indeed is the need of this moment and place, Alida. I would not toy with such a grave matter, for then I would be a foolish leader. If you want my help, you, too, must instill my trust. Do not act like a nursery maid. Tell me fully of your need, and I will seek to assist thee, but do not be foolish in thinking that such help comes without a price. For whether you, I or my men pay it, a price is always required."

She jumped as he snarled, "Now, again, I ask of thee a simple offering to place this dealing in the perspective of a pact if nothing else. What will my crest receive as an offering for its protection?" He released his grasp on her.

Alida stood face-to-face and toe-to-toe with him—a princess and king at war with one another. "I will offer thee jewels that were my mother's. I found them in our family cache at Castle Falda. Plus, I will be forever in your debt as an ally should some military need of your own arise."

"Nay. Something more."

She stubbornly stuck out her jaw staring into his eyes. "I *have* nothing else!" She longed for a sudden breeze to come again from around the windows and cool her hot cheeks, the scent of pine from outside already enticing her to run away, leaving the madness of her mission behind.

He was quiet and then said softly, "I will take, in exchange for my army's protection, seven years' worth of the land's full production, whether it be in livestock or harvest or offering of the earth such as metals and precious stones." His soft words and deep voice belied the steel that underlay every word he spoke.

For a moment, there was only silence and the hiss and sputter of the candles as she mentally calculated the worth of what he was asking. Finally, with great horror she said, "Falda is a rich land! Seven years' worth of production equals near a king's ransom!"

He shook his head in exasperation, but maintained eye contact. "You ask the aid of a king."

She was instantly angry. "You are as much a blackguard as Kellen. Everything I own now for seven years will belong to you! How am I to amass wealth enough that when the land reverts I am able to build my own army? True it will be safe from other armies, and it will eventually revert to me, but you would not have even known of Falda's abandoned state had it not been for me. You might as well have lost it to another."

He reached out and gently took her chin into his large, warm, calloused hand. Everything in his stance and his gaze showed his levity. "Don't ever compare me to Kellen, Princess. Now that being said, nothing else you could offer interests me, as I will need a way to explain the siege to my people. Guarding the lands will take wealth, and if we can gain from the land during the process, then so much the better. It will still be in your name, and by keeping that which we produce, no uncomfortable questions will be raised by my people until later about the identity of the true benefactor."

"It is as if you ask for my very soul!" Her voice was small in the power of his presence. "I have no family, Ulrich—no friends, nothing to claim except for my heritage lands, lands that my family has fought for generations to protect."

"No family? How can you say such a thing? You will bear children soon enough, and even if your match to Kellen is not all you dreamed of, it is the lot you have drawn. You best make the most of your marriage." He raised his eyebrows at the strangled sound she made low in her throat and the hopelessness in her eyes he thought he saw when he mentioned children. "I do not ask you for much, Princess."

She snorted quietly. "You are SO generous to ask such a *small* boon."

"Fine, a small compromise I will make. I will guard the land in the eighth year without drawing any wealth from it. The land and all its wealth will revert to you in the eighth year so that you have a year's earnings with which to amass an army as well as safety while you do so. "Then quietly again,

"Promise me, Alida. I will take no other offering."

She pulled away and paced to the window her mind in turmoil. "How can I offer you the one thing that I am not sure I would be willing to give again to a man–that is his power over me. For surely by making a pact, I am tied to you and your governing for seven years."

His anger simmered beneath his brow, and his words were clipped in response. "You know that I am unlike that *union* you now enjoy with your present spouse. You know that I would not take advantage of you, such is my respect for you. All I ask is equal appreciation for my position and responsibilities. Now agree to the terms that Falda might have my protection."

She was silent for a moment longer as she recounted the exact state of her current union, and then she turned to him. "You shall have your desire, and from it, I shall have mine." *Freedom,* she said silently in her mind. She would regain that which her family had lost. She would pay the price. She had promised herself freedom, and freedom she would have.

Ulrich watched a range of emotions pass over her face while she promised away her life. He did not feel any remorse for what he had made her promise, for he would make sure that Alida never regretted their hasty treaty. He stepped towards her, and his eyes burnt down into hers for a single instant before growing shuttered and businesslike once again.

Then he leaned to the side of her and taking up a thin, nearly transparent sheet of leather and a sharpened reed began to write out their pact using a pot of red dye as ink. When he had accomplished his aim, he took up wax and an engraved seal displaying the emblem of a wolf. Gruffly he commanded her, "Sign this agreement and get thee gone."

She stared at him, her hesitation obvious. "It looks like blood."

"This treaty is no small thing, Alida. Be sure that it will require blood to enforce. Now make your seal, or we'll have no bargain!" This time there was no request in the words. He looked over at her and did not make a move towards her, but instead awaited her response.

She faltered for a moment and then leaned forward, reaching for the smooth dry reed. When she was finished writing, she dripped a small mound of wax at the bottom of the page. Then she pressed her hand to the sheet to seal the bargain. The hot wax steaming up over her knuckle warmed her signet ring and made the treaty that much more real.

When she finished, she boldly held out the reed for his use. "Sign the treaty as well, Wolf, for neither would I have you trick me or falsify our bargain!"

At this, he gently covered her hand with his own, letting the electricity of their fingers blend for a moment before removing the twig with his strong, roughened fingers. He then turned away with inscrutable features to scratch his own name into the agreement that tied their lands together, whatever their individual fates may hold.

She swallowed as she watched his hand move across the leather sheet, not knowing how to react. For this was no game, and the man she made it with was not a simple fool. He was a king, the chief of his men, and she was at his mercy. His special scent of rosemary soap and male musk again assaulted her with its pure maleness and warmth, and she suddenly found the large chamber too close for comfort.

Ulrich briskly arose and pointed to the window. "Our bargain is complete, and I will fulfill my promise."

His sudden movement left Alida feeling hard. "You are the coldest man I know. You gain from me my very life and then act as if we spoke only of something trite, ordering me to take my leave like some servant!" Her voice blazed out into the silence, and he could see her frustration written in every line of her flesh and bone.

He looked at her, anger and tension written in every line of his face, the emotion brought swiftly to the surface by her inflammatory comments. "Look again, fair little bird, am I as cold as you claim? From you, at least, I would think there would be some knowledge of my nature! I cannot even touch your hand without being burned—and to complete the madness of this pact I have just signed away my army."

She brushed her hair from her face and sighed for necessary apologies were often difficult for her. "Nay, cold you are not, and I think you feel the levity of this as much as I." She was silent a moment, and then looking down at her hands said softly, "I suppose I just need someone to blame." Then even quieter, "Do you think us foolish for our pact?"

He moved the few steps toward her, his bare feet making little more than a soft rasp against the stone, and she was reminded again of a predator. His voice gravelly with his own questions and fear, he said softly, "I believe that if we were truly meant to rule together then by Creator's own hand it will happen. Maybe this is all that was meant for us. If I have acted foolishly in asking this of you, I will know it when at one hundred and five only a landlord have I been to you!"

She raised her eyebrows at him and pressed her lips together holding back a chuckle. "At least I'll be assured that the taxes I pay you are well spent." Her laughter died in the heat of his levity, causing her to bite her lip in silence.

He straightened and tried to collect his thoughts, gazing intently at her beauty and vulnerability. He cupped her cheek and ran the pad of his thumb along the noble lines of her high cheekbones, fighting the raw emotions that flooded his heart. The scent of roses and lavender and night air rose from her skin, leaving a heady trail where his thumb had been. Removing his hand hastily, as if dropping a live coal, he said, "We have a bargain sealed this night by our own hands, and you will find me true to my word. Now let us speak no further, and get thee gone from here before either of us can change our mind." He turned his back and prayed silently that Creator would have His way in whatever form it took.

"Contact me should anything go awry," she said softly to his turned back. Then she gazed around the room for a moment longer, freezing the scene in a corner of her mind to review when she wasn't so overcome. Shaking away the sudden clarity of the moment, she transformed in the silence of the night. Ulrich felt his heart lurch as the sound of her wings touching the casement reached his ear.

———————————————————

When Alida had returned to Kinterden and had fully transformed back into her human form, she fell onto her pallet and wept hot tears into the soft, lavender-scented folds of the furs, her body shaking with inexplicable emotion. She felt like she was wrapped in webs as an uncertain meal for the spider of her future. Surely, she would be consumed!

After allowing herself a moment's pity, she swallowed her tears and wearily sat up, her stomach hurting from the tears and emotion. She must not give in to such thoughts. Was not Creator the one who formed her? What had she to fear of man's plans? With her resolve tremulously in place, she clothed herself in a sleeping tunic and crawled wearily beneath the covers, sadly aware of the warm folds that would have been welcoming should a loving mate have accompanied her to bed.

From the heavens, Creator watched the dangerous game that his two servants played, knowing that they were but steps away from a crucial move. They had given Him power by their own will, despite their penchant for creating interference. Their flesh was barely restrained, but as small children trying their best to obey their parents, they, too, had offered what they could, and things were well in hand.

The next morning found a restless and irritable Ulrich at the head of his ranks that had gathered outside. From amongst them, he chose his captain, Landres, and several of his most trustworthy warriors. He then took them into the keep and discussed their exact placement and duties while protecting Falda.

They could tell by his demeanor that he would not suffer any mistakes in the carrying out of their mission. He did not divulge any details as to his interest in the abandoned lands, but his men knew that the domain of which he spoke was a rare and fertile piece. He was wise to have gone after it.

When the plan had been discussed and everyone fully briefed, the bulk of the men departed to gather their belongings, the sounds of their deep voices ringing off the cobblestoned courtyard. Landres, wasting no time, followed Ulrich through the main doors of the castle and pulled him aside.

"Do you think that such a small rank will be sufficient for this campaign?"

Ulrich wearily rubbed his hand over his face as if to wipe away fatigue. "I do not know, but I have tried to prepare for any eventuality. A messenger will ride between us weekly, and at your command, I will bring the entire force should some mishap occur. We cannot afford to leave the homeland unmanned. I will send a train of supplies with separate escort, and it should arrive shortly after you. This will allow you and the men to proceed as quickly as possible. I trust you with this mission, Landres. I know that it is not the most exciting or dangerous of charges I have entrusted to you, but for my own reasons, I need you on this one. I pray that it will proceed without incident."

Landres saluted; then with his heels clicking together crisply, he turned to leave. When he was out of harms way, he called back over his shoulder, "Find yourself a mate and make good on your vows. You have been a beast of late and your demeanor would benefit greatly from finding love in the soft arms of a woman!"

Ulrich growled at his captain's retreating back. "There are more important things to think on than lovemaking, Landres."

Landres laughed gustily, and then despite his liege's glowering face, he retorted, "You are thirty and five. I think that it is high time you thought of it."

Ulrich muttered and turned away. Landres had no idea! He had not found the opportunity yet to discuss his new beliefs with the captain, though he had openly shared his newfound belief with Drachmund's high advisor.

He picked up his own leather bag, worn to a buttery softness, off the trestle table before him and stalked out into the bleak winter day. Titan was his only hope of working off enough physical energy to forget a future that stretched endlessly ahead without Alida.

He moved rapidly to the stables, glad that the brisk air was taking the edge off his exhaustion. The night before had been sleepless, long, and nerve-wracking in bouts—his mind unable to lay to rest the sight of Alida dwarfed by that ridiculous robe, while relating to him the astounding proposal that had accompanied her visit. Those that passed him left him to himself, some even giving him wide berth.

The open doors of the stables offered up warm air, fragrant with the smell of hay and grooms oil. The stablehands and warriors' attendants bustled about readying the mounts that would carry the small contingent to the borders of Falda. Again, no one spoke a word to him, most of the lads ducking their heads and moving on their way when he made eye contact with them. Opening the largest stall door on the front block, Ulrich chuckled darkly when his steed snorted at him and turned about in a nervous circle. Was he really behaving so badly?

His answer came moments later when Eldridge walked into the same stall. His pace was measured and stately, which agitated Ulrich even more. If only he had his advisor's self control.

The man's smooth, warm voice called out welcome, and he firmly grasped Ulrich on the shoulder, his hands strong despite his years spent in nonphysical endeavors.

"What ails thee, Ulrich?"

Ulrich swallowed the immediate answer that came to his tongue, covering up his choked reply with a cough. He was not used to being anything other than completely honest with Eldridge.

"I'm just restless. Not enough activity." He turned his back so that the advisor could not see his face.

Eldridge snorted in a definite departure from his usual decorum. "You fool yourself, Ulrich. People have been talking. They say you're in love, though no one knows who the mysterious maid could be. I tend to agree with them, but I have avoided participating in the gossip." The advisor settled in for a chat in a nearby chair while pulling out a fragrant stick of licorice from his tunic pocket.

"What do they all want?" muttered Ulrich pulling too hard as he combed his mount's tail. The horse stamped and bared his teeth reminding his master to be careful. "It is *my* life after all, Eldridge. I need not display all my thoughts to all our people at every occasion." His scowl deepened.

"My, aren't we in a mood? I'm not asking that of you, Ulrich, but I am concerned about you and your well-being." The advisor smiled holding up his hands in mock surrender to show that he meant neither harm nor intrusion and then returned to sucking loudly on his licorice stick.

Ulrich sighed and turned to face him, his head hung low. "I have always trusted your wisdom in matters which troubled me. Therefore, I will speak with thee, but it must not be bantered about as common knowledge. I would hate it if . . ."

Eldridge raised a hand stemming Ulrich's speech and said, "Choose your words, Ulrich, and do not feel obligated to tell me anything. Just assure me that you are well and then match your behavior to your words."

Ulrich, greatly agitated by a subject he'd been trying to avoid, left off his horse's tail and began currying the beast. His strokes along the horse's sleek back were short and rapidly, matching his frustrated energy. Eldridge waited in the silence and watched the man he had known from boyhood.

"It *is* indeed a woman. The only woman I would ever have. She drives me to madness, and I cannot rid myself of the thought of her." Eldridge continued to wait. "She is like breathing to me, and yet I cannot fully take a breath. She is as necessary as eating, yet this meal is denied to me. In all ways, I am restrained and crippled from acting on my desires for she belongs to another man." He nearly choked on his words for they were bitter gall to him.

Eldridge's heart skipped a beat as he struggled to hide his reaction. It was very unlike Ulrich to seek a woman already married or taken. He was a king. Handsome and powerful enough to have any number of eligible maids to wife and conquests to bed. Eldridge continued to hold his tongue, though he burned to speak. He knew it was restraint that made him invaluable, for restraint gave him time to think and calculate before reacting.

The silence stretched on, and finally Ulrich turned to his advisor and friend, his face mirroring his deep frustration. "Add to her unavailability the fact that she is also my lands' sworn enemy, but *still* I cannot think of any other woman. It has been months since I have even looked at anyone else. My body cries out for the release that a marriage or conquest would bring and for an easier path, but I am driven to follow God and inexplicably to wait for *her.*" He threw the currycomb down, infuriated at his cuckolded state and was greatly satisfied at the loud crash it made against the stall door.

Eldridge decided then to speak, but proceeded slowly choosing his words with caution. "So you have contrived a siege to fill up your mind and time?"

Ulrich chuckled wryly, "There will be no siege. It is a peaceful take-over, for the land is hers and she has begged my protection."

Eldridge chuckled softly. "You never have been one to do things in partial measures!" Then more seriously, "This must be the single heir of Falda, not your direct enemy but niece of the infamous Savine of Lyrnne, a distasteful connection to be sure, but not one which would have rendered you unable to make a match. No, 'tis her married status that I would warrant has truly cuck-olded you! I cannot think how you would have come to know her."

Ulrich sighed and rubbed the back of his neck. "I am as good as gelded 'tis true, for not only is she married but married to Kellen Grost of Kinterden Dell!" At this announcement, Eldridge's eye grew keener for now he clearly understood the gravity of the situation. Ulrich continued as if Eldridge were not present. "But does this change my heart? Nay, for she is perfect, wild, and beautiful. I met her by chance when Lyrnne still stood as she hunted in the lands surrounding that city, and I have found that I cannot live without her. Though I have tried to tell myself to forget her, I sin daily with sudden thoughts of her skin and hair and words."

Eldridge said softly, "Tell me you have not lain with her!"

"Nay!" Ulrich's vehemence startled Eldridge.

The advisor breathed a sigh of relief and slapped his knees. "Then no transgression has been committed, Ulrich! 'Tis not a sin to be tempted, although dwelling on such thoughts would be. Temptation comes to us all in one form or another. And though in matters of love and romance, you'll find me at a loss, I know that loving someone but refusing to act on your desire when the connection is not advisable shows only restraint and good judgment. I would continue on this route if I were you. I've never met anyone who interested me more than political matters and legalities, so I'm completely basing all of this upon conjecture, you understand."

Ulrich laughed at his advisor's wry expression. "You may yet have such a siren in your future!"

Eldridge sniffed and lifted his chin. "I have avoided these unpleasant emotions that many fools have had to suffer, and I do not feel in the least bit cheated!"

Ulrich chuckled and said, "Creator would not be so cruel to the rest of us and spare you!" Then his face grew grim again. "What am I to do, for I would not disobey my God, but neither will I live in such misery!"

Eldridge stood, crossing to where his friend attended the warm sides of his mount. "Follow your heart, for you are no fool, Ulrich. There will be a solution. Creator does not allow us to walk about without guidance. It is you who has so recently reminded me of this!"

Ulrich smiled tiredly and said, "Which is it, Eldridge? Follow my heart or continue to ignore her—for you have just recommended I do both. And believe me, she is not easily forgotten so I'd rather do the first."

Eldridge smiled, "You have been following your heart by making choices despite temptation. Following your heart does not always mean you make the emotional decision. Sometimes it means you are making the better but more difficult choice."

Ulrich nodded then said distantly, "Do not expect me in this afternoon. I'll be out riding."

Eldridge bowed slightly and gave his fare-thee-well whispering a prayer as he left. His charge was surrounded by men who did not understand him. The rarity of his devotion to a god not made of wood or stone or ivory as many of their land served was a foreign idea at best. He had watched over the years as his king's friends had pressured the man to take what he wanted using his kingship as an excuse. Eldridge was amazed that Ulrich had stayed so steadfast to his family's beliefs, which had blended beautifully with this new found spirituality. Somewhere along the way, those earlier morals had actually led the king to his more recent belief in a single Creator, who had been Eldridge's own persuasion for years. The advisor had assumed that it was his guidance over the years that had made Ulrich choose The Way. He prayed this young woman would not lead his precious charge astray!

Disdaining a saddle for Titan, Ulrich mounted bareback in a graceful leap and headed out into the misty grey countryside robed in a warm, woolen cloak, leggings, and tunic–serviceable gear that could do nothing to warm his spirit.

———————————————

Landres and his group of warriors headed out for Falda that same day, moving quickly and quietly as individual shadows through the concealing woods.

When night fell, they did not allow themselves the pleasure of a fire and warm food but pushed on after watering and feeding their mounts and after quickly partaking of dried lamb and brown bread. Enough time had passed at Falda that any number of rivals might have noted its empty façade and made plans of their own for invasion. A full moon, gracious and smiling, lit their way that first night as they moved gracefully like so many of its piercing moon-beams through the cold, winter shadows.

The next day, too, found smooth traveling though the sunlight was still thin and the air overly crisp. It wasn't until the second night that Landres began to grow uncomfortable. He had noted earlier, at the beginning of their march, that the main road they flanked was packed down hard and covered in hoofprints and manure. With a commander's instincts, he kept an eye on the direction and age of the markings that lead to a similar heading as his own band. His concern lay in the fact that the markings grew more obviously fresh as if they were pulling astride a slower moving contingent—slower inevitably meaning greater in number.

His wariness was further piqued when he saw thin trails of smoke rising from an area up ahead that he knew lead to an immense plain. Waving his men into deeper silence, they approached the outskirts of the plain on full alert.

Then he and his band heard the distinctive clink of weapons and the low voices of men. There were no sounds of women or merriment that would have marked an innocent merchant's band. These were the sounds of an army.

Landres pulled his charger to a halt and silently directed his men to gather around. When they all had given him their full regard, he directed them quietly in a hoarse whisper to fully flank the field. He warned them of the likelihood of guards and told them only to gather as much information as they could. He wanted no confrontation if they were greatly outnumbered.

Within moments, Drachmund's warriors had taken position in the flank of the field and counted at least ten well-ordered battalions with a possibility of more hidden within the rolling dells, concealing twists of the valley and surrounding forests. Landres' band numbered only seven score and ten. Silently signaling his men to spread out, they moved quickly ahead. They allowed enough space between so that they became an insignificant trickle amidst the shadows and trunks of the forest. When they had gone a safe distance, Landres dropped back into the company of his own guardsmen, addressing two who had been used occasionally as spies due to their ability to gather detailed observations. There purpose was always clear.

"What information did you obtain?" His voice held the hard edge of a commander who knew the potential gravity of the situation.

The first said decisively, "They are headed to Falda, and their keen references to the land make me wonder at their claim to ownership. Such knowledge of the city's fortifications and surrounding properties can only mean a long-standing intimacy with Falda."

The soldier next to him shook his head in agreement. "I heard similar information, and it is safe to assume that only an army with claim would take the time to set up camp as if they had all the time in the world."

Landres thanked the two and picking up his reins urged his mount into a trot, the only sound a muffled jingle. He moved on down the line to anyone else who could offer him news until he had gathered all the available information. Several had noted the emblem of Kinterden Dell on pack leathers, though there were no banners claiming the same. Another soldier had noted that they escorted large supply and weaponry wagons that were overkill for the mere thousand that comprised the contingent—possibly a greater number to follow? There were also young lads and old men that acted as minions to the commanding ranks of the army. It was obvious that they intended a long stay at their proposed destination, for no army would take along unnecessary bodies unless the campaign was indefinite.

Landres found his fastest mounted guardsman and sent him back immediately to Drachmund Heights with the message that another party sought to claim Falda. This would be no peaceful habitation. The warrior become messenger fled silently back through the dark surrounding arms of the forests, which had hidden their advancement thus far. Should he not reach Ulrich, his fellow warriors who were greatly outnumbered had the very sobering chance that they would lose the land that Ulrich sought to possess.

———————————————————

At Kinterden Dell, the cool and misty day turned into a bleak, frost-covered evening. Kellen sat with his feet resting on a hide-covered stool, his musings lost to the mesmerizing gleam of a blazing fire. The popping sizzle of the flames kept him company long after most of his castle had settled in for the night. He could still see Alida with her dark hair, moist from the dewy air outside, as she covertly tried to enter the castle. She had not known that she was being watched, and he chuckled darkly at the thought of his latest move for power in the chess game of their marriage.

Without her knowledge, he had sent a band of his men to secure the lands and city of Falda. He planned to claim all of her remaining property and rights. She had no more family left to fight him, and it suited him perfectly that she was now completely at his mercy. An adjudicator that he kept in his pocket with adequate monthly funds would suit him well in reverting the agreements between Lyrnne and Kinterden, for there was no council larger than the allegiances made between warlords. Even adjudicators that served the people impartially, often found that most of what they had drawn up became invalid with the right maneuvering.

He absentmindedly rubbed the smooth, worn wood of the arms of his chair as he considered his new approach to their bond. With the invalidation of their earlier agreements, he would take his rightful place in making all decisions concerning her and the future of their holdings. Settling in deeper to the velvet-lined embrace of his great oak chair, he decided to wait a little while longer beside the fire before climbing to her chamber, making his latest plans known to her.

As the hours passed, the fire died down slowly, the coals beginning their descent into embers while thin slips of fragrant pine smoke rose up from the growing mound of ashes beneath them. Kellen, feeling it was time, rose and made his way to his wife's room, the heels of his boots clicking softly on the stone floor of the great hall.

The door to Alida's chamber opened softly without as much as a creak or groan. She lay sleeping deeply with her hair spread over the furs and her hand against her cheek. The cold air in the room brought a rosy bloom to her cheeks, which glowed warmly already from the light of the candles. But then all such details were lost on her husband, for he felt nothing for her besides ownership.

Kellen crossed to where she lay and quickly removed his boots with their soft clunk to the floor as if he was a friend settling in for a moment's visit. The cold air chased his progress, and he wormed his feet and legs comfortably under the wrappings inhaling the scents of the furs. She was no doubt spending too much of his money on such frivolities. Releasing his irritation towards her, he wasted no time in forcefully wrapping his hand painfully through her long hair.

Alida came awake, her muscles bunched in fear as a scream rose in her throat, but Kellen's calloused hand over her mouth quelled any sound. Kellen jerked her to her knees, her face inches from his. His moist beer-scented breath was revolting as usual, and though Alida had stilled her screams, she was terrified still, floating in a half-awake state. He had thoroughly startled her, and his forcefulness brought back memories of his past abuse. She began to fight him, tearing at his strong arms attempting to loosen herself from his grip. Stinging nail marks and bruises left a trail of pain along his arms and back while he too reacted.

Ignoring his discomfort, Kellen smoothly grabbed her arms and used his legs to pin her warm length beneath him, spoiling for a grand fight with her. Realizing that her resistance was sparking that sinister streak she had noted too many times, she went completely still beneath him, willing her muscles to go limp.

Kellen started to laugh. A sound that was filled with madness and hate. "You women are so sure of yourselves and your value, though we prove over and over again how low you really are. You cannot even fight equitably, acting like spoiled pets that when cornered are all teeth and rolling eyes. You never even smelled the trap I was laying for you, and don't think that I am not aware of your comings and goings, *fair lady,* for I have eyes and ears everywhere, all too ready to come to my aid!"

She started to speak, her eyes growing wide with the course of his diatribe. "Silence!" His voice grew instantly harsh empowered by her obvious humiliation. She did in fact fear him. How amusing and delightful. With a sneer, he backhanded her hard across her cheek and then yanked her from the pallet dragging her across the cold, stone floor.

Her head felt like it was going to explode from his stinging blow, and although Alida wanted to fight him, she knew that any action on her part would drive him further over the edge. Shaking off the ringing in her ears, she did her best to prevent further injury as the rough floor snatched at her barely covered skin, praying all the while for an opening in which to escape.

When Kellen saw that she was refusing to fight him, he stared at her for a second before throwing her down. Then he stood for a few moments with his back to her panting quietly, as he allowed his composure to restore itself. She began to inch away from him, fearing any movement would catch his attention.

Like a cat with an injured mouse, Kellen took his time catching his breath, willing his emotions further to a deadly calm. Then without warning, he turned, bent over her, and grabbed her head by her hair so that she was forced to look into his eyes. Alida barely had time to swallow the squeal that had risen in her throat at his painful grasp of her hair when he kicked her in the stomach as hard as could. The force was so violent that she immediately retched on the floor. He laughed at her increasing humiliation, his voice cold and remorseless. "You are my chattel, and I'll see that you behave as one of such a low position. It may take a great deal of time and effort, Alida, but I'll see you tamed and fully at my mercy until I can rid myself of you completely. Your aunt was a tool to be used to further my advancement, and despite the little agreements drawn up following our union, I continued in my plan to regain both Lyrnne and Falda for myself. The war with Quirin was a rather fortunate event taking care of my needs in a more public manner, ridding me of your aunt and ridiculous nursemaid in a most tidy packet." His smile grew more sinister. "Still, the *coup de grace* is this–I have sent my army to secure Falda, their ranks nearing the city while your spittle dries on my boot! It won't be long before I have the final piece of the puzzle allowing me the final move, making sure that you do not pop up again to challenge me!" Then he brought his fist across her jaw and the blessed black silence of unconsciousness took her in its arms.

CHAPTER SEVENTEEN

Ulrich looked up from teaching an agile young whelp the use of a dirk when the ringing sound of hooves on the hard cobblestones of the castle court-yard outside caught his attention. Though muffled by the walls of the castle, he could tell that there was something urgent in their rapid cadence.

He hurried from the warmth of the main hall out into the snow-covered yard and watched as one of Landres' guards approached with his charger in a full gallop. The young warrior rode with determination, his hair wild and expression grim. Flecks of lather and foam from the rider's horse had soaked through his battle leggings, and the smell of horse and human sweat surrounded both rider and mount with a greater urgency than words could have formed as the guard pulled alongside Ulrich. After quickly dismounting and saluting, the warrior launched into his message without further preamble, his voice hoarse and rough with exhaustion. When the message had been given, Ulrich turned and hurriedly reentered the smoke-tinged air of the great hall, sending servants to gather the commanders of his army.

A short time later, when all had been assembled, he instructed them to begin the process of collecting weapons, gear, and men under their command. Drachmund's force was going to war.

The massing of the men was rapid and efficient, for the Drachmund forces were well ordered and worthy. Ulrich's time that had seemed so measureless in the light of morning, was instantly consumed in the drawing up of engagement plans with the various battalion leaders as well as gathering reports on their readiness. He also saw to it that a lesser but experienced force would be left behind to keep the castle and city protected in their absence.

The remainder of the day had passed speedily when the gates were finally ordered shut and secured as Ulrich and his bands of warriors headed off into the late afternoon light that slanted across the frozen ground. They took only limited rations of food and water, knowing that the supply train Ulrich had ordered originally was being amassed in greater quantity to follow soon thereafter, for they could not risk the slowing effect of the cavalcade. Whatever time they had been given was spent in collecting their weapons and mounts.

Ulrich did not keep his army to the forests as had Landres' band. With Kellen's army already well ahead of them, they had no further reason to hide their intentions and took the broad common road instead. When night fell cold and dark, the force broke its endless cadence of hoofbeats and marching soldiers to make a light camp amongst the twisted pines and snow-caked fields of the outer borders of The Heights. They would start out again early the next morning for they knew that Kinterden would not easily release its hold on Falda's vast, rich properties.

Ulrich kept to himself, refusing the quiet conversation and rousing war stories of his men as they psyched themselves up for battle. Musing quietly over a tankard, he was honest with himself that he needed to prove to Alida that he could be trusted to succeed under any manner of adversity. In private contemplation, he wondered whether this could be the very event to bring her to his side and prove his worth. Then with great effort, he focused his thoughts and prepared himself for the grim realities of the battle to come. His cold steel blade glimmered menacingly in the light of his spitting campfire as he readied its surface with a cloth and oil.

Back in Kinterden castle's family quarters, Alida came to with the bitter iron-tinted taste of blood and vomit coating her mouth, as well as the scents and sounds of women all around her. There was something almost bird-like about their rustling tunics that offered up fragrant reminders of everything from roses to baked bread. They seemed so comical compared to the broken ragdoll condition of her own body and soul that she nearly laughed. She noted without interest that at some point since her beating she had been lifted to her pallet where every line and fold of the furs seemed to press painfully into her injuries. The intrusion of a young maid pressing a cool cloth to her battered face also became apparent as her consciousness increased.

She gazed at the bright headcloths and aprons around her and felt a sudden rise of rage in her chest that came in a hot surge to the surface of her skin. She arose with great difficulty, her face flushed and vivid, ignoring the pain that rushed to her limbs and stomach with the effort.

"Get out!" Her newly found voice wept in withheld fury—her normally cool, even tones spent in the pain of her awakening.

The two women closest to her pallet jumped and stared with big eyes at the easy play of lithe muscle beneath her delicate tunic and at her foreboding glare. They edged gingerly away from her towards their companions, none wanting to be too near. She was the strongest woman they had ever known, and they all feared her ability to back up her orders. They were gentlewomen in the truest sense of the day without the training and fury of her warrior's blood.

Alida snorted quietly. The kinswomen of Kinterden Dell lay divided between jealousy and fear of her. She had formed no close bonds with any of them and found their presence to be more of a nuisance than aid. They were self-righteous gossipmongers, and she wanted none of their involvement. They had remained indifferent to her or openly hostile, and their feigned interest in her health now needled her beyond endurance. As for the maids included in their mass, she was too humiliated to face them.

"GET OUT!" This time her voice boomed out into the silence that had followed her initial command.

Brightly woven aprons and skirts twitched as their owners scrambled quickly from her chambers, the heavy, well-oiled door sliding shut with a sigh behind them. As the silence of the quarters enveloped her, Alida dropped her head into her hands and wept.

The sobs were heavy and anguished, and she gingerly lay back on her pallet trying to stem their flow to lessen the floods of pain that washed over her body at the exertion.

From the corner of the room, a voice whispered, "Pardon me, miss. I did'na leave with the others." Alida gasped, wiping at her hot tears as she struggled to sit up. Her piercing gaze rested without welcome on a soft-voiced, petite woman who stood not far from her.

Faced with Alida's ferocious expression, the serving woman straightened her shoulders and curtsied. "Forgive m' boldness, but the last thing you need is ta b'left alone. Badly injured you've been, and yoor in need of careful attention, not isolation."

"I neither want nor need your attentions!" Alida's response ground out rustily from between her teeth—her rage and impotence unchecked and nakedly apparent in the tears that continued to slide like a molten river down her hot cheeks.

The woman stood her ground nonetheless with her chin in the air and a sympathetic gleam in her eye. Alida rose gingerly, and after faltering a moment, she advanced on the woman, her stance fluid and graceful despite her obvious pain. "Do you remain to take the delicious stories of my pain to the other chits in the castle or just to rub in the fact that I have been humbled before all of you?"

The servant's ability to withstand terror was apparent, for Alida was formidable and had taken up her sword from beside the bed with an anguished moan. "Yoor in pain, and I'm 'ere to 'elp ye. That is all! I d'na gossip, miss. 'Tis my greatest fault or so cook says." She backed up slightly at the cloudy anger that swirled in her mistress's eyes, but then refused to retreat further.

Alida halted her advance and was about to leave the woman to her frustrating notions when the exertion overcame her, and she collapsed once again in an unconscious heap on the ground.

When the woman was certain that Alida wasn't moving, she crept to her side, kicking away the sword and clucking like a mother hen, saying to herself, *Poor thing's been through ell n' back.* Then to Alida, "But d'na worry, lovey, I'll na' let the others bother ye." Her lilting words rolled off her tongue easily, telling the origin of her birth. She was from the Isles of Mist and knew all too well what it was like to be desperate without a soul to rely on.

She carefully hefted her mistress under the arms and dragged her slowly to the bed, her size no detriment to her scrappy strength. Then she retrieved a cool, damp cloth and waterskin that the previous attendant had discarded. She bathed Alida from head to toe, her jaw tightening at the deep bruises, lumps, and abrasions that marred the fair skin. She, too, had felt abuse at a man's hand, only she had not let the cretin live. She both admired and loathed her mistress's apparent composure in the matter. She had heard that this was not the first of such occasions.

When she had finished bathing Alida and had dressed her and tucked her in beneath the soft scented furs, she leaned over her and whispered, "Me name's Gwynn, or Gwyneth if you prefer. Sleep well, and I'll check back wi' ye' later." Then in an utterly tender motion, she smoothed away a wispy strand of hair that had fallen across her mistress' cheek. Alida didn't utter a word, for long before the ministrations had begun, she had gone to a place that was dark and utterly without sound or pain.

Old man moon had risen and was treading his endless path across the sky when Lordifyn appeared in the great hall of Kinterden, carefully whisking his way past the forms of sleeping servants. When he had come to the one he sought, he noted with surprise that the woman was already wide awake and staring directly at him. There was no fear or disbelief in Gwyneth's brown eyes, only curiosity and composure.

Lordifyn's deep voice hushed out into the room, "Have you been given the sight?" Gwynn propped herself up on her elbow, her fingers busying themselves with the brittle straws of hay that surrounded her. "Aye. 'Tis not the first time I've been fey, and 'twill not be m'last if I make m'best guess."

Lordifyn hesitated then whispered, "Then you will perform a task for the one who has given you the sight?"

"I never said that now, did I? How'm I ta' know just what sort a person ye be and what master you serve?" Her retort was both cautious and noncommittal.

Lordifyn started at the woman's quiet response then hesitated before continuing. "Alida is my charge, and no one else save she has ever seen me. You, Gwynn, have apparently been chosen by The Master–for He is the only true Master - whose name means Love." He paused for a moment and then said even more softly, "The task is this—Alida is in need of her one remaining friend. He is the chieftain of Drachmund Heights and is this land's enemy. He currently rides into battle with Kellen's army at Falda, but she is in need of him more now than his well-ordered ranks. Pray heed this call and send him a messenger to summon him back. Tell him to find Alida's paradise. He will know what it means."

"No one else will go?" Gwyneth asked, her question more to the air in general than to Lordifyn while her dark eyes hid her thoughts.

Lordifyn shook his head and waited. Gwyneth nodded then and arose not wasting any time, though the dawn had yet to peek out its tawny head. She knew that she was embroiling herself in danger, but she also knew that neglect of God's call could bring only greater folly. She didn't truly believe in being "fey" or magic as her people called it. She had one allegiance only these days and that was to the one true God.

Lordifyn reached out and touched Gwyneth's arm, God's own spirit flowing to her in peaceful assurance through the heavenly messenger. Then in a ripple of light, he disappeared.

When she was alone again, Gwyneth crept from the hot, muggy hall where the snores of warriors and servant girls reverberated, her focus being the under-smithy at the stables. Bryon, whose company she sought, had a big brawny frame, quiet dark eyes, and a loyalty only to her. They had a history together of friendship and protection. They had arrived separately on two different days to Kinterden so that no one would connect them, but they had known each other long before during the dark years after Gwyneth had killed her husband and fled for the main continent. She had met Bryon on the ship then, and he, being in dark circumstances himself, had formed a fast union with her.

Bryon listened to the night's hushed story and without comment rallied his mount, his thick fingers adroitly saddling the beast for a long ride. When she had left, he awakened the apprentice to tell him that he would be gone for a few days "to attend to a matter from higher up." He asked the young lad to alert the master-smithy of his absence when the sun had risen.

Gwyneth watched from the shadows outside the hall, the cold air forming funnels of vapor from her warm breath. She watched as Bryon mounted his horse and hurried from the keep out into the city, his mount's clipped departure noted and accepted by the guardsmen as unusual but necessary. Bryon had told the guard he had been sent out most urgently on a confidential matter directly handed down from the lord. Of course, the guard thought he meant Kellen, but Bryon meant God Himself. The maid pulled her scratchy, serviceable cloak tightly around her shoulders as a shiver of fear worked its way along her spine.

Saying a soft prayer to diminish the fear and loneliness Bryon's departure had caused, Gwyneth again found her bed on the comfortable, fragrant hay pile in the warmth of the great hall and fell into a troubled sleep, her dreams riddled with the screams of her mistress and sudden arrival of a bright lord to Alida's rescue.

Under that same moon, awaiting a similar dawn, Landres and his men lay concealed within Falda's walls. They counted themselves blessed. For having arrived first, they had been successful in securing the walled city and castle against any external siege.

His band watched as Kellen's men down below them, one by one, climbed from sleeping rolls, stretching and moving on to a specified area outside the camp limits for their personal needs. It had been less than a week, and Kellen's men who had finally arrived had begun the process of setting up an efficient camp. Including the latrine, they had areas for all manner of needs including a cooking post, a war games practice field, and racks for skinning and curing game caught in the surrounding forest.

The Kinterden force had moved on their scout's original correlation that the city and castle were deserted. They had brought their caravan along the road at a leisurely pace assuming they could move in and finalize Kellen's hold of the lands. They were, therefore, surprised and waylaid by the bolted impenetrable doors of the city. However, since no challenge had been sent out to them, and since there had been no sign of life from within the walls such as smoke, sound, or movement, the captain of Kellen's guard assumed that the place was indeed deserted and had simply been secured by Kellen's command via an original scouting dispatch after the fall of Lyrnne. Surely, their master's bride would know of secret passages into and exiting the city and could be called upon to open her walls to Kellen's colonization. So rather than sending a messenger back to Kinterden asking for aid and risking a second set of Kellen's orders, the captain had simply issued the command that the troops make an orderly camp that would suffice until the city walls could be reopened.

Landres and his men, even in the face of the obviously peaceful encampment outside, did not relax their guard and continued to go about their defense alert and quiet. They knew that to send out a challenge at this point would be foolhardy, and since their rivals had not yet ascertained their presence, it was to their benefit to remain patient and ready until their own force arrived.

They had yet to hear any news from the messenger they had sent to summon Ulrich. Landres' only worry was that Ulrich would not know that his men had arrived first and were in possession of the castle and city, for the messenger had returned to the Heights before their possession of Falda. He would have to devise a plan to alert Ulrich without alerting the encampment outside. He decided to start with the most obvious plan of action, which would be to locate any secret passageways the city and castle might have.

The next night when a sliver of moon appeared from behind a cloud, he and his men began a systematic search of Falda's walls and rooms to find any possible openings to the outside fields.

They located a hidden door leading from what looked to be a war room in the castle down to a back door in the keep wall and summarily to a door out of the city. However, it wasn't good enough, for Landres knew that Kinterden guardsmen patrolled every side of the castle including the thickets that had grown up along the walls. Kellen's men would also be in search of secret passageways until they had received their full force. Landres' men, therefore, needed an escape that would lead out into the forest itself, bypassing the surrounding army altogether.

Meanwhile, Ulrich and the rest of his army were making good time. They expected to arrive at Falda in a day and a half. As they came round a sharp turn in the snow-frosted road, a man in a hooded cloak rode fast towards their leading mount. Ulrich automatically placed his hand on his sword preparing for an attack, though he was not at the head of the force but surrounded by battalion leaders towards the forefront. He heard the figure arguing with his men, and so he rode forward cautiously at the side of the decoy *liege* (his armor bearer, Gradon) to see if he could be of aid. His own mount's breath puffed out in a white vaporous cloud around them as he surged forward the beast's handsome quarters brushing against the stamping sides of Gradon's mount.

When the figure caught sight of Drachmund's insignia emblazoned on the leather chest guard of the decoy, he pointed and argued more vehemently. One of Ulrich's archers turned his mount and rode towards Ulrich and his supposed "leader," while several other warriors prevented the man from following.

Namod pulled astride the two men, and nodding his head back over his shoulder, he said impatiently to Gradon, "Sire, he wants to see you and only you. He won't give his business or his name. Do you want us to send him away?"

Ulrich, turning to Gradon said in a low voice (as if in conference), "I'll handle it. Have the men fall in place at the ready." Gradon spoke in low tones appearing to give commands after which Namod rode off.

Ulrich rode through the ranks of his guard at the decoy's side, presumably as an armor bearer, and approached the man placing his helmet on his head as he went. His senses were alert now, for it could be an ambush with an archer or spear thrower in the brush ahead ready to take out the decoy when he cleared the ranks.

He made sure to approach with the man between him and the road ahead and his own men in a safe "u" shape around his and Gradon's back and sides. One line of well-trained ranks to the sides of his approach faced the brush along the road with bows at the ready while a second line kept a keen eye on the groves of trees up ahead their own bows poised for battle. It would not do for his army to lose their leader this early in the game.

From beneath the hood, Bryon watched Gradon approach, the clipped hoofbeats of their mounts ringing in the brittle winter air. Bryon was not duped. He would bet his life that the "armor bearer" at the chief's side was the real king. Here was a mighty man, mightier by far than the one who wore the insignia. There was nothing to be wanting in his figure or mounted seat. Here was the formidable defender of Gwyneth's mistress. Ulrich's powerful chest and arms played easily with the control of the spirited mount, and his legs expertly guided the beast in a measured pace that could almost be a war dance. His battle gear was worn and well-fitted without any telling insignia, but his carriage was too royal for a mere guard. Bryon briefly speculated whether there were any romantic involvement between Kinterden's mistress and this powerful warrior before him. It was all too dangerous, this covert mission to get the attention of Kinterden's staunchest enemy. Abruptly, the smithy forced his attention back to the immediate task.

Ulrich called out a clipped greeting on behalf of "his sire," nothing but reserve and caution in his tone. Bryon responded openly without malice and held out both his hands palms facing upward. Ulrich ordered that if it pleased his guest, he would like the cloak thrown back and any weapons displayed. Bryon showed his short sword and mace, but refused to throw back his hood.

He wanted no one to know his identity.

Ulrich, leaving Bradon behind, drew abreast of the figure and thanked him for his cooperation. Then inquired why the man was so secretive about showing his person to the king.

Bryon's deep voice sounded out quietly. "'We both know you are the one I seek, and I carry a private message, milord, from mistress Alida."

Immediately Ulrich was alert and trained on the man's every action. In a stony voice he commanded, "What news of her?"

"I have been sent to say that you are urgently needed and must meet her as soon as possible in 'her paradise.' She is not doing well, sire."

"Who sent you?" Ulrich's mount danced beneath him aware of his master's tension.

"'Twas one of Alida's serving women who asked to have her identity remain a secret as well."

"You worry that you will be cast as spies by Kellen?"

"Aye. It's where we must live and work. We want no trouble from anyone, but we must do as we are bid."

"Are you alone here in this place, or did you bring a guard?"

"I came alone." He looked anxious to leave, and Ulrich could not blame him. He would not want to be from the opposing side up against an entire army.

"Is Alida dying?" Ulrich fought to keep his voice from shaking as he asked this final question, for he knew of no other reason why she would allow there to be any tie between them while she remained married.

"Nay. But she has been badly injured. Please ask of me nothing more. Do as you are bid for no one save the four of us is privy to this matter. I must return soon!"

Ulrich nodded, giving Bryon his leave and watched as the figure took to the forest with cape flying and his body hunched in flight, the sound of terse hoofbeats fading away into the forest covering. Ulrich then quickly rode back to his army alongside the decoy once again and instructed the leaders of the various bands, through Bradon, to proceed as planned to Falda. There they would divide and settle into small camps around Kinterden's forces in secrecy until he could return to them and plan the siege. He let no one know of his destination and said only that he had been called away on a greater emergency.

His men shook their heads in disbelief as they watched their leader ride into the night. What could be more important than a campaign to secure more land? Muttering amongst themselves, they gathered nonetheless into disciplined lines and proceeded again quickly towards Falda, especially after Ulrich's top commanders quelled any attempt at surmising their master's business.

Alida was awakened mid-afternoon, two and a half days after the beating. She was still in excruciating pain, but her cuts had tentatively sealed themselves. Those that were bad enough had been stitched shut by Gwynn so that Alida was feeling slightly more able. She was amazed at the extent of damage done to her body. For other than a bruised jaw, sore and badly bruised stomach, and abrasions on her leg, she should have had no more injury according to her memory of what had happened. However, she did and this meant that Kellen had continued to beat her after she had gone unconscious. Alida shook with rage at her impotence in the matter. She should have been able to defend herself better against the brute. She told Gwyneth as much, but the serving woman had only shook her head and reminded Alida that though she had much prowess in hunting and horsemanship, she was yet much smaller than Kellen and had already been at the mercy of his physical force when she awoke. Abuse was that much more sinister for one's guard was not constantly up in one's own home. Home was supposed to mean safety and peace.

Alida had been surprised at Gwyneth's lack of respect for Kellen. As a result, a cautious trust in Gwyneth had begun. Should she continue to trust the serving woman, she would at last have a confidante and friend in the castle where she had been lonely for so many months. Yet should Gwyneth turn on her or show a truer loyalty to Kellen, then the danger to Alida would increase. She considered ending the friendship before it truly deepened, but there was something in her that believed in Gwyneth's authenticity. She wished for the hundredth time that Deive were around to guide her. She said a prayer instead and allowed her body and soul to ease in the Creator's tender comfort through the able hands of the maid.

Gwyneth spent the day occasionally checking Alida's wounds or fussing over her comfort. Alida was restless, but Gwyneth's company was soothing, and she knew her body couldn't take activity yet.

Her trust in her serving woman was tested that night, however, for when the sun had gone down, Gwyneth opened the door. When she had thoroughly checked the chambers and hallway, she came back to her mistress's side.

She whispered, "You must meet *him* tonight in you're 'paradise.' *He'll* be awaitin' ye." Gwynn looked at her mistress pointedly, her body language more of an indicator than what she had said.

Alida's face twisted in consternation. "What on earth are you talking about, Gwynn? You speak in riddles."

"Nay. Lordifyn said that you must meet the wolf tonight in the forest in your secret place."

Alida sat upright ignoring her body's groans. "How do you know of Lordifyn and the secret cove?" *And of Ulrich,* she thought silently.

"He appeared to me the night after your beating. He said you'd despair and would be in need of comfort from your only livin' friend. The good man's been sent for, and you'll need to meet wi' him. He's worried, I na'."

Alida didn't offer any information but sat quietly gazing at Gwynn.

"Ulrich, my mistress, should there be any doubt to whom I'm referrin'."

Alida bit her bottom lip and then gingerly rose looking for her most comfortable tunic and darkest cloak. "You know that if you aid me in this and Kellen is alerted, you'll be beaten and possibly killed."

"Aye. I've known it from the start, but I'm wi' ye just the same!" Gwynn remained unshakable.

Alida paused a moment, allowing herself to make the decision. If Kellen had planted Gwynn to catch her, then the maid wouldn't suffer, but Alida herself would most likely die at his hand. If what Gwynn said were the truth, Alida would be putting both of them in danger. As if reading her thoughts, Gwynn gently squeezed her mistress's arm. Alida decided not to look back and dressed hurriedly in silence. There was a curious knot inside at the thought of depending on Ulrich. For he was indeed her only true friend besides the kindness of this maid.

The two women slipped out of the castle and then the city into the black night, and Alida was reminded of her excursions with Deive. Perhaps this was a good omen. They traveled in relative silence with Alida leaning heavily on Gwynn, requiring numerous resting periods. Presently they arrived at a grove where Gwynn had hidden away two small, thick plow horses. The mounts were shaggy and sturdy, and Alida chuckled as one whickered softly to her and tossed its head. She patted both their broad faces, and with Gwynn's help, she mounted gingerly on the back of the smaller, her usual strength astonishingly diminished.

From there they made their way to the deeper glens, and Alida relied on her inner sight and her falcon's night vision to direct their way. Halfway there, Gwynn stopped and said she'd bed down for the night and would await her mistress's return. Alida did not argue and was secretly glad that the glade would remain her own.

When she reached the spot, she tied up her horse and made her way to the brush barrier. She saw no sign of Titan or any other activity. Then she stopped dead in her tracks as a thought surfaced suddenly. How did Ulrich know of this place? She had never told him. Perhaps Lordifyn had relayed the directions. She continued on, but had grown cautious, for too many people seemed privy to her secrets.

With hushed steps, Alida came out into the glade and saw no sign of Ulrich. The moon chose that moment to break through the clouds, but it wasn't full enough to see the entire glade. She lowered herself carefully to a rock by one of the springs and rubbed her eyes, which had suddenly grown very heavy. How delicious it would feel to bathe in the warmth of the springs. Surely, her muscle aches would subside, and she'd feel at ease. Nevertheless, she sat up straighter and decided to wait for a while, for she did not want to give Ulrich a view of her naked flesh. She'd been too free with him as it was.

She watched silently as the night moved sluggishly along and still she did not see any sign of her wolf. When a couple of hours had passed, she decided that she could wait no longer and carefully stepped out of her cloak and tunic, remaining attired in her thin, dark underslip, her bare feet encased only by the silky strands of new grass. She flung her hair over her shoulders and braided it so that its curly, satin length hung down her back. She was forced to pause several times for her right arm ached deeply.

Sliding one leg and then the other into the depths of the pool closest to her, Alida slowly submerged herself until her head disappeared beneath the hot water the smell of the mineral springs enlivening her senses. When she broke from its surface moments later, her braid had come loose and water cascaded gloriously from her silken, moon-drenched head.

In the nearby shadows, Ulrich released a breath for she had a glorious silhouette, all alabaster and silk in the white rays of moonlight. He had just arrived with careful tread lest this be a plot to capture him. He was therefore surprised by the vision afforded him. Turning his back, he waited until he heard the telltale sounds of splashing as she settled into the pool once again. When he dared to look once more, she was resting with her head lain across her bent arms and her stomach against the side of the pool. When her breathing became deeper and some time had passed, he stalked silently forward, his stomach knotted with restraint. He gently ran his warm hand down her glistening arm, calling her name as he touched her. Her head immediately came up, and she cried out in surprise.

He gentled her with soft reassuring words and ran his other hand along her jaw, puzzling that it felt fuller than it had before. His own jaw hardened when she made a little sound of pain at his caress. He grabbed up her cloak from off the ground. Kneeling, he opened it, pulling her from the water into its warmth and nestling her safely onto his lap once seated. She argued softly with him, but she didn't even attempt to physically wrest herself from his grasp. He knew then that something was terribly wrong.

As he tenderly dried the drops from her hair and shoulders, he noticed how the shadows seemed thicker around her neck and the upper part of her left arm as well as low on her legs and shins. Even at this distance, her skin didn't glow quite as brightly as he remembered. When his touch smoothed over her elegant neck and collarbones, she muffled a throaty whimper of pain. Ulrich couldn't take anymore.

"What is wrong with thee, love?" His voice held more concern and fear than she had ever heard.

"Naught." She said it into his shoulder, for even with his ministrations being as gentle as they were, her body throbbed painfully from its wounds and the exertion of the walk and ride to meet him.

He wanted to take her chin in his hand and force her to meet his eyes, but he knew that this, too, caused her pain. Unable to take anymore mystery, he removed a pouch at his side and extracted flint and cloths dipped in fat from its midst. Working carefully, he made a small torch and then settled it into the ground next to them. When he looked up from this small duty, Alida had turned away from him, and on her back where the underslip slung low to her shoulder blades, he saw old scars and rows of newer more jagged ones.

How did she gain such horrible scars? he wondered. *Why were there new ones marring her still silky skin?* His teeth clenched together, and he none to carefully turned her in his lap. It was then that he saw the "shadows" across her face, arms, and legs. The shadows were bruises. Bruises so thick and dark that they looked like her skin had been dusted with soot.

His wrath burned red behind his eyes, and his voice came out so steely and quiet that she had to strain to hear him. "It was that fiend you're married to, wasn't it? I'm going to kill him for doing this to you, Alida. No man is allowed such handling of thee!"

She cried out, "How do you know that it was he?"

"Tell me that it wasn't! Give me reason to hate another!" His eyes had turned into blazing daggers in the weak light of the torch. She trembled at the rage that shook from his strong form reverberating into hers.

"I cannot." She hung her head, for surely disaster would come of this. She had no strength to deal with Ulrich, his deep anger, Kellen and his fury, or her own pain. She felt like an idiot, but right there on his lap she began to weep—great choking sobs that were wrenched from the deepest part of her. She bravely tried to wipe away the tears and stem her sobs, but they would not be held back. Ulrich softened at her misery. He would save the burn for when she was gone from his presence. Kellen would not survive when the blazing rage was released once again.

He cozened her and murmured every reassurance that came to mind, his voice a thread of warm caramel in the cool air. Her grief and fear were beyond any he had seen. She had been nearly crushed beneath the events that had dominated her life in the past months and years since leaving Falda. This, added to the heavy hand of her cruel spouse, would have completely broken another woman. Her strength to continue amazed and drew admiration from him. She was so immense in her power and brightness.

When her tears had been nearly spent, she spoke softly, her words again murmured into his rock-hard shoulder. "Will you guard me and aid me in my healing, for in order to do so I must change form. The body of a falcon is stronger and more given to mending than this awkward human skin."

Ulrich gently raised her chin and smoothed away her hair. "I love thee in all thy forms and would be honored to aid thee. But answer me this query, why have you not done so sooner?"

"It takes too much energy and strength to transform under such conditions. I am vulnerable even in my healthiest moments. To do so when broken would render me as useless as a babe in arms." She swallowed and then looked at him with directness and pleading. "You will have to hold me down and keep me from flight, and then you must hood my eyes and wrap me in some bit of cloth, perhaps my cloak. I must not be allowed movement of any kind. I may hurt you, and I may scream, but you have to continue on as instructed."

He nodded without comment, swallowing back the bile that rose in his throat at her treatment and again gently stroked away her hair, carefully avoiding contact with her damaged flesh.

Then silently he arose, and lifting her into his strong arms, he found a place away from the springs and rocks. He gently deposited her onto the soft grass of the cove, and tearing a bit of cloth from his tunic, he fashioned a hood that would suffice for the duties asked of him. Alida watched his movements and marveled at his gentleness and willingness. She had nothing to fear this night.

When all the preparations had been made, Alida lay back in his arms and gazed into the sky, feeling her body recede and her spirit take over. Then screaming and thrashing began as she lurched into her falcon form, and it was then that she felt the extent of her injuries. Her left wing was broken or cracked, and the bone's damage had not been fully felt until now. A cracked collar bone, sternum, and rib were added to this. Her innards felt like fire and ice such was the extent of their bruising, which made it difficult to concentrate. Now completely transformed, Alida thought no more as a human but as cousin to the wolf and the air and the earth. All she knew was pain, and she sought escape.

Ulrich cried aloud at the unexpected strength that flowed from the injured bird in his arms. She was all cutting talons and beak buoyed by a flashing agony. As carefully as he could, without relinquishing control, he extracted her from her black crumpled overslip and covered her smooth feathered head with the hood, wrapping her up tightly in her previously discarded tunic.

Then he proceeded to his horse. He would take her from here for a few days and allow the old woman, Birch, to administer herbs and bone setting. Alida would not have permitted it should she have known before, but her injuries far exceeded mere rest as their prescription.

The cove stood still and empty behind the odd pair as the moon's pale light turned silently into a cold dawn.

On his way from the glen, Gwyneth met up with him, her soft voice consigning the care of her mistress to be transferred to him. Gwyneth did not know that Ulrich already had Alida in his arms in bird form, for she assumed that her mistress still lay back in the cove ready to join him shortly, and that the falcon he held was his own hunting bird. Ulrich chose not to alert the servant woman of Alida's changeling abilities and rode quietly away, assuring the dark-eyed foreigner of his return.

Deep within the shadows behind the little troupe, angry eyes watched, coldly calculating the exchange. Cackling fiends patted and pinched—their hot, stinging fingers encouraging rage. They had been dealt a mighty blow the night of Lyrnne's fall, and they sought revenge in the form of this dark-haired man. Perhaps he would rid them of the bright one's presence.

CHAPTER EIGHTEEN

A stately older woman opened the door to the resounding knocks that rang out just hours after dawn. Ulrich was immediately invited in, a rush of cold, moist mountain air following him through the door, as he was offered a rough seat at a humble but sturdy table.

Ulrich quietly rejected her offer of a drink or nourishment, and when she saw how upset he was, Birch settled in to listen quietly to his tale, her fingers tapping absentmindedly on the table at which they sat. He told her that he had found the injured bird in the forest and had decided to rescue it. He also stated that he did not intend to keep the bird, but would release it when its healing was complete. When he was done with this explanation, she patted his cheek with her dry, rose-scented hand and said, "Now tell us the real story, m'dear."

He ran his hand over his face. "I never could fool you. You and Eldridge have much in common."

She laughed, her teeth flashing in the firelight and said, "That old fool just pretends to know a great deal. He couldn't tell the difference between a bull and a cow!"

Ulrich chuckled outright, allowing himself to settle into the familiar surroundings. They could have chatted for a while about many things that mattered little, but Ulrich fell silent for a time. The only sound in the room was the pop and sizzle of the fire and the whisper of fir fingers over the roof of the abode. He could feel her dark eyes on him, and being wooed by the pungent smells of herbs and leavening, he began to tell his heavy tale of Alida and his growing passion for her. This time he knew better than to leave out any detail.

Birch listened quietly, punctuating her silence with murmurs and nods when necessary her hands busy with a twig that pried at the spaces between the table's planks. She remembered making the funny costume for a masquerade. She had thought it odd at the time that Ulrich had not elaborated on the feast's location. Now she understood his cautiousness. She knew all too well the bloody history of the feuding between Kinterden Dells and Drachmund Heights, having seen much of this history herself.

Just as Eldridge had, not so long ago, she asked carefully pointed questions. Ulrich had never behaved in such a manner in her entire memory of him, and by this, she knew the graveness of the situation.

She was glad when he did not seek her advice, and she used the empty moments after his speech to make up a cot for him to sleep on since he had declared that he would not be leaving, wanting instead to remain at Alida's side.

A short while later, as Birch mixed a tonic on the table, Ulrich gently lifted the light-bodied falcon onto his lap, smoothing the silky feathers down over Alida's breast that had been disturbed in the movement. Doing as he was instructed, Ulrich removed the hood and helped Birch administer the odorous concoction she had just made by filling a small bladder full of the liquid and gently forcing the fluid through the falcon's open beak. When the bird's head had dropped wearily back upon her softly feathered breast, Birch gently set the silken wing and rib as best she could. The broken sternum was left as it was, and Birch prayed that the shattered ends would not pierce a lung or the innards.

Then she gently squeezed Ulrich's shoulder, signaling the momentary end to her ministrations. He sighed and absentmindedly passed his finger through the flame of a cinnamon-scented oil lamp, remembering how simple things had been when he had come here as a boy.

They continued their application of tonic and aid for three days, and in mid-afternoon on the third day, Ulrich picked up Alida's tiny form and rode back the way he'd come, keeping her nested against his warm chest until he could deposit her safely into the cove with an extra supply of Birch's healing formula.

He had also brought along with him a cage in which two young bantam hens had been placed. In a casement attached to one of the bird's legs, he had included a note to Gwynn. It merely read "She's home." Then he hunkered down to watch the road until a fat farmer with a load of dried goods and tools approached. Ulrich stopped the man and made a bargain that in exchange for gold coins and a fine, sharp blade, the farmer would carry the cage beyond Kinterden walls and see that it was delivered properly.

This was done so with little effort. The man was clearly benign and was of the assumption that others were as innocent. He thought himself very clever for having made such an incredible bargain. He was not keen enough to wonder about the contents attached to one of the biddies.

The eyes that watched from the forest as they had on the previous night could not readily discern the details of the transaction. However, they had seen that Alida was back in the cove, for the watcher had seen the tall man deposit her there. What was of greater interest was the fact that a most unusual transformation had taken place afterwards.

When Gwynn rode out secretly that night in dark attire, the eyes of this watcher were upon her. Ulrich, too, secretly watched the maidservant. When she had come close enough for him to see that she was unescorted, he led her to the cove and handed Alida's care over to her. Then he made his own departure leaving a small, gentle kiss upon his love's smooth forehead. He rode straightaway back to the battle he had deserted, feeling a deep urgency to complete the mission. He wanted Alida with him and sought to settle his discontent by ending his enemy's power.

The moon at Falda crept beneath a lone, dark cloud as Landres, and his guard slowly made the rounds again that night using the darkness to cover their search for a hidden passage. They had been at it for about an hour, when one of his men quickly approached and motioned to an upstairs room. Quietly the two made their way up the tower, leaving the rest of the guard to continue their search.

Landres clasped the warrior on the shoulder in silent thanks after they entered the tiny room and the cleverly hidden door's mechanism had been demonstrated. A monstrous oaken closet that would normally take six men to move had been placed into a niche of comparable size. There was no way to grasp the sides of the closet without giving up leverage, almost as if it had been pushed in from the front. The warrior had spent a great deal of time poking and prodding at the thing before discovering that one of the hooks within could twist sideways setting a simple mechanism into motion. The works were made of wooden and iron gears that caused the entire wardrobe to slide forward out of the niche, exposing a door behind it in the granite wall. When it was opened, a rush of dank, cool air blew past them. They drew their swords and proceeded cautiously and silently down the damp, stone staircase by the dim light of a small lamp all the while drawing in breaths of stale air tinted by moss and mold. After only going a few feet, the unreliable little torch guttered out, and they were left in total darkness.

Landres encouraged his guard to continue, though they were now without the benefit of light. Each scrabbled their way along, touching the moist walls and stairs. Soon the staircase's hard surface gave way to a more spongy footing. Landres knelt and removed his glove, feeling the ground beneath their feet. It consisted of damp rotting leaves, moss and dirt.

Knowing that it was yet early for the relief of their army, Landres continued his progress through the tunnel with his warriors en towe. Presently they heard the unfamiliar voices of another guard's men. Landres grasped his companion's hand and pressed their sign for silence into his palm. Then they crept forward, each straining to hear the exact location of their enemies through the tricky gusts of the tunnel. All at once, they could see light up ahead, and they dropped to a crawl, peering out at the scene before them.

A half-dozen of Kinterden guardsmen stood around a small fire warming their hands and chuckling over each other's bawdy tales. They were heavily armed and well muscled, a sign of the total readiness of Kellen's entire army.

Landres was instantly thankful that their lantern had not suffered the gusts of wind, for the light would have been obvious through the bramble and stone that over time had concealed the opening to the tunnel. They lay for some time observing the enemy and watched as the moon grew even fuller overhead. When they had completed their inspection, they retreated up the winding staircase and into the tower room.

Once the door had been secured again, the two men rushed down to their own guard below. Plans for a message relay to Ulrich would have to be set up, and as immediately as possible.

Landres chose Gowen, one of his lancemen who was swift of foot, to be their relay. The man was given an inscription on leather, secured in a compact casement, as well as a flask of water. His comrades worried silently that he included no weapon, fearing for his safety, but he insisted that he would be better served in an unencumbered state.

Two other men were sent along as escort through the tunnel to watch Gowen's back as he exited into the forest. Landres had estimated by the visible stars that Gowen would exit through the tunnel on the westerly side of the castle and city, leaving but a short route to the main road and freedom.

The three men lay on their bellies much as Landres and Burtoch had, watching for any opportunity to slip unnoticed by Kellen's guard. Their vigil paid off. For an hour later, the guard was changed, and Gowen's slender, dark-cloaked form passed silently into the surrounding forest, using the moon and stars overhead to direct him to the road as planned.

Landres' directions proved precise, and Gowen was able to meld silently into the night. When he was sure that he had passed all of Kellen's guard, he veered off into a small cove. There he stripped silently to his bare skin, wrapping the casement, flask, and clothing into a bundle. Then in the moonlight, his form morphed into that of a lean, wild-eyed dog. When the transformation was complete, the bundle was grasped up tightly into the mouth of the beast as it fled towards home.

'Twas only some hours later that the horses at the head of Ulrich's army began fretfully breaking rank. Their restless whinnies and chuckles caused ripples of unease throughout the guard. These were well-trained warhorses not given to the natural unease of most mounts. Ulrich's captains whistled and soothed, bringing the steeds under hand, but now their own defenses were up, for they knew better than to ignore such a warning. Then as quickly as the disturbance had begun, it was over. Some moments later, a tall, slender man walked towards the mass of drawn swords.

Greetings were called out as soon as Gowen was recognized. He was breathing heavily and sweat beaded on his brow. Swords were replaced with offered flagons and a flurry of questions. The captain of the mounted archers held his hand up for silence. When this was given, he quietly directed inquiries about the battle up ahead.

Gowen concisely related both the positions of the two armed forces as well as the location of the secret entrance before handing over the inscription from Landres. For the sake of his cover, he feigned a greater exhaustion than he felt, for only Landres knew of his changeling blood. No one thought to ask how long it had taken to travel from Falda's imposing walls. He was given one of their extra mounts as the captains drew together to make a plan of action. They conversed heatedly for several moments, many being loath to advance under such circumstances. The uneasy balance currently held at Falda could be overturned by an indelicate move, endangering their force within Falda's walls.

Little time was lost before an agreement was reached, and a temporary camp was made for the bulk of the army. As a precaution, a small battalion was sent ahead to strengthen the forces within Falda. Gowen headed up the battalion due to his greater familiarity with the terrain and enemy encampment. Those left behind found themselves praying for Ulrich's swift arrival back.

In the soft light of Kinterden candles, Alida allowed herself to be soothed. Gwynn had drawn Alida a fragrant herbal bath, and the warmth encompassed her completely. Her bruises were fading to an ugly yellowish-green, and her cuts had healed to much-reduced scabs. Her arm and rib did not pain her so abominably, and her jaw and head no longer ached. The deepest remnant of her injuries was mental rather than physical.

She longed for both revenge and safety. The man whose keep she shared had become the object of her nightly fantasies in which he was slain in some meticulous and horrible manner. She would fight to shake the images from herself, knowing that any door to anger and bitterness would open her up to the gleeful and manipulative presence of darkness. Nevertheless, there too was a place for justice, a call that she was hard pressed to ignore.

Gwynn, remembering her own loathing of the man she'd been espoused to, held her tongue as she watched her mistress's struggle. She could offer no advice, for in such grave matters a person was forced to make her own path. Her choice had led her into danger, loneliness, and regret, but she was finally free. Long ago, she had offered repentance though she still believed her actions unforgivable. Now she sought to serve others as a gift in return for absolution.

Seeking to calm her mistress, Gwynn bathed Alida's back and told her fairytales. The stories were soothing to Alida's overwrought mind, and she concentrated on the maid's smooth voice as the dwindling pain was washed from her body. When Alida had fallen asleep, Gwynn quietly left the room via a back passage. She would return to awaken her before the water grew too cool.

Alida slept lightly, allowing the warmth of the bath to wash over her. Just as she felt her sleep deepening, she felt hands other than Gwynn's caress her wet back. Wearily her eyes came open, and she heard a deep intake of breath behind her. Hands slid silently over her stiff shoulders and none to gently pinched the tender muscles near her neck. Alida instantly knew her husband's thickly muscled hands.

"Sleep well, little one? You glow with rest and care and *something* else." His voice was almost a sneer in the calm silence of the room.

Alida shook her head, eliminating the cobwebs that sleep had left behind. She struggled to sit up, but Kellen's forceful grip disallowed any movement. Abruptly, she willed herself to relax under his touch, loath to incite his anger and violence again. Her eyes were wide with terror, and she fought hard to quell the fearful twist of her gut, her knuckles like iron on her knees beneath the lapping surface of the water.

"Where have you been? I have greatly missed the companionship of my dear little wife. Have you enjoyed your time away?" Alida forced herself to remain calm, but dread was starting to seep through her facade. "It must have been so *lonely* for you all these months, locked away from any familiar faces. It is important for us all to have *friends*. Do you have friends, Alida?"

This time she could not contain the shiver of fear that caressed her spine. She could have sworn he implied much by his tone. Then, the moment seemed as quickly gone as it had come. Could it be that Kellen's madness was growing?

Her response was quiet as she used a soggy sponge to hide her shaking hands. "I . . . I don't know by what you mean when you say 'gone.' I have been resting, my . . . my body was . . ."

He interrupted chuckling darkly, "Somewhat damaged?"

She swallowed. "I picked up some herbs and potions from the kitchen and made use of the cold streams in the surrounding dells."

He chuckled. "How brave, clever, and *resourceful*. My little wife is indeed so *very* clever. No one else would think to bathe in a stream during the biting cold of this season. Most would seek a warm bath, perhaps similar to the one you enjoy at this very moment—even better yet, the comforts of a soak in a warm spring. And what of friends, Alida? You never answered my query about your lack of friends. Have you enlisted the trust of one of my servants or kinsmen? Perhaps even the tender ear of a *male protector.*"

Alida, unable to contain her response stiffened and climbed from the water. "I . . . I am cold and need to dress. Forgive me, for I do not ignore you, 'tis only that the room is dreadful drafty."

Ignoring the obvious fact that she would still remain tender from his latest violence, Kellen grasped her tightly about her ribs, crushing her to his body against the impenetrable wall of his chest. "Do you know what grieves me the most, my dear?" Mutely, she shook her head.

"Not only have you sought the company and mostly likely the bed of my enemy, but you have enlisted the aid of one of *my own* servants." Then in a near whisper, "She will not survive your betrayal."

Alida cried out, tears instantly springing to her eyes. Not Gwynn! She could not suffer the loss of another friend. He turned her roughly in his arms so that she faced him, their profiles so close that they breathed one another's breath. His eyes were sharp and almost gleeful for a moment as he took in her terror and pain and then he said, "Next time choose your friends more carefully." Then as quietly as he had come, Kellen was gone—a mad dog into the mad night.

She stood shivering in the cool air with her fear cascading from her eyes and down her cheeks in great salty sobs, the tears drying, cooling on her hot cheeks as water on coals. Then roughly, though the sobs still racked her breast, she brushed away her tears and dressed shakily. She didn't know what she would do, but she would not let him harm Gwynn.

From the back passage, Gwynn grasped her cloak tighter to her neck, the itch of the wool tickling her along the ridge of her jaw. She had opened the door just as Kellen had begun his torturous game with her mistress and had overheard the entire conversation. Action quickly replaced surprise, and she fled down the passage to a small door she had discovered not long ago. Its tight hallway filled with freezing air from the outer walls took her from the upper levels of the keep to the open courtyard below. There she shakily sought out Bryon, and without delay, he hid her in the smithy, beneath a pile of scratchy, moldering burlap.

Out in the courtyard, Kellen gazed coolly about, having lost track of the petite, dark-haired maid that had incited Alida to find shelter with his enemy. He blamed the servant, for he could not believe that Alida would willfully go against him after having suffered so much at his hand. She would become more womanly and timid with time he thought, especially once her maid was disposed of.

Bryon watched from the shadows, going about his work as if nothing were out of the norm. His muscles were tight and heated at the thought of confrontation, but he soothed his nerves, reminding himself that few if any of the keepsmen knew of his and Gwynn's attachment. Should any be discovered, he was able to handle both his own safety and hers. His beefy hands flexed over his work, and the rush of protectiveness he felt for Gwynn turned them into iron.

Much to Bryon's relief, Kellen wandered away after having found no sign of the maid. Shortly thereafter, Alida burst through a side door, peering wildly about, her heels rapping a quick staccato in the midst of the other sounds, both human and beast, in the courtyard. Though Bryon longed to assure her of Gwynn's safety, he would not give away the maid's location. He quickly looked away from their frantic mistress, seemingly concentrating on a steaming scythe he was carefully testing, having just pulled it from the cold water barrel.

Kellen turned just in time to see Alida hurrying through the shadows, and quickly crossing to her side, he took her in hand with a look of warning before delivering her safekeeping to one of his guardsmen. As instructed, the man remained very alert, never giving her any opening for escape. When she grew very bold and tried to face him down on the way back to chambers, he cuffed her roughly on the cheek. Her eyes flashed as she warned him with a hiss of Kellen's fury, but he chuckled darkly and then spit on the ground. "He said to handle you the way he would himself!"

She wanted to scream in fury, but would not give the cruel guard or her own husband the satisfaction, so instead she swallowed her anger and continued to watch for an opening.

CHAPTER NINETEEN

Kellen, with the help of his men, began a systematic search of the halls, grounds, and outlying areas of the keep for the "dangerous" and disloyal maid. Much to Bryon's relief, they started with the servant's quarters, which were opposite ends from the smithy. Watching cautiously, he waited until a loud body of men had passed by, the sound of their feet and deep voices ricocheting off the stone keep. Then stealthily he removed Gwynn from the rucksack pile and secretly deposited her outside of the keep walls.

From there she fled to the shelter of the surrounding dells and forestland, her brown cloak and diminutive size camouflaging her from the eyes of the watch on the wall. Her jaw was set tightly, and no tears fell in the bitter cold. She knew how to survive and knew that now was not the time to give way to fear.

Thinking for himself and Gwynn, Bryon made use of the guard's occupation elsewhere to quietly gather up supplies that were necessary for a small journey. He took things that were sturdy and not easily missed, and later that night, when the search had died down, including a thorough search of the smelting room, he told the head smith that he would be leaving to aid his relative who had been sick some weeks before. Apparently, this unfortunate "relative" had fallen ill once again, and he would probably be gone for a longer duration this time. The smith, though unhappy to be shorthanded, alerted the guard and sent Bryon on his way, never guessing for a moment that Bryon's casual manner belied his intent to escape permanently.

Once free of the keep walls, Bryon headed along the main road on his shaggy mount knowing that he was still in direct view of the guard. Though no connection had been made between him and Gwynn, she was a fugitive and his gear had been checked over for any sign of her presence or person. When none was found, they let him pass. By behaving normally, he assured that his freedom would continue. He kept on in this way, his mount's feet rustling at a casual pace through the rocks and dirt clods of the well-worn road until he had gone past the bend in the byway, which took him from the watchtower's view.

Once there, he quietly melded into the forest shadows, heading silently for a prearranged place of meeting.

Gwynn's muffled cry when she saw his approach was all he needed to tell him how much she depended on him. All her good intentions of bravery fled at the sight of his brawny frame. He spoke in deep, husky tones to her after having dismounted, and before he could react, she was in his arms hugging him tightly. Though he knew she was loath to express such emotion, tears soon soaked through his goat's hair vest.

He patted her back awkwardly, for they'd had little physical interaction, even after having been companions for so long. Then he felt it—pleasurable warmth that started from his toes and moved up to his chest and cheeks. He felt passion for her come in this silent way, and in that moment, his resolve to keep her safe increased until he thought he would burst from the power of it.

Gently and without breath, he tipped her chin up and kissed her softly on the lips—his own dry and warm. They remained quietly like that for some time before he cleared his throat and distanced himself from her, leading the way to his horse. He would see them safe and secure before exploring this new development. She was soon mounted before him with his arms tightly about her trim waist as they headed for Drachmund Heights. Both hoped for asylum against Kellen and his force.

―――――――――――――――――

In the frosted evening air, Ulrich bent near to his steed's neck, knowing he would soon come upon Falda's byway. He was alert as always, noting as he had so many weeks before the many tracks cluttering the path beneath Titan's feet. He assumed by the lack of fresher marks that these were the hoofprints of his own army. Because they had not been crossed over, Ulrich prayed that this was a sign of his force's dominance in the situation.

As he and Titan pushed on, fat, cold flakes of snow began tumbling down around their heads. Neither man nor beast paid much heed to the thickening flurries. Had Kellen's captain posted a guard along the stretch of road, he would have seen the urgency of the powerful beast and golden-haired rider dancing through the thick cold to the cadence of the impending war.

Many furlongs up ahead, the guardsman on watch for the Drachmund encampment gazed out into the blinding flurries, his senses straining for sight and sound. The waiting and cold made him tired, but he still he continued on, his pacing making deep marks in the snow. This vigil was rewarded much later that night, for Ulrich was greeted by the menacing point of spear and sword as he burst through the blinding downfall.

Ulrich called out, "Ho there, watchman! Be thee friend or foe?"

The man immediately lowered his weapons and grinned. "Friend to thee, you overgrown apparition!" Ulrich laughed and saluted as he rode briskly by, his cloak and beard completed caked with snow.

The news of Ulrich's arrival was quickly passed around, and his captains merged en force to the center of the encampment. They all took what little warmth they could from their cloaks and weak lanterns, for fires were still outlawed by the captains to preserve their location. The gathered men quickly updated their leader on the current events of the siege and then fell silent as he mulled over the information.

Presently, Ulrich said, "We have surprise as our boon. It would not be too difficult to make our force within Falda aware of a plan to attack simultaneously, trapping Kellen's force between us. I am surprised that you have not advanced already."

A few of his captains shuffled about uncomfortably, and then one swallowed and straightened, saluting as he spoke. "Forgive our delay. We were loathe to advance without your command, milord. A lot can go wrong unexpectedly, and we did not want be without your guidance and approval."

Ulrich nodded, the weight of responsibility sitting lightly on his knowing shoulders. "Very well. We will let the guard within the walls know of our intentions to attack at moonrise tomorrow. Ready yourselves." The captains left, melding like ghosts into the weakly lit flurries, the howling of the wind masking any recognizable sounds of weapons clinking or human conversation.

Up ahead in the Kinterden camp, Kellen's captain of the guard, Murok, and an advisor sat comfortably ensconced in a pavilion discussing their inability to breach the city's outer walls.

"'Tis odd that we can find no opening into the city, and that it is locked from the inside. I am ready to break down the doors."

The advisor shook his head, "Nay, t'would be too much trouble. Besides, if there were a force within, no matter how small, they would cut us down in the doorway like hay before a thresher. We have already discarded the idea that it was occupied, Murok, but ye must realize that even a small force could be within, so small that they don't want to give away their weakness."

"Aye, but what presence in this area would use so small a force? The most powerful keeps would want to display their military might. They would not pass up the opportunity to flaunt their strength."

The advisor was quiet only a moment. "Our best move is to send a messenger to Kellen. We didn't use the opportunity before, but we can use it now. Then we will have a point of decision. If it was Kellen that ordered Falda locked, he will know how to unlock it as well. In addition, the waiting will only deprive a force inside of their much needed supplies, especially if that force is one of an unfriendly nature,."

Murok rose quickly, being a man of action. He ordered a messenger who was given rations and a sturdy long-haired mount. The man was instructed to keep off the main byway and make his way to Kinterden as speedily as possible.

After full preparation, the young man wheeled the thickly muscled charger about and took off for the forest. He valiantly attempted to keep close to the byway without traveling it directly, but the snow and the darkness made it nearly impossible to track anything. Soon he gave rein to his mount, tucking his frozen hands into his cloak. He let the beast make its own way towards home, the sound of the wind around him his only companion.

Through the muffling presence of the snow, the messenger and Ulrich's army passed each other in the night, neither party realizing the presence of the other.

Far away, a man and woman on horseback clattered up the frozen path to the imposing doors of Drachmund Heights. All at once, they were surrounded by spears pointed menacingly at the sides of their homely mount. Both Gwynn and Bryon held their ground, neither shrinking from the guard.

"What is your business?" demanded a gruff, red-haired warrior.

"We seek asylum within yonder walls." Bryon's gaze did not waver, his eyes intent but non-aggressive. He shifted his hold on the reigns, putting the rough leather straps into one palm that his other might be free to fight if necessary.

"From whence do you hail?"

"Kinterden Dell."

The guards shook their heads in disbelief, one boldly speaking out. "You seek asylum within these walls when you are from the keep of our most loathed enemy? You come to our gates with the stench of Grost's aura still strong on your pale hides! Get thee gone beggars, and seek asylum within some other holding. We've no interest in allowing the likes of you to mingle with our good folk."

Despite the haranguing, Bryon responded quietly, his brogue thickening with stress, "Then we ask one boon of thee, when thy master returns, ye give to him this scroll to read. It is meant for no other eyes than his own."

The red-haired guardsman advanced on Bryon. "What source tells thee that our master is away?" The prick of his spear in the mount's side caused the beast to dance beneath the couple.

Bryon remained closemouthed. Gwynn unable to bear the silence and the increasing glowers of the guard, said softly, "He told us 'imself of 'is plans."

This was not entirely true, but Alida had told Gwynn that Ulrich sought to gain Falda back for her. Gwynn had assumed that he had already ridden to do as he was bid having passed along the information to Bryon. It was a dangerous chance to take.

The guardsmen remained unmoved for a few moments as they exchanged eye contact and the unspoken signals of men at arms who have served long with one another. Finally, the bold one who had spoken before said, "Ye may camp outside our walls under the watchful eye of the wall guards. We will seek the wisdom of the keep advisor and our master."

Both Bryon and Gwynn caught the hesitation in the voice of the young guard and knew that Ulrich must indeed be away. Nevertheless, they did as they were bid and made a small camp beneath Drachmund's walls, the thin fire that they made doing little to guard them from the wail of the wind that beat against Drachmund's battlements.

The guardsmen turned their mounts and reentered the walls of the city intent upon locating Eldridge. They found him hunched in his usual place over the musty, dust-filled records of the castle. Before any of them could interrupt him, his smooth voice inquired of their well-being.

"We did not even know if you had heard us enter, Master Eldridge."

He chuckled, "I am a lot more aware than any of you think! Now what do you so earnestly seek? All of ye look like a breath of wind t'would send thee scampering away."

The red-haired warrior stepped forward, clearing his throat respectfully. "There are people outside of the walls seeking asylum from the reach of Kinterden Dell. They know, somehow, that Ulrich is away. There are only two; the woman said she was told so by Ulrich himself. They gave us this scroll to pass along to him."

Eldridge, in an unusual show of nervousness, dropped the blackened twig with which he was scribing and stood up quickly; the clang of the writing tool against his tankard a sharp punctuation to his movements. In moments, he stood before the guardsman and snatched away the hide-covered scroll. Then he proceeded to inundate them with questions. "Where are these people? Why did you not bring them to me for questioning? I want them brought in immediately. No—wait! Take me to them instead!" Then again with indecision, "Nay, bring them inside, t'will be safer for all concerned. The poor souls must be frozen to death in the gale outside."

The guards with carefully schooled faces did not react to the stress of the flustered older man and moved quickly to bring the two vagrants to him. Bryon and Gwynn looked up as the great gates to the city opened once again without so much as a squeak or groan unfolding the ranks of the band around them like satin bonds. The red-haired guardsmen motioned them to dismount and led their horse while following on foot in the center of the mounted group.

Once inside the city walls, the guardsmen visibly relaxed, but their strides remained businesslike as they marched their charges through the streets. They were given immediate entrance to the castle, with wide-eyed children and keepsmen whispering around them about the couple in the middle of the guard. None heeded the questions as they took precautions to secure the "guests," leading them to where an anxious and pacing Eldridge awaited. To their surprise, he asked all the guard to leave and had Bryon and Gwynn sit before him on a sturdy wooden bench in the warm anteroom. When the doors to the room had shut, Eldridge began immediately with his interrogation.

"You have spoken with Ulrich before?"

Gwynn and Bryon exchanged a glance. Then Gwynn spoke up, her voice filled with indecision and mistrust. "Aye, I have spoken with him in the forest outside of Kinterden Dell."

"Be thou, Alida?" The air around the threesome ground to a great and silent stillness for the space of a nanosecond before Gwynn laughed. "Nay, if ye saw milady ye'd recognize her at once by her carriage and wellborn speech. I am Gwyneth, her handmaid."

Some of Eldridge's nervousness dissipated before he demanded of Bryon. "And who, pray tell, are you?"

Bryon straightened his back. "Me name's Bryon, the under-smithy at Kinterden."

Eldridge found a stick of black licorice root, his eyes narrowing in thought as he sucked loudly on the treat. "And what is your business with Drachmund Heights?"

Bryon remained silent, and once again, Gwynn led the way, her bright gaze guileless and intelligent. "We have fled for our lives, or rather I have. We aided our mistress, Alida, against the wishes of Kellen Grost. He is seeking to end my life as an instrument of discipline to his own people lest they should at anytime in the future do the same. Bryon is innocent of this entire affair, but has chosen to never return, for we have an inseparable bond between us."

Bryon scowled at her, but could no longer hold his tongue, his husky voice offended. "Nay, I am not innocent. I took a message to your master from Gwynn and her mistress. I was a party to the entire matter as well." He scuffed his toe on the ground and then stilled his movement lest it reveal his nervousness.

Eldridge stood and grabbed the scroll from where he had placed it. "May I? You were right about Ulrich being away, and we do not know when he will return. It could be weeks before he reviews it. Generally, in matters of the city, I am the next after our liege to be informed. You can trust me entirely with this matter."

Bryon and Gwynn scrutinized him separately and then glanced at each other again, finally motioning their approval. Everyone remained silent as Eldridge read the contents of the scroll, his eyes passing quickly over the entire story of how the two before him had come seeking refuge. Then rolling the scroll up crisply, he held his warm, smooth hands out to each of them and welcomed them to Drachmund Heights, apologizing for the cool reception.

Arrangements were made, and they were given more luxurious quarters than their stations would command. As a silent, non-offensive precaution, Eldridge also instructed several servants to keep their eyes on the newcomers and had additional guards posted near their doors "for their own protection."

In the hilly lands of Kinterden that smelled of slush-laden flora, Kellen and his men gave up their search. Because of their inability to find the handmaid after so many days of seeking her, Kellen was in a foul mood. He had allowed his hatred towards his wife and her maid to build, and only a violent release would soothe his mind.

Seeing the predatory carriage of her husband and knowing that his anger had increased due to Gwynn's escape from his guards, Alida had become a phantom in the halls of the keep. She refused to present herself to him after his madness in her chambers those few nights earlier. Should she come face-to-face with him again, one of them would die. She fingered the cold steel and ivory handle of a wicked-looking dagger that told her so.

She found a tiny room in the loneliest section of the castle where she laid out a blanket and fur. She did not allow herself even a tiny fire, not wanting smoke or heat to give away her location. In the wee hours of one lonely morning, after nights and days of prayer and anguish, she finally made the decision to leave the keep and be rid of her fear and hatred forever. She would not cower like a trapped beast beneath Kellen's shadow. The Ancient One would never require of his child this constant misery. However, with her decision came also the knowledge that she would never be free to love again as long as her husband lived. The thought of living as an old maid was more attractive than acting out the part of a wife to a madman.

When night had fallen, three days after Gwynn's departure, Alida found a high parapet and allowed her transformation to take place. There, in the curling howl of the winter air that had come back in full force after a brief teasing thaw, Alida felt the downy warmth of oiled feathers replace the raw chill of her bare skin. Having gathered her bundled possessions into her beak, the winged creature flew high, fighting the cold that had taken away the smoother thermal winds of daylight. No sound followed her, save for the whistling wind in her wings, for she would not give her position away to the guards below.

Like an ant on the road to the keep, Alida saw a tired horseman rapidly approaching the main gates. By his gear, she could see that he was one of Kellen's warriors, and by the cadence of his hoofbeats, she knew it was urgent. It was a guardsman she had not seen since he and others had left some weeks earlier on a mysterious mission. She shrugged off the trickle of curiosity and animal warning that the warrior's arrival had created. The keep and its business were no longer her concern.

With directed strength, she fought her way towards Drachmund Heights, her falcon's eyes gazing into the hazy night colors, seeing no sign of the spirits that normally attended her. She had no way of knowing that they had left her to defend Ulrich's honorable cause in a battle that would be fought over the soil of her homeland, a bidding that was given by Creator Himself.

On the rich, snow-covered lands of Falda, Drachmund's army gathered in anticipation of battle. Ulrich's written instructions were delivered to the force within Falda by the same lone cur that had traversed the miles to find Ulrich's troops. He went unhindered past Kellen's warriors, save for a single stone that was thrown at his retreating tail. The warriors did not think twice about how he disappeared into the prickly undergrowth, for such was the nature of any beast, especially one as gaunt and indescript as the dog that had skulked by their ranks.

Once inside, he transformed and quickly located some keepsman's discarded clothing, having been unable to bring his bundled attire as he had on the road before. Then he hastened to locate Landres. The captain of the guard received the message with great relief. For the patience of his men was wearing thinner by the day, and they had begun to conserve their supplies, not knowing the duration of the siege they'd have to endure.

CHAPTER TWENTY

The moon that rose that night shed its cold blue light over the creeping forms of Ulrich's army. Within a portion of an hour, they had completely surrounded Kellen's encampment. In the moment that the moon broke free from low-hanging winter clouds, their battle cry with all of its chilling clarity rang out over the frozen land like starving wolves hunting in the night.

A simultaneous cry rang out from within Falda's walls as the gates burst open and poured out their dagger-like wave of death.

Kellen's men were too well trained to run screaming from their bedrolls, but there was still a certain chaos to their movements as they gathered up weapons in the eerie cacophony that surrounded them. Sleepy shouts and the tinging sound of weaponry rang out in the night, as did the sounds of stumbling feet and hissing fires.

The howls continued as Ulrich, leading his men, advanced with great fury, his own voice raised in a bloodcurdling cry. To the warriors of Kinterden, the mass of men that advanced upon them looked like the rippling folds of a dark wizard's cloak.

The clash of the first men to battle resounded in the already noise filled air–metal deflecting off metal mixed with the stench of sweaty anticipation. Moments later, every sword whistled death and every arcing arrow its whine of pain. The pull of battle deafened any human softness, and though bodies fell and bled, warriors from both camps fought with single-minded intent for both their own lives and those of their living comrades, their horror had to be waylaid for the practiced strokes of war.

Kellen's battlefield advisor and Murok fought back to back, astounded by the fierce expertise of the overwhelming force that dropped their men one by one. 'Twas not so much that they were greatly outnumbered, for Murok had brought the greatest strength of Kinterden to the field, but they had been caught unaware, and few of his men had time enough to clothe themselves in their protective gear.

Nearby, Gowen unsheathed a small throwing blade from his boot, hefting its cold, pearl-encased weight while his eyes trained in on the richer attire of

Kellen's advisor. He was glad now that he had left the minute weapons behind in the sheltering walls of Falda. Mayhap with luck, he'd bring down this man and leave Kinterden's army limping from the lack of at least one of its leaders.

The small blade left Gowen's hand with a hushed whistle, even as he drew another from his snow-covered boot, his hands warm with battle and thus immune to the cold. The first found its mark, directly in the temple of the unfortunate advisor with a sucking sound that dropped him with a leaden thud to the slushy earth. The second remained quiet and deadly in his hand as Murok turned on him with a roar. Rather than face down the heavily armed warrior with only his small blade in hand, Gowen turned and sprinted away leaving Murok trapped between two other battling groups. Gowen's darting moves gave testament to his dog-changer muscles.

Landres, having seen the whole affair, laughed darkly as Gowen moved to his side. "You, sir, are no warrior but a tricky assassin. I do not envy that poor fool." With a smile and sweat dripping hotly over his brow, he tossed the extra sword that Gowen had left behind with his own, stabbing backwards into the screaming approach of an unfortunate Kinterden guard, the scream ending in a half gurgle as the man fell slain to the ground.

Gowen's bright teeth flashed in the cold light, his eyes hard and cocky. "Aye, I am a dog with teeth and claws and no sense of pride. I dash in and bite, and then I run with my tail well tucked."

Landres' chuckle turned to a growl as he swung his sword again, this time parrying a blow from a warrior that had lunged in their direction. A man seeing his companion's disadvantage in the face of two Drachmund soldiers joined swiftly in the fight. Gowen had no choice this time but to stay and defend life and limb alongside his friend. The blows came heavy and hard, their ringing force causing ripples of fractured pain down the Drachmund warriors' arms and shoulders. It was a barbaric dance of art and prowess between men of deadly intent and deadlier aim.

Some distance away from the fury of hand-to-hand combat, bands of archers protected by ensigns carrying shields rested in the relative security of their outlying position. Their deadly quills rained down with cruel force on the shoulders, necks, and backs of Kinterden's best with beautiful precision. Here and there, a soft throat or belly was found and the gurgles of pain gave hideous testament to the gaping maw of death that hungered for the lives on the battlefield.

Spear throwers, too, remaining detached but alert, sent their lightweight skewers into men who were foolish enough to come within range. Not one of Drachmund's ranks showed weakness or lack of training–these were men born and trained for the bloodiest of arts.

Then a shift in the battle became apparent as Murok bellowed for his captains to gather their bands. The ranks of Kinterden men were rallied into lines of sword-encased threats, fighting against Drachmund's double-edged attack. There in a suddenly cohesive wheel Kinterden turned their vulnerability to their compatriots and the threat of their weaponry on all sides towards the enemy.

Ulrich's mouth pinched into a stern line as he watched the initial moments of surprise and advantage melt away. Now t'would be a fairer and tougher match. Now he would see all his army's strengths and weaknesses in the most gruesome and truest of lights.

His call, too, echoed over the fields as key adjustments were made to his already well-ordered ranks. The advances and retreats from here on out would be more predictable and harsh. This was not like the attack on Lyrnne that he had witnessed with the berserker ranks of Quirin's band. These were armies trained alike in the well-ordered rules of combat.

Back at Kinterden, Kellen and the few captains who remained listened to Murok's messenger.

Kellen scowled at the missive that had been included, and had he been a dragon changeling the thin leather scroll would have been consumed by the fire of his breath. However, a dragon of a different kind haunted his heart, a black hate with razor sharp jaws and fowl miasmic breath.

The creature that inhabited him unfurled into his very blood, and as a result, everything looked dangerous, and everything was rife with hidden meaning. He could not believe that it had taken the captain of his guard so long to enquire about the locked fortress. The devious nature within whispered at the threat the letter implied. Kellen's nostrils curled, and he crushed the leather folds of the missive in his fist. He would have Falda, for it meant the crushing of his wife's only remaining power. He did not care about the fields or the possibility of wealth, he wanted only to enjoy her misery.

The hate compacted more tightly in his chest. Turning to the head captain of the remaining force, Kellen growled out as if to a child, "Take the rest of the men and execute Murok. The fool took too long to contact me. He may have cost us Falda."

The captain swallowed at the thought of having to kill his fellow warrior whom he had come to admire. "Milord, I realize Murok's position, but he is not entirely responsible. Did he not have your advisor to rely upon?"

Kellen grinned, "How right you are. Dispatch Koln as well."

The captain turned green, stuttering with surprise, "But, milord . . ."

The point of Kellen's sleek silver dirk was quickly pressed to the captain's throat. "Shall we make it three?"

The man saluted, and along with the other captains left the hall, their shoulders stiff with the weight of their orders. Once outside, quiet grumbling roiled amongst them.

"Kellen is becoming more foreign to me as the days pass."

"Aye, he's not been himself since marrying that little cow."

"We'd do better to dispatch her than such worthy men as Murok and Koln."

The head captain disliking the seeds of subversion barked out, "It must be easy for all of you to speak when *your* pride is not on the line. 'Tis just the move needed to humble the wench." He hastened his stride, pulling ahead of the group. He would not risk death. *He* would obey *his* orders.

Then from out of the hallway, Kellen himself strode. He had decided not to leave such important business to his men. He would join them on the battlefield. Besides, he did not want them to have the chance to discuss his politics behind his back. Danger licked at his senses. His head twitched slightly as he made his way to the stables, unrest apparent in every motion.

Small, sulfurous fiends clustered around their host, holding on lovingly to his ears and the back of his neck. His growing hatefulness and paranoia dripped like honey from their lips. They talked aloud to their parent force that whispered and aided them. He would introduce himself fully to Kellen when the time was right. His black chuckle sent the small fiends into a frenzy. This favored child of Creator, the winged woman whose husband they now tormented would not survive their menace.

This thought that had spun through the legion's mind for centuries continued its endless revolving. They had known about her birth and her place before she had been the seed in her father's groin. They had planned her death before she was quickened. This special duty that they had been given would succeed. Kellen unconsciously licked his lips, his jerky movements becoming more and more mated to the sulfurous cloud.

The only creatures witness to its horror were the terrified horses who were being saddled in preparation of the journey. They did not silence their bugling until a piece of the legion that threatened them grossly with scratches and jeers entered into Kellen's own mount, leaving them in peace.

On the fields of Falda, Ulrich and Landres looked out upon the fifth withdrawal of the battle, kneeling together over a leather map of military logistics. Their forces, still on either side of the Kinterden army, remained their greatest advantage. It had dissuaded Kellen's force from gaining too lengthy or complete of a rest. With every withdrawal, the Kinterden army concerned itself more with wary watchfulness than any expenditure of energy on tactics.

Ulrich and Landres divided and redirected their forces until the Kinterden wheel was not only enclosed on two sides as it had been initially, but was now fully surrounded. The noose of Drachmund Heights would in this way grow tighter and more impossibly broken with each bloody and successful attack.

The seventh advance saw the empowerment of their plan. For Ulrich's men were not only intent on the individual combat before them, but the success of their entire force. They minded the call of their captains, and their battle cry that resembled the heavy howls of wolves kept them well banded and intense with each new wave. Communication flowed easily in the circular advancement, and the added mental game of such complete unity tore away at Kinterden complacency and focus, even after their foes' regrouping. All around them, the air was rife with the smells of blood and gore and the smoky oil of flaming arrows.

The Kinterden army was immense to be sure, but the Drachmund force ate away at their numbers with unrelenting advances. Ulrich had called his men armed with maces and swords to the innermost ring of the army. Here such weapons were at their most useful. For Ulrich's army had drawn too close for Murok's men to use arrows or spears against the inner lines without fear of injuring their own. Reports from the front lines that trickled in to Ulrich and Landres also provided great relief, for it had been discovered that the Drachmund swordplay was more advanced, throwing Kellen's men off-balance. Add to this, the passion of Drachmund's army to succeed for their liege, and they were matchless. Ulrich believed that the fallen advisor to Kellen had been key in confusing and weakening the army, for they were used to performing orders rather than devising them.

Conversely, for the Drachmund force, the archers and spear throwers had been moved to the outermost ring finding the perfect enlistment there. Well-cast strikes were flung into the very midst of the Kinterden force. It was horrific being packed in with the odorous corpses of fallen soldiers. Though these were hardened men of battle, the situation was dire. For it was difficult even to maintain their footing in the slick pools of blood and human remains. They had to fight twice as hard to do the same job as Ulrich's men. Kellen's army was becoming mad with alarm. None amongst them had a faith in Creator to fall back upon and from which to derive strength.

Landres and Ulrich had left their outlying positions of strategy, preferring to be in the midst of the heaviest warfare. They fought valiantly side by side in the masses of sweating, writhing bodies, their jeers and well-aimed blows testaments to their assumption of success. Mixed in with the sounds of sheer bravado were their prayers to The Ancient of Days for swift victory and warnings to the men around them to continue to persevere.

Ulrich's blade alone found well over two hundred men that night, his hand glued to his sword grip by the sticky warmth of blood and the sheer inability of his hands to uncurl after such use hour after hour . As his jaw clenched yet again with the force of a parry here and a thrust there, still more men did fall, all feeling the heat of the red wolf's blade.

Landres, with aching arms and back, continued likewise to parry and thrust. His lunges were deep and sure in the spongy, damp earth, even with his fatigue. He found nearly every mark, cutting down a greater number than even his leader. 'Twas his place to remain by Ulrich and 'twas his every well-aimed blow that had kept his leader standing and in good health. Upon occasion, these two worthy blood and sweat soaked men grinned grimly at one another as the noose tightened and their strength increased.

Kellen being yet a good day away had no way of knowing that his well-trained army had begun to appear somewhat less capable beneath the new light of early morn. When this watery light had grown somewhat stronger with the strengthening of dawn, Ulrich withdrew his men once more, and this time they retreated far enough back that at first Murok thought they'd been given reprieve at last. Then the weary and grim archers of Drachmund stepped forth with aching shoulders and throbbing necks for the final whistling rain of death. To a man, the last of Kinterden fell bloody and defeated to the wet, red-brown soil of Falda.

The selfsame sun whose face did shine on the grim fields of Falda shone without apology in the mists of Drachmund Heights. Alida, having awakened from a fitful night's rest on Ulrich's luxurious pallet, paced to the chieftain's window. Her linen robe whispered around the length of her body as she turned to the bright warmth of the sun.

When she had covertly arrived the night before through Ulrich's window, the voices of the castle that past by her in the halls whispered about the tumultuous war at Falda and the presence of her love at that place. Because of it, her heart was in turmoil, and with the dawn, she had made the final decision to attend to him there. She undressed once more, packing up the bundle of the night before, and then she transformed lightly in the wet air, turning towards the place of her birth. This time, in the cool fingers of the mist, hundreds of watchers appeared at her wingtips calling silent secrets out into the warmth of the dawning light. She listened and answered with knowledge of her own which Creator had imparted.

Little by little, the hundreds of watchers became thousands, and presently Alida saw the canopy of war that had spread out through the sky's shell. Colors of hate and beauty mixed and roiled in the otherworldly silence above the earth. Alida, struck by its power, watched in awe as the force of beauty overwhelmed hate in what looked to be nothing more than rivulets. Nevertheless, it took very little for the drops and rivulets to become streams until the earth was covered in a gauzy mist of blue with the silence of victory falling complete.

Alida dropped down through the covering just in time to witness the final rain of arrows being loosed from Ulrich's archers. As always, she was awed by how the things of the natural mirrored those of the spirit world. The woods enveloped her plummet to the earth, and in the cocoon of a ring of tree roots, her transformation was made complete. Still the watchers attended her, until the dew of her sweat from flight had dried powdery and useless on her skin, the cold air battling with the warmer updrafts of the mossy roots of the great tree.

Some leagues away, Kellen feeling a deep urgency in his blood, spurred his riotous mount towards Falda. He wanted nothing more than the blood of battle and the sweet odor of victory. His fingers curled around the reins as he called his remaining ranks in tighter. Again, the battle called to them as mysteriously as a pounding in the chest and a whisper on the wind, and this time he nearly lost control of his steed. The destrier was fractious and as anxious for the war ahead as he was.

The legion doted on its host, making him feel safe and powerful. It put the taste of war on his tongue and sent myriad visions of victory through his muddied mind. The parent power sat waiting in between heaven and earth. It was almost time. Then with a shuddering surge, the legion was vomited from the bowels of that place, and there on Falda's byway, he, the puppet master of the legion, appeared in a great and glorious divination to the half-insane lord.

Kellen wavered on his mount, seeing a shining man dressed in woven linen with a crown of stars ringing his head. Kellen allowed his eyes to close, trying to clear away the vision, but still it remained. In a trance, he and his mount continued forward toward the beautiful being. When they had drawn nigh, Kellen saw that what he thought was stars were entrapped souls tortured in an unnatural orange light. Instead of finding them hideous, his cruel heart thought it mesmerizing, and he reached out his hand to touch them.

It was then that the prince of the legion spoke, his voice honeyed and soothing. "Most pleasing of all my subjects, you shall stand above men filled with greater knowledge and fairer to behold than any man before or yet to come. Every warrior who crosses your path shall envy your comeliness and your might. Women and children will fear your presence. No beast on earth will escape thee, and even the walls of your home shall call thy name. Your might will be remembered and your lands vast. In every place, at every table, your name will be raised on high, and on every lip, your valor will be praised. You shall be as a god."

Kellen, mewling and greedy, called out, "Who are you that I may give my due?"

Behind the honeyed tones, the prince hissed, "Call me 'lord.' "

"Of what are you the lord?"

The creation paused and grinning deeply called out, "I am the lord of noise and the air is my dominion."

"What do you want of me?" Kellen's voice was eager now, his lusts overcoming any suspicion.

"I want that my realm should be free of the whelp Alida. I want her death, Kellen, and though I know that you have yet your use for her, I would ask that by your hand her death would come."

Kellen swallowed the chortle that rose in his throat. This foolish deity did not realize that he already had planned his "adored" wife's demise. He turned away as if in deep contemplation, his brow creased appropriately with worry and regret. Then solemnly shaking his head, Kellen said, "I cannot deny thee."

The power, tasting the deceit, grew more mighty and licked at the peaceable air around him. Then he moved back towards the bowels of the in-between land, his voice growing dimmer in retreat. "Do not displease me."

Kellen's army, whose ranks had halted, watched in confusion as their master reached out his hand to nothing but air. He moved this way and that, his voice talking to no one, as his eyes like the eyes of one in a fever darted to and fro. His mount held absolutely still.

The captain to Kellen's right moved forward towards his master, but being unable to bear the chaotic gleam in his eye, he backed up quickly once more to the saner companionship of his rank. Then as suddenly as it had come, the moment was gone, and Kellen, with a mighty roar, spurred his mount forward.

"To battle!"

His men, willing away their unease, surged forward in unison though they knew not of which battle he spoke. The messenger they had seen said nothing of a battle. The messenger had only said that Falda was locked and requested assistance in opening her gates. However, the guardsmen, being well-trained, did as they were beckoned by their liege.

The sight that greeted Kellen and his men upon arrival at Falda a day later was fearsome indeed.

The sky, though a riotous blue to those of the spiritual realm, was in the physical realm a dark roiling black, for clouds had appeared from out of the mouth of the in-between land to swallow the newly risen sun. It was no more than a cover created to deceive and confuse, but Kellen and his men, being not aware of those things spiritual, felt the dampness of the black clouds to their very souls.

For this weapon, which had been formed against Ulrich's band, in turn, had worked doubly on the band arriving from the south. All around them lay the twisted and lifeless forms of their kinsmen and friends. Gaunt faces stared unseeing into the gullet of the black clouds and gnarled hands that had frozen in place poked up from the battlefield like horrible flowers. A dusting of snow covered the older corpses and the fresher were pink as the snow mixed with the remains of somewhat warmer blood. The horror of the scene was fresh to the arriving battalions, and their minds, not having been warmed by the battle itself, screamed out in disbelief.

Ulrich's guards had begun the retreat towards the walls of Falda immediately following the final rain of arrows. For the next interminable hours, they proceeded to eliminate any wounded survivors of Kinterden. Ulrich had commanded that all of the belongings and weapons of the corpses remain untouched, for they would be gathered and burned on the morrow. When the day had come and gone and another rising of the sun appeared, one of Ulrich's number turned to look back at the aftermath of battle and saw at the edge of the far-off copse, Kellen's fresh battalions. His voice screamed out a warning before a well-aimed arrow pierced his throat.

Immediately, Ulrich's captains began whistling and shouting for their men to regroup, the majority of the remaining ranks headed for safety within Falda's walls. Then Ulrich himself, shouting more fully than any other and with a voice hoarse from command, instructed his freshest bands to remain facing the oncoming force with weapons at the ready. They would protect his exhausted army's retreat.

They were greater in number than Kellen's men and all fought valiantly with Ulrich at their head, but the past few days events wore at them. Ulrich, wondering if the outcome was indeed assured, called out to Creator to aid them and give them final victory. He kept up his shouted prayers as his sword swung like the scythe of death. In those moments, he felt his hope and strength renewed.

His exhausted men who fought closely with him felt, too, this spreading power, and soon they chanted together Ulrich's prayer of safety and victory, their blood-covered knuckles grasping their weapons with a renewed strength. The fiends on Kellen's shoulders and those that resided in the breast of his mount screamed in agony at the power of this invocation. Full of malicious desire, they struck back by aiding the hate of both their hosts and the men that rode with him.

It was during this moment of advance that Alida came from out of the forest. She had donned battle gear taken from fallen soldiers including a quiver and arrows, and carried a slender long blade firmly in her whitened grasp. She could see the red glow of fiends and warriors on Kellen's side and the shimmering silver of the watchers and warriors from Ulrich's bands. The two forces looked like ocean tides advancing for a final, calamitous meeting.

In a voice filled with pulsing faith, Alida shouted to the winds, "Ancient of Days, I seek that which you freely give. May the hands of mine enemies be stayed, and may your conquering princes give us aid."

A sound like the roar of winter rushed from behind her out of the forest, and she saw warriors from the bosom of Creator encircle the field of battle. They stood seven cubits high, gowned in silvery mist and light. Their faces were indistinguishable such was their illumination, but she could discern green long-fingered hands that plucked out fiends from the fabric of the earth. In their shimmering hair, which was spun like a fine, glass web over the globe of the field, escaping fiends were caught and mercilessly dispatched by smaller warrior spirits.

Alida, shouting her thanks at the top of her voice, dashed out into the melee to help the beloved of her heart. She jumped into the fight with hacking swings of her blade, sparing as much energy as possible until she could reach her goal - the vantage of a nearby rise. After fierce swordplay, she was finally rewarded with the rapid climb to the little hill, using the time to prepare arrows as she went. These she used sparingly, picking off only captains and aids in Kellen's three battalions.

Kellen, having spotted the keen-eyed warrior woman, wheeled his horse in her direction. The possessed steed responded with great glee, and the prince of the air cackled despite a growing number of wounds in his side. His soul blood would dry soon enough once her menace was destroyed.

Ulrich, having spotted Kellen early on, watched as his archenemy wheeled his charger. He made a move to follow, and in that instant, he caught sight of Kellen's target high on a rise to the east of Falda. Ulrich swallowed the fear he felt at seeing his love in danger. He delivered a fatal slashing blow to the warrior who had engaged him and galloped off, his path an intentional interception to Kellen's.

The Prince of the Air settled deeper into Kellen his murmurs and cries a constant prod to his host's sick mind. Ulrich, unaware of his own shining escort, allowed every muscle and breath to strive along with his steed. The two men arrived at the point of interception, and the Prince of the Air screamed out hatefully when he caught sight of Ulrich's shimmering escort.

Lordifyn, his eyes glowing silver in the mists, felt his might increase, for Ulrich's army had not given up their prayers and songs. The protector made a beeline for the Prince of the Air, but was engaged first by his summoned fiends. The Prince of the Air, faltering for a moment in his surety, suffered another blow. Then with the force of fire and wind, the bowels of the in-between land vomited more shadows onto the earth. Yet still, even with these fiery reinforcements, the hand of hate was held back for prayer contained the greatest power.

Alida, completely aware of the spiritual warfare before her, added her own prayers and songs to the rising praise. Her watchers contended for her against the crawling shadows that nipped at her feet and spirit. The awesome sight of the massive warriors sent from Creator distracted Alida, and she did not see that Kellen, with a deft movement, had gone around Ulrich and was now bearing down on her.

With high-pitched trills, her watchers warned her of his impending arrival, and Alida was able to throw herself out of the way as Kellen's destrier tried to trample her. Immediately, when he realized that his steed had missed her, Kellen jumped from off of horseback and tackled Alida just as she began to stand. The wind was knocked from her, and her head hit a patch of protruding rocks. Instantly, she was unconscious.

Ulrich, meanwhile, had wheeled his horse, adjusting for Kellen's feint and advance and was only paces behind Kellen. When he saw Alida go limp, his stomach lurched into his throat, and it was all he could do to keep the bile from leaving his mouth.

Kellen in a smooth movement and with superhuman strength threw the light body of his wife onto his mount's back and preceded to mount behind her, just as Ulrich caught up to them. With a frantic motion, Kellen's mount began to trot, though his master had not yet gained his seat.

Ulrich slashed out at his nemesis, and his well-slung blade sliced through Kellen's cloak and into his side. However, Kellen hung on and further encouraged his mount until the stumbling beast was at a good canter. Ulrich had turned to make another pass just as a loose arrow from out in the battlefield drove into his left arm. The pain delayed his turn, and he fell several paces behind again as he watched Kellen take his seat firmly, all the while grasping at Alida's still form.

Ulrich watched as his mount fell further and further behind. It was then that he realized his horse had been shot as well. An arrow from the same barrage had found its way into the black charger's hindquarters. Ulrich, refusing to give up, watched the direction of Kellen and saw that the half-crazed man was taking to the thickets behind Falda.

When he and his mount had finally reached the back corner of the castle, they saw Kellen's mount prancing nervously around without sign of Kellen or Alida. Ulrich dismounted and watched grimly as his and Kellen's mount advanced on each other snorting and bugling. Ulrich knew that they would fight to the death as they'd been trained, and he was powerless to stop them. He said a quiet, anxious prayer that his would be the victor.

Then he began the search for any clue as to Kellen and Alida's disappearance. He found a small trail of blood and prayed yet again, but this time for the safety of his beloved. All around him, the protectors darted and danced. They did their best to direct Ulrich, but he was not as sensitive as Alida to their call. It wasn't until a touch from Creator on his shoulder that Ulrich knew which way to go.

The view that greeted him between a thicket and Falda's wall was a decidedly more revived Alida and a wrathful Kellen. They battled hand to hand, her small fine blade nearly breaking beneath the gigantic tremors of Kellen's broadsword. Her's being a finer metal withstood the pressure, but she knew it was only a matter of time until Kellen's frustrations made him the victor.

She immediately sensed Ulrich's presence, the distraction causing her to lose her focus on Kellen's well-aimed blows. Her reflexes were good enough that the blade whose arch had been intended for decapitation whistled by, but the blunt, heavy grip caught her temple, and she was knocked backwards reeling from its blow.

Ulrich surged forward, his adrenaline carrying his war-torn and exhausted body. Blow for blow, the two great warriors met each other. No sound was heard from either, save grunts and the occasional deep, gasping breaths of pain. Then with powerful clarity, Ulrich's gravelly voice hummed through the clearing.

"I've waited for the day that your blood would mark the length of my sword. Come closer, you vile worm, and surely my joy will be complete."

Kellen giggled, his voice oddly pitched and mad. "Do it, you son of the dog, and you'll have every dark desire that you have thus far been denied. Can't you taste the need? You want her and everything I own so badly that it must rest on your tongue very sweet indeed!"

Alida reached unspeaking towards Ulrich, her eyes pleading with him for some unknown thing. Then she slumped to the ground totally still. Ulrich swallowed, surprised again at how much desire and pride he felt for this slender woman at his feet. He could do without more land and power, for it was her that he truly desired. Then softly like a mere whisper, Creator's voice swept through his troubled mind.

Ulrich straightened, his eyes boring into those of his enemy. "As much as my fleshly desire has driven me, I will not become you. I will not sink to such a level. You will be captured and held in my dungeon's jealous grasp until all you have worked to build is given to Alida on that day she herself will declare your fate. Your wife will then be kept here with a full guard to live out her days as she sees fit. I have sworn my protection of her, but no more than that."

Kellen grinned. "You are sadly, sadly mistaken. I am going to cleave you in half and then kill Alida as well. Neither of you will survive; the Prince has prophesied."

"Your 'Prince' has misspoken, Kellen. Creator is with us this day and will use your evil for our good. I do not wish for anything that is not given me by Creator. You would be wise to do the same."

"I wish for everything, and everything in excess," Kellen laughed, his voice shrill with madness. "There is nothing that I shall not have. For I am powerful, and you and this woman are nothing compared to my expanding greatness."

Ulrich, wishing to expend no more energy on speech, was silent; his eyes trained in on his enemy.

From the south of the clearing, a man broke free of the brambles and approached quickly his sword drawn and ready. From the east of the clearing, another man stepped forward, and from the north yet another. Neither Kellen nor Ulrich ceased their concentration on each other, but Kellen's face had turned a sickly white.

Ulrich smiled, "You took long enough, Gowen. I was beginning to fear I'd never see a friendly face again." Gowen and the two guardsmen chuckled as they drew nigh to the dueling pair.

It wasn't long before they had Kellen firmly beaten and at their mercy. They had no rope with which to detain him, but they had backed him against the wall, all four of their blades jabbed firmly against his vulnerable neck. Kellen in fury and fear spewed forth the vilest of curses and taunts, his eyes bloodshot with the brown having turned to a deep purple.

Ulrich finally dropped his sword point and moved away from this scene, his wounds aching and bloody. His men carefully began to move Kellen away from the wall, seeking to direct him towards the battlefield and more of their comrades where presumably a length of cord or chain could be found.

The Prince waited and watched, his anger filling Kellen from head to foot, and then his opening came. A little too much room appeared between the guardsmen, and Kellen, with a smooth motion, grabbed a hidden blade from his waistband. Before the dirk had fully left his hand, his head was severed from its perch by Gowen's swift reflexes and the matching strike of Lordifyn.

The men—witness to Kellen's death—felt sickened by the diseased corpse that lay before them. From out of the bloody neck and decapitated head, white, thick maggots made their squirming way. The inner flesh, too, was discolored putridly as if he had begun to rot from the inside out.

Gowen was more deeply affected. For had the guardsmen any spiritual insight, they would have heard the ungodly scream that echoed from the Prince's severed crown, for he was destroyed as well with the downward arch of the sword. Only Gowen heard and saw this result, and he knew that they had been rescued from a great darkness. A prayer, shaped like a ray of light, left his mouth and streaked into the heavens.

Creator smiled down from the glowing arch of the sky and whispered secrets into the soul of the changeling.

CHAPTER TWENTY-ONE

The black clouds that had billowed up from the center of the in-between land cleared away almost as quickly as they had come. When their black, muddy mists had dissolved, the sun shone through, striking the earth full force. It would be said in later years that never had spring come so quickly, for it was only a week later that green shoots and tender flowers poked through the stained soils of Falda.

The war had taken blood and lives to win, but the force, which had dogged Alida's path since birth, was forever crushed. When Ulrich, Gowen, and the guardsmen left the clearing and had made their way back to the battlefield with Alida cradled against Ulrich's chest, they witnessed a great turn in the battle. By the time the sun had reached mid-climb, Ulrich and his army had destroyed Kellen's last battalion.

There was no watery winter light that day or biting chill. The presence of the hosts from Creator's bosom carried his light with them, and it was a heat great enough to warm the earth and its inhabitants.

Alida herself remained in a silent state, unconscious and terribly pale. She was not able to see the tender ministrations of the hosts to Ulrich's people, and she was unable to hear their victory songs.

For days Ulrich stayed by her side, and when the fields had been cleared of corpses and the whole lot burned and their remains buried, he decided to move her to Drachmund Heights. He promised himself in the light of morning that he would bring her back to her homeland, but at night, when everything was silent and still on the road home, he fought the desires that whispered to him to keep her by his side forever.

Laying deep in the grip of a coma, months passed before Alida stirred or opened her eyes. Eldridge and Birch, throughout the duration of Alida's coma, worriedly watched as their master and friend began to lose weight. The lines around his eyes deepened, and many realized that he had aged greatly over the past year.

He did not rest well and left much of the running of the keep in Eldridge's capable hands. Some days he left before first light to ride, not returning until the evening had aged to embers and song. These were the worst times to approach him, for many feared the sharp gleam that would take root within his eyes.

His gaunt face had never looked so beautiful, than the day he leaned over Alida to softly kiss her good morning. All at once, she opened her cloudy dream-filled eyes to his tortured gaze. He was so startled and pleased that he grasped her hand up quickly and pressed it to his lips.

Strangely enough, she resisted. Thinking that she must be merely hungry or disoriented, he ordered a bevy of servants to tend to her. They had only been able to force liquids such as broth, mead, and rich juices down her throat. She had been able to swallow feebly during her internment, but Birch had been unable to do anything else for her. The older woman was thrilled soon after her awakening when a harried servant beat on her door with a summons to come to the keep.

The next days were spent bathing, feeding, and tending to Alida's bodily needs. Nevertheless, no one could breach the silence behind her eyes or the sorrow that flanked their creases. On the seventh day, she asked to be dressed and taken out for air. She was very weak and was only able to last for a few brief moments in the hot summer sun. Birch and Gwynn spent hours combing Alida's hair while chatting amicably with one another, in the hopes that Alida would join in. Nevertheless, their mistress failed to acknowledge their presence, a fact that greatly disturbed both the serving women.

Ulrich, who withdrew further into himself with every denial of her eyes and touch, watched her beloved form instead from a distance as she pushed herself to become strong again. He did not understand her need to do this and longed to hear her private reasons.

Finally, two months later, as fall had begun its progression through the land, she requested that he take her to the conquered land of Kinterden and allow her to remain. She did not say Kellen's clan, nor Kellen's keep, but instead alienated Ulrich with her soft references to *her* keep and *her* people. He silently did as she requested and had a well-stocked wagon brought around for her to ride in. This, too, she disdained and rode bareback on a humble horse that Bryon brought forward for her.

In a last minute fit of rebellion, Ulrich ordered his own horse brought round and rode far ahead of the small cavalcade consisting of him and Alida,

Bryon, Gwynn, twenty guardsmen, and seven servants.

Even when they reached the walls of Kinterden, Ulrich did not hang back but entered the gates confidently and quietly as lord of his own keep. For Kellen Grost's grisly head had been presented on a spear to the Kinterden watch during the weeks following the victory at Falda. Within days, the walls of Kinterden had been opened to its new master for fear of being razed to the ground by Drachmund's full power. Since then Ulrich had begun the process of turning the keep to his wise and competent ruling.

Ulrich allowed Alida a measure of privacy as she made her rounds through the keep, speaking with the most humble of servants and old soldiers who had never known anything but Kinterden and its protection.

Ulrich overheard her talking with a group several nights later and was sickened by what she said.

"I want you to know that the rumors of my passion for the new lord are nothing but dust. I was as much a pawn in his game as was my husband. I do not confess to a great love for my buried lord, but I will do right by his name and legacy. I will not be a traitor to the land I wed nor to you, my adopted people."

Ulrich, still reeling from her words, watched as a harsh-voiced man rose from the group and menacingly made his way to her side. "Had he not been galli- vanting about all over the countryside for your useless hide, lady, our lord would be sitting here with us in the stead of you!" His words were backed by several other disgruntled voices in the crowd.

A crone much older than Alida rose and stood by the smith's side. "You're too late with your mewling apologies and half-made promises, chit. We get news here in these parts too, you know, and we've been told that our new 'lord' will be marrying you within the next fortnight. He has a great passion for you, regardless of your mewling intentions!"

Alida bowed her head in shame and then rose quietly. "This may very well be the case, but I will not marry the man of my own volition, and he will never share a marriage bed with me unless I am forced."

With these words, she rose gracefully and left the circle making her way to her old chambers.

Guilt, shame, and questions plagued her breast. Night and day, she could not break free of the fog that surrounded her. Before Kellen had died, she had felt her growing passion for Ulrich and had even left her home to be with him, but now she clearly saw that he was no better than Quirin.

Ulrich, having heard from her own lips a confession of disdain and disownment, felt as though his heart had been shattered. That night as he lay on a simple pallet high on a deserted parapet, he dreamed a dream that would forever change his life.

In it, he was led through a thicket of brambles. All around him, thorns and whipping branches tore at his flesh. Though he did not understand it, he felt himself determined to break free from their midst. The harder he pushed, the thicker the brambles became. A voice kept calling, "Remain steadfast; do not waver." He answered it by continuing on, but still he did not know why he followed its lead.

All at once, he broke free from the brambles, and he found himself on a ledge high above a breathtaking canyon. Out over this height, a falcon of pure white spread her wings dipping and rejoicing in the warm air.

Presently, she came his direction and then with grace and majesty landed on his shoulder. The wild gleam in her eye left and as he gently lifted her from her perch, she transformed to be held close against his chest. All the wounds from the brambles began to heal and the air was filled with joy.

The voice that had encouraged him to continue through the brambles called out, "Take this woman-changeling to wife. For I have laid out a plan that will span beyond the years of your lives together and into those of your children."

Ulrich awoke sweating but glad. Then he sat on his pallet with tears streaming down his cheeks. Far in the distance, he heard a scream, and he looked towards the rising sun where Alida, in falcon form, flew against the morning rays. Resolutely, he wiped away the tears, rose and rolled up his mat, making his way to the lower chambers. There he quietly ordered a gathering of the entire city below the balcony of the castle.

They came together sleepy and yawning, grumbling at his early command—a mass of discontented foes. When they were all gathered, even down to the children, Ulrich began to speak in a deep and even voice. "I have come to let all of you know that in three fortnights from now, I will take your mistress to wife. The wedding will be held at Drachmund Heights, and I expect all who remain to attend. Those who stand before me now can make the choice to remain in the city and keep of their heritage or to go as freed men and women. I want only those who can find humility and grace enough to join my rank without malice to continue as keepsmen of Kinterden Dell. These who remain will be expected to earn their way as well as my respect. Those who rebel and wish to go as freed men and women will never be allowed to return to these lands. If you do, you, your husbands, wives, and children will be cut down the moment any step foot over my borders. Do not forget that my borders shall reach from here to Falda and east to Lyrnne—the booty of war acquired when I am wed."

A strong voice from the midst of the crowd called out, "Then you will not be wed." Immediately the keep was filled with the jeers and catcalls of the gathered crowd.

Ulrich immediately recognized Alida's voice and watched as she moved through the crowd of Kinterden's keepsmen and nobility. Ulrich smiled a small half smile and then continued. "Alida and I *will* be wed. Guards take her carefully out to the wagon and prepare our band for return to Drachmund Heights. As for the rest of you, make your choices wisely."

Just then, Alida broke free of the encircling guards and ran swiftly towards a bareback mount. Ulrich's command was quicker, and by the time she reached for the nag's mane, Landres' strong arm had pulled her back. After having seen to her unwilling ascent to the balcony, he gently but firmly forced her into the circle of Ulrich's arms where with his weight and strength she was pinned between his body and the balcony wall. There, with a steely edge to his voice, he ground out softly enough only for her ears, "Do not run again. I desire you enough without adding this kind of close interaction to the mix. We will be wed. You will be treated with every consideration until the day comes that you accept this union, however tremulously it may have started. Do not forget a bargain made many nights ago between a certain man and woman. He promised his protection and she, her land for seven years. I have in no way, mishandled thee or our bargain, and I never will. I will seduce you, but never take you. One day you will desire me so much that you of your own choice will come to me. In the meantime, we will be wed and fulfill the agreement set in writing. Should seven years come and go, you will be free to live your life out alone at Falda, and you will regain those lands for yourself."

Alida had no cocky retort or brazen address with which to silence him. She felt only sadness—a great, deep sadness. For this man before her, whom she had thought beautiful at one time, would never reach her heart again. He grasped her hand and allowed her time to straighten her somewhat ruffled garments. All around them, the people of Kinterden gaped in openmouthed surprise. They had never seen such open defiance treated in this manner. Any male amongst their group would have beaten her to within an inch of her life for the embarrassment of refusal. However, here their new lord stood looking calm and in complete control without ever having put a mark on her.

That day, three hundred additional servants from the keep, all women, joined the cavalcade back to Kinterden. Their respect for Ulrich was much improved.

Preparations for the wedding began with clothing choices and room assignments. Guests from neighboring lands, including a rebuilt Lyrnne and somewhat reluctant Kinterden, were sent summons.

Birch and Gwynn were kept very busy making all the choices, for Alida refused to help. Gwynn kept her silence, though she longed to tell Alida to straighten up. Finally, the lass was given a man who would love her heart and soul, and she wallowed in dregs of self-pity. This wedding was a sign that good could come from war and pain. She only hoped that Alida would come to see this. Both the women, as well as a visiting Ansel, made everything as beautiful and choice as possible, trying to tempt their beloved mistress.

On a soft autumn night, a couple weeks into the preparations, Alida made her way down to the kitchen garden. She was bored and restless, her remembrance of her first marriage clawing at the corners of her mind. She sought diversion, and so she had decided to find some form of manual work to occupy her time. The gardens were where she had earlier witnessed the servants making new wine—a delicacy at Lyrnne and Kinterden with Ulrich being the only nearby supplier.

It had amazed her that the servant men and women actually climbed into the vats to tread barefoot upon the grapes. Though she would not admit it to anyone and though the wine would be used at the wedding, she found her fascination with the process too much to contain.

From the shadows, Ulrich watched as she drew near the vat, encircling it and staring down into its midst. He wryly shook his head, for it had just occurred to him that he was, for the moment, forced into his old place as voyeur.

His breath went to double time as he watched her gather up the ends of her tunic, fastening their length at thigh level. Then she bathed her legs and feet with a ladle full of water, which had been boiled and cooled. The clear droplets glistened all over her skin as she stepped into the vat. What began as a serious rather thoughtful expression on her lovely face changed into something much more free and joyful. The squish of the grapes and the rhythm of her pace nearly comical.

To Ulrich's great amusement, it was only a short time before he heard her mutter, "Who would have thought that grapes could tickle." Then with a gleeful chuckle, she said, "Ha! Such a fancy pair of purple legs my liege will be presented with on our wedding night, the great lout!" It was a great joy to him to see her smile for the first time in weeks as she sped up the process of stamping.

The next morning a somewhat confused kitchen staff looked at the vat of well-trod grapes. After several useless attempts to find out who had completed the job so thoroughly, they all gave up and went back to work. Ulrich smiled quietly to himself, the picture of the kitchen elf firmly imprinted upon his mind.

The wedding day was bright, crisp, and lovely. Alida, sitting alone at her window, tried not to remember the last time she had gone through the process of nuptials—that hazy day so long ago—made of the stuff of nightmares.

So depressed and deeply alone was she, that she could not see the host that had come to joyfully administer peace to her. When they saw that she did not recognize them but looked through them to the sight beyond, they withdrew quietly. The acknowledgment of such beings was becoming less and less common for her. She had withdrawn deeply into herself and had not even taken flight since that morning at Kinterden when Ulrich had announced their upcoming nuptials.

Creator was saddened that He had not heard her soft voice amongst those who regularly sought Him. Though she did not acknowledge His presence nor actively seek His help, He was there nonetheless.

Alida arose from her seat sometime later and was adorned in her wedding attire. It was far simpler than her first gown, for she had not been brave enough to tell her friends that she was still a maid. It was a pale green tunic that reached to the tops of her feet in soft folds. All over, it had been embroidered with wild flowers and falcons with their wings spread in flight. To its center, Birch attached

Roushti's pin with its stylized wolf. The joining of this pin to a tunic representing her own crest was almost too much for her overburdened pride to bear.

When Gwynn wasn't looking, Alida brushed away a tear that had formed at the corner of her eye.

"What is wrong with me?" she whispered. "Normally, I am not so weak." From somewhere deep within, an answering voice said, "He is the first you have loved."

When she had been completely prepared, she was led down to the main hall that had been decorated with autumn leaves and late-blooming flowers. On long trestle tables covered in fine linen, a feast was laid out. Alida was surprised, for all of the castle's best silver and gold platters, utensils, and cups were displayed.

As she watched from behind hooded eyes, the noble guests that were tardy in arriving gathered around the tables with those already seated. The seating where they were led, formed several nested U-shaped lines of tables around the area where Eldridge and Ulrich awaited her. She was surprised, too, to see the castle's advisor standing in place as magistrate over the proceedings. She was informed quietly by Gwynn that Ulrich's advisor had trained as a keeper of the law before he took up duties under Ulrich. She was mildly disappointed that there would be no question as to the legality of the proceedings.

To Alida's surprise, there was no attempt at a facade with flowery vows or promises, for Ulrich and his house had declared her a bride under siege taken as part of the bounty of war.

It pricked her pride that Ulrich had allowed such terms to be used for their union, but she also knew, as did he, that she would have refused any love vows required of her, thus negating the union from the start. Under the laws of war, no matter how she refused or fought, she would be given to the groom along with all her possessions. The hall roared its approval when the ceremony was finalized.

Ulrich, ever the gentleman, took his love's hand and led her to the highest dais in the center of the U-shaped gathering. He did not offend her sensibilities further by forcing physical contact or affection. In fact, as the day went on, Alida clearly recognized that he was all but ignoring her. Not to say that he did not expertly attend to her needs, but this was done so in a very subtle way. A mere twitch of his hand and her tankard was refilled; a long gaze at a servant and her plate was piled again with the choicest pheasant, swan, quail, and boar. There was always some serving wench close by to hand her a bunch of grapes or an apple tart. At one point, a young woman, no more than fifteen years, bathed her hot brow and then feet, for the hall had become very warm amidst the merriment.

It amazed Alida to no end that Ulrich's people had every confidence in him winning her over. They took it in stride that he had gained a bride under such circumstances. Alida tried quietly to quell any thought that this was a love match, for she was very cool to Ulrich all day long and into the evening. When he asked her join him in a dance, she declined, and he moved on to a much more gracious noblewoman.

As soon as it was possible, Alida retreated to her new chambers. Ulrich was the one that led her from the hall, but he made it very clear that there was to be no bedding ritual. When he came to her door, he softly kissed her hand and bid her good night. Then he turned on his heal and headed back for the lively entertainment of the hall.

She stared after his long stride and broad shoulders, a little place of sadness welling up in her heart. Then she straightened her spine and walked into her chambers, softly closing the door.

She undressed and climbed beneath the soft linen coverlet whose top had been piled with the softest, whitest furs she had ever seen. They formed a large, warm blanket and had been treated with a powdered violet for fragrance. It was not long before she dropped off to sleep. For though she was in good health, the weight of the day had sapped all her strength.

The next morning, some of her doldrums gone, Alida rose early and sought out the stable boy to help her saddle a mount. He agreed without any nervousness, which surprised her. Didn't he know that she could ride away and never return? He seemed to trust that this would not be the case. When she followed him into the fragrant stalls, she soon saw why.

Ulrich stood beside his own destrier with a soft smile on his lips. He elegantly strode towards her and brought with him a steed as grand as his own. The horse was a bay with deep red highlights in his glossy coat. He had not been gelded, and this small acquiescence to her taste in mounts softened her to Ulrich's unwanted presence.

He did not issue any orders but simply rode out ahead of her, keeping some yards to the head or side of her so that she was always in his view. Remembering the pleasant and exhilarating rides they had shared, Alida should have relaxed into the morning's exercise. Then she recalled how changed he was when the time had been at its most dire, and her resolve was set fixedly back into place.

By the end of the ride, her frustration over his presence was exceedingly apparent in her rapid dismount and angry retreating stride from the stables. Ulrich watched her go, and then he chuckled to himself. He knew all too well the disturbing effect he had on his wife, for she had the same effect on him. Then he uttered a quick prayer for the return of her joy and for his wisdom in dealing with her.

Alida, meanwhile, stormed into her chambers. She surprised Gwynn whose dreamy smile quickly turned stern. Alida took one look at her, pointed her finger, and said, "Don't say a word."

Gwynn followed her. "Ye should be pleased wi' 'is attempts to win ye over. Ye should be dancing in joy that ye 'ave the love of such a worthy man. Instead ye storm about and lie listless, imagining some great harm 'es done ye, not caring to share this dire insult wi' any of us."

Alida turned on her handmaid and stalked towards her with all of her predatory prowess plain to see. Her finger nearly touched the maid's chest as she ground out from between clenched teeth, "you think he is *so* perfect, but what you don't know would change your mind just as it has changed mine."

Gwynn standing just as firm, her brogue growing deeper, pointed her own finger. "There was 'ordes of the 'osts at yer wedding, miss. Great gleaming masses of 'em. Do ye think they'd come to a union what wasn't blessed of the Ancient of Days 'imself? Did ye not see them? And what of the master's tender care of ye when that brute of a man ye married had beaten ye to oblivion. Does it na' count for anythin'? And what of the communion ye two 'ave between ye? What of the shared secrets and knowledge of each other?"

Alida backed away. "You don't understand!"

"Then 'elp me to understand, lass. Tell me what could 'ave gone so wrong since the war."

Alida, forcing back her tears, said, "It is of no use to discuss it with anyone. What's done is done, and now I am married."

Gwynn gently grasped her arm. "I would'na encourage a match that did not 'ave some hope of survivin'. I would'na push ye towards a man of questionable character, but Ulrich is good, and ye need to open yer eyes t'see it!"

Alida continued to stare out her window until long after Gwynn had left. The same memories Gwynn had just recited flooded back over her. They were in direct rival with the beast she had witnessed in the war. Alida swallowed back her tears, which threatened more and more often these days. Then shoring up her strength, she made her way back down to the main hall of the castle.

Throughout the morning, she explored the castle hallways, surprised at the breadth and depth of its structure. From the gates, it looked imposing and certainly large enough to house a good number of inhabitants, but she would never have guessed at its true size—for much of the castle was built back into the mountain and this without the feel and discomfort of a cave.

Ulrich's ancestors had built the rooms with high ceilings having had masons at their behest to cut the stone smooth on the walls, floors, and ceilings. Large fireplaces ensured warmth while chasing away the damp. From all appearances, these massive hearths were kept blazing day and night by numerous servants. For light, huge candelabras hung and lowered by chains were situated gracefully in many of the rooms. Some of the smaller dorms held numerous sconces as well as individual candleholders for personal use.

The rooms had been made not only livable but also luxurious with heavy, thick, wool tapestries cast about on the floors and hung on the cold stone walls. There were always comfortable seats to be found as well as curiosities from exotic lands. Alida went through room after room and was astounded by the displayed wealth.

All the servants she met along the way were exceedingly gracious, a new experience for her as both Lyrnne's and Kinterden's staff had been hostile or divided upon her arrival. Ulrich had instructed his already good-natured staff as to her care and entertainment. They were happy to answer any number of questions she had about the castle, lands, and people. Their only reluctance was to answer questions about Ulrich, and many were boldfaced enough to suggest she seek him out and ask him herself. The few who seemed mildly offended by her questioning made great efforts to shed their master in a good light, giving only positive information about him.

She eventually made her way to the storerooms where she was shocked at the sheer amount of the supplies. Never before, even at Falda, had such care been taken to provide for the long-term needs of it inhabitants.

Everything had a system to it, and for every bushel of fruit or grain or dried meat, there was a tally made in a ledger. From these small ledgers, a greater one was filled, and the completed books were given to Eldridge for his final accounting. These storerooms were at the very back of the castle so that in the event of a war their supplies would not easily be threatened.

Alida, quietly storing up all of this information about her new home, was surprised at how truly well planned and thoughtful Ulrich had been in the running of his keep. As she had so many times in the last few days, Alida brought back her deeper feelings of animosity towards him when his goodness sought to overwhelm her sensibilities.

When she had toured all there was to see, she made her way back to her bright chambers. Her window offered one of the most extensive views of the surrounding lands and the bright fall light was shameless in its cascade through her room. She had turned to go down to the kitchens, when something wrapped and lying on her pallet caught her attention.

She cautiously picked up the hide-enclosed package and gasped as a beautiful, ivory-inlaid ewe bow was extracted. The wood was gleaming and polished and the ivory winked out subtly from the fine pattern. She turned it over and over in her hand, running her fingers over its smooth length and across silver-tipped ends. With it, a quiver of finely shaped arrows had been included. Each quill had been set expertly, and she was surprised at the great worth of the gift.

Ulrich's compelling voice shattered the silence of the room and washed over her like wine.

I know your old bow is your favorite, but perhaps with time, this new bow will fit your hand and sight as well. It could use your touch to truly make it worthy."

She tried to ignore him, but within a few steps, he was by her side. He tenderly ran his hand along the back of her hair and over her forearms where the tunic left them bare. "My huntress will also need a mount, and so I have decreed that the destrier that she rode this morn would be hers as well."

"Think ye to win me over with gifts and flattery, milord?" Her voice had never been so cool or furious.

His was calm in return. "Nay. I will win thee over because you cannot ignore me. Because my eyes and my lips and my voice haunt you, and because you know me as I know thee."

She whirled on him, extracting her throbbing skin and hair from his touch. "We are wed in name only, milord. Do not forget this."

He laughed quietly, and his eyes pierced hers as if they were arrows themselves. "What you say is true, lady, but I know a secret that you do not."

He paused, and then circling her, he continued, "Your spoiled and willful behavior is new to me. I have seen you strong and sad, joyful and intent. I have seen you wistful and furious and gladsome and in anguish, but never spoiled and never petulant. Bear in mind that such behavior can be unattractive." With that, he quickly grasped her and laid his mouth on hers, his firm lips taking kisses from her like unwilling nectar.

When he pulled away, she hissed out at him, "You take that which is not yours, Wolf. You are a thief and a traitor. Do not so touch me again."

This time he did not laugh, but instead bowed cockily and swept his arm out in mock subservience. His voice was steely and grating, "Your desire has been my every command." Then he left the room with lazy, long strides.

She nearly screamed in frustration as the door closed behind him. With an agitation borne of desire as old as time, Alida again sought out the stables and rode across the hills and fields. This time, as Ulrich followed her, he kept his location secret from her.

She was out until the sun began to drop and was so weary and hungry by the time she returned that she requested her food be brought to her chamber rather than seeking out the boisterous trestle tables in the main hall.

She had gathered several pheasant and a young boar that day using her old equipment. Though it rankled her greatly, she had been forced to use the new mount that Ulrich had given her since she had no other. When she dropped her kill off at the kitchens and gave them her order for supper, Ansel softly patted her arm. " T'would do ye every good to lie wi' your husband, lass."

Alida turned furious and disbelieving eyes on him. "What business, pray tell, is it of yours, cook?"

He chortled at her offense. "We all know the circumstances betwixt ye, miss. I just want your happiness, and the rumors round here are that your husband is a thoughtful and gracious man. That usually carries over into the furs!"

She flushed deeply at that. "I do not believe that Creator would have us so lightly banter about a matter as serious as the marriage bed."

Ansel laughed even harder. "Then, Priestess, you do not know the Ancient of Days as well as we all believed, for it was he who made us and our desires and 'twas He who called the marriage bed blessed!"

Alida, at his words, was downcast. Why was she allowing everyone to get such a rise out of her? Ansel was right, Gwynn was right, and Ulrich was right. However, she had heard and seen a thing that she could not forget, and she was trapped by her inability to explain it away and by her pride.

Gwynn, passing her in the hall, was troubled by the sight of little fiend attached at shoulder level to her mistress. His expression was vainglorious and mewling and his claws were firmly ensconced somewhere around her mouth.

CHAPTER TWENTY-TWO

Gwynn hastened after her mistress and caught up finally with her in chambers. "Ye have a little attendant, miss!"

Alida looked up, her eyes cloudy and introspective. "What are you talking about, Gwynn?"

"Ye are carryin' evil about wi' ye."

Alida, though having been rescued from the Prince of the Air, was still subject to the machinations of the in-between lands and their ceaseless attempts to dampen her spirits, to lead her astray, and to cast down her hope.

Alida shivered, hearing the warning in her friend's voice. She turned her head slowly, and her eyes were opened and stared straight into the now-fearful eyes of the spirit. "Get thee away! You have no place here!"

The little fiend hissed, "Oh, do I not? Have I not been given room in your pity and your pride and your withdrawal from *Him!*"

Again, she shouted, "By the name of the Ancient of Days, I cast thee out! Get thee gone!"

The little spirit screamed as bright spirit fire came from her mouth. Alida fell onto her bed exhausted by the days and the weeks of trying to carry her fear alone. When had she become so blind?

Gwynn glided softly to her side and smoothed the hair from off her brow. "Ye 'ave ministered to all of us, miss, and we've all but ignored yer needs. Forgive m'apathy towards ye, love. Please share wi' me what has turned ye so sour on the devotion of your goodly lord, and what wall has been keeping ye from the Master!"

Alida cried softly, tears rolling down her cheeks. "I swore I'd never give the breath of hate any room in me. I promised both Creator and my own soul that I would not allow pride and fear to stop me. But I have, and I have wasted this many months because of it!"

Gwynn clucked softly, her voice strong and straight. "Ye are human,· . as we all are, miss. Though ye 'ave the changlin' blood in yer veins, an ancient blood that gives ye more of the inclination for things of the spirit, ye are still weak unless ye seek that which is stronger. All yer trainin' and all yer knowledge and everythin' ye've seen means naught unless ye strive wi' the Master." She stroked her friend's brow once more and then rose quietly. "A servant comes wi' yer food. Eat something and then think on what I've said." The handmaid left the chambers with a soft click of the door.

Alida lay for a while, her mind adrift on Gwynn's words. Then she arose, and when she had eaten her fill and had bathed and changed into a soft wool tunic, she climbed the heights of the keep until she looked out at the misty moonlit mountain crags. The wind whipped through her hair and through her robes, cooling her skin.

She turned her face to the heavens and softly began to sing. The melody was ancient and rhythmic designed to set reverence in the air and given utterance from the deepest places in her soul that had harbored fear, pride, pity, and malice over the preceding months. In the whipping chill of the wind, she rooted out all the subtle evils that had held her back. Creator's presence, with a fire borne of her song, shot whistling from out of the heavens and burnt through her. There was nothing gentle about His presence, for He was jealous of the time lost. He seared the deep reaches of her being and burnt out every remaining remnant of her sorrow and strife.

Ulrich, from the shadows, prayed softly for his beloved, seeing the abundant light and fire from the heavens arch down and through her. He smelled the clean, hot fragrance of fire and knew that, as he watched, Alida was being immersed in both repentance and renewal. He was angry still with her, but it was pure and without sin. All could be wiped clean with a few simple words from her mouth.

When she lay still and contrite upon the stone of the keep, Ulrich made his way to her side. He lifted her gently against his chest and muttered, "Brambles."

Alida moved against the wall of his chest and chuckled disbelievingly. "What did you say?"

He told her softly of his dream and of his recent prayers for her. She pulled away, and into his moonlit face, she whispered, "Forgive me."

He was silent and then reached out stroking her hair beneath his palm. "You were already forgiven."

Then Alida took a deep breath, rose, and began pacing the walkway around the parapet. Ulrich, seeing that she had something to say, waited silently. With a shaken voice, Alida quietly recited out into the air, "I've waited for the day that your blood would mark the length of my sword. Come closer, you vile worm, and surely my joy will be complete." She turned then to look into his face.

It took Ulrich a moment to understand what she was talking about, and then in a flood of sound and color, the moment at Falda between he and Kellen came rushing back.

He rose quickly and crossed to her side. With sorrowful eyes, she cried out, "Will you deny that he was slaughtered so that you could posses me! It was the means to entrap me in the bargain between us, a way to make the years pass by with your possession of not only my lands but of myself."

Ulrich was quiet, still abstaining from saying anything. Her fists beat against his chest. "It was the last thing I heard and the first thing with which I awoke. It has been such great anguish living with the belief that you would cast aside everything, including your own valor and purity, for love! I had left Kinterden to be with you as a friend, but even I was willing to wait until death, however long away, would separate my vows with Kellen, freeing me to be with you."

Ulrich caught her hands and pressed them into silence against his chest. "You fainted, Alida, you did not hear the rest of what I told him. 'Twas not my sword that took his life, though the temptation was great. He sealed his own fate on the blade of Gowen! Seek out my soldier and confirm if this is not true!"

Alida stared at him, warring with her memory and her innate desire to trust him. Then in a very small voice she said, "I will."

Ulrich nodded his head and ran his palm along her cheek, stopping to run his fingers over her mouth. Then he turned on his heel and made his way slowly down the stone stairs to the hall below before making his way out into the night.

It hurt that she did not know him well enough to believe that he would throw aside his faith in Creator. He had made mistakes before he found her. He had lived on pride. He had sought after war and after power. He had known somewhere in his heart that he was not happy and was not free, and he remembered the long nights when he would ride and shout and pace trying to find what he was missing. Then, he had met her and had seen what was lacking in his existence. Not just in her as an object of his adoration and desire, but in what she embodied later as a priestess of God.

He had seen his own impurity and had been faced with a new direction. He had put his trust in Creator and his heart into her hands. He knew that his place with Creator was sealed, but now he would see whether his heart, too, rested well. He longed to have his horse saddled so that he could work off the fretful energy that overwhelmed him, but he was loath to leave Alida to her own wiles. Breathing out a quiet entreaty, he reluctantly made his way back into the castle and sought out his private chambers.

Alida, meanwhile, had reentered the lively hall seeking an audience with Gowen. He sat amongst several of his compatriots drinking and discussing something with great animation. He felt his cousin, the falcon, before she had even reached the table. When he looked up, he saw the surprise and questions that flitted across her face.

Making a quick and gracious exit, he walked out into the night air with Alida at his heels. Before she could utter a word, he turned and grinned. "I take it you just now learned my secret, fair mistress?"

She smiled too. "I cannot believe it took me so long to know you as a changeling, sir."

Gowen bowed low. "A mangy cur at your service!" Alida smiled, but Gowen could sense her worry and hesitation. "Why did you seek me out?"

Alida gathered her strength, and with her usual directness, she forged ahead. "I need to have the answer to a question that has haunted me since the battle at Falda. I need your utmost honesty in the recall of the events that surrounded the death of my buried husband."

Gowen frowned and was silent a moment as he allowed that day to wash back over him. "The clearing was silent, save for the striking ring of blade against blade. The moment we approached and saw Ulrich and Kellen hand-to-hand, I knew that it was no common battle. In all of our years of combat together, I have never seen him fight with such desperation and direction. He was badly injured, but he protected your position as a wolf protects its cubs. Then we heard him say that he would know completion with the death of his enemy. I think I knew then that he loved you more than his own life."

Alida did not comment, keeping the privacy of their relationship intact. Gowen, respecting this silence continued. "All of us wondered at a hesitation in his advance, for one moment he was all fury and force and the next he was relinquishing a chance to conquer. Then he caught sight of us and ordered silently that we surround your husband. He left off his own attack then; perhaps he did not trust himself. We were directed to take Kellen hostage, but he was enraged, and when the moment allowed, he withdrew a blade with which to slaughter Ulrich. I was the first to react, and 'twas my blade that brought him to the grave."

Alida mulled over his tale. Then she smiled weakly and softly said, "Thank you." She had turned to go, when Gowen stopped her with a soft retort.

"I know that it is not proper of a soldier to offer guidance, but I also know that yours is not a common union. You have been taken as a bride under siege, and as such, it is painfully apparent that you do not seek my lord as he seeks you." He cleared his throat nervously and continued.

Landres would probably show more decorum and would not offer advice where advice was not sought, but I am not he, and I suggest that you lay aside any grievance towards Ulrich and seek his true heart. I swore that I would never give my loyalty to any man, but I was wrong, for a very great leader and friend was there before me for the taking, and now he is there as well for you."

Alida dryly commented, "Yes, but it seems that my taking of my husband will be slightly different from yours."

Gowen had the good grace to blush and was charmed by his mistress' next words, for she was uncommonly strong and capitulation did not seem to be her style. "I have wronged my lord, Gowen, and I intend to make right my grievance. You, as well as others, have made clear your loyalty to Ulrich. By all rights, this adoration is deserved."

Gowen grinned, relieved that she was not angry. He nodded and made his "Fare thee well."

Alida slowly reentered the castle, undecided as to what she should do next. She said a silent prayer for the intervention of Creator.

That night Ulrich had an abominable time falling asleep. When the hour had moved into the dark of morning, he groggily arose and made his way to Alida's chambers. The door that opened silently to her room revealed a fire reduced to coals and a melody of soft moonlight that filtered through the window to her pallet.

The room was very chilled, and Ulrich quietly went about stoking the fire. When a small blaze had been reestablished, Ulrich went to the pallet and gazed down at his wife. In sleep, her skin glowed with a dewy softness and her lips begged for his attention. Ulrich passed his hand over his face, wiping away weariness and desire.

Alida, in the midst of some dream, rolled over and softly laughed. Ulrich's gut wrenched with the musical sound that had been too long in coming over the past few months, especially in his presence. Then he heard a whisper in the room.

When he turned, a watcher stood nearby with a smile on her face. "Creator says to tell you that all will be well. The thorns have not yet given up their pull against you and your desire. Continue to stand fast."

Ulrich chuckled softly. "I will, for the prize is very great. She is more than I could have hoped for in a mate and friend."

The watcher sighed softly and then touched his arm. "Creator has called me back to his bosom. Take care of her and thee, and do not allow anything to come between you. If only He would let me tell you of the wonders I know."

The room grew suddenly darker as she was pulled away in a whisper of wind. Ulrich watched in fascination as the room began to fill this time with other smaller spirits, different in nature who took their places around the chamber.

They did not acknowledge him or speak to him, but he felt a great peace in the presence that they pulled with them. Then his insight faded, and he was alone again with his wife. Not knowing if it was a dream or a truth, Ulrich sat down on the pallet in the curve of Alida's body. Exhaustion overcame him, and he moved her over gently to allow him room to sleep. His last view was of her softly smiling lips and dark curls.

Alida fought to awaken from the nightmare in which she was once again being pinned down by Kellen's weight. In her dream, he was just lifting his hand to strike her when she forced herself to open her eyes.

To her surprise, she was being pinned down, not by the malevolent Kellen, but by a heavily sleeping Ulrich. By all appearances, he had fallen asleep atop the furs and had rolled close to her during the night until he was all but on top of her.

She was unsure of whether or not to awaken him when the question was answered for her.

With a lazy yawn, he opened his eyes and was taken aback by the appearance of his attractive wife's sleep softened face. In a reaction borne of desire, sleepiness, and opportunity, his lips immediately came down over hers.

It was not a deep kiss, but instead, it consisted of soft, dry flutters over her mouth. He was drunk on her scent and her nearness and the ease of their location. He allowed his mouth to wander tenderly to her cheeks and her eyes and her ears, blocking out the little voice that reminded him that he had said he would not force his affections.

Alida lay very still, seeing the sleep befuddled look in his eyes. She tried to ignore his tender ministrations, but the truth was that it felt very nice to awaken to such a pleasant reality, especially after such a terrifying nightmare. She allowed it for a little while only, and then when she felt his kisses begin to increase, she softly caressed his cheek.

"Ulrich, wake up."

He chuckled deeply. "I'm wide awake already, love."

Her expression changed. "You mean that you have been lying here kissing me, and you have been fully aware of your actions the entire time?"

He grinned. "I am still a little sleepy."

Alida groaned. "Get off, please. You promised."

He touched her lips with his once more and then rolled over. "Very well, but it is widely known that kisses and other such interaction between a husband and wife in the morning can result in a very pleasant day to follow."

She couldn't help chuckling in return, though she forced her next expression to become very dour. "To think that I was going to ask you to ride with me today and hunt in a new valley that I discovered from my window."

He did not say a word but simply gazed down into her eyes. "Oh, very well, despite your misbehavior, we can still be friends and spend the day exercising in the fresh air." She playfully squeezed his arm.

He grinned and then said with deep sarcasm. "I want your friendship indeed, lady, but the kind of exercise that I would like to enjoy with you is more conducive to a spousal relation."

She stuck her tongue out, rolled her eyes, and hopped out of bed. "Well, time is wasting."

He smiled wickedly and said, "Then let's commence with the activities."

Alida rolled her eyes again, correcting herself, "Time is wasting *for our ride!*"

Ulrich's husky voice was full of smiles. "I want desperately to respond to that!"

Alida, not ignorant to his train of thought, said, "You need help."

"Then assist me." His brows arched suggestively.

This time she merely pointed to the door, afraid to incriminate herself further.

With a gentle kiss to her cheek, Ulrich took his leave of her chamber. They would both change into their hunting gear and commence with the day. He was cautiously optimistic, for she had seemed softer than he had seen her in a year.

The wind whistled past Ulrich and Alida as they made their way gingerly down into a valley that Alida had seen the day before. There were a few flakes of snow mixed in with the wind for they were much higher than Kinterden, Lyrnne, or Falda.

Just as they rounded a cove of trees, Alida caught sight of a glorious white stag. He stood with his side towards them, fleetingly unaware of their presence. Ulrich turned to his wife and motioned that she should take the kill. She removed an arrow from her quiver and placed it carefully and quickly into her bow. Ulrich was overjoyed to see that it was the set he had given her. Just as she lifted the bow to take her aim, the cold wind shifted, and their scent was immediately carried to the stag.

With a majestic leap, he cleared a fallen log and headed deeper into the forest, his rapid retreat being marked by the thrashing of bracken that fell under his winged feet. Alida and Ulrich, with a swiftness borne of experience, had already begun to follow, their horses responding to the merest pressure.

The chase was on. Through mighty gusts of wind and the whipping branches of fir and alder, the riders proceeded. Alida kept sight of the flashing white flanks ahead. Then, all at once, the white flanks disappeared. Alida spurred on Hercules, her mount, into the shadowy bend where she had lost track of the stag. She laughed delightedly as she saw the obvious destination of the beast, for up ahead a large cove of white alder would camouflage his flight. Indeed, it was all but impossible to see him amidst the snowy white trunks of the trees.

She slowed her mount, for she knew the stag would no longer run. He would rest so that movement or sound would not give his position away. In the forest behind them, his color had been a beacon, but here it was his safety. She silenced Hercules' footfall in the heaviest beds of leaves. Her eyes scanned the trees for the beast's shape, and soon she was able to discern his rounded rump and shoulder.

She signaled silently to Ulrich who was immensely enjoying his outing with her. He was more intent on watching her movements than the stag. When he signaled back, she took aim again and loosed her arrow to the place just behind the stag's front leg. The animal, when struck, burst from its position and ran, but Alida's aim had been true, and he was felled after a few feet by the barb.

They rounded on the stag and saw that no further action was needed. Reverently, Alida dismounted and kneeled beside the majestic creature. She placed his five-pronged head into her lap and gave an excited shout of thanks to Creator for the kill. Then she and Ulrich gutted, skinned, and quartered the magnificent carcass, carefully packing it onto the backs of their mounts.

It was late afternoon when they returned with the stag meat and seven rabbits. All the pelts were white and would be used to make winter gear for Alida. Ulrich had also planned to take the antlers and have jewelry, a wine horn, and tools made from their sturdy stock.

They had not talked much all afternoon, exchanging only the occasional friendly word or comment on the hunt, but there was something more at peace between them. Alida smiled softly as Ulrich squeezed her hand in pride when someone in the hall commented on the fortuitous kill. White stags, especially, were considered very good omens.

Many saw the affectionate exchange and were heartened by the possibility of a growing union between their lord and mistress. None was more gladdened than Ulrich, for Alida had not pulled away.

When the evening feast had ended and the nightly song and dances had begun, someone requested that Alida share the tale of her kill with them. She did so, and very dramatically, to the delight of her husband's people. Ulrich rejoiced in the picture of his keepsmen comfortably relating to his wife. If all continued to go well, he would soon have the completion of his dream.

The hunt was the first of many outings that the couple took together. They went fishing and exploring, as well as the occasional ride without destination or intent—these pleasant meanderings adding to their kinship. Some of the days were spent riding around Drachmund's various holdings to see how the harvest had progressed and to make plans for the next year. Alida was very curious about every facet of the running of Drachmund Heights. She hoped to apply some of the methods to a renewed Falda and Lyrnne as well as to the more traditional Kinterden Dell.

Nevertheless, to Alida's growing frustration, these numerous outings did not bring the closeness she sought, for Ulrich had not made the move to come again to her room. On occasion, he would touch her softly with his hand, but she longed to be kissed again and to feel his arms around her in a way she had never allowed.

He was not immune to her, for he saw the increasing edge in her personality and caught the broad feminine hints towards closeness. However, he had given her a bargain and expected it to remain until she broke it. Neither of them brought up the conversation on the parapets. Ulrich, because he was unsure whether her questions had been answered, and Alida, because she was loathe to admit the wasted time.

Other couples in the keep were not so awkward with each other. Gwynn and Bryon had discovered their own love so long ago in their escape.

As they had promised themselves, they further explored that kiss given long ago in the forest as they fled Kellen's wrath. To both their surprise, they found a hidden, deep passion for each other. Daily they walked and talked with each other, gladdened by shared interest and love.

Alida was surprised at her bittersweet feelings when Bryon announced in midwinter that he and Gwynn were to be married. By all appearances, she joined whole-heartedly in the wedding preparations, but in her heart, she mourned the lack of affection between her and Ulrich, of which Bryon and Gwynn had an obvious abundance.

When Ulrich gave away the petite handmaid amidst a cacophony of blessing from the keepsmen, Alida could not stop tears from trailing down her cheek. It was in those moments that she realized how foolish she had continued to be. She had asked Creator's forgiveness and had increased her friendship with Ulrich, but had not brought down the walls that would allow the new intimacy of marriage.

In awe, she remained very still, as flood after flood of humility washed through her heart. Had she not been standing before a whole assembly of keepsmen and visitors, she would have dissolved into a soggy heap of tears.

When the vows had been gladly given and sealed, and kisses and hugs exchanged, Alida slipped silently out of the hall and made her way back up to the parapet where she had nearly reconciled with the man who loved her.

Night had fallen and most of the guard was downstairs in the hall. Quietly, though it was freezing with the wind whistling by her, Alida transformed. Ulrich, who had followed her, rounded a corner of the wall just in time to see her fly off into the night. His heart caught in his throat, for immediately he feared that she was leaving for good.

He gathered up her clothing and ran down to the stables, where he quickly saddled a mount. Then without explanation to the guard at the gate, he headed off in the direction he'd seen her fly.

The night around him was very clear and the plate of the sky was covered in bright stars. However, stars were not what he sought, and when his eyes finally caught sight of a white gleaming form high in the heavens, his heart leapt into his throat. Without hesitation, he urged his mount into a gallop, ever mindful of the path Alida continued to follow, the plunge of his horse's hooves in the snow evident by the crackling of the snow and ice around them.

It grew very late and his horse had begun to tire before he finally saw her plummet down towards a clearing up ahead. Ulrich approached quietly, not wanting to send her off into flight again from fear. He dismounted and entered the clearing, watching as the final stages of her transformation took place. When she opened her eyes, she lay naked in the snow looking up at the stars.

"Not only am I a fool in the devises of love, but I cannot even remember my clothing though it is the dead of winter," she whispered mournfully to herself, rocking back and forth with her arms around her knees.

Ulrich, who stood nearby, heard her comment and approached cautiously. "For the record, you are not a fool in the devises of love, you are the embodiment of it. Especially sitting there with your dark hair flowing down to the snow and your skin pink from the cold."

This husky voiced retort from the man she adored sent her into a fresh torrent of pain, and the tears began to come more rapidly than she could stem.

Ulrich forgot his good intentions and his self-inflicted restrictions. He paced forward and gathered her up into his arms. "Shush now. Don't cry; it breaks my heart when you are sad."

When she did not stop crying, he continued, "If you are sad because you are not free, I will give you freedom. You can leave and I will not follow. This has gone on too long, Alida. I need not wait anymore."

She cried harder, and he felt the crush of his heart as it died within his chest. Then she said the most amazing thing. "I love you. I'm sorry, and I—I hope that you will forgive me, yet again. I spoke with Gowen the same night that I accused you of killing Kellen to posses me. He told me the truth of what happened. I do not want to be free. I've been so foolish and cannot live any longer without your touch and without your tenderness!"

He pulled her nearer and then bent over her, kissing her more deeply than he had ever done before. She tasted like honey, wine, and sweetmeats. Her hair was lightly fragranced with lavender and rose, and he drank in every scent, every flavor as if he needed these to survive.

When the kiss had begun to melt her bones, Alida felt his hands pull her tighter to his body. Then he broke contact with her mouth and whispered, "Please allow me to make love with you tonight. Not here, not out in the cold and the wind, but back at *our* home in *our* bed. You will feel cherished and warm and satisfied, I promise."

She laughed softly and ran her hands over his face. "I thought you said I would be the one to beg for affections."

He groaned and kissed her mouth. "This is not the time to remind me of stupid declarations and foolish pride. Now kiss me back."

She did so and with great passion. Ulrich, feeling his desire rise with the demand to be sated, pulled away and huskily instructed her to dress herself in his cloak and outer tunic. Then he picked her up tenderly and with her still in his arms mounted his horse settling her onto his lap.

They stayed crushed together on the ride back while Ulrich whispered promises in her ear and touched her intimately—his love deep and apparent for her.

They did not reenter Drachmund's gates until it was well into the wee hours of the morning. The guards, being astute and well trained, made no comment and did not even look up as the lord of the castle passed by with his wife firmly ensconced on his lap.

Tenderly, Ulrich lifted Alida from the back of the horse and carried her up to his chambers. Rather than waking a servant, he insisted that she allow him to look after her needs.

When he had her comfortably seated before a roaring blaze, he went down to the kitchens and found a loaf of bread, fruit compote, and sliced meats. He carefully balanced all of these on a tray with pitchers of mead and honeyed milk.

When he softly opened the door, her welcoming gaze and tender smile sent his heart and stomach into spirals. This woman who sat before him with her dark hair curling untamed over her shoulders, was his every desire and hope.

He placed the tray before her and then leaned over her for a kiss. The meeting of their lips, pure and gentle, warmed rapidly, and he was left breathless in her presence. His desire for her was very apparent and sweet.

Alida, surprisingly, felt no embarrassment though she well knew what was ahead. This was the man that The Ancient of Days had intended for her; there would be no fear or shame this night. She was, however, a little unsure of how to proceed, whether she should take the lead or allow him. She need not have worried, for presently he released her ordering her to remain still with her eyes closed.

Then after making some mysterious noises on the other side of the chamber, he finally came to her. He asked her to continue to keep her eyes shut, and taking her hand, he led her to the sleeping pallet.

When Alida opened her eyes, an exquisite garment made of a material she had never seen was carefully laid out over the furs. She reached out and touched its soft surface, marveling over the texture. Throughout its powdered blue tinted weave, birds and flowers had been woven so that they shimmered in the light when she raised it up to have a closer look.

"What is it?" she asked wonderingly.

"It is called silk and comes from the Far East. I sent for it when I first met you, in the hopes that one day I could present it as a gift. A merchant from the south brought it to me from his storehouse." He paused. "I would like for you to wear it." He motioned to a screen on the other side of the room. "Will you?"

She nodded and then smilingly kissed him on the lips, running a free hand up over his chest.

When she emerged sometime later, he thought he had never seen a more glorious vision. The blue of the sheath and robe made her eyes sparkle like sapphires. Against her skin, the texture looked perfectly matched, and Ulrich felt his joy soar. Here was his wife, gowned in a gift he'd given her, with eyes only for him. This was truly their wedding night.

The food and the fire were forgotten as he pulled her somewhat roughly against his body, covering her mouth and face with passionate kisses. From the heavens, The All smiled down at his perfect creation, and then with joyful laughter, He released for their ears alone a sweet melody.

Late the next morning, Ulrich squeezed his wife gently around the waist as she softly came out of slumber. His kisses and full-length hugs preceded his words. "Good morn to thee, fair wife."

"Good morn, husband," she smilingly crooned back.

When his face grew suddenly serious, Alida pulled back slowly, watching his expression as he murmured, "why did you not tell me?"

"Tell you what?"

"You were yet a maiden when I took thee last night."

Alida bit her lip. "My union with Kellen was never consummated. His tastes ran against those of a natural man."

A huge smile broke out over his face. "Then you are mine and mine alone."

She leaned forward and bit his ear gently. "It would have been thus no matter the previous circumstances," but Ulrich could not erase the silly grin from off his face.

It was this picture that greeted surprised servants, who opened the door to attend to their duties. Their stuttering and hasty retreat was testament to the lord's disapproval at having suffered an intrusion.

Within the hour, the entire castle knew that the lord and mistress were now on the best of terms.

Over a leisurely repast later that afternoon, Gwynn and Alida whispered quietly with each other. Soft laughter occasionally punctuated their murmurs. From across the room, Bryon and Ulrich merely smiled at each other, their chests puffed out like bantam roosters.

The weeks flowed one into the next as smoothly as honey for the newly joined couples. Alida had never felt so fulfilled or satisfied, and her mate was sure he would burst from the joy that followed him from morning to morning. Their most treasured moments together were spent talking and learning, sharing bits of their lives that were new and untold.

The castle itself had never looked so good or run so smoothly, for the inhabitants basked in their lord and lady's unified justice and wise direction. Eldridge, muttering over his cups one night, claimed he was sure to die from the sickly sweet atmosphere, before he was firmly cuffed by Birch who had overheard his mutterings. She was quite enjoying the lovely picture her beloved boy and lady made.

CHAPTER TWENTY-THREE

It was into this peace and prosperity that a scraggly band of men rode one afternoon. As was usual, they were stopped at the front gates of the city—the castle just a dream beyond the iron walls of the fully geared guard of Drachmund. They presented themselves to the guards as common travelers weary from the road. They begged the hospitality of a few nights' stay as well as some simple provisions. They were searched, and it was requested that their weapons be left at the city gate; then a cheerful servant pointed out quarters for them at a nearby inn.

When they had refreshed themselves and made their way to the castle proper, the men marveled at the richness of their surroundings and at the merry atmosphere in the castle hall. One man introduced himself as a minstrel and was allowed to play and sing for the keepsmen of Drachmund Heights. He sang songs about the gathered assembly, and by the end of the night, he had the inhabitants of the keep laughing and singing along.

There was nothing alarming about these men or anything that would have alerted the seasoned soldiers in the hall to guess at their arrival. Thusly, they were well received into the gracious open arms of the great city and castle alike. Other than queries placed by one of the quieter men regarding Bryon, their stay in the keep went along without incident.

Two days later these men went on their way with newly restored provisions and rested mounts. They headed south with thanks and good wishes. Once out of sight of the castle, they cut into the forest and backtracked coming out again on the road far north of Drachmund Heights. Grimness and determination set the pace for their ride home. There would be no rest until their aim was fulfilled.

"You're sure it was him?" A giant man with flaming red hair and a thick red beard gazed out through an archer's slit into a blizzard that howled around his domain. There was something strained about his stance and lightly flexed hands.

"Yes, sire, it was the very man."

"We will ride out after the storm, and my peace will be complete." He did not say anything else, and the slender quiet man who had addressed him left the room without a sound.

That night in the broad stone hall, far to the north of Drachmund Heights, the conversation that was on most nights rowdy and merry had dropped to a tense hum. The gathered soldiers who served The Red prepared themselves to follow their leader, a desire for harsh northern justice burning in their hearts.

War chants and ancient songs rang throughout the hall the next day as preparations were made for battle. When the snow had slowed from blizzard to driving sleet, the battalion headed out from the dark grey battlements. At their lead, The Red rode a massive, shaggy horse with wool blankets covering its back and a tasseled bridle and rein for a lead. At his side, a pair of wolfhounds constantly abided, giving their every loyalty to his call.

It would take at least a month before they had made their way through wilderness and over the sea to the richer lands of the south and to the sweet finality of revenge. He had ensured that his men had packed enough provisions and a goodly amount of war gear to suffice against the weaker, soft fools his men had spoken about. Should they need further goods or gear, they would plunder small villages along the way. His massive form was enough of a beacon to lead his men through bitter storm after bitter storm. They knew none mightier than this, their master and lord.

That night the same wind that had blown at Brögen Fjords, though greatly lessened in its travels south, whistled over the Heights. Alida, strangely restive, paced her nuptial chambers.

Ulrich already peacefully ensconced beneath the furs opened one eye and called to her, "Come back to bed, love. What ails thee?"

She shuddered, "I do not know, Ulrich, but even our watchers are agitated. They whisper strange things to me; they warn me of something to come."

He rolled over and threw open the furs on her side. "Come back to bed and rest. Naught is afoot from which Creator shall not save us all."

She lay down with him, but when her tossing and turning threatened to disturb his rest, she arose again and very softly left the chambers. She climbed to the open parapets above, with her cloak tightly wrapped about her. Her head lifted as if attempting to catch a scent, but to all appearances, the castle lay in its normal silent slumber. Then she allowed her transformation to occur and lifted into the chilling winds fighting their stringent currents.

Here in the cavern of the sky, the agitation of the watchers was even greater. Their silver-blue forms darted about her, tugging at her wings and whispering some warning that she could not discern. She peered down to the earth below, but could see no evil stirring in the forests or upon the roads. Here and there, she caught sight of some night creature in its vigilant search for food, but there was nothing amiss.

She stayed in flight until the sun was well risen in the east. Then exhausted, she dropped back to the castle. Ulrich let her sleep, but was disturbed by her odd behavior. Gwynn and Birch did not laugh off her discontent either, but told him not to worry overmuch about her. Birch even suggested that perhaps she was with child.

Ulrich, upon hearing this, immediately went up to sit by his wife and work quietly on the ledgers until she awoke. It was very difficult for him to concentrate on the numbers when he could well picture her holding his small, rotund cub many months from now.

When she finally did awaken, he swiftly moved to her side. "Why are you so tired?"

"I was up all night until the sun rose."

"Your behavior is very odd."

Alida sighed, "What is it you really want to ask, husband?"

He paused and grinned slyly, "You aren't with babe, are you?"

She laughed, shaking her head. "You have an overactive imagination. I am not with babe."

He looked crestfallen. "Then something really is wrong. I have not seen you so agitated since the days when you were yet with Kellen."

She hung her head. "This feeling of fear will not leave me."

He gathered her up into his arms and lay down on the pallet; then whispering softly he entreated God for protection and for an answer to her worry. In the warm silence of the room, the watchers darted about shaking their heads, now was not the time for peace.

Alida rose somewhat calmer, but still tense. "Do not fear husband; the answer to our requests will be made known over time. I am going to bathe, eat, and then ride for a while alone." She kissed him sweetly and went on her way.

Ulrich paced the chambers for a while, and then he took the steps two at a time to the hall below. He had the guards check and recheck the weaponry and food stores. They also were instructed to ride the perimeter of the keep, verifying that all escape routes and entries were intact and secured. Battlements were strengthened and the gates oiled.

Landres approached Ulrich while these duties were being carried out. "Milord, why this attention to readiness? Have you been alerted to a possible attack?"

Ulrich did not reply at first, his eyes looking somewhere off in the distance. Then quietly he responded, "My wife is very restless all of a sudden, as if some inner alarm has been sounded. I know how this sounds, Landres, but I trust her instincts."

Landres clasped his friend on the shoulder. "She is worthy of such trust and respect. We all should pay heed to her instincts, for she is one of the greatest warriors I have known. She is not simply some silly female to us, Ulrich."

Ulrich's white smile was thanks enough. He was deeply appreciative of his clan's ready acceptance of Alida and more importantly Landres' approval.

For weeks they stayed at attention with all watches doubled and every soldier at a keyed ready, for without cause the scouts that were sent out from the city one by one did not return. Ulrich knew now that something was terribly wrong. Alida, who had thought the feeling would lessen with time, found herself more restless than ever, though Ulrich had not told her of the missing scouts. She did not intend to avoid anyone, but she felt such gravity over this unknown battle that all she could do was pray. Most often, this took place while walking the parapets of the city walls with Landres or Ulrich standing nearby, quiet and strong.

It was here that The Red first saw her. Of course, this was from some distance away with his army hidden in the forest. He could not distinguish any features from his position, but he could tell by the robes and hair that it was a female figure.

The gates of the castle were firmly closed and there were more posted guards than his men had described. He poked the scout next to him, "I guess the gates are not thrown wide to us like every other lazy southern province. I am mildly impressed."

He withdrew, leaving the scout to vigilance while he sought out his captains. "There are at least two score guardsmen visible on the front walls. Who knows how many more wait behind the gates. Mayhap our attempt at killing all their scouts has not paid off."

"What is our plan of attack, sire?"

"Bring me Grog, Cardul, Dren, and Cerdu. They are to attire themselves as the travelers they were when first they breached those walls. They will need to approach from the south. Have them age their gear with mud and water. When they have begun to enter the gates, we will attack from the sides. Allow them some hours to prepare. We will make an attempt at a breach late into the night."

Unaware of the conversation below, Alida stayed upon the parapets until the lanterns had been lit and the guard had changed. Then she made her way to the hall. She found Ulrich and after a warm meal, they retired to their chambers. The castle around them settled in for another restless night as they had so many nights over the past month.

Ulrich, tired of the tension and tired of the worry, ordered a huge bath for their room. He gently undressed his wife and took her into the bath with him, enjoying the feel of her skin beneath his fingers as he massaged her shoulders and neck. Then they cozened down into the warm fragrant water, talking softly with one another.

When the water began to grow cool, Ulrich helped Alida from the bath and gently dried her off, welcoming her into their warm bed beneath the furs, their intimacy a reprieve in itself.

They had begun to drift off to sleep when he heard the castle alarm sound. Instantly he was out of the bed. Alida, too, jumped from her place and readied herself in a serviceable tunic, leggings, and gear. He wanted to ask to her stay where it was safe, but he knew that it would be useless to argue with her. This was as much her home to defend, as it was his.

They went quietly together to the head of the stairs and looked down into the hall. The staircase curved away from them blocking some of the view, but they could see and hear the raucous sounds of preparations taking place below them. Alida moved forward just a bit around the bend, scanning the teeming mass of people. To her left she saw four men who were vaguely familiar. Just as she placed them, Ulrich caught sight and remembered them as well. All at once fighting, broke out.

He was sick with anger as he watched the men who had been welcomed into his keep, run through servants, guards, and even a young lad, no more than a child, who had been awakened by the strange noises. The four were joined by more and more foreigners until Ulrich and Alida knew that the outer defenses of the city itself and then the castle had been breached.

Ulrich scanned the crowd once more and found Landres just below. They made eye contact, and Ulrich with a silent signal to attack joined the fray simultaneously. Alida followed closely behind.

Ulrich's men flocked in from all areas of the castle, fighting for their home until the hall rang with their calls and the sounds of blood. During the fighting Ulrich and Alida were separated. Every once in awhile he would look for her dark head, and when he could no longer see her, he made his way in the direction to which she'd disappeared.

Suddenly, the hall, which had once had been raucous with warfare, grew deathly silent. For at the door, standing head and shoulders above even the tallest warrior, was The Red. More important than his stature, however, was the fact that he held Alida unconscious in his grasp.

The silence broke as his men let out a great cheer, for they knew that the wench whom their lord held was surely of some worth. The Red was not known for his undue attention to the fairer sex. Especially in warfare, the leader cared very little for a female's wellbeing.

In direct opposition of the coup, Ulrich's clan let out horrified gasps of fury. A young lass ran to Ulrich's side, tugging at his arm when she saw the approach of The Red. Then in a breathless rush, she related the events surrounding Alida's capture, her sobs and shaking barely stilled by Ulrich's encouragement. He lifted the girl into his arms where she buried her head into his shoulder, and finding a nearby servant, he commanded that the young lass be taken from the hall before harm came to her.

The Red had been furious when he saw Alida slay four of his men. Women did not fight from whence he came, but this hellcat attacked with a fervor he had rarely seen even in a man. From a nearby servant he had extracted the unwilling information that she was none other than the mistress of these holdings. The servant had then been quickly dispatched, and Alida had been faced with the sight of the huge man bearing down upon her.

Their battle had been surprisingly entertaining The Red thought with a secret smile, for the wench was agile and strong. It pleased him that he should find the crown jewel of the land within moments of the siege.

In a powerful deep voice, he called his men to his side and then addressed Drachmund's fuming force. "It seems as though I have gained the one thing that would stay the hand of an entire army." He paused and ran his sword along her unconscious jaw. "But I could be wrested of my prize should the one I seek be offered in exchange. If he is relinquished to me, I will release her and you and your precious home will be saved."

Ulrich with a growl paced forward, blood in his eye and his lips curled in a ferocious snarl. The Red, wanting to keep his hostage out of enemy hands, threw Alida to the ground behind him and ordered that his men guard her well. Then he faced Ulrich, his brows rising in surprise at the insignia on Ulrich's breastplate.

"You are The Wolf," he said softly. "I have heard tales of thy valor and plenty. You are a worthy opponent. It appears I have entered the very den of the legend and now find myself in fear of the fangs."

Ulrich's teeth ground together. "If you are so in fear then relinquish my wife to me, and I will spare some part of your pitiful life."

The Red laughed, his gleaming teeth bright in his scarlet beard. "Make it easy on thyself, and give me what I seek."

"Every man within this keep is under my protection. I will not exchange one life for another."

"Even if I were to tell you that the one I seek is a murderer? Would you exchange his worthless life for that of your priceless mate?"

Ulrich felt his stomach drop. "I do not consort with murderers."

"Then you have been a fool, for my men did find the wretch here some weeks ago. He is called Bryon of Goodlock."

Ulrich paled and stood straighter. "You are mistaken about the man's character."

"Nay. He slaughtered my brother in cold blood. I seek vengeance."

Landres had drawn close to Ulrich's side and whispered, "Bryon has been gone this past three days with Gwynn to Kinterden Dell."

Ulrich stepped forward. "I will not bargain. The man you seek is not here, and even if he were, his life is as valuable as my wife's. Be he murderer or not, he should be given the opportunity to stand trial for this accusation, not handed over to be destroyed." Landres, along with Ulrich's other men, knew how much that statement cost their leader, for Alida was the dearest thing in the world to him. Nevertheless, he was also a just leader, and his valor could cost him everything he valued.

The Red roared his agitation, his eyes hateful and closed. "You have just lost your wife."

Ulrich clutched his sword tighter. "Take my life in her stead and in the stead of Bryon."

The Red glared hotly at his opponent. "Nay, you are worth five of the man. He is no more important than a woman, and so this woman I shall take. It may be I can gain from her hide enough satisfaction to stay my hand for a time."

Ulrich snarled and leapt forward, his loosed anger hot in his chest. Again and again, he attacked the giant warrior, drawing blood in only a few of his well-aimed blows. They parried and thrusted like the rhythmical arms of a pendulum neither gaining purchase over the other. Presently, The Red and his men began their descent towards the gates with Ulrich and all of Drachmund's force in pursuit. The Red, making a calculated move with a great arch of his sword, slashed Ulrich's right side. The cut was so deep that Ulrich instantly fell to his knees. His last sight was of his men being held off by the threat of Alida's pale throat. None dared to be the one to cost their leader this woman who meant everything.

Landres and a bold guard set out after The Red, but when a sudden cold sleet turned into a thick blizzard, they lost the pursuit and were forced to return to Drachmund's protective walls.

They found Ulrich very pale, lying in the care of Birch and her serving women. When Landres walked into the room, Ulrich motioned all of the women out. Then he turned cloudy eyes on his captain and gritted out, "You have lost her?"

Landres lifted his chin and responded gruffly, "Aye, milord."

Ulrich turned his head then and covered his eyes with his strong hand, but not before a tear slid from behind the barrier. Landres swallowed the emotion that welled up in his own throat for he had failed his best friend and leader. He swallowed again. "You know that whether she lives or dies I will pursue him."

"Aye, and I with thee. Has a messenger been sent to collect Bryon from Kinterden."

"Yes, milord."

Then in the silence of the room, Ulrich turned tortured eyes back on Landres and their resolve returned, this time accompanied by a great anger. "When he arrives, bring him to me. We are lost to the storm these few days, but I will ride after that." Landres saluted and left the room, fear and hope giving speed to his stride.

In the heavens, Alida's protectors awaited their release. The hand of Creator withheld them, for a part of his plan had yet to be carried out. Creator grieved at the temporary sorrow his creations would suffer, but he knew that very soon life would come from these ashes.

Alida, unconscious yet but alive, was carried along in front of The Red where he had thrown her over his mount disdaining any care for her comfort. At The Red's signal, the battalion of northern warriors gave their horses unrestricted rein and were pleased when the steeds found a series of caves. Packs were searched for flint, and soon small fires blazed deep within the protective caverns.

The Red took a small, round room off the biggest cave and rolled out his traveling pallet. His dogs lay down at the mouth of the room and awaited his command. When Alida came to, she lay on a stone floor with her hands tied tightly behind her back. The Red saw her eyes open and chuckled as he lifted her to her feet. "You are a strong little wench, aren't you? I hit thee hard enough to silence thee for an entire day, and you awaken within a few hours."

She did not speak, but looked at him without cowering, her eyes like hard pieces of flint. He circled her slowly, appreciating the curves he saw subtly hidden beneath her tunic and leggings. Boldly he ran his hand over her form. "It appears the little warrior has a shape. By her valor, I would have guessed her to be as squarely hewn as a man." With a flick of his wrist, he loosed her hair from the confines of the sturdy leather thong she wore. His breath came out in a soft flare as he saw how lustrous the length of her hair.

Then without further ado, he proceeded to dishonor her. Alida did her best to fight him with her teeth, feet, and bound hands, but he was infinitely stronger at this range and dwarfed her tiny frame with his height and brawn. After he had his way with her, she found enough room to surprise him and bit into his hand, drawing blood and flesh from the limb. He backhanded her and knocked her onto the ground. He then lifted her onto his bedroll and waited until she could focus on him. He leaned over, her pinning her to the ground and whispered, "You should have killed me instead of my men, for I am going to make you pay for every one of their lives. Little cats should never enter the battles of titans."

He cast her aside and ordered her to clothe herself. While she dressed, he watched her coolly, no emotion apparent in his mask-like gaze. When his voice echoed out into the room, she flinched and then took a deep breath covering her fear. "You did not cry and plead as other women would have. I admire such strength. The Wolf has good taste."

Then taunting her rebellion, he called out, "Your fate has been decided. You will become a serving wench to my wives, and your wild ways will be tamed by the humility of a pauper's cause. The sins of others will be cleansed through your pain. "

Still, Alida did not reply, a trickle of his blood running in a cold rivulet from the corner of her mouth. He rose, making his way to where he had thrown her. Leaning very close, he whispered, "Don't try to leave while I sleep, or my companions will rip you to shreds." Then he returned to his pallet and quietly ordered, "Guard." The wolfhounds growled and looked at her with their steely yellow eyes.

Alida knew that though she was a changeling these hounds would not be made friends, for their loyalty was greater than their blood. She considered for a moment changing while the giant slept, but the dogs would rip her falcon body into pieces. She would have to wait for a better moment.

Exhausted from an already long day and paralyzed by her disgrace and injuries, Alida fell warily asleep. She did not awaken again until a rough hand slapped at her cheeks.

Bryon strode into the main hall amidst the buzz of anxious conversation. Ulrich's gaze burnt into him from the end of the great table where he sat surrounded by his fiercest warriors. It was in the best of moments a very intimidating arrangement, but for Bryon it felt as if he were headed towards certain doom. He did not allow his eye contact to falter for a moment from the man whom he now called lord and friend, but his insides had turned to liquid.

Ulrich rose and his fists came down on the table. "Everyone who is not a part of my present guard is dismissed, and close the door on your way out." A flurry of movement encompassing the sounds of boots, skirts, and nervous conversation occurred as everyone hurried from the hall leaving Bryon to his fate.

Ulrich strode around the table and approached the burly smith whose thick, clenched hands were the only outward sign of his fear. Stopping barely an inch from his nose, Ulrich growled, "explain, or by God, I shall not spare thee."

Bryon nodded and swallowing deeply hesitantly began his tale. "I was a cocky youth of seventeen, with a weakness for every kind of combat. Whether in games or courting or in hand-to-hand battle, I sought competition as if it were my blood's life."

He swallowed forcefully and continued. "I suppose it is a very common tale, but my passion overcame my good sense, and one bitterly cold afternoon, I challenged the chief's youngest son to a duel with staves.

"We chose a newly frozen fjord as our jousting site to make it more interesting, and then we left before the game could be halted by saner men. We began to spare amidst the bleak wind and snapping ice, and as the match wore on, my anger became greater and greater, for I could only equal Stivak's pace, I could not best him.

"Round for round, we went without any sign of dominance or weakness. He just laughed at me from his frozen beard, his eyes too merry and bright for the competition I was feeling. Then he mocked me, imparting to me the news that he had taken my newest lover to his own bed and that she had preferred his attentions to mine.

"I could not contain the forcefulness of my will, which burst forth at that moment, and I began to intentionally back him towards a dangerously thin place over the frozen water. Stivak, being as heavy and large as his brother, broke through the ice and plunged to his neck in the slushy water screaming for my help, for not only was it cold enough to kill a man in moments, but he did not know how to swim.

"I thought to teach him a lesson, so I stuck out my stave pretending to extend help. When he grasped its length, I released it into his grip without pulling him back, waiting for the glory of true panic to show on his face. However, my anger was my downfall, for he slipped beneath the surface and never reappeared.

"I had been searching for his body alone for hours when I heard a group from the keep calling for us. By this point, my anger had been replaced with a great fear, for Stivak's family was known for their lack of mercy, and I did not deserve any, even in the best of circumstances. Like a coward, I ran. I watched from the banks, as they continued searching for both of us.

"Eventually, they found him frozen just beneath the surface of some ice near the mouth of the fjord. They cut him out of the ice and were surprised to find my staff in his grip. I knew then that my fate had been sealed. I fled their land with the vow never to return. I stayed very far south for years until the story of my misdeed was no longer passed amongst merchants from that land. When I could not bear the heat and easy ways of the southern provinces any longer, I returned to a point as close to my original homeland as I would ever be allowed, The Isles of Mist. After more time had past, I was enlisted as a smithy by warriors from Kinterden Dell.

They obviously did not give up their search, for now I have again cost a great family someone of value."

Bryon's voice died out in the hall as if he were choking, and then much to Ulrich's surprise, the rough man before him wiped tears away from his clouded eyes. "Forgive me, milord. I love Alida as if she were my own kin. I am a grown man tired of running and tired of excuses. I will stand whatever justice you meet out."

Ulrich raised his hand as if to cuff the smith, but then lowered it just as quickly, his eyes a burning blue. "I will not offer you up to the barbarians from the north, for they would surely slay you, but you must pay for your crime and cowardice though it was wrought in your youth." He paused with his mouth in a steely line. "You will become my bond slave for fourteen years. At the end of that time, your debt will be considered paid, and you may live where and how you like, along with your wife, for God only knows that Gwynn doesn't deserve to lose her husband. If you do not fulfill your fourteen-year bond with me, I will run you through personally. As it is, pray to God that my wife is safe." He whirled away from Bryon and stalked out of the hall, his muscles quivering and damp with rage.

Bryon dropped to his knees, completely unaware of the humility it portrayed, choking on deep sobs that racked his body. Then he felt the strong hand of one of the warriors on his shoulders.

"Rise up, smith. Our lord is known for his justice, and justice has been meted out this day though it has cost him everything he holds dear. Consider yourself blessed that his justice met with mercy."

Bryon nodded, wiped away his tears, and rising on unsteady legs, he headed out of the hall. Curiously, though he was now a slave, he had never felt freer.

The blizzard and several successive storms, added to Ulrich's sorry state, kept them from beginning their travel until a full month had passed.

CHAPTER TWENTY-FOUR

BERYNTH, IN THE PROVINCE OF BRÖGEN FJORDS

The horses and riders bent against the freezing onslaught of the storm, their shoulders and backs aching from the strain and their heads throbbing from the constant roar of the winds and the slapping sting of slush and ice-laden snow.

Alida, her eyes a steely grey in the gloom, stared straight ahead, refusing to express her exhaustion or any form of weakness to the rough, brawny men around her.

The Red, who had left her alone since that first horrible night in the caves, suddenly broke free from the head of the command line and rode back to where she was. Without comment, he grasped the lead reins of her mount and led the shaggy horse to the front of the slow moving battalion.

Alida sat up straighter, her heart hammering away in her throat. There was a gleam in the massive man's eye that nearly matched the light that glimmered from his ice-crusted beard. His voice, hoarse from the conditions and pride alike, commanded with a sneer, "Woman, cast your eyes upon a sight infinitely greater than thee." His hairy, powerful hand gestured to some point up ahead.

Alida looked up, and suddenly from out of the blowing flurries of snow, a great black city rose like a beast from the frozen rocks, the winter winds moaning horribly around its walls.

"Welcome to Brögen Fjords, your new home." Alida shivered inside at the sight of the imposing walls before her, for this place made of dark stone looked as if no warmth could ever penetrate its walls.

They rode the rest of the way in silence until the great black iron gates of the castle loomed directly before them, their ride unremarkable through the· . winding, filth-laden streets of Brögen's township. She'd never seen such a lack of concern for the disposal of human, animal, and vegetative waste.

When they had entered into the sheltered grounds within the walls, Alida was ordered to dismount and follow her new lord. She did so with great bitterness of heart and fear for what lay ahead. For the weeks upon weeks, it had taken to arrive at this place, she had called upon Creator to aid her and to come to her rescue, but there was no answer in the fiercely cold winds of the north.

She was unable to save herself, for The Red kept her guarded by his hounds and men during the night in a rough, oddly egg-shaped tent made of smelly animal hides. During the day, she rode between the same guards and hounds. Any further hope of escape was lessened by the winds of blizzards and bitterly driving rains that kept her from transforming and taking flight. She would not last under such conditions.

Now in this castle, at the heart of an imposing city, she would be thwarted yet again, for only arrow slits here and there on the walls provided a view to the outside. From what she could see, not a single window graced the facade of the keep.

The Red roughly directed her to stand with him as she was pronounced a serving woman to his harem of wives. Here she would be no more than a piece of chattel locked away in the women's quarters without the freedom to move about the city and castle that other servant's enjoyed.

The Red, with the harsh voice of a king devoid of mercy, instructed a sullen maid to take Alida to the women's quarters and left with his men without further comment to his newest acquisition.

Alida, on travel weary legs, was led to a great series of chambers where the chatter of women could be heard through the thick doors. It was a new arrangement for her. She was accustomed to the cohabitation of male and female nobility, as it had been done in all the homes she had encountered since childhood.

When the heavy oak door swung open, a woman with black hair and large green eyes gazed silently at her from a hide couch the heavy odors of scented candles and old perfume beckoning her into the choking gloom. Alida's only relief was that by all appearances these chambers seemed more comfortable than the other living areas she had glimpsed on her tour through the castle.

Another woman, no more than seventeen years, with blonde hair and pale blue eyes nervously hovered near the couch of the black-haired female, her young white hands passing over and over a piece of crumpled silk causing the fabric to hiss and crackle with static.

Alida shuddered. She could feel a great deal of animosity pouring from these females who were very fine and delicate, all having cat's eyes and sullen expressions. When the servant had left, a third female with dark brown hair and brown eyes strolled forward, running her hands through her straight locks and keeping direct eye contact with Alida. Her buxom form threatened to burst the fine cloth of her tunics, and despite her lazy stride, Alida's keen observation saw and smelled the thin sheen of sweat that rested on her brow.

"By the gods, you are the worst I've seen yet." Her melodious voice rang out into the room like a smith's hammer strike off cold iron.

The black-haired female chuckled. "Leave off the comments, Hilde. Can't you see our lord's taste grows more indifferent with each new servant he brings to us. Who asked for your watery explanation anyway?"

The timid, young woman with the blonde hair squeaked out, "She looks like a man."

Alida did not make a sound. Her stance was relaxed, and she offered up no sign of her emotion as she took her time surveying the room. The black-haired woman arose and approached with a graceful stride, only slightly way-laid by the soft, telltale shuffle of a weak leg. "I am called Deirdre, and the one who spoke first is Hilde. The whelp behind my couch is Juniper. We are the wives of The Red, and I am his first. You will do as I say during your stay here, or I will make your life a living hell. The others will annoy you, but have no real power. The gossip is that you enjoyed a noble status not long since past; though I can hardly fathom how such a poor-looking wench as you could have ever been called noble."

When Alida did not comment, Juniper said, "Perhaps she is mute or speaks another language. She looks very foreign."

At this Alida turned toward Deirdre and said with steely softness, "I am Alida of Falda, and I do not take orders from anyone but God and occasionally my husband."

Deirdre smiled as if she had just licked a bowl of cream. "Then you will find your stay here very short indeed. Oh, and he is not your husband, he is your lord–for none as pitiful you could capture his attention."

Alida, unwilling to explain that she meant Ulrich rather than The Red, turned on her heel and strode over to the wall where an arrow slit had been placed. Near it, a small spitting lamp with fat and wick strove to remain burning in the chilling gusts that swept through the slit.

Deirdre's creamy voice slithered out into the room, "There is naught to see that you will ever want to see again. We are well guarded, for we belong to The Red and The Red alone. No other men are even allowed to gaze upon us, and our serving wenches may not entertain males in these quarters lest we be introduced to their brawny presence as well. These four walls are all you will ever see."

Alida did not turn and did not make a sound. She merely began to remove the heavy cloak and outer coverings that had protected her against the storms. When her cloak, mittens, and underwrap had been removed, she slowly undid her hair from her braid and ran her fingers absently through its length, her mind already seeking a plan of escape.

Deirdre, burning holes into the new acquisition's back with her catty gaze, cursed silently to herself as she saw the curling, glorious length of Alida's hair and the smooth firm muscles that rippled on her upper arms. It was true, that looked foreign and not at all tame. Deirdre's eyes narrowed. This one would take some thought. She turned and limped back to the soft layers of her couch, returning blithely to the delicious gossip that had embroiled them before Alida's arrival. It would not do to seem overly focused on a mere servant.

Silent tears rolled down Alida's cheeks. Because her back was turned, it went unnoticed by the other women, a thing in which Alida counted herself fortunate.

When some time had passed and her melancholy was under control, Alida turned and asked where she might gain a bath from one of the numerous underlings that hovered about the skirts of the room. Her request was met with open disdain as well as curiosity.

"You'll catch your death, you stupid female," hissed Hilde.

"Better her than us," called out Juniper.

Deirdre did nothing but watch. She had heard of these soft pleasure-seeking southerners. Many of the men in the keep wove horrendous, ribald tales about them and their indolent ways. Alida was both amused an amazed that they should make such comments—she merely wanted a bath. Lazily, she said, "From the odor in these chambers, you would all do well to follow suit." The satisfying sound of offended gasps were followed by no other comments—the cats momentarily silenced of their mewing.

Alida then carried and dumped bucket after bucket of her own water into a rough-hewn tub that was no more than a barrel sawed in half. The first task having been completed she then made her way around the chambers gathering linen towels and other supplies. Alida, after all the preparations had been made set about enjoying every minute of the cleansing. She mourned the lack of warmth and scenting agents that she would have been given at home for her bath, but the tepid cleansing ripples of the water that had been drawn from a cistern in the chambers felt wonderful after such a merciless trip. It was her first chance to wash away her dishonor, and she felt somehow more human for the doing of it, though she could barely stand to look at the bruises and telltale signs of violence that The Red had left on her skin.

The Red's other wives took cursory glances in her direction, altering their initial judgment that she was manly, for there was nothing male about her lovely rounded features and obvious femininity.

When she had bathed and clothed herself in the serviceable tunics that arrived mysteriously from below, Alida asked which pallet was hers. Deirdre, still fuming over Alida's last comment, disdained from replying, choosing instead to stare at her fingernails while lazily running a long, gloriously plumed feather over her cheeks, the sound like the annoying rasp of a mouse cleaning its coat with its paws. Alida shrugged and walked to the nearest pallet. From behind her, Hilde shrieked like a banshee caught in high winds, her hands grasping for a nearby dining knife. Enraged that Alida should seek to strip her of her one symbol of status, the third wife of The Red attacked!

Alida was much stronger and faster, and Hilde felt herself propelled into the nearest wall with horrifying speed as the wind was knocked out of her in a painful whoosh. Then Alida strode to her side and bent over her, her face mere inches from the crying woman, her voice steely and unrepentant. "I do not want to be here anymore than any of you want me here! I was brought against my will to serve as mere chattel, when I am possessed of the greatest man I know, having lands and wealth of my own. I would endear myself to all and any of you that would so choose, but not if it requires me to demean myself or to submit myself to puling women with nothing better to do than gossip and whine. I'll suffer at the hand of The Red, for his stature and weapons allow me no recourse, but I'll not readily suffer an attack from any such as you." She straightened, and with some hesitation, she offered a hand to the shaken woman, her anger causing her grasp to be unnecessarily hard. Hilde hesitantly accepted the aid and was smoothly lifted to her feet, shaken and not at all sure what all had just transpired, but certain of this woman's strength.

From across the room, Deirdre glared balefully at the surrender that she perceived in the other woman. Alida asked again, "Which pallet is mine?" With some reluctance, Hilde said, "Servants are not given pallets to lie upon. You will make a space for yourself on the ground with the other maids, pointing to the farthest wall from them under the arrow slit. Alida did not smile but did her best to sound somewhat grateful murmuring a succinct, "Thank you."

From the door that had opened silently, a deep laugh spread out into the room, its harsh sound echoing off the tapestry-covered walls. "I think my women shall find that the newest addition to their chambers is not at all what they expected." The Red strolled over to Alida and roughly grabbed her arm, ignoring her protest. His eyes roved where they would as he asked with some disdain, "Enjoying your new quarters?"

Alida felt her stomach quiver. She said softly but with strength, "He *will* come for me."

The Red chuckled again and then turned to leave, pulling her along behind him despite her best attempts to fight. They arrived in a huge chamber with furs covering the floors and a massive pallet made of oak. He casually tossed her onto the floor at the base of his pallet, beneath the hiss of numerous candelabra that lit the room, as if her weight and strength meant nothing. The places where he had held her arms throbbed painfully. "He may come for you, but until that time, you are mine. Do not forget, little one, that you are the sacrificial lamb. Others' sins are your burdens."

Alida winced at his comments then turned away—the hot blush of anger coming onto her cheeks. He commanded her to gather up a platter of food from across the room with which to serve him.

Grinding her teeth together, she rose and crossed the room, his mere presence like a bane to her wildly roiling stomach and heart. Would she see abuse at this man's hand as she had at Kellen's hand should she refuse to act the part of a servant? Thinking to protect herself until she could find a means of escape, she obeyed, doing every menial chore he required. She found herself hard pressed to follow his commands, however, when at the end of the humiliating session he ordered her to kneel on all fours before his chair. For he then proceeded to place his heavily soiled gargantuan boots upon her back, laughing all the while at his human footstool.

She fought to hold back her frustration and anger, but tears dripped down her nose before she could stop them. To her chagrin, The Red saw them fall. He laughed callously and said, "Even when you cry, it does not seem that your will has been broken, a fact I find intriguing. By the look in your eye, you would run me through in a second. Nevertheless, know this—I have never taken a woman nor have I ever purchased a beast that did not one day submit to my hand. There are worse things than force to make a woman or beast alike, obey a man's command."

She turned away embarrassed at the visible sign of weakness she had shown. The Red was indifferent over her obvious humiliation. She was confounded at his casual dismissal of her and tried to avoid his gaze, cautiously bracing herself for every one of his subsequent commands. When later she looked up at him, he refused to look away, and his gaze burned with a twisted form of humor at the defiance he saw displayed. "Not only does The Wolf have good taste, but I find myself entertained by his whelp of a wife!" Then shrugging his massive shoulders, the whole affair was dismissed. "Whether you submit or not is really of no concern to me for you are trapped here, and no one will come to your aid. You'll find being forgotten is worse than all the force I could ever wield against you!"

Without further comment, he commanded her to crawl to a pallet of furs set beside the fire, for he did not want her to leave should he desire to be served by her hand during the late hours. He fell asleep nearly instantly, and Alida remained stiffly where she was for a moment before finally laying tensely on her side. The arrogant declaration he had made before falling asleep rang through her restless dreams.

The next day The Red himself returned her to the women's chambers, the heated calloused band of his grasp ever a deterrent to her escape through the maze of hallways. His personal attendance back to the chambers was apparently a very unusual occurrence, for Deirdre's glances grew even darker and the other women looked at her in awe.

The rest of that horrible first day dripped slowly away amidst the high-pitched gossip, steely glares, and ribald stories of the other women. Alida, feeling the constraints of her bondage and the soreness of old wounds, paced like a she-lioness before the door. She would hold back the tears until the dark silence of the night. Later in frustration and rage, she paced forward and wrestled with the large door, finally getting it opened far enough to see out into the hall, her muscles quivering with the thought that the hall should be unmanned. The air in the hall was cooler than the air in the chambers, and like a chilling hand, it swept down over her robes and skin just before the steely black eyes of an attending guard did the same.

Hilde came out behind her and said with a tremor in her voice that spoke of real fear, "You had best return, Alida, for none of us are allowed out of these chambers unless we are summoned."

Alida pulled her head back in and said scornfully, "What would you have me do to while away the time, besides the useless activities that I have already witnessed?"

Deirdre, hearing the comment, rose and advanced like a terrible goddess of vengeance, her hair flying about her in a black silky cloud and her robes hissing with the rapidity of her stride. She caught up a precious vase in her hand from a nearby side table, her long sharp fingernails tinging off the surface briefly before it left her hand as a projectile towards Alida's head. A screech of rage followed the body of the ornament before it shattered with a ring off the cold stone walls, scattering at Alida's feet with music of its own. Deirdre was a horrible shot. "You snide, little venomous snake! Who by the gods do you think you are?" Her voice trailed off with an enraged squeak. "You are the newcomer here, not us. You give answer for your actions not the other way around! He may have chosen you to come to him last night, but it will wear off, and he will take his turn with all of us as he has done time after time when the freshness of each new conquest wears off." Spittle from her mouth flecked out with each word, the soft warm spray touching Alida's cheek and forehead, for now they stood nearly toe-to-toe.

Alida waited at the ready for any violence, but Deirdre had learned that her tongue would be her best weapon, for she had witnessed Alida's prowess against Hilde. Although it was difficult, Alida refrained from speaking for she pitied the violent unhappiness of the woman whose beauty was marred not only by anger, but also by something darker that Alida could not name. Instead, she used the sleeve of her gown to wipe away the spittle, returning Deirdre's glare with an unrelenting gaze of her own. They stood this way for some time, toe-to-toe, without moving or speaking—Deirdre's chest heaving with anger and heat coming off her body and from her breath as a testament to her rage. Finally, the other woman sneered and spat full in Alida's face and then turned and strode back to her pallet.

Alida did not utter another word, but using a piece of linen sheet, she wiped away the oozing spit from her hair and face and then kept to herself for the rest of the day. That night, as she feared he would, The Red sent another summons for her.

This time in the oppressively warm environs of his chambers, he watched her the entire time as he ordered her about to do one or another demeaning task, carefully cataloging her every emotion. When he had finished with her, he waved his hand, dismissing her. She was then commanded to sleep again on a pile of furs that had been laid beside the fire. She would sleep where his dogs had lain for many a cold night. She wiped angrily at the hot tears that had wet her face without her bidding, and with all the dignity she could muster, she said softly, "Please allow me to return to my chambers. You'll have no more need of me this night."

The Red said quietly, "Nay. I will not have any appearance of your loathing for me leave this room. Get thee to thy bed." She did not immediately obey him, her feet frozen to the spot and her desire to argue with him expanding in her chest. He was silent for a moment, and then strolling forward, he looked at her for a single instant before grasping her chin painfully in his large hands, his eyes boring holes into hers. Then he turned her around and pushed at her buttocks with his boot heel kicking her to where she would not willingly go. "You will come to respect me, little harpie. I saw the way The Wolf looked at you. Do you not want the same glances from me? He and I are, after all, warriors of equal and admirable valor."

Alida rose slowly to her feet from the humiliated bundle she had easily become. With every ounce of nobility, she brushed away the dirt of the floor from her skirts and then straightened back to her full height. She behaved as one who knew her worth. Carefully watching him, she backed towards the fire, her voice deceptively low though rage ate at the heart of her belly. She clutched at her tunic skirts with shaking fists. "You . . . you uncivilized beast! A man of no honor! You have nothing in common with the likes of Ulrich! You have stolen me away from a man who is the greatest among men. You have taken me from everything that I respect and hold dear. You have tried to turn me into an animal trapped in a cage of your making. Then, following my rape and humiliation, you dare to ask why I despise thee? Your heart would not begin to know how to look at a woman the way my husband looks at me."

The Red rose and majestically descended on her, his height and muscle like a bull's. Fully ignoring her tirade, he said almost to himself , "So The Wolf is greater than I or so claims his little woman." He snorted, motioning largely like a bard telling a drama. "Here she stands no better than a servant or a slave, and she plays the part of nobility—a fascinating and yet pitiful sight." Again, he turned her around and booted her to the rugs by the fire. A game he played in order to take her measure.

Alida rose again as slowly as the first time. Brushing away the dirt, she straightened her noble frame and turned once more to face him. She was hard pressed to keep from talking. With great effort she remained silent, her eyes like burning coals in the firelight and her limbs quivering from the warmth of the fire. Every lick of the flames tasted the cooling sheen of sweat on her skin that had come from defying The Red. She stood her ground. Three more times he pushed her to the floor and three more times she rose.

He descended on her a fourth time and nausea forced itself up her throat as The Red ran a hand over her face and hair in a manner very similar to Ulrich's. It was as if by touching her, he could somehow understand the stuff of which she was made. Alida pulled away, for it cut too close to the quick.

This time there was no sarcasm in his voice. "Perhaps it is your newness that fascinates me. Although, even with the others, I do not remember such displays of strength for they behaved as women and I used them as women. Now, I use you and command you as I would my staff, for you refuse to show any hint of feminine weakness. Give me your answer if you have one. Tell me what makes you so much stronger."

Alida was quiet for a moment, deigning how wise it was to respond with truth. Then with a quiet boldness she said, "You are fascinated with that which you have no power to obtain. Or perhaps it is that you see in me the surety of your death, and it titillates you. It is well known that my husband does not suffer injustice against those of his house. The Wolf will come for me, and your blood will soothe the snarling of his teeth."

The Red looked down at her without any sign of acceptance or dismissal on his face, and then throwing her down with his fist entangled painfully in her rich hair, he ordered her to scrub the floors of his chamber as if he could prove to her that he could obtain anything he desired. Their relationship in that odd dance of captive and captor, continued in this way night after night and day after day, until time swirled into itself like blood into water.

Then one day, startlingly, the sun finally gleamed through the arrow slit for the first time in Alida's memory, and it was then that the pattern was broken. The Red shook the chambers awake that morning with his loud voice, and rather than ordering her or one of the wives to his chambers, which was her immediate exhausted thought, he ordered them all gruffly to dress for a hunt. She would participate alongside for the entire day as an aid to his wives and himself.

Alida, like the other women, hurriedly prepared herself, for she refused to miss any occasion of freedom and exercise even if it were in the presence of her enemies.

If his men thought anything of his wives' and their servants' attendance at the hunt, no word to that effect was spoken. They did not so much as glance their way nor was there any pause to the ring of metal and deep voices in the courtyard as the full entourage of them walked to the mounts that had been prepared by the servants. Hilde in her coldest voice said, "They act as if we do not exist. Every year our exodus from the chambers for a single attempt to entertain our lord at this dull event is treated without the bat of an eyelash. You'd think we had not been cloistered for months on end. Aren't they even curious about us?"

Deirdre laughed sneeringly, "Even the whisper of attention our direction would bring The Red's wrath down on their heads. They aren't foolish Hilde, and to him there is no such thing as casual flirtation. He takes and keeps that which is his! Consider it an honor that we are ignored."

The day was glorious and full around them, and she drew in the cold air of the land with great pleasure. Alida, free for the first time from the confines of the women's quarters, rode alongside the women's entourage, fighting the joy she felt rise up within her breast at the brisk air and warm sunlight. Her heart was pricked with guilt over her enjoyment of anything in this barren place. Then as silently as that thought had come followed the whisper of God. Everything good and perfect came from Him. Alida put to death the self-pity, guilt, and bitterness she felt and just rested, taking in every soul-healing moment around her—from the rare twitter of birds to the sound of wind moaning off the tall towers behind her. Presently they had descended down into the city, the dirty snow of past days covered with a fresh layer so that the filth she remembered was invisible. She listened closely to The Red's proud boasting from up ahead regarding his domain, putting to memory every last detail. The landmarks and stories might come in handy should she ever find the chance to escape. They wound through the townships a different way than when they had first come to the city, and in the small portion of an hour later, they had exited the walls of the city for the rough terrain beyond.

He was enjoying the presence of his females who all fought for his attention, when he realized that Alida, who had kept herself apart from the conversation, had suddenly stiffened and was driving her horse quickly ahead. She veered away from his own mount and that of the guards', the crunch of her beast's hooves in snow turning into the sound of a torrent. Immediately, his pleasant intent changed to one of great anger as he dashed towards her, for surely she meant to escape. Then he caught sight of her target. It was not a place of escape, but rather the fact that she had caught sight of a great shaggy ram posed majestically on the steep ridges above them. Alida's intense concentration on the hunt had driven away any thoughts of the men and women beside her or their translation of her actions.

He watched fascinated as she smoothly removed a long-shafted spear from Deirdre's carrier as she dashed past the dark-haired woman's mount. In the next instant, she let the lean weapon loose in the direction of the ram. The beast was struck through its neck and stumbled from the force of the hit. By the time the ram had recovered, Alida had prepared to let loose yet another spear, but the strong hands of The Red were on hers in an instant, pulling up her mount before he brought the ram down himself, the beast bleating to its death from the frozen heights above them. His men laughed at the thwarted kill, and The Red laughed along with them before stating, "You see, I have not underestimated the little hellion. Watch your weapons men, lest she steal from you and kill you with your own steel."

Alida, though proud of the fact that she had drawn first blood, did not comment on her ability. She dutifully rode on, ignoring the hateful glances of some of the other women, for she was completely comfortable with her prowess. Her quiet dignity drew respect from those others who did not immediately react with jealousy or humor over her humiliation.

The day did not end with that first kill, but proceeded through a thick, overgrown forest for other signs of winter life. When the entourage rounded a bend together ahead of the slowly moving band of servants, The Red shouted a warning, for up ahead he had spotted a young white bear. Its sharp claws and open mouth were magnificent to behold, and all the riders felt an instant rush at the sight. The Red, sensing a great battle, prepared his huge broadsword and battle-ax. Then he rode down the beast as if fiends pursued his path.

The bear having nowhere to turn stood its ground, roaring in the clear air. Its claws swooped in a dangerous angry arc as The Red careened by on his sturdy mount. Then The Red did something so daring it bordered on foolhardy, for he dismounted with a mighty leap to face the bear.

Alida did not utter a sound but sat quietly at the ready on her own well-trained mount. It occurred to her that she could use The Red's distraction to make her escape, but she feared that his servants and the accompanying warriors who had fallen back would contain her flight. Instead, she forced her attentions on the battle before her.

The Red made good leeway against the beast at first, for his ax cut deeply into the side of the enraged bear. Alida, noting its height, hair and fat stores was certain that it was young enough for this to be its first contention. Then the tables were turned, for the beast suddenly came alive with a passion that was thrilling to see, and in the same instance, The Red lost his footing. His men, close enough to see the danger, surged forward in a nervous mass. With a great leap, The Red's captain landed on the back of the bear, and drawing a long dirk, he drove it deeply down into the beast's neck before being cast off with a roar.

No one save Alida saw the white mass of snarling fur that hurtled from the depths of the forest off to the side of them, the deep growl ending in a scream of maternal vengeance. The cub, although nearly full grown, had not yet left its mother, and she was intent on blood. The she-bear picked Hilde as its target, and the woman was quickly unhorsed as the heavy animal tore at the neck of her mount, the sound of rending flesh enough to bring the men's attention to the site of the new attack. Up it rose on its shaggy legs, the smell of wild animal hide rank in Hilde's nostrils and the roaring like a war cry setting all her hair on end.

Alida had wasted no time in bringing her horse around and reached The Red's bride at the same time that the bear was rending Hilde's mount useless. Alida had pulled more spears from the women's armory packs and was throwing one after another into the beast's hide—the stings of the weapons like massive hornets to the enraged bear. Then rounding again and taking up a bow and arrow, she shot three successive arrows through the throat of the beast and a single, well-aimed blow into the gaping maw. The bear sunk in on itself with a defeated gurgle, the smell of her musky hide even stronger in her fear and exertion. Alida immediately jumped from her mount, and taking up a handful of rank, snow-damp fur, she pulled the beast's wiry-haired head back, slitting the throat for good measure—a spurt of warm, sweet smelling blood quickly covering her hand.

The Red, along with his men, called out with a loud, simultaneous cry, beating their metal chest plates with a rapid, two-beat salute, their calls showing excitement and respect alike. Whatever mockery they had sought to make of her before had been drowned out in the prowess that even now spilled out scarlet on the crisp snow. In the breast of their king, something powerful rang, for the woman he had stolen had unwittingly saved his last hope of producing progeny and had therefore made herself more than just another body in his castle.

Hilde, looked up shakily from the ground where she had fallen ungracefully. She was hard pressed to hold back her tears at the close encounter with death. She felt both humiliation and relief as she rose to unsteady feet, her backside cold from the melted snow beneath her, knowing that fundamentally something had changed. Alida came to Hilde's aid shortly following a quiet whisper in the bear's ear to make its way swiftly to the lands of paradise with her brave cub. Alida was feeling uncustomarily empathetic for the creature she had brought down.

That night The Red did not call for Alida, a strange sort of respect replacing his previous humiliations of her. Instead, he paced back and forth through his chambers afire with something he could not reason away. How could he relent towards The Wolf's bride without losing face himself, for he was beginning to admire the scrappy warrior, and more importantly, he was now beholden to her.

Ulrich, cursing the long, original delay and the bad luck they kept encountering once underway, suffered equally with his men from the biting winds that cut through their thickest winter gear with the practiced agility that only a storm can perform. Day after day, they endured this razor sharp wind, stinging sleet, and depressing gloom that revolved endlessly, one after another, and sometimes in tandem as they made their slow way north, almost as if the grip of the otherworld bade them not continue.

Ulrich could not shake the great fear that gripped him, the fear that Alida would not be found alive. This quiet terror would snake its way into his heart in the darkening of the day or at odd moments when he felt too weary to continue.

Landres who rode constantly at his side worried over his master, for Ulrich's wound, having been infected off and on during the weeks, seeped continuously. They packed it and put the poultices on it that Birch had prepared, but this did not seem to curb the weeping from in between the neat rows of her tight stitches and the pink tender flesh of newly made scar tissue.

Landres and Ulrich both knew that should Ulrich not find rest soon, he would be lost. Their aim was to arrive at the docks of an ally far to the north, finding a ferry to the land of The Red on a warship. Ulrich would use the trip over for some much-needed rest.

When their aim finally came in sight, Ulrich was only barely able to dismount without aid, his sharp moan coming far too quickly from his mouth to be curbed. As efficiently as possible, his men ensconced him deep within the berth of the sailing vessel, the sounds of their boots hitting with deep thuds on the rolling decks. The seaweed-tainted spray was a stinging welcome in their nostrils. They were halfway done with the first leg of their journey.

The captain of the vessel was accustomed to carrying passengers and cargo through the worst of conditions, so he waved off Landres' concerns over safety. In the blustering, salt-laden gusts and beneath more of the endless grey sleet, the sturdy little vessel set sail. In the dark berth, Ulrich closed his eyes and whispered a prayer yet again to Creator to save the life of his bride and to give his band safe passage to avenge her capture. His massive hands curled childlike in the rough gunnysacks that he lay upon for he had no strength to hide his exhaustion and fear. True to his nature, he prayed for his own life only at the very end of the whispered pleas.

In the heavens above, Creator's watchers flew along with the vessel, but none were sent to release Alida of Brögen Fjords. She was safe in their care, her body not available to the jaws of death, but her trials would not be stayed until Creator's hand released the warriors to her aid.

Landres, standing at the head of the vessel near the captain, tentatively released his own request to the heavens in the hope that all would be set to rights. His whispered prayer was caught away on the loud, howling gale around them, but made it nonetheless to God's ear.

A sliver of moon shone through the arrow slit in tiny flashes as clouds raced over its surface. Alida came awake suddenly, feeling a hand brush her arm. From the darkness, Hilde's face appeared barely visible in the weak light. She leaned very close to Alida, her hair brushing her cheek as she whispered, "Wake up. I need to talk to you."

Alida sat up and brushed the sleep from her eyes her body wary and sluggish. "What is it, Hilde? Are you unwell?"

Hilde shook her head. "Nay, but leave it to you to enquire after another's health. I have to tell you the story of the wives of The Red, for secrets as dark as the stone of the castle could easily prey upon your ignorance. As time goes on, you become the object of growing hate."

Alida ran a hand over her eyes groaning and said, "Could you not give me your tales during the day?"

Hilde shook her head again. "It is not safe to discuss things with you when the others are around. Since we are not allowed to leave these chambers, you and I would have no other opportunity to speak. Juniper has very good hearing and is excellent at ferreting out information to give to Deirdre."

Alida nodded and then waited for Hilde to begin. As she waited, a huge yawn, hummed up through her own ears, until finally finding release with an accompanying stretch. Hilde climbed onto Alida's pallet, drawing up her knees to her chin. "Deirdre was the daughter of a very great chief far to the East, past the great sea and into the deep forest land. The Red, foraging for riches, spices and slaves, had captured her when she was only twenty years. When they arrived, back at Brögen Fjords The Red found that Deirdre was anything but docile. Rather than drawing from him a natural male interest, she inspired something malicious within his breast. Many have said that the bitterness of his brother's death and the weight of having become the only heir had already ruined him.

"Deirdre longed to return to her homeland and constantly bickered with him over her freedom. One night out of desperation, she tried to kill him while he was sleeping. He awoke before she could drive a knife through his heart. He beat her severely for the small wound he'd incurred. Her injuries from the ordeal numbered as a broken leg, arm, and something much more insidious. Deirdre could no longer bear children.

"Since she knew that her only value to The Red was the hope that she would produce heirs, Deirdre convinced the physician to hide her barrenness from The Red. She did this by giving the physician physical "favors" as well as small treasures wrested from around the keep, a difficult thing in her cloistered state.

"Over time, our master became very restless, for she showed no sign of fattening with child. He rode out on another campaign for supplies and treasures, and when he returned, he had brought with him a very young girl from a rich southeastern province. Juniper was married to The Red as soon as her menses had proven her to be of childbearing age.

"Deirdre, bitter and afraid for her place in the keep, made a friend of the frightened lonely girl. She convinced Juniper that if she ever had children The Red would kill her, for her purpose and usefulness would end with the production of heirs. Juniper was so afraid that she took Deirdre's advice to drink a potion that renders women barren for a short span of time. However, the dose was much higher than normal, and Juniper's newly ripe womb was rendered useless forever. This, too, Deirdre had the physician hide from both The Red and from Juniper."

Hilde's soft voice died away in the darkness.

"And your own tale?" said Alida softly.

Hilde cleared her throat, continuing. "I came here shortly after Juniper, for The Red captured me when he found me sick and alone beside the road. He no doubt thought to use me in his kitchens.

Nevertheless, when I had bathed and was attired in new clothes, he found me favorable. He decided to take me as a concubine. Time passed, and he did not take his rights with me for one thing or another kept him away from the keep.

"When he returned, he again set about getting his first wives with child, disdaining my chambers. Months found him frustrated and still without sign of an heir. One day his captain casually mentioned that the master's concubine could well be the hope of heirdom. The Red overheard the comment and so again, my lot was changed, and he took me to wife.

"But Deirdre and Juniper, out of jealousy and self-concern, conspired together to keep him from lying with me often enough to produce an heir. So far, they have been successful. I do not seek to change the way things are, for I neither hate nor love The Red. I do not care whether he desires me or not or whether an heir is produced. My only concern is that I am provided for. In the years I have been here, I have lain with him no more than I could count on my hands and feet." She paused for a moment, and then tilting her head like an intent bird, she said, "Now you enter our little cloistered world, full of fire and independence. The Red, during the span of two fortnights, has sought your comforts more than he has ever sought ours. Deirdre is furious, with a mimicking Juniper close behind. I—well, I learned my lesson the first day you came. I have decided that you would better serve as a friend than foe, plus I'd be hard-pressed to disdain anyone who had saved my life." A dimple marred her cheek at this comment.

Alida smiled back. "Why *did* you attack me?" she then asked curiously.

"The only status we have is as potential bearers of Brögen heirs. The people of the fjords do not value women, as do some provinces. What we receive, we hoard, for we do not know when our usefulness will end. My pallet is a symbol of status, for it is better than either Deirdre's or Juniper's and certainly many stations above a mere servant's pallet. The Red himself had it commissioned in the hopes that I would soften towards him and become more wifely.

"Past concubines or hopefuls for the position of wife have been cast to your very bed which the rest of us agreed was of lower desirability, only fit for a servant." Then she said concerned, "You haven't been overly cold here, have you?"

Alida smiled. "On the contrary, I love the breeze, however chill it may be. It reminds me that there is such a thing as freedom. As for your pallets and clothes and jewelry and status, I would give all I have to leave it behind."

"I have never been homesick," confided Hilde.

Alida shook her head confounded. "Have you no lands nor family nor friends who would occupy your time away from here?"

Hilde dropped her head. "As I said, The Red found me beside the road. I do not remember how I came to be there. All I remember of those dark days is that I was starving, cold, lonely, and very sick."

Alida patted her arm. "When he comes for me, I'll take you with me."

Hilde looked puzzled. "The Red only ever calls for one of us at a time. We do not entertain him with duets and games as do some women of other lands."

Alida laughed at the woman's comment. "I speak of my husband of the southerly lands, not The Red. I have every confidence Ulrich will come to rescue me. And though I have been weak in my faith, should he not come, I know that The Ancient of Days will be my deliverer."

Hilde again looked puzzled. "A man rescuing you I can comprehend, for he is flesh and blood, bent of ego and property. Yet who is this "Ancient of days" who would come for you? Is it a secret sect of warriors?"

Alida chuckled and grasped Hilde's hand in her own. "Hilde, Ulrich will come for me because he loves me, not because of ego or because he views me as a possession. Though our love is very strong, should something fierce keep him from me, I would wait on the true power that has never been hidden from me, though His mysteries are slowly discerned. This is whom I call 'The Ancient of Days.' He is the One True God. I have viewed His glory first hand. He is not only an ancient tale or a clever fantasy, but is a reality."

Hilde looked away. "If there is a power for good greater than us, why would it allow us to suffer? Why would it not rescue us before trials could assail us? And what of the evil that roams this earth and harms children and grown men alike?"

Alida put her arm around the woman. "The trials are not from the hand of Creator, but from the hand of the in-between lands that stir our world like a cauldron. 'Tis this maleficence that brings suffering. Sometimes Creator withholds immediate deliverance from these ills, because his aid has not been requested or because the time is not right and He has a greater plan. Our paths are much changed by what we suffer and overcome, but He would save us from trials that kill. When we can bear no more, it is in this moment that He comes to our aid, for usually it is in this moment that we remember to ask and are at our most malleable." As she spoke these words, Alida felt a sudden calm descend upon her like a mantel. She had spoken aloud the answer to her own bitterness and fear and was no longer afraid.

Hilde did not respond but sat for a moment longer looking at the arrow slit. Then she said, "I will see you on the morrow?"

"It is already the morrow. Besides, we are here together every day." Then after a hug, Alida said, "Good night, Hilde." Alida lay on her pile of furs unable to sleep with the stories that Hilde had told her strung before her like a web. She felt great pity for these women who had let these chambers become their whole existence. Yet what choice did they have?

When she finally drifted off to sleep, she heard a very soft whisper in her ear and recognized the voice of Creator. "In time," was all he said.

She awoke again late that morning with a ray of sun piercing her sleep. When she opened them, turning away from the light, the first thing she saw was the calm visage of The Red. The second thing she noticed was that the chamber around them was silent and empty.

Chapter Twenty-Five

"Where are the other women?" asked Alida warily, drawing herself up into a fetal position against the wall with her blankets wrapped tightly around her.

"They have been taken to other quarters so that they will not witness what occurs this day."

Alida wrapped her arms protectively around herself. "What do you mean?"

He stepped forward and brushed her hair off her shoulder. "Don't be afraid. I am merely having these chambers made into your own private abode. All of their possessions and pallets will be moved to another part of the castle."

Alida's brow creased. "But these are the only rooms that they know, and I am a mere servant. Surely one of the others is more deserving."

He shook his head. "Nay. Your worth is far above any of them."

Alida was quiet and then softly said, "Why this sudden change, milord?"

He mused silently over her tone and then said, "You have never addressed me with anything close to respect, woman."

She raised her chin. "My name is Alida."

"Very well, in private I shall call you by your name, little winged one. An appropriate name for a fleet-footed warrior."

Though gracious, there was not intimacy to her reply, "And in public?"

He paused and then stepped even closer to her. "You will be called The Head Mistress of Brögen Fjords." His smooth tone could not hide his emotion and pride over the change in her status.

Alida was silent. She knew that her place in the keep had risen to a dangerously high level. The other women would not take kindly to the change.

"Again, I would ask why?"

He was silent and then stepped forward, rising far above her like a massive tree. "You are worthy of it. Not only have you endured the upheaval from your homeland without complaint and with great bravery, but you are also beautiful and skilled. Many have tried to outhunt and outsmart me, but you—I cannot even put into words what I feel."

She shrugged, her shoulders falling gracefully once again and her eyes clear and wary. "You feel nothing. You said it yourself; there is nothing special about me. Trust me, the newness will wane as it has with all your wives, and you will forget me."

He was adamant and calm. "Nay. You and I both know how in control of your prowess you are. Not once since the battle have you taken up arms against me. Perhaps, with time, *you* will come to remember me."

Her voice was very soft in the room. "Given a chance and a blade,

I would kill you. Do not elevate me to a status I do not deserve. You are my enemy, and I do not fear you. I pity you, and you will die for what you have sown."

His voice grew dark and he growled. "Pity? Why pity?"

"Because you lack wisdom in the treatment of things finer than yourself. Because you crush the beauty of women within your hand as a flower in the mouth of a goat. Because you have never known that it was possible to love a woman so much that your own voice disappears into the unity that is created."

He took to pacing, shaking his head and circling her like a predator. "Such odd mysterious words, but these notions you have are not fitted to reality, Alida. You are nothing more than a woman, and I nothing more than a man. Women were created to please the flesh of man and to bear his children, nothing more. You talk as if we are equals."

She straightened her shoulders. "We are."

A scowl covered his features. "Women, my dear little wren, are devious and strange. They are illogical, complex, silly beings without any knowledge of things that are weighty. I would never want to stand beside any woman in combat or peace as I would beside my best captain."

Alida rose to his taunt with a light in her eye. "You took not a second thought to your captain or any other man yesterday, for the day belonged to me and my protection of your wife. As for being a woman, if I am so devious and strange, illogical, complex and silly, why do you give me such special attentions, and why did you include the women in the hunt with thee. If I am so weak, why was I able to dispatch four of your men before you took the matter into your own hands the night of the siege?"

He scowled again. "Do not tread upon my good graces."

Alida grew still. "Nay. That I would not do. If it were my choice, I would be given back to my own lord with my lands spread out before me and with all of the running of it in his hands and mine. If it were my choice, you would have no worry of me, for I would be ensconced in the arms of my husband and lover with our only recreations being of those most happily married. I would not tread on thy good graces nor would I seek any favor, for I would that I had never known thee. For me, you do not exist."

The Red struggled to avoid the rage that rose in him at her words, for they were spoken truthfully without malice or guile. It was as if she were a man that he met in battle, blade for blade. Nevertheless, something deeper pulled at him for in his heart. He wished that it were he who she spoke of and not The Wolf.

"I have no more to say to thee." Turning, he proceeded to leave. Then some feet away, he came to an abrupt halt. His shoulders were stiff with wounded pride. "As an aside, I came here today with the intent to let you know that you have the freedom to come and go anywhere you like within the city, as long as you are escorted. I thought that it would please you."

Alida went completely still and said in a very quiet wary voice, "It does, milord." Then even softer, "Thank you."

He spoke over her comment, continuing as if she'd never uttered a word. "However, if you try to escape and are captured, I will kill you. As for my men and the men of the city, they know that it would be unwise to look upon thee lustfully or attempt to win thy good graces. I have kept my wives away from the unworthy all these years, as did my father and his father before, but I cannot see the wisdom of keeping you locked up. The others are tame enough, broken to my hand, but you—well, let my word stand." Alida stood unmoving as the door clicked shut softly behind him.

On the darkened sea far to the south, waves like mountains tossed the little vessel about like a twig. Ulrich was so exhausted that the storm-pitched boat only succeeded in rocking him to sleep.

The entire trip across the sea gave him time to rest with strange dark dreams fluttering like dark moths through a moonlit cavern. Twice they were blown off course, and twice they had to set the way again, yet the wounded man in the berth slept as if wakefulness was no longer a possibility.

Landres and Gowen watched over his beaten form, splitting their attentions to the events above board as well as down in the hold. For his own good, they had tied him down loosely enough that he could free himself if needed and tightly enough to hold through the pitch of the mighty seas they sailed.

When the time occasioned it, they would assist with the rowing, baling, or turning of the sails to the shouts of the fearless captain. Again and again, Landres prayed that they would safely see the land, for he longed to gain back for his master that which he had lost, as well as the simple fact that he did not like the turbulent and dangerous waters in which they sailed.

One night as he sat dozing beside Ulrich he thought he heard a voice say "In time," but he couldn't be sure.

Alida, back at Brögen Fjords, having been given new freedom, set about exploring the castle and lands, sometimes with the aid of The Red's people and oft times without, but always with escort, for she had bowed to The Red in the one respect that she not go alone.

Her life was relatively good now with this increased freedom and with the special care he gave her. The chambers, which she had once shared with the other wives, suited her well, for they were appointed much, as his were, with every possible necessity for such a cold land.

The furniture was heavy and roughly hewn, but having been worn smooth with time, it was quite comfortable, and the furs that graced her room were of the highest quality. She no longer slept on the floor but on a pallet that was even more magnificent than Hilde's, having been carved and inlaid with brightly colored flowers, stylized horses, and clever little birds and animals. Whenever possible, he had more luxurious tunics sent up for her, but she rarely wore them for she did not want to become comfortable in her place as borrowed mistress of the castle, and as she had told Hilde, she longed for nothing more than her own homeland.

It was in this gilded cage that she awoke one morning feeling as if the weight of the sky pressed in on her body. Her eyes and hip sockets hurt, and her mouth was very dry. All morning long, she nursed a chamber pot as sickening heaves washed over her body, leaving sweat, exhaustion, and weeping eyes in their wake.

When The Red came to escort her on some errand, he found her curled up beneath her covers in a little ball, her face green and pallid.

"What ails thee, woman?"

"I know not, milord." Alida turned her face from him, her reply all but swallowed in the bedclothes.

He crossed to the pallet and felt her head. "Perhaps it is the menses. I have not known you to deal with one since your arrival here."

Alida froze as a horrible thought trickled across her consciousness. Mentally, she counted the time since she had last had a menses. 'Twas just the week before the siege on Drachmund Heights. She sat up and tried to leave the bed, horror taking up residence in her mind.

"I will call a physician for you, little wren," he said softly, his own words not registering as significant in his mind. "Lay back and rest."

Alida jerked. "Nay! I will be fine. 'Tis naught more than a small illness easily come and most easily gone. Don't waste your time on such a silly matter."

"A doctor *shall* be sent up, Alida. For you were hearty and hale just last night, and now, in the morning hours, you grow suddenly sick. I also came to thee last night to bid thee lie with me, but found thee asleep, no sign of fever or illness upon your skin. Something is not right!"

Alida fought the panic that was rising in her belly; at the same time, the relief at having been unavailable to him hit her consciousness. She had no argument to give The Red that would convince him that she was fine. She could not afford the diagnosis from the physician that she would most likely receive. Even more so, she could not afford this diagnosis to be given to The Red. She did not say a word, her eyes tightly closed.

"I am sending for him now!" Without another word, The Red strode from the room seeking out the physician to come to her.

When the cravenly doctor arrived, Alida sat upon her pallet with her head in her hands. She was weeping silently, because of the fear that gripped at her heart. Should the child that she most undoubtedly carried be Ulrich's, The Red would surely kill the babe upon its birth. Should she carry the seed of The Red, he would never release her, even with a battle against the Drachmund forces. An heir, and one gotten through her, would mean more to the lord of this castle than anything that he had as of yet claimed or seen.

The doctor probed at her body for over an hour, his quick dark eyes peering into and over her body like a crow, and his fingers like hard prongs poking where they had no right. Alida shivered at his touch, but knew that her fate was now being woven in the air right before her eyes.

When he finished his exam, he rose and quietly gathered up his various urns and tools. He delicately cleared his throat as he stared at the young woman sitting stiffly before him. "There is no illness to be found other than what is natural. It is obvious that you are with babe and are a healthy several months into the process. My lord will be immediately informed, of course."

Alida swallowed. "Could we not keep the information from him just for a span of time until it is—well, until I am ready to relate the news?"

The physician's eyes grew even sharper. He tapped his chin with his finger and slowly walked the length of the room, eventually grasping his hands behind his back. "I would be willing to withhold this information under certain—conditions."

Alida shivered, remembering Hilde's tale about Deirdre. She rose and squared her shoulders. "Never mind, I will tell The Red myself. Thank you. You are dismissed, and if you please, send The Red to me immediately."

The man frowned and left the room, his odd gait scratching against the stone floor. Once outside the door, he did not immediately proceed to The Red but turned at the next stair heading for the women's chambers now situated to the east. He wrung his hands together with the delicious news, for Deirdre would undoubtedly pay highly for this information.

He walked into the chambers without knocking and sent the little maids and servants who attended the women, scattering. He then quickly drew Deirdre aside and quietly informed her of the news.

Within the span of only a few moments, her eyes turned into a thunderous jade. "She is supposed to be dead or missing." Her perfect teeth ground together. "No wonder our little maids would not give us news of her whereabouts. She has taken over the nest like a thieving cuckoo."

She slipped a silver pendant into the doctor's hand and then leaned close to his ear. "Come tonight and tomorrow night for your usual—payment."

He gripped her slender arm painfully in his grasp. "The usual payment is not enough."

Deirdre's eyes narrowed. "Unhand me, or I will call the guards with evidence of this abuse."

"You are in no place to threaten, milady. Don't ever forget that."

Deirdre set her jaw. "Very well, what do you desire?"

His grin, like a black troll, spread across his face. "I want double the usual treasure, and I want a week's worth of nights alone with you."

Deirdre shivered, for she knew first hand his cruel nature. "Very well."

He released her arm and strode from the room without a backward glance.

Juniper sidled close to Deirdre, and when she had caught her attention, she said worriedly, "Are you ill again, milady?"

Deirdre backhanded the young woman. "Mind your place. I will give you information when I choose and not before."

Juniper's eyes glistened with tears, and then she turned and ran to her pallet.

Hilde, seeing the storm brewing in the head wife's eyes, called a servant covertly to her side with a message to give to Alida. The serving maid tried to argue that she was no longer accessible, but Hilde glared at her and said, "Just do as I have commanded." With a nod and curtsy, the young woman hurried out efficiently sidestepping Deirdre.

The message from Hilde arrived moments before The Red himself. She had written that the physician had been in to see Deirdre that morning and that when he had left, Deirdre had been furious. There was also a side note bearing well wishes and relief that Alida was well.

Alida was carefully rolling up the missive when The Red strolled into the chambers without knocking, his heavy step and presence growing more familiar each day.

"The physician never returned to me to give news of your health," he said impatiently.

Alida cleared her throat. "I asked him to call for you."

The Red waited, and when her silence grew too lengthy, he asked testily, "Well?"

"I am with babe." Her slight fingers twisted the bedclothes in nervousness, and she could barely keep the tremor from her voice, though a warrior's own heart beat in her breast.

He stood completely still, gazing piercingly at her. "You do not jest with me, little wren?"

"Nay."

"Did you know this before his arrival?" His voice was a little softer, and he remained as still as a statue.

She turned her gaze from his. "Aye, milord. I guessed it this morning before you sent for him."

"Why did not tell me then?"

She paused and wrung her hands together. "There is a question as to the babe's paternity."

The silence that fell over the room was fraught with tension. Then The Red's voice crawled out darkly from his throat. "This cannot be."

Alida seeing immediately his mistaken belief hastened to explain. "I was taken by both you and my husband on the night of the siege. Since then, I have lain with no one, but that still leaves the question between ye and he."

He strode to her side. "It is mine, of course, though the gods know how it was begotten with a single night with you."

She glared at him. "How can you be so sure? I, too, pray that it was on a night with love, begotten, and not as the result of your sin."

"I am undoubtedly more virile than any southerner." His reply came from his mouth with a prideful sneer, completely ignoring the fact that she had addressed his abuse of her.

She gazed up at him. "I was married to Ulrich and all that implies for months before your arrival! And milord, it can happen after only a single attempt."

Crimson streaks stained The Red's jaw. "I will not believe that my final claim for an heir has been gotten through another man."

"'Tis his claim more rightly than yours," she said softly.

The Red strode to her side and pulled her against his body. "It will be mine regardless of its features or parentage, if it be a male. If it is a female, it will die, and you will conceive yet again another time, for it is known now that you are able. A bastard son can be molded into the image I desire, but a bastard daughter is useless at best."

Alida's eyes grew wide, and then she hit him across the face with as mighty a blow as she could muster. "No babe of mine will be slaughtered for the sins or rights of men, for it is a life nonetheless and a treasure to me and God. If the babe be male or female, its life will not be separated from my own." Tears choked off her words, and she shook with both fear and worry.

The Red's eyes turned a steely grey, her blow further darkening his jaw. "My word is still law in this keep, Alida, regardless of the freedom you enjoy. Pray that your child is a boy."

She gathered up every bit of hope within her. "I could not bear to give a child of mine to you. My husband will claim me *and* our son or daughter, and you will pay the consequence of your sin."

The Red did not utter another word, but grabbed the front of her tunic, all but lifting her from the pallet. Alida flinched, awaiting his misuse of her. The Red gazed at her for only a moment. "I will not call for thee to come to my bed as I had planned, though by all rights I have cause to until the child is borne. You have been called my wife and mistress of the keep and it is only matters of state and responsibility that have kept me away from using your flesh as I would. But now, I will not risk this child's life when it is so newly gotten."

"Yet you would kill it when it serves thee no purpose," she rejoined.

"Enough." His thundering voice died out slowly in the room. "Be thankful for your reprieve, woman, perhaps motherhood will make thee more biddable."

Alida wept quietly has the door clicked shut behind The Red. She prayed that she would be allowed such a treasured role as motherhood.

The weary yet still fiery band of Drachmund Heights landed in the frozen North the night after Alida's discovery. Ulrich, being much rested, was fit for battle, but he feared for both his own life and that of his men, for the northern warriors were known for their fierceness and strength. Add to this the weather and the natural aggressiveness that was borne of defending one's homeland, and Ulrich had a right to be wary, for he had brought only a small contingency with him, leaving the bulk of his force to defend their widened homeland.

He ordered that they take up residence in a neutral province near Brögen Fjords while he devised a plan of attack. Meanwhile, he and his men disdained wearing the distinctive Drachmund emblem and carried themselves under a story of mercenaries returning home to some vague location to the northeast of a neighboring region. He hoped to dissuade any spies or kinsmen of Brögen Fjords who would carry their presence back to The Red's keep.

They ensconced themselves at a modest inn where the goodwife and her mate seemed more occupied with turning a coin than any local gossip. This was both beneficial and detrimental, for Ulrich would have liked news of other regional occurrences without having news of his own team carried about.

Since this was virtually impossible, he set about creating a plan for Alida's rescue with what little facts he had gleaned, as well as Bryon's aged knowledge about the keep.

Deirdre, for the first time in all the years she had been at the Fjords, sent a message of summons to her lord a few days after Alida's pregnancy had been made known to the keep at large.

The Red entered the women's chambers looking thunderous and irritable. "What is thy concern, woman?" he asked without preamble to Deirdre.

She delicately smoothed her tunic over her legs and without rising said softly, "Thank you for answering my summons."

The Red scowled, a wary flicker passing through his eyes at her gentle tone. "Well, out with it!"

"Milord, might we not speak elsewhere? My news is best given to thine ears alone."

He reached out, and without ceremony, he pulled her to her feet, jerking her out the door. Then with long strides, he hauled her after him to his own chambers where, once inside, he pushed her into a chair. "Now that your every wish has been fulfilled, speak!"

Deirdre fought the urge to rail against his power, but she knew that patience would better suit her purpose. Her responding smile, therefore, was almost sickeningly sweet. "I have heard the news of Alida's condition, and though I know 'tis a happy time for thee, I felt that my conscience would not let me rest without imparting some particularly important news to you."

The Red's fists clenched, for he could easily see through his first wife's facade. "Get on with it, woman!"

She delicately cleared her throat. "It was my understanding, through word of mouth, of course, that Alida has been allowed certain—freedoms. I have also heard and witnessed with my own eyes, her indiscretion while enjoying this freedom."

The Red's eyes narrowed. "What do you mean indiscretion?"

Again, she cleared her throat. "Well, ah . . . you could say the unlawful use of her body as a bartering tool."

The Red approached the chair slowly with anger boiling in his eyes. "Do you fully understand what you imply?" Then after a pause, he leaned even closer. "Of course you do, how foolish of me to assume otherwise. You will lose much and have already lost much with her presence here in the castle. I have nothing to gain from believing you."

Deirdre fought again her urge to scream and hit and instead forced her voice to a deep calm. "I knew you would not believe me, and that is why I came prepared with names and places, milord. I learned my lesson from you many years ago; now I only seek to keep your name unsullied."

When he didn't respond, she continued. "Gilnor, while hunting, and Liedre, in the back rooms after an evening feast. Oh, and I mustn't forget the captain of your guard, Griffin. He sought her comforts on all the nights when you did not. He has also lain with Hilde. Apparently, milord, your bevy of *adoring* females is . . . slightly used."

The Red's roar of fury at her gall and open lies shook the walls of his chamber. He withheld his hand from her, but without ceremony, he jerked her to her feet and pulled her roughly down the hall after him until they'd reached Alida's chambers. There he flung open the door and pushed her through so roughly that she fell to the floor.

He then strode to Alida's pallet where she had just sat up from a nap. Her hair was tumbled about her shoulders, and her eyes were still soft with sleep. He looked back and forth between her soft strong visage and the bitterly lined face of Deirdre.

He then sat on Alida's pallet and pulled her onto his lap. Instantly, she was wide awake, her body feeling his tension and her eyes focused on the hateful gaze of the head wife. She did not like his close proximity nor the harried, cornered look that Deirdre was wearing, despite her attempts to mask it.

"Wife, this pitiful creature on the floor before you has accused you of laying with all three of my most trusted warriors and friends. She claims not only one indiscretion, but numerous as if you were naught but a harlot for purchase." He gently stroked her arm, but his fingers felt like lightly restrained steel.

Alida carefully stood, removing herself from his grasp and walked to a midden area between Deirdre and his seated position. "Ask her why the doctor left my chambers immediately upon finding out my condition and sought her company rather than summoning you as I had requested."

Deirdre paled visibly, her eyes wide with sudden terror. Then she took a deep breath and rose, her expression growing shuttered and the moment of weakness apparently gone. "I had a bout with dizziness, and he was only stopping by to give me a potion."

Alida's quiet voice issued, "If this is so, why was Hilde alarmed enough to send me word that you were very angry after he had pulled you aside for a private discussion?"

Deirdre grinned satisfied with what she perceived as a trap for Alida's words. "Milord already knows of his other wife's indiscretions. I would assume she sent you word because you are in league together, and she feared her actions being brought to light."

Alida did not say anything but walked over to a large trunk and lifted the lid, removing from its depths a fine roll of papyrus. She then made her way to The Red's side and let him read for himself the words written from Hilde's hand.

The Red, after having perused the entirety of the missive rose silently and ran his hand along Alida's cheek. In a soft, rarely used voice, meant only for her ears, he said, "Forgive my intrusion upon your rest. You need as much as possible so that our babe is brought forth healthy. I have changed my mind, however, on another matter—that of our relations. I desire you in every way, and have decided that we would be better suited to living in chambers together. As for this other matter, she will not concern thee again."

Alida shook at his words, for all his gentle references to her condition and place as his "wife" could not dispel the horror of what he had proposed. Oh, for a sword to thrust into his black heart. Then across her consciousness a voice whispered, "Life is mine to give and take. Trust in me." Alida sank down onto her pallet watching as The Red ordered Deirdre out into the hallway. This time the woman with the black hair and green eyes might not fare so well at her lord's hand. This time she might not survive.

The Red, after having left Alida's chambers, returned a shaking Deirdre to the women's hall. Then he left without further word to her. Deirdre shuddered and was not able to calm herself for there was something very still and deadly in his treatment of her. She ordered her handmaids to leave and lay upon her pallet, her breath becoming very shallow.

When night had fallen and he still had not returned, Deirdre began to relax. Perhaps he had believed some part of her story and was even now investigating its truth. Feeling better with this thought, she rose and prepared herself for the physician's arrival. During her preparations, the thought occurred to her that she should cancel the physician's visit after such a harrowing day, but she pushed away her nervousness and continued as planned.

From a niche out in the hallway beside the women's chambers, The Red stood covered in shadow, his large form hidden by the darkness and the depth of the walls around him. He had been watching Deirdre's door keenly for activity all afternoon and through the progression of eventide.

When a slightly stooped figure reached for the door and pushed it open without ceremony, The Red knew it had been well worth the wait.

He gave them some time to settle in with each other, and then quietly he went down to the hall and gathered Griffin, Liedre, and Gilnor. Within only a few moments, they arrived back at the chambers. The Red threw open the door, and before him were the physician and his first wife in a most compromising state. He promptly snatched the stuttering physician off Deirdre and threw him into the waiting arms of his men.

Deirdre whipped up a batch of tears, claiming that she had been raped and that the doctor had threatened to kill her if she ever told The Red. Her husband silenced her with a single look that cut straight through her. He ordered her, in a very soft voice, to dress herself, and then he told his men to bring her down to the main hall when she was properly attired.

The physician and Deirdre were chained side by side in the main hall to rings built into the massive dark walls. All the serving wenches and maids were sent out, and all that remained were The Red's scribes, warriors and keepsmen. Then to the surprise of his men, he had Alida brought down from her chambers. She was given a seat next to, but slightly below his own, on a raised dais near the end of the hall, amidst the whispers and loud murmurs of the gathered men and keep managers.

When everything had grown silent at the raising of The Red's hand, he rose and strode down the hall stopping at the point where Deirdre and the physician were grappled to a high, smooth place on the most visible wall. "These two traitors were found in union together in the women's chambers. Add to this Deirdre's sin of accusing my new wife of similar adultery as well as her charge that it was with my three most trusted men, and I have cause for justice."

The murmurs both angry and surprised of the warriors filled the hall. The Red again silenced them. "At no time have I believed her charges and instead sought occasion to trap her in her own lies. I will seek the advice of Griffin, Gilnor, and Liedre as to the exact nature of the punishment meted out against this prostitute and her lover. They also have the right to justice and to clearing their names."

Again, murmurs and accusations filled the hall while The Red and his advisors discussed the punishment. Eventually, The Red raised his hand for silence. He turned to the dais and ordered, "Wife, come here to me."

Alida gracefully descended the steps, her stomach roiling with fear for the chained woman and man. There was no indication of her inner turmoil in her stately stride or in her calm visage, but she felt the small rise of bile at the look in his eye. She approached The Red and he took her hand. Into it, he placed a curved gold knife with a finely honed blade.

"Kill them," he ordered her.

Alida gazed silently into his eyes, and then bending down she knelt upon the floor and said, "Nay, milord, the smear against my good name is naught compared to their lives." This was spoken softly and in a deferential manner for she knew how ego bent The Red could be.

He hesitated only a moment and then removed the knife. "Since my fair wife cannot find it in her heart to kill those who plotted injustice against her, I will take her cause as my own."

Without further ceremony, in the midst of Deirdre's screams and the physician's cries, The Red strode down the hall and promptly slit their throats. Alida looked away, for though she was accustomed to the gore and blood of battle, this was entirely beyond her experience. She felt vomit rise up into her throat and quickly begged The Red's leave. It was granted, and she walked, almost at a run, from out of the hall, her light boots tapping against the stones and the brush of her fine tunics like the flick of a horse's tail.

Outside, the stars shone crisply, and new dark clouds threatened another blizzard. She gasped in great portions of the cool air and dropped to her knees, seeking to alleviate her dizziness. She heard him approach on the frozen ground behind her as another wave of nauseousness washed over her.

"T'was the only way, little wren."

"Nay," she croaked out a wash of tears pouring hotly from her eyes, "you should have banished them or made them slaves. Taking their lives was barbaric."

"They would have been glad of the freedom banishment offered and making them slaves was better than they deserved."

"Why?" She was very quiet, broken before the depth of his hard heart.

"I will not explain myself further. Come and I will escort you to our chambers."

Alida felt a moment of panic. He had been serious about joining their chambers. Now she would never be free of him. He lifted her to her feet and pulled her body to him. "You are worth much to me. I will not allow the slander of your name in this place. I will have many children from your womb, and in time, as I have declared before, you will grow to love me."

He then picked her up in his arms and carried her exhausted form up into his slightly altered chambers. He laid her on his bed and began removing her clothing. Alida, with tears washing her face, declared to no one in particular, "I can take no more."

CHAPTER TWENTY-SIX

"Now!"

The hand of Creator moved and the heavens trembled as a cascade of spiritual warriors poured from its bosom. Creator stirred every protector and watcher to life, and soon the blue, cold dome above Brögen Fjords was filled with the darting forms of deliverance. Creator turned his back on the fool, and the sheer and complete absence of light pierced through to the hard heart of The Red.

The Red roared in pain, his body on fire from the blue light of Creator's presence. Though he could see nothing, he felt as if a furnace had been lit in the tenderest parts of his flesh. Alida sat up as the pull of unconsciousness was replaced with great strength. Before her on the floor, The Red writhed and called out for aid. Behind his closed eyelids, every atrocity he had ever performed danced in gruesome play. Creator's voice resounded in his head, and he was asked to account for each sin.

The Red, as royalty, had never been brought to account for any single action in his lifetime. He had been born with every consideration and every care that his father's wealth and cruelty could obtain. Over time, the coddling had crippled any softer nature he might have had. He mourned, as did Creator, the loss of innocence from Deirdre, Juniper, and Hilde. He saw the abomination of his rape of these women and the darkness in which their lives had been formed because of his actions. He saw the murdered faces of the villages he had plundered for sport and gain. He was present before the great call of their misery, and he was at his deepest level, terrified, utterly and horribly terrified.

His limbs had never felt so heavy, so immovable. Every part of him was foreign, and he was no longer mighty. Yellow and white watchers darted between Alida and The Red, soothing her and moving songlike about her body, while others burned his flesh and seared his eyes with their mere presence. When The Red felt he could bear no more, the air around him stilled and Creator spoke, his voice a ringing understanding within The Red's heart. "Choose to ask forgiveness, or go your way as you always have. Choose bitterness and anger, fear and brute desires, or choose eternal life beyond what your flesh knows. You have been shown all there is to see in your life. Make your decision with wisdom. However, know this, should you choose the way of purity and strength, you will still suffer retribution for the wrongs you have committed. Armies will come against this place seeking revenge and justice, and you will answer with your life and that of your army. Should you choose to continue on the path you now follow, you will have little more of this life with the next hailing very dark indeed. The things you will know then are too horrible to reveal, but they will be manifested when your last breath seeps from your body. Now choose."

The voice disappeared as quickly as it had come, and Creator removed the spirit beings from the chamber of The Red. The mighty, flame-haired king wept upon the dark stone of the castle that he had always thought the most mighty and most worthy protector of his form. His body was exhausted, and he was soaked in sweat.

Alida gazed silently at him, covered modestly again from his view, her heart pounding in her breast like a skin drum. Her eyes were no longer wary or sad or overcome. She knew she was being rescued, as had been promised to her. She would be removed from this place as surely as she had been brought into its walls, though she did not know Creator's timing. She heard The Red's sobbing breaths and the quietly muttered words not meant for her ears. She understood the pain he had felt from bearing Creator's presence or even more darkly the lack thereof.

Very softly she called out, "I should have warned thee that the righteous are always a cause upheld."

He chuckled with hoarse irony in the midst of a sob, "I would not have believed. I would have thought thee insane."

"You have witnessed the might of the power which is my protection, and though I could not know of its completion, I knew that one day it would be manifested."

He drew a tired hand across his eyes and asked, "Is one always faced with one's sins in such a manner?"

She shook her head. "Nay, Creator chooses to approach us all in different ways."

He stood upon shaky legs and reached for her hand. As soon as he had touched her, she knew his decision.

"I will take thee back to thine own chambers," he said softly.

Alida, seeing him up close, watched as his hair turned white before her eyes. She clutched her cloak about her, trying not to stare at the fiery marks left by the protectors. "You have chosen well."

Ulrich awoke from late afternoon slumber. Something in him pressed urgency upon the plan he and Landres had devised that morning. He arose with the usual shafts of pain emitting from the slash in his side. However, they were overcome by something greater. As he had seen Alida do hundreds of times, he stilled his body and listened.

It was then that a voice whispered, "Now. Do not wait!"

He knew exactly what it meant. His exhaustion quickly melted away, and Ulrich raced down the narrow inn steps to the great room below. "Gather your gear; we ride as soon as everyone is packed."

Ulrich's men never argued against any action of their lord, for they respected his instincts and leadership. They rose en masse and headed for their horses and equipment. Landres gathered his gear while calling out directions to the rest of the men. He filled in details when and where the men required it, as well as carefully organizing their ranks. All together, they numbered a score and five of his most trusted.

Gowen took care of the inn expenses and graciously thanked the innkeeper and goodwife while quelling their inquiries over the haste of their departure. He was more than happy to be taking his leave into the fresh air outdoors, for the odorous smells of grease and of unfamiliar surroundings were a disruption to his doglike nature.

When they had assembled and were mounted, Ulrich gave the signal, and they set their horses at a fast pace for the walls of the great black keep. The blizzard that Alida had seen hovering over the castle after the execution never came to fruition for Creator stayed the winds and snow.

The men from Drachmund Heights made good time over the unfamiliar landscape with Bryon at their lead, directing them past great frozen fjords and past treacherous hillsides. Everywhere the scent of gnarled dwarf pines accompanied the clipped and then muffled sound of their mount's heavily feathered hooves as they plodded through slush and frozen rock alike.

Watchers accompanied them, giving Bryon much needed memories of this trail or that inlet in order to speed their cause. Creator also sent small dancing earth warmers to ease the path beneath the horses' feet. Their startling colors of green and red were only apparent to the beasts and to Gowen. Though they had no power of their own, they were very proud of the work they performed on God's behalf and were therefore delightful to watch.

Gowen, laughing inwardly at the miracle he saw unfolding, silently gave thanks to Creator. He knew that their path was well fortified.

After speedy travel, they arrived at the keep in the wee hours of the morning. Bryon directed them to compass the walls, hiding below great overhangs of dripping ice and snow. Though the runoff beneath the ice plunked away with a hollow melodious sound and though they had to cross small chortling streams beneath dangerous-looking crevasses, they made good leeway, remaining relatively silent in their communication. As planned, Bryon progressed to the north along with Ulrich and Gowen, searching for the tunnel that took them beneath the city and eventually led to an underground gate into the castle.

When they located the tunnel, Ulrich directed Bryon to stand guard and allowed Gowen to enter first. The warrior transformed into a dog and crept down the passage with scuttling feet until the steel gate stood just a yard away. Beyond the bars of the gate, he could see two guards laughing over a game they played with rounded bones and black rocks. He whined as earnestly as he could, and one guard rose and made his way to the gate, peering out into the dark tunnel.

"Lyron, come see what I've found!" The second guard rose and came forward, his eyes squinting at the shadows. "Can you see him? Look there in the shadows. It's nothing but a mangy cur!"

Lyron laughed. "By the gods, what is a beast like that doing about these parts? It's odd, but he doesn't look malnourished or frozen. He must have left the city and could not return when the gates were closed." Gowen whined louder, giving a small additional yip for good measure.

The guards shook their heads. "He probably found a warm hole to sleep in and has been dining off the snow hares and ptarmigan."

"Should we let him in?"

"No. The Red wouldn't like it. He isn't fond of dogs."

Lyron squinted harder, his face all but pressed to the cold iron bars and his breath puffing out in small, warm exhales. "Fine, but if the thing dies and starts to rot down here, it's your responsibility."

The first guard moved away from the gate, waving his hand dismissively. "If he is smart enough to find his way in, he can find his way out." They returned to their game, ignoring Gowen's high-pitched whining and yips.

When he saw that they were fully engrossed in their game again, he returned to the mouth of the tunnel where Ulrich waited and took him back in. Ulrich silently made his way along the black walls, keeping his eyes fixed on the light ahead. When they drew close enough to the gate, he gave Gowen a silent signal and watched as the dog transformed and dressed quickly, gathering up his little blades.

Ulrich removed his own dirk, and they moved into throwing position. Within moments, the two guards lay dead with knives in their throats, silencing any alarm they would have given. Ulrich then approached the gate, listening for any other sign of life. When nothing but silence and the occasional drip from the wet stone greeted him, he raised his broadsword and brought it down on the lock of the gate. The gate groaned under the blow, but would not come open. He waited for a count of fifteen trying to refrain from making repetitive sounds that would catch the ear of alert watchmen. He then lifted his sword a second time, finding with this blow that the lock gave way.

They moved quickly into the space and checked the guards for any sign of life. Then Ulrich moved to the steps, peering quickly and covertly up their length to the top where yet another gate stood, presumably locked.

Ulrich removed the keys from off Lyron's body and approached the locked gate. Gowen, standing below, saw Ulrich's body stiffen and then watched as his lord flattened himself into a niche in the wall. Gowen, too, stepped back into shadow and watched in silence as two guards progressed past the gate at the top of the stairs. They paused shortly to test the gate with a rapid jangling shake and then continued on, the spit and roar of their burning torches giving no sign as to how new the watch was.

Ulrich tried every key on the ring, but not one opened the gate. He quickly turned and went to where Gowen stood. "I will go and gather the other men together down in this chamber. Then we will wait for the guards to pass again. The bars are wide enough this time that you can slip through as a dog. Once you are past the gate, find a shadow to hide in, and we'll pass you your blades. The guard that touches the gate will be mine to dispatch. The one against the wall on his opposite side will be yours." Gowen nodded and watched as Ulrich went quickly to summon the others.

When Ulrich had gathered everyone and had them standing quietly in the shadows of the chamber, he and Landres consulted quietly with Bryon. Landres peered about at the layout of the room. "How do they expect their men to leave this chamber?"

Bryon was quiet for a moment, searching his memory. "When I was here, the guard was changed every five hours. At that time, the guards above would open the gates for guards below and switch places with them to prevent the very thing that we attempt. They must continually patrol their areas during the five-hour wait. There are four levels to this system. The gate at the top of the stairs is the first in this series."

Ulrich said, "Are there anymore than two guards per gate?"

"Not on the first, second, and third. The fourth, of course, opens into the main hall in full view of everyone."

Ulrich resisted the urge to swear. "How many men inhabit the hall at this hour?"

"Normally each warrior retires to the barracks that are outside the hall. Only servants and a handful, maybe seven, of guards remain in the actual hall. Brögen Fjords is a very massive and extensive keep. The main hall is not for sleeping as it is in many places. There is a war room, barracks, servant's quarters, upper chambers, women's chambers, and guest quarters. The main hall is used primarily for judgment, feasts, and entertainment."

Ulrich was quiet. "The women's chambers are our objective then." Bryon nodded silently, his heart squeezing again with the reminder that Alida was here due to his folly.

After they had spoken quietly with the rest of the band, Ulrich moved forward and gave Landres enough room to slip Gowen's clothes and knives through the bars with a whisper of leather and no other telltale sounds. It was enough for the hearing of a dog. They were quickly snatched up, and they heard him growl, "What took you so long? I'm freezing!"

Landres chuckled and then whispered, "Stop your whining. You're not a dog any longer. Do we or do we not have business to attend to?"

Gowen ignored him and stepped back into the shadows. Then they waited for the guard to approach. In less than a half hour, the second set of guards were neatly killed and handy items removed from their persons. Ulrich, Gowen, Landres and the rest of the men all made their way to the second upper level gate. Again, their plan was carried out expediently, as it was with the third. They moved as efficiently as possible the whole time, for they had to work beneath the cover of night when things would be at their most silent in the castle.

When they reached the fourth gate, they sent Gowen in to scout the hall and determine how many guards were about. He returned with the news that five guards and three serving women occupied the far end of the hall. They had not noticed his presence as he had stayed to the shadows.

Ulrich sent him back in, and when two of the guards passed by to check the gate, they were handled swiftly and the gate was unlocked. Ulrich, Landres, and one other warrior quickly eliminated the rest of the guards who had their backs turned to the gate. The serving women were knocked unconscious before they could scream or flee, and they were then neatly bundled together with ropes and gags.

Ulrich was headed for the stairs to the upper chambers when Bryon waylaid him. "Milord, I am concerned that the location of the women's chambers has changed since my last stay here."

Ulrich already looking up at the stairs impatiently said, "Why?"

"The Red, as all the rulers before him, is very protective about his wives. He was never satisfied with the location and safety of the chambers."

Ulrich paused only a moment before making his way back to the serving women. He extracted a gag from one and had cold water poured on her until she came to, sputtering and frightened beneath his hand. Ulrich kept his palm cupped over her plump cheeks and mouth and leaned in very close, "Where are the women's quarters?" The maid shook her head refusing to answer.

"If you do not give me the directions I seek, I will kill you and the women who lay beside you."

Her eyes filled with tears and he removed his hand. She sputtered, "I don't know why I protect them. I don't like any of milord's wives."

Ulrich growled, "Where are the chambers?"

She gave him quick directions and promptly found the gag shoved back in her mouth along with a piece of her stringy brown hair. He had started to walk away from her and then changed his mind.

He again removed the gag, "There was a woman from the South with dark curly hair brought here four months ago as a hostage, is she amongst the women in those chambers?"

She paused, her small dark eyes darting back and forth, and it was long enough for him to see that she was debating over a lie. He held his knife close to her throat and signaled Landres and Gowen to do the same with the other women.

She choked and said, "Please, milord, she is in her own chambers. At the first turn, I told ye about, go right instead of left. You'll find her at the last door at the end of the hall." Landres promptly sent her back to unconsciousness.

Ulrich's warriors secured her again, and then half of them spread about the hall disappearing like ghosts into niches and shadow to watch for and warn of any change in the guard. The rest went with Ulrich to the upper chambers.

Guards that they encountered along the way, were swiftly and quietly killed. When they finally came to the turn described by the maid, Ulrich motioned his men to await him and then proceeded into the chamber, his footfall hushed on rich fur and his presence hidden by the gloom of guttering candles and torches.

The maid, however, had given him directions to The Red's own rooms, and Ulrich found himself gazing at the massive man as he slept. Anger and months of frustration rose within his chest in a mixture of fire and ice, the burn for retribution and fear for his bride each a powerful motivator. In three strides, he stood beside the bed and laid his broadsword's blade across The Red's throat. He hesitated a moment when he saw the head of white rather than red hair that now graced The Red's massive crown, but his hesitation lasted too long. Within a part of a moment, he himself found a blade at his throat.

The Red, aided by years of battle experience whispered, "So The Wolf comes at last for his mate."

Ulrich's lip curled, and he growled without preamble. "Where is she?"

The Red laughed and then choked as the blade pressed against his neck, his own making itself known to Ulrich in the process. Ulrich's faced blazed with anger, "You will give me directions to her chambers, and then I will kill you. You will not be allowed the pleasure of rising from your death-bed."

Then behind Ulrich, The Red watched with growing anxious energy as Bryon and Landres entered the chamber, their faces hidden in shadow. He had no idea how they could have entered his domain without sounding an alarm. The Red paused, and all at once, old hates threatened to return, for he recognized the broad man in his chambers. He said quietly in Bryon's general direction, "Why did you do it, you son of a pig?"

Bryon started at the lord's appearance, for only months before his hair had still been a gleaming red. Then covering his shock, he cleared his throat, his tone open and contrite, "'Twas a game fought with youthful zeal and jeal-ousness, ending in a terrible accident. There was naught I could do when I'd realized my folly - though to be sure that realization came too late. Forgive me."

The Red gazed at him and some hardness left his face. Without a word, he nodded knowing that he may well meet his brother on this very night.

Ulrich growled from behind them, "This reunion is very touching, but I want my wife."

The Red knew that his life balanced on the thin hair of fate. He would fight for he had no choice. All it took was the initial twitch of The Red's hand inflicting no more than a deep knick to drive Ulrich into action, who simi-larly drew his payment of blood. The clanging blows that followed were well matched, but Ulrich having the longer blade and being in a vicious rage had fierceness to his movements that would not be stayed. Their breath heaved forth with the exertion and the thunk of their thick bodies, and Ulrich's boots echoed hollowly about the room, sometimes in quick step and sometimes in a shuffle as they fought like two bearded lions, their roars muffled by the attempt to save breath and limb. Within moments in a single, well-placed and unex-pected blow, The Red's massive head lay severed beside his pallet. With a sigh, his soul left his body to be escorted into the afterlife.

Ulrich wiped his sweat-covered brow and turned for the door growl-ing. "We must find Alida."

His men followed him from the chamber and down the halls, splitting off for separate chambers.

When Ulrich had searched several adjoining areas, Landres rushed to his side and said, "I believe we've found her room." They hastened together to a massive door in a wing opposite from The Red's. Ulrich hastily opened the door and crossed to where his wife lay, gently pulling back the furs from off her body. He lifted her into his arms, and she came awake with a start.

"Shush, love, it is I," said Ulrich with tenderness and relief. "Thank Creator you are safe."

Alida flung her arms around his familiar musky neck and buried her face against the part of his thick hair that curled softly inward. She stroked the back of his beloved head and powerful shoulders and did not utter a word, but Ulrich could feel her warm, thick tears soaking through to his skin.

He held her tight against his body and then slowly released her until she stood flush against his chest and thighs. His hands ran over her curves, remembering her shape. "You have gained a little weight," he said softly, "at least they didn't starve you. This whole place will burn for every one of The Red's sins."

Alida touched his lips, "do not curse this land or its leader whatever your anger husband."

Ulrich was adamant, "Do not beg of me good will, Wife. Never on his behalf."

She peered at him a moment and then sighing nodded. "If only you could know the dues he has paid. Creator revealed himself fully to The Red, and Ulrich, you should have been there to see it. He was seared and brought to trial. A more terrible and awesome fate my eyes have never before seen."

She paused, a shiver coursing down her back, perhaps in foreknowledge, and then she clutched his face with her soft, warm, slender hands. "By your leave, I have something to tell thee."

Ulrich tipped her chin up until he gazed directly into her eyes. "Speak, for if he has caused you any harm, his lands and people will pay the price."

"I am with child."

Ulrich froze, his eyes fleetingly disbelieving before turning into a roiling blue thundercloud.

Alida repeated softly, "I am with child," and then added, "and I know naught the father of the babe."

Ulrich snarled, his voice very calm and his hands falling away from her face. "Explain by God, or I shall slay every last man in this kingdom this very night."

Alida tugged at his arm keeping him from leaving the chamber. "We must forgive and move on, for all grace is due him and his people. If Creator can grant mercy and spare his life, so can we."

"I don't agree." His voice curled from out of his throat. "Tonight my name is Justice, wife."

"Ulrich, please." Her voice was very calm, softly pleading. "Please, by God, stay thy hand."

His hands clenched around the grip of his sword, and she could feel his anger throbbing through the thick tense muscles of his forearms. Landres' face was very grim in the dully-lit room, for he knew the nature of Ulrich's fully unleashed wrath. He had only witnessed it once before in battle, and now he almost pitied this land to which they'd come.

Ulrich's jaw clenched and he whispered, "He is already dead, but I will spare this land for your sake." Her gasp was swallowed by his movement. Landres and Ulrich's men watched as their lord strode from the room, his face a furious mask, with his wife en towe.

One of the men muttered, "By all that is good, I pray I never have to face our lord in full sail as he is now."

They all made their way down to the hall where they joined up with the rest of their group, awaiting Ulrich and Alida's return. Into one of the rings to which the physician and Deirdre had been tied the day before, the Drachmund banner was strung as a memento of their visit.

Ulrich came to the gates of the tunnels then, and with a curt nod, he was followed by his men. As quietly as they had entered, the score and five men, this time with two women en towe, left the tunnels of the great black city behind. Brögen Fjord's magnificent keep lay dormant hidden by ice and snow— a beast not yet willing to rise. Alida was carefully placed in her husband's lap after he had mounted Titan. There she found safety with the edges of Ulrich's warm and itchy woolen cloak wrapped securely about her.

His burning possessive kiss was enough to tell her of his relief. If Ulrich was curious about the bundled form of another woman seated before

Gowen, he disdained comment, for his anger had not yet fully cooled, and he remained silent on all counts. Alida was as quiet as possible for she had never seen him burn like this before.

Back along the walls of wet stone and thawing ice, they made their way silently until they had reached a ridge of concealing rock. Then, with great energy borne by the thought of home, they sped off for the inlet and summarily the docks.

Hours later to ease the remnants of tension that haunted the band, Landres softly began to sing a song of deliverance that rang out with his haunting baritone voice, matched by the throbbing cadence of the horse's hooves. Beneath the flow of music, they drove onwards towards the vessels that would carry them back to the sweet wild winds of Drachmund Heights. The cold breezes that whistled past the parapets and crevices of Brögen Fjords, whose sight quickly faded behind them; had lost their power to blow as fierce for the fiery band was on its way to warmer lands and their quest showed every sign of good success.

CHAPTER TWENTY-SEVEN

Seven nights later in the berth of the same vessel that had brought the Drachmund band across the stormy sea, Alida and Ulrich lay next to each other. Ulrich could smell her sweet scent and was on fire from the soft heat being produced by her skin. He desired her touch and warmth after not having seen her for so long, but made no move to initiate contact with her. He feared that after her handling of the past months she would be revolted by the thought of intimacies. He had spoken little to her during the week, for much of what he felt could not be verbalized. He had nearly lost her, and now that she was regained. He didn't know how to breach the walls of terror that had given him wings and iron in his back.

Finally, tired of the silence, Alida pressed herself as close to him as she could manage and gazed up at him, her eyes large with vulnerability while tempered by a strange formality. "Are you angry with me, milord?"

Ulrich scowled and then ran his hand over his face. "Nay. You have done no wrong. I am just tired, love. Let us speak no more this night, and do not address me so formally, for God's sake. I am your husband after all."

She tried to compose her features. "But Ulrich, we have said little to one another since leaving Brögen Fjords. I have missed the sound of your voice and your presence—here." She touched her chest and then his chest, her uncertainty making the caress timid like the flutter of bird wings. She sought to let him know that though he was present with her physically, she felt as lonely as she ever had.

Ulrich, unsure of whether he could restrain his desire a moment longer, awkwardly removed her arm, patting it absentmindedly before rolling over and mumbling. "Good night, I pray thy sound sleep." Alida stared at him disbelievingly, her visions of comfort in his arms turning to dust. Without a sound, she curled into herself and turned her back on him as well, cool tears rolling from the corners of her eyes and down the bridge of her nose.

The next few days Ulrich spent above board with his men, avoiding Alida's presence altogether, making her loneliness complete. Now she could not even touch him to reassure herself that he was real.

It wasn't long before she became violently ill within the berth of the constantly tossed vessel, for the pregnancy had already given her a bent towards nauseousness. It seemed that her misery would never end.

Hilde attended her diligently, using cool water to mop Alida's brow and keeping her bedclothes and urns freshly rotated.

One morning, Hilde entered the hold and found Alida sobbing desperately into the linens and furs. She immediately rushed to her side. "Alida, darling, what is wrong?"

Alida turned her face toward the wall trying to wipe away her tears. She did not succeed, and instead Hilde's soft, concerned tones made her cry harder, the tears and effort pounding through her ribs and the bridge of her nose and forehead like a storm. Finally, she admitted, "He finds me utterly loathsome now for I have been handled by another man. Not only that, but I carry a babe of unknown paternity, and am constantly sick. Perhaps he regrets having made the trip for such damaged goods." Her anger and sadness held equal parts in her voice as her emotion trailed off into yet again another hopeless moan.

Ulrich chose that moment to enter the hold, and overhearing the entire thing, he felt his heart lurch. He strode forward and touched Hilde on the shoulder. At his fierce look, she rose and left Alida to his care, praying to Alida's god that his words would be soft.

Ulrich wasted no time and gathered his wife into his arms trying not to crush her, as he was longing to do. Her sorrow touched him deeply, and he caressed her tear-stained cheeks with every tenderness of his lips, fluttering his love against her eyes, cheeks, and throat. She tried to pull away from him, but he soothed her with his tender words and drew her closer. "By God, I have been such a fool. Forgive me, please, my love, my sweet! I desired you so much, but I feared your rejection of me. You have been greatly mishandled by men, and I did not want to see loathing in your eyes when I came to you as a husband and a man myself. Instead of giving you comfort, I made your trials greater."

Alida choked on her tears and beat against him with her closed fists. "You are not just any male, *you are my husband* and the man I love! I do not see any other man but you behind my eyelids when sleep is ready to take me but wakefulness is too stubborn to let me go. I cannot loathe that which I adore. Did you think that I, too, did not feel anger and fear and worry in the time that I was away from you? 'Twas *my* body he used and *my* sensibilities that he crushed, but I am *not* fragile. I *have* survived everything that has tried to crush me, and it is because you are such a great part of my strength. To have you remove that strength destroys my soul. Do not think to remove it from me again!"

He held her more tightly as his own pent up tears were given release, flowing like a warm veil down his cheeks and onto his beard. He whispered softly to her and rocked her in his arms. "The babe that you bear, whether it be his or mine, male or female, will know nothing but love in its lifetime, for it has the most treasured of women as its mother. It will also know all things good, for it is a gift, a thing of beauty grown in the ashes of your trials. A chance at turning our shame, mine for having lost you and yours for having endured, to joy." He wiped away her tears, kissing her softly and then quietly lay back on the bed with her.

Wrapped securely in each other's arms and in the full knowledge of their love for each other, she told him all that she had endured. When Ulrich could contain himself no longer, he whispered, "Please let me make love to you. Let me soothe away the ugliness you have faced. Let me remind you of our love." She nodded, her eyes filling again with tears.

With a soft smile she whispered, "Refresh my memory." He took every care then with her, and in those hours, some new hope was born.

The rest of the trip back to Drachmund Heights passed uneventfully, though it was fraught with stress. Once again, Ulrich found himself awed by his wife's constitution. Though she was jostled about and uncomfortable in the saddle they had to share, she did not miscarry the babe, as he had feared she would. She also did not complain, his only clue to her weariness being the fine, dark lines around her eyes.

He took great pains to make sure that she was given as much rest during the ride as he could offer and stopped much more often than was usual for his men. He also made sure that she had the best morsels of the meat from kills they made and always gave her the first draughts of water from the streams at which they stopped.

At night when they would bed down under the stars, he would massage her back, feet, and ankles though he was exhausted to the bone himself. She was only about five months into the pregnancy by his calculations, but to him it seemed that she was near bearing the child for her stomach was very large. He politically avoided mentioning this, but her discomfort was apparent to everyone.

When they finally reached the Heights, the gates of the city were thrown wide to the joyous shouts of the guards, and the inhabitants poured forth in greeting. It did not surprise Ulrich that they were so pleased to see the return of their mistress, for he was sure that they had missed her warm leadership. Nevertheless, he felt oddly protective of her in the midst of the crowd, especially when he noticed the whispers and gazes of some at her distended belly. Fiercely, he ordered the streets cleared, his brow filled with thunder.

When they reached the massive gates of the castle itself, he dismounted and gingerly removed her from the saddle taking time to cozen her into his arms. He carried her up to their chambers, the knowledge that they were home together at last giving him an uncommon strength and causing the silent, deep tears of a man to come unbidden once again to his eyes. When they reached the warmth of their chambers, he found a breathless Birch, Gwynn, and the most experienced women of the castle gathered en totale to help welcome their mistress.

Down below, in the courtyard, Hilde stood off to the side suddenly out of her element until Alida, tired as she was, remembered her and had Birch bring her to the chambers. Ulrich loathed letting her go, but finally he was sent out to see about a physician. After he left, they all fussed over their mistress, trying to avoid talking too loudly, but they were very pleased that she was home and their conversation rattled over her like the cackles of hens.

When the entourage had finally left the room, Alida lay back on the soft, warm pallet and closed her eyes breathing deeply. To no one in particular she whispered, "Unless I fly, I never want to travel again."

She heard a chuckle from her left and turned her head seeing the warm smile of her husband who had returned unannounced and who had seen to the continuing peace of the chambers. The women of the keep might be strong-willed, but he was the husband, and this was his home.

He gathered her hand in his big, warm palm while letting her body lie undisturbed on the comfortable bed and simply said, "You're home to stay forever. For by the One who gave us life, I will not let you leave again. Now rest and rest again for as long and as heavily as you like. I am going to occupy the guest quarters and leave this entire pallet to you." A tender warm kiss followed his declaration.

This time she chuckled. "Are you employing the double entendre with your use of the word 'heavily?' " Then she laughed even harder when she saw his sheepish expression. "The face of innocence does not suit a wolf."

He grinned tentatively. "I just wanted to give you the maximum amount of comfort I could offer."

She turned slowly on her side and slugged him in the arm. "You had better go before I beat you, but return to me when my ire has had time to cool. Do not lie anywhere else. I need you as much as I ever have."

He ran his hand softly across her cheek, erasing her merriment and replacing it with passion and tenderness. "You are so pretty when you smile. I am glad you are home with me again."

She squeezed his hand and watched as he quietly exited the chambers. Within moments, she had dropped into a deep sleep. All around her, in the silence of the room, watchers and healers spun a web of sleep around her, drawing dewy droplets of peace from the air around them. Into this web, they also placed joyful memories and dreams. Softly sleeping with a smile on her face, the mother-to-be took her rest in the cradle of Creator.

The last months of her internment passed slowly, for Alida's belly grew very large indeed, until her skin itched from the endless stretching required, and her breasts sat like heavy globes upon its top. Towards the very end, she found herself loathe to leave the bed and sat miserable and ill-tempered in the growing heat of early summer, a constant bevy of servants surrounding her with fans.

Birch, Hilde, Gwynn, and the serving women became her constant companions, for Ulrich grew very restive and distant the longer her condition continued. She knew that privately he feared both her harm in childbirth and the appearance of a babe not his own. And though he had told her that the child would be well cared for, she prayed that he would not only treasure the child for being a fellow creation just as valuable as any from God, but also being a child borne of her body into their home.

She did not know of his late night visits to her bedside where he would sit and pray for her as well, sometimes softly touching her hand or face. Though he spent little time during the day with her and avoided conversation, his occasional smile or gift given through her serving women reassured her of the strength of their relationship.

Then the time was called. Protectors swept down from the heavens cleaning the grounds, city, and castle of the Heights of every disease carrying fiend, preparing for the birth of the believer's child. They cavorted and whispered secrets that Alida could not hear. To Gwynn they looked like frenzied nursemaids running about, and she could feel deep in her bones the imminent arrival of the babe.

Birch, too, was held by the grip of anticipation. For though she was not given the gift of sight for spiritual things, there was a feeling in the castle that prefaced the coming birth. Early one morn when dawn had barely touched the earth, Alida came crying from sleep, her huge smooth belly upright and racked with contractions and her body pouring sweat as from a bucket.

She heaved herself up from the bed and began with a lumbering gait to pace the length of the chamber, unsure of whether or not to alert the serving women in the chamber next to hers of her discomfort. When she felt some relief in the walking, she decided to leave the stuffy rooms and headed for the open hall, feeling sure that the discomfort would soon pass, and she could return to bed.

It took her a great deal of time to make her way down the steps, but she eventually found herself in the silent great room. The moment she stopped to rest, contractions racked her body, and so again, she began walking to help alleviate some of the pain. The hall seemed as hot as her chambers, and so she disdained the high-vaulted room for the cool summer dawn outside of the castle.

She nodded to the guards who managed the gates to the castle gardens and chose to hide her discomfort behind a pleasant smile. It just couldn't yet be her time. They watched somewhat worriedly as the mistress of the castle left the safe halls, where serving women abounded, for the trees and gardens beyond, her waddling walk unsteady and a strange pallor upon her skin.

Landres who was seeing to the change of the watch hurriedly sent word to his lord after receiving a worried impartation of the news from a young guard. He did not want to offend Alida or her sense of freedom, but he was worried about her vulnerability out in the open gardens. As soon as word had been sent, he shadowed her progress being careful to stay anonymous.

Ulrich was up and dressing before his mind had fully gathered what the servant had told him. All he knew was that Alida was presently unescorted. When he had wakened and was thinking more clearly, a flood of anger and anxiety washed over him. He was out of the guestrooms that he'd begun to occupy and into the hall in a few strides, yanking open the doors to the court-yard.

The guards on the parapets pointed out her general heading, but by then had lost sight of her slow meanderings under the thick canopies of the trees. Ulrich was quick to pick up her trail and soon had overcome Landres. His voice was gruff with the lingering effects of sleep. "Where is she?"

Landres pointed to a clearing not far ahead, where Ulrich could just see his wife's retreating shoulders. "Thank you, Landres. I will see to her safety from here."

"Go easy on her, Ulrich. Women close to childbirth do strange things."

Ulrich nodded absentmindedly and headed off at a quick pace, intent on bringing her back while the song of awakening birds carried him through the soft grasses. When he reached her side, he watched as she doubled over in pain and caught up air into her lungs in deep gulps, her body trembling and unsteady. Then amazed and angered, he watched as she again began to walk, headed for the great oak at the center of the clearing.

He dismounted and strode to her side, his eyes on her pale, damp skin and wet hair. "Alida, I am taking you back. This is foolishness. You are obvi-ously not thinking clearly. The babe is coming."

Her blue eyes, dark with pain, turned on him, and he had never seen such a black scowl. "Do not order me about, husband. 'Tis my body, and I am not being foolish. I just need to rest a moment under this tree. It cannot yet be time."

His fists balled up at his side, and he slowed his speech attempting to sound nonchalant. "You call walking outside of the castle's protection and serving women, while you are heavy with babe and unable to navigate easily, a wise choice?"

"So now you question my logic!" Her voice cut through the air right before she fainted.

Ulrich, at her side, caught her, halfway dragged her, and halfway carried her the last few feet to the soft ground at the base of the oak tree. Its great roots heaved out of the ground, creating a cocoon or basin of sorts, and it was perfectly situated for surrounding both her body and his.

Though he was strong, Ulrich also knew that he could not carry his pregnant wife for such a distance back and was glad that Landres knew where they were. He decided to leave her where she lay, walking back for aid. Just then, her soft voice grew hoarse as a groan racked her body. "Don't leave me, Ulrich!"

He instantly dismounted and was by her side again, soothing her. "Alida, I must return to get help. We have to bring you back to the castle where it is safe and the women can help me care for you. Please let me go."

She shook her head then clutched her stomach and pulled her knees to her chest the smell of the earth and her own sweat and moss surrounding her. "There is no time. The child comes now, and unless you help me, I will bear it alone while you seek assistance."

Ulrich felt beads of sweat break out on his brow. He knelt at her side and laid his cloak under her. He massaged her sweat-slick legs and talked softly to her, completely at a loss of what to do.

Within moments of her declaration that she was having the baby, a great contraction moved the upward pitch of her belly, and Ulrich watched as water and a little blood gushed from between her legs.

She groaned aloud as her body shuddered with effort and fresh sweat coated her neck and face.

Ulrich thought she would break his arm, such was the strength of her grip on him. Each time she bore down, he had to grit his own teeth to keep from crying out for she had transitioned to pushing.

Presently a rhythm grew from her labor, and they waited together for each new cycle. It seemed that a great deal of time had passed when Ulrich suddenly saw the child's head crowning from her body. He encouraged her, his voice heavy with excitement. Then the deep contraction passed, and he had to choke back fear as the child's head receded back inside.

"Alida, the child will not come," he said worriedly, his forehead creased and a telltale vein throbbing near his temple. How could his mouth feel like cotton when water poured from every other pore?

Alida was breathing deeply, waiting for the next heavy contraction. She absentmindedly patted his hand. "'Tis normal, Ulrich. It will come. It is two steps forward, one step back."

He sat back on his heels and again wiped away her sweat using a corner of his cloak, the cloth leaving an itchy trail in its wake. When the next contraction rolled down her belly, Alida pushed with all her might and held the force for as long as possible deep in the lowest part of her pelvis. Her eyes were closed with the concentration, and she felt that every blood vessel in her face and neck would pop. The pounding of the blood in her ears would surely deafen her.

Again, the crown of the babe receded. Alida opened her eyes, feeling that she could not do anymore, and suddenly, before her, she saw the darting forms of the protectors and watchers. Their mass was suddenly excited, and she could almost not distinguish the form of one from another.

A small, pinkish one darted from the mass and gently touched her lips, its eyes tender and joyful. Then Alida was strengthened, for she knew that they heralded the arrival of the babe. She gathered herself together and shifted her position slightly, her body quietly signaling what she could not have logically deduced. When the next contraction came, she again bore down with all her might, the pressure trailing off at the end, and this time she heard her husband's excited whoop!

The babe's head came from her body with a rush. Next followed the shoulders, which Ulrich helped to turn. The child's red skin was covered in birth, and its arms flailed in the bright summer morning, a swimmer suddenly out of water. All around them, the smell of blood and birth and the cocoon of earth flooded an already sensate occasion.

"You have borne me a girl!" Ulrich shouted again and removed his wife's cloak from her shoulders to wrap up the shivering, delicate babe. He removed mucus and film from the baby's mouth, and smiled as it wailed aloud, forlorn for the red room of solace it had just left. Then with great reluctance, he handed the baby to his wife, kissing her as he did so.

However, her face was contorted with pain, and she was not focused on him. Ulrich looked down at the ground between her legs and saw a chubby leg protruding from her body. "Ulrich, help me!" Her head rolled back against the tree, and her teeth ground together, her wobbly and barely upright seat testament to a faint coming on.

He quickly and carefully set their baby girl on the ground beside them and reached for his wife's body, fearing the sight before him.

Born out of instinct and his experience with animals and though he knew it would hurt Alida terribly, he was sure that unless he pushed the other babe back up inside her and turned it, she and the second child would suffer injury or worse. Alida was crying out, her eyes tightly closed and her knuckles white where they grasped at the tree roots. Tears poured down her cheeks, and she was frantic.

Ulrich made an instant decision. There was not time to push the babe back in and turn it. With his other hand, he reached up inside of her and pulled the slippery little legs of his baby until both pointed downward. Then he wrapped one hand around both the babe's ankles, pulling down carefully but firmly in the rotating direction in which he'd seen the other babe come. The other hand pushed on Alida's stomach from above the baby's head. He prayed to God that safety surround them.

Their son came into the world with a gush of water and a piercing scream that mirrored his mother's, the cry not at all delicate and mournful like his sister's.

Ulrich quickly cleaned the new babe and then bundled the two children together, watching in amazement as they sucked one another's thumbs. With tears streaming down his face, he reached for his wife. He comforted her until she had passed the afterbirth and was resting more quietly, her sobs making the job difficult. Then holding their two precious gifts between them, they alternated continuously between tears and laughter.

Ulrich said, "Where, by all that is good, are the hundreds that never leave us alone normally."

Alida guffawed harder and then gasped, "Oh it hurts—don't make me laugh."

438 R. A. WINTERS

Ulrich was still worried about Alida, for blood leaked from between her legs. She reassured him that she felt fine, considering her ordeal, and was anxious to return to the keep. Ulrich, gathering as much volume in his voice as he could, called out, "Can somebody help us?"

Alida looked up at Ulrich with great trust in her eyes. He smiled a bit wobbly and dropped down beside her once again, his sweating face against her sweating brow and their breath being breathed in by one another.

He did his best to help make her more presentable by gently wiping her body and pulling down her tunic modestly. He folded up his bloody cloak so that the stains and contents did not show on the outward sides and wiped her hair from her face with a careful hand, feeling every emotion known to man assail all his logic and good intentions at being in charge. "Honey, I know that you don't want to be alone, but we need help. I'll be right back."

Then he stood, taking the children with him. He carried them to a bright, sunlit spot in the grass. His wife joined them soon after, having been lifted into his arms and deposited in the same spot of warm light.

Shortly thereafter, Landres and an entire bevy of frantic serving women found them there, covered in new sunlight with the babes nursing greedily, if somewhat awkwardly, at her breasts, their small mewling mouths trying to learn the rhythm old as time.

It was late that morning when Ulrich and Alida were able to take the time to study their children's faces together. For Birch, when she had arrived at the cove like a general, had insisted on a boiled water bath and herbal wash immediately for preventing infection.

When they had arrived back in chambers, Birch, Gwynn, and Hilde had baths and clean clothes brought up for the entire family. Alida and Ulrich were bathed privately in their chamber behind oaken screens, while in another room Birch and Gwynn washed away the signs of birth from the tiny, squalling babes.

Ulrich helped Alida dress in a sleeping gown and tucked her snugly into their pallet, his awe at what they had experienced surrounding him like a dream. Then the children were handed to them gleaming and tired while the women silently exited the rooms, the fragrant scents of the herbal wash lingering over the foursome.

With the babies so clean, it was easier to distinguish features and to nuzzle at the sweetness behind their ears. Ulrich and Alida marveled at the downy white hair of their girl. She was fragile boned and tiny, though apparently quite healthy. After some soft discussion, Ulrich leaned over her and whispered in her tiny shell-like ear, "Your name is Yoninah, for you are our little dove, pure of wing, whose voice is lovely to behold." Their son, who was then taken up promptly by his father, outweighed her by at least double and had a smooth red down covering his crown. They knew without discussion that one child had been born for each father, for the girl's face reminded Ulrich of his mother, and the boy was built like The Red with fiery hair which neither Alida nor Ulrich carried in their blood. Both babies had their mother's mouth and eye shape.

Alida touched her husband's face, seeing the bittersweet realization of this miracle pass over his features. Then without a word, he lifted the boy tenderly into his arms and held him tight, a tear dripping from the bridge of his nose onto the babe's smooth cheek. His dry warm lips brushed the little face repeatedly before doing the same with his tiny daughter. Then with the hitch of a sob in his voice, Ulrich whispered to his baby son, "You shall be called Rory, for you are as red as the father who begot you, but certainly no deeper or richer in color than my own blood and the soils of the lands that will be given thee." Any fears that Alida had harbored during the pregnancy melted away. For she knew that without a doubt Ulrich had accepted the workings of Creator, however inexplicable they may have seemed, in that moment.

They lay together talking softly until sheer exhaustion pulled Alida into sleep after the natural rush of adrenaline gave way. Then Ulrich moved closer to his family, his mouth moving silently in prayer and praise. He was greatly blessed.

From the towering skies, powerful music and rejoicing poured down to the province as Creator and his creations celebrated the births of two nations, which were bound together forever by blood and faith.

Contact author R. A. Winters
or order more copies of this book at
www.rawinters.com

&

TATE PUBLISHING, LLC

127 East Trade Center Terrace
Mustang, Oklahoma 73064

(888) 361 - 9473

Tate Publishing, LLC

www.tatepublishing.com